Too Good To Be Real

ALSO BY MELONIE JOHNSON

Too Good To Be Real

MELONIE JOHNSON

ST. MARTIN'S GRIFFIN
NEW YORK

First published in the United States by St. Martin's Griffin, an imprint of St. Martin's Publishing Group

TOO GOOD TO BE REAL. Copyright © 2021 by Melonie Johnson. All rights reserved. Printed in the United States of America. For information, address St. Martin's Publishing Group, 120 Broadway, New York, NY 10271.

www.stmartins.com

Designed by Devan Norman

Library of Congress Cataloging-in-Publication Data

Names: Johnson, Melonie, author.
Title: Too good to be real / Melonie Johnson.
Description: First edition. | New York : St. Martin's Griffin, 2021. |
Identifiers: LCCN 2021002064 | ISBN 9781250768803 (trade paperback) |
    ISBN 9781250768810 (ebook)
Subjects: GSAFD: Love stories.
Classification: LCC PS3610.O366334 T66 2021 | DDC 813/.6—dc23
LC record available at https://lccn.loc.gov/2021002064

Our books may be purchased in bulk for promotional, educational, or business use. Please contact your local bookseller or the Macmillan Corporate and Premium Sales Department at 1-800-221-7945, extension 5442, or by email at MacmillanSpecialMarkets@macmillan.com.

First Edition: 2021

10 9 8 7 6 5 4 3 2 1

For my nanny, who refused to watch the second VHS tape of Titanic.
She made me feel so cherished; her love shines in me still.
And always will.

CHAPTER 1

JULIA

"His penis looks like your shrimp."

Julia Carpenter paused, chopsticks hovering near her lips as she stared at her friend Andie, seated on the other side of their regular lunch booth in Tasty Thai. Next to Julia, their friend Kat hid a snicker in her noodles.

"What?" Andie reached across the table for Julia's phone. "Am I wrong?" She tilted the image on the screen toward them for comparison. "See?"

"Well," Kat snickered again, "maybe her shrimp looks like his penis."

The shrimp in question slipped from between Julia's chopsticks and landed back in her bowl with a squicky splat. She set the utensils down and made a grab for her phone. "Stop waving that thing around."

Kat and Andie both snickered this time.

Julia resisted the urge to join in their juvenile appreciation of the unintentional innuendo and plucked her phone from Andie's grasp. But when she glanced at the screen, she had to admit the male anatomy currently on display did bear an unfortunate resemblance to the shrimp in her pad kee mao. And now she was snickering too. Really, it was either laugh or cry. Shaking her head, she deleted the image sent by her most recent dating fail. "Why do guys think we like looking at pictures of their junk?"

"Because they like looking at ours." Andie shrugged. "How often does a dick pic come accompanied by the eloquent request to"—she paused and lowered her voice to dude-bro level—"*send me your nudes?*"

"All the time." Kat rolled her eyes as she sipped her tea.

"And how often do you comply?" Andie crossed her arms and rested against the back of the booth, one dark brow arched.

Kat's full lips pursed around the rim of her cup. "Never." She swallowed and added, "Well, there was that one time . . ."

Andie's other eyebrow jumped to join its twin as she leaned forward. "What?"

"I'm kidding." Kat's smile was wicked. "What about you, Jules?"

"Not on purpose." Julia picked up the teapot and poured out a measure of steaming liquid.

"Now *you're* the one who's kidding," Kat insisted.

"It was one time, and it was just my butt." Julia lifted her teacup, inhaling the soothing scent of jasmine while enjoying the looks of fascinated horror on her friends' faces. "And it was an accident."

"I've heard of accidentally butt dialing someone." Andie shook her head, her dark fringe of bangs falling over one eye. "But sending a butt pic by accident?"

"Forget sending it. I'm still confused about how you managed to take a selfie of your naked butt by mistake in the first place," Kat admitted.

"Oh," Julia confessed, "that part was on purpose."

"What do you call a butt selfie, anyway?" Andie mused.

"A belfie," Julia answered immediately.

"For the record, I knew that, but I refuse to ever use that word," Kat declared.

"Also, in case you were wondering, yes, there is such a thing as a belfie stick."

"I refuse to use that, too," Kat amended.

"For someone who claims it was 'one time,'" Andie made quotation marks with her fingers, "and 'an accident,' you sure know a lot about butt pic stuff."

"In my first year at *TrendList*, I wrote an article about the top five ways to get the best angle for your belfie," Julia explained. "And yes, it was an accident, and it really was just that one time. I can't believe either of you are surprised. This is me we're talking about, remember? Murphy's Law on two legs."

"Oh, come on. You're not that bad." Kat patted her on the shoulder. "You make yourself sound like a walking disaster."

"I mean, she kind of is." Andie blew her bangs out of her face. "No offense, Jules."

"None taken." Julia grimaced good-naturedly. It was true. In her experience, anything that could go wrong, did go wrong. Murphy's Law incarnate. If there was a way she could screw something up, odds were, she would. Case in point: sending a dude she'd gone on a few casual dates with a close-up of her bare ass by mistake. "I never told either of you about this?"

"Trust me, I'd remember," Kat assured her.

"It's not really a big deal." Julia recalled the incident, cheeks heating from more than just the tea. "I had a bug bite on my butt, and it was swelling up and itching and I was worried it might be a deadly spider or something that bit me."

"So you took a selfie of your *dupa*?" Kat shook her head. "Why not just look in the mirror?"

"It was at an odd angle and I wanted to send a picture to my mom for her opinion." Her mother was a dermatologist who saw plenty of weirder things in her average day on the job.

"Too bad you didn't have a belfie stick." Andie smirked.

"Anyway . . ." Julia ignored her and continued. "Let's talk about the plan for Friday night."

"Hold on." Andie raised a hand. "I still have questions."

"It wasn't poisonous," Julia assured her. "Just a mosquito bite."

"Uh-huh, yeah, great." Andie waved that aside. "What I want to know is who'd you accidentally send the belfie to?"

"Yeah," Kat chimed in, blue eyes twinkling. "Who got the literal booty call?"

"Funny you should call it that." A reluctant smile tugged at Julia's lips. She really did have a talent for messing things up. "Because that's exactly what Derek thought when he got it."

"Derek?" Kat tapped her chopsticks together in thought. "The *I just bought a boat* guy?"

"The *I took an hour to make my hair look like I slept funny* guy?" Andie added.

"That's the one." Julia nodded. "He showed up at my door so fast, I still didn't have my pants back on."

"What did you do?"

"I told him the truth. That it was a mistake. That I'd meant to send the pic to someone else."

"Uh-oh." Andie winced. "Did you explain to him it was meant for your mom?"

"I don't know if that would have been better," Kat chortled.

"He bailed before I could." Julia shrugged, then stopped, eyes widening. "Oh, God. He thought I was sending the pic to another guy, didn't he? No wonder he was so mad!"

"You're just putting that together?" Kat made a noise in the back of her throat, half disgusted and half amused. "Honestly, Jules, I don't know how you manage any sort of love life."

"Easy. I don't."

"But you go on dates all the time," Kat insisted.

"Yeah, and they all end in disaster." Julia poked at the remaining food in her bowl. "Or with dick pics."

"Or both," Andie added.

"Definitely both," Kat agreed.

"Then why do we keep doing it?" Julia asked, as much to herself as to her friends.

"Because we keep hoping we'll find the one," Andie said.

"Which one?" Julia wondered.

"She means *the one*." Kat fluttered her fingers. "You know, the one meant just for you."

"Oh." Julia stabbed a chopstick through the shrimp. "*That* one."

"The right one is out there," Andie promised. "We just have to keep looking."

"It's what we have to keep looking *at* that bothers me." Julia held up her chopstick, phallic shellfish speared on the end.

"Does this mean it's a *no* to seeing shrimp boy again?" Andie asked.

Julia twirled her chopstick, sending the little crustacean spinning. "I think so." She sighed. "I need to enact a strict no dick pics policy. If they send me an unsolicited shot of their wiener, I'm out."

"That'll narrow down your dating options real quick," Andie snorted.

Kat's face took on a dreamy, pensive look. "What if it's a really good one though?"

"Nope." Julia shook her head.

"Like, *really* good," Kat insisted.

"*Still* no," Julia said, equally insistent. She twirled her chopstick faster. Hell, no. She was tired of that line so casually getting crossed.

"Well, send them my way, then." Kat reached out and tapped her chopstick against Julia's, knocking the shrimp back into the bowl. "But only the really good ones."

Julia and Andie both stared at their friend.

"Relax. I'm just messing with you." Kat met their gazes, a sly smile in the corner of her mouth. "Though maybe it's not a bad thing to know what the package looks like before it's delivered."

"Yeah, but you should be allowed to order the package first." Julia's peeved tone turned teasing. "Nobody appreciates junk mail."

"Wow." Andie snorted. "You two make it all sound *so* romantic."

"When's the last time *you* went on a romantic date?" Kat shot back.

"Honestly, at this point I'd settle for someone who wasn't looking for me to play mommy." Andie made a face. "For him *or* his kids."

"Uh-oh." Julia shared a glance with Kat before asking, "Did you try dating another team dad?"

"I don't know why I keep doing this to myself." Andie shook her head. "I mean, if I fall in love with a guy, I'd be fine having a relationship with his kids, but I need to have a relationship with *him* first. All these dudes seem to want is a babysitter with benefits."

"That's like one step away from banging the nanny." Julia bit her lip, holding back from saying more. Her friend had a habit of going out with the single dads of girls she coached. Widowed, divorced, separated—whatever their story was at the start, inevitably they all ended the same.

"Definitely not romantic," Kat agreed, frowning. "Though I'm not really one to talk. I can't remember the last time a date felt romantic or the last romantic gesture someone did for me. I'd blame my notorious ability to be attracted to assholes, but it's not like the odds are in our favor."

"Why do you say that?" Julia asked.

"Jerks are everywhere." Kat spread her arms wide. "I sell way more *I screwed up* bouquets at work than I do *Let's make this night special* ones."

"How do you know which is which?"

"Someone has to type up the messages that go on those little cards." Kat leaned closer and lowered her voice. "You would not believe some of the shit I've had dictated to me."

"Maybe if guys started sending flowers instead of dick pics, they'd get more action," Julia suggested.

"Or they could send flowers *with* their dick pics," Andie observed drily.

Kat clapped her hands. "You might be onto something. That would make a great marketing campaign for the shop!"

"It would make a great article for *TrendList*," Julia agreed, pulling a pen from her purse along with the mini notebook she always carried to jot down story ideas.

"How to make your dick pics more romantic?" Andie crinkled her nose.

"Would you click on that article?" Julia challenged.

"You know I would," Andie admitted, face splitting in a *You've got me there* grin.

"'A Dozen Ways to Up Your Dick Pic Game,'" Julia muttered, writing the possible title down in her notebook.

"Up your game?" Kat shook her head. "Uh-uh."

"What? Too dude-bro?" Julia tapped her pen against the edge of the table. "How about 'A Dozen Ways to Say *I Love You* With Your—'"

"Actually," Andie interrupted, "I'm more concerned about the number. Isn't a dozen rather optimistic?"

Julia doodled on the corner of the page. "Planning this article in the first place is optimistic."

"Layoff rumors again?" Concern softened Andie's voice.

"It's journalism. There's always layoff rumors." Julia scribbled over the titles, pen scratching back and forth in jerky, irritated movements. "But I have confirmation from a reliable source that another wave of cuts is coming."

"You're the hardest-working person I've ever met." Kat put an arm around her shoulders. "You've survived every layoff so far. Do you really think this will actually affect you?"

"The ax could drop any day," Julia sighed, shrimp and noodles squirming unpleasantly in her gut. She'd told herself she wouldn't bring this up at lunch, but she could never hide anything from her friends for long. "And I don't think I'm going to escape the chopping block this time."

Kat sighed too. "Shit, Jules." She squeezed Julia's shoulder. "Maybe this is a good thing."

"How?"

"You were just complaining about being tired of writing yet another quiz on how to use your horoscope sign to determine which candidate on *The Bachelorette* would be right for you."

"I like writing those quizzes. I'm tired of writing about *The Bachelorette*," Julia amended.

"Then why torture yourself?"

"Because for some inexplicable reason, people really seem to enjoy reading about *The Bachelorette*."

"Excuse me." Kat poked her. "*I'm* one of those people."

"If I didn't write it, they'd find someone else who would." Julia paused and glared into her teacup. "Though it looks like that's about to happen anyway."

"If you're creating stuff people want, why do you think *Trend-List* is going to lay you off?" Andie asked.

"I don't *think* they will; I *know* it. I told you. The news came from a very reliable source." Julia shook her head. "When I first started at *TrendList*, freelancers were the exception, not the norm. But they've been cleaning house. Firing writing teams and replacing them with part-timers who are cheaper and don't qualify for benefits."

"That sucks." Kat frowned.

"Honestly, I'm lucky to have survived there this long."

"Your career is just getting started," Andie scoffed. "Maybe now, with some experience under your belt, you'll find a better job somewhere else. One door closes another opens and all that."

"Like every other job prospect in journalism isn't struggling with the same issue. How do you think I score so many side gigs?" Julia didn't make any attempt to hide the sarcasm in her voice. Her gut twisted again. She tried not to think about how taking those freelance writing assignments meant she was probably taking a job from someone just like her. But it was the nature of the business, and she depended on the extra income from those gigs to make ends meet.

"You summarized it perfectly, Kat. It sucks." Andie scowled.

"And it's not just journalism. My mom's said similar things about teaching positions at her university. They're retaining fewer full-time professors and hiring more adjuncts."

"Who get paid a lot less and don't qualify for a benefits package," Julia grumbled.

"I can't imagine *TrendList* paying anyone much less. You've been there almost three years and your pay is still peanuts." Kat paused when the server returned to clear their table.

"The pay *is* peanuts, thanks for the reminder," Julia agreed. "But the benefit package is solid, and you know how much I need that." The words summoned forth the weight of her parents' judgment from hundreds of miles away. She slumped deeper into the booth.

They didn't agree on much, but when it came to Julia's life choices, her parents formed an irritatingly unified front. At the top of *Fifty Reasons Our Daughter Shouldn't Pursue a Career in Journalism* was their concern over a lack of steady full-time jobs with health benefits. Perhaps even more irritating was the fact they were right. Though Julia was determined to do whatever she could to prove them wrong.

She'd been so proud when she first scored the position at the popular digital media company, sure that it was the start of great things. Julia liked her job at *TrendList*. She enjoyed creating lighthearted content that offered entertainment and distraction to the masses. But she'd been churning out lists and quizzes for nearly three years and didn't seem to have much to show for it. She had to admit she was starting to feel stuck.

Maybe Kat was onto something and getting canned would be a good thing. The thought hadn't even finished forming in her brain before Julia was already dismissing it. Being underappreciated and occasionally understimulated was more appealing than unemployment, definitely easier than losing her health insurance, and infinitely better than having to head back home and acknowledge that her parents had known best all along.

"Whoa, I'm getting some very negative vibes from you right now," Kat said, nudging Julia with her shoulder. "Bright side time. You still have your job at this current moment, correct?"

"As far as I know." Only Kat could use the phrase "bright side time" without making Julia want to inflict bodily harm. The waitress dropped the bill and Julia fidgeted with a corner of the receipt. "We'll see what happens when I get back to the office."

"That's it?" Kat pressed.

"What do you mean?"

"You never give up that easily." Kat grabbed the check out of her hands. "What are you going to do?"

"Um, what *can* I do?" Julia flipped to a new page in her notepad. "Let's see . . . ten ways to avoid getting canned." She began to make a list. "Number one. Beg. Number two. Cry."

"I'm serious, Jules."

"Number three," Julia continued. "Plead."

"Isn't *plead* the same thing as *beg*?" Andie asked.

"Not helping," Kat growled. She took the pen from Julia. "Number four." Kat scrawled, adding to the list. "Show them your worth."

Julia snorted. "Okay, Miss Bright Side. I've had enough of your positive energy for today."

"I'm serious, Jules." Kat underlined what she'd written. "You said anybody could make those list things."

"Listicles. And maybe not *anybody*—" Julia began.

"Fine," Kat cut her off. "Anybody with an internet connection and a decent understanding of pop culture. Whatever. My point is you're more than that. You're worth more than the peanuts they pay you. So much more. You're a great writer. You're smart and funny and ridiculously creative. Make them see it."

Andie brightened. "That's actually a really good idea."

"You're on Li'l Miss Sunshine's side too now?" Julia groused, but it was halfhearted at best. Hard to be annoyed at your friends when they're showering you with compliments.

"I deal with this on the field all the time. A hundred or more girls vying for the same handful of spots on a team. All of them are competent. All of them could get the job done. Who's bringing something a little extra to the table?"

"I'm not bribing my boss," Julia warned.

"You've been watching too much reality TV, Jules." Andie rolled her eyes. "I'm talking about the TADA factor."

"You lost me," Kat said.

"TADA." Andie ticked off her fingers. "Talent. Ambition. Determination. Athleticism."

"You can forget about that last one," Julia said, laughing.

"Well, it was created for soccer players. How about we swap it out for something highly valued in a journalist." Andie's face scrunched in thought. "Accuracy?"

"Sadly, not as important as one would hope." Julia shook her head. "I get what you're trying to say, though."

"I ask my players all the time, 'What are you bringing that the others aren't?' They're performing at a level where phenomenal skill isn't just expected, it's the baseline. Which means, if they don't want to get cut, they have to prove themselves valuable to the team in other ways." Andie leaned across the table, dark eyes intense. "Do you wanna get cut?"

"No."

"What are you going to do about it then?"

"Um . . ." Julia squirmed in the booth. It was hard to ignore Andie when she used her coach voice. Julia bet if her friend demanded that everyone in the restaurant stand up and start doing speed drills the entire place would be on their feet in seconds. "Show my boss I'm a valuable team player?"

"You got it, MVP." Andie pounded the table with her fist.

"Exactly what I was trying to say." Kat squeezed Julia's arm. "Make your ass invaluable to them."

"How did this conversation circle back around to my butt?" Julia teased. The alarm on her phone chimed. Julia jumped and crammed her notebook and pen back in her purse. "Shit. I won't have a job to save if I don't get back to work." She scooted out of the booth. Dropping some cash on the table, she turned to her friends. "So, Friday . . . I'll take care of the movie?"

"And I've got the drinks," Andie added, standing as well.

"I guess that leaves me in charge of snacks." Kat wriggled out of the booth. "I'm on it."

Once outside the Thai place, Julia gave each of her friends a quick hug. "Thanks for the pep talk."

"You're going to schedule a meeting with your boss?" Andie asked. "Show 'em your TADA?"

"Yes," Julia said, striving to sound more confident. "Definitely."

"Today." Kat wagged a finger at her. "You promise?"

"TADA today. I promise. I'll tell you all about it when I see you Friday." With a wave, Julia turned and headed toward her L stop. A moment later she laughed out loud when she heard Kat shout, "Remember to show them you're an ass . . . et!"

CHAPTER 2

JULIA

When she arrived back at her desk, Julia was still chuckling. Her friends' unique approach to motivational speaking might be weird, but it was also effective. She was in a much better mood now than she'd been in all week. And she was going to keep her promise and talk to her boss today. She glanced over at the door to the editorial director's office. Yep. Definitely. Sometime today.

But maybe just a teensy bit later. She had an assignment to finish first.

Julia pulled up her current project, "16 Ways Magnetic Eyelashes Will Change Your Life." Clicking through the file, her thoughts drifted back to the conversation at lunch about how her own life might be ready for a change. Despite what she was promising in her article, magnetic eyelashes weren't going to cut it.

She finished the eyelashes story and hit Send. Time to keep her promise. Julia slid from her chair and headed for her boss's office door. While most of the *TrendList* staff worked in an open floor plan, some of the upper-level employees had offices. As Julia maneuvered through the beehive of coworkers, she tried to act calm, cool, and collected. But her heart was pounding and her mouth had suddenly gone completely dry. This was no good. She couldn't have her TADA moment when she was like this.

Shifting direction, Julia circled back to her desk for her mug and then headed for the break room. She was going to keep her promise. Soon. After she'd had her traditional afternoon pick-me-up.

She plopped a compostable coffee pod into the machine and started it up. While waiting for it to brew, she closed her eyes and tried to plan out what she would say. But all her brain kept coming up with was the smartass shit she'd written on her notepad while at the restaurant. Beg. Cry. Plead.

"I think it's done now," a voice called from behind her.

"Huh?" Julia's attention jerked back to the machine. "Oh, sorry." Flustered, she quickly popped out the pod and grabbed her mug.

"Three p.m. slump, huh?"

Julia stared at the grumpy-faced cat on her mug, too embarrassed to make eye contact with the person behind her. She stepped out of the way, fiddling nervously with cream and sugar. "I know this stuff is terrible, but I can't seem to break the habit."

"I used to be the same, but now it's only hot water for me." The woman stepped forward, closed the empty pod chamber, and started up the machine again. "Sometimes I spice things up and add a slice of lemon."

Julia almost dropped her coffee when she realized who she was talking to. Cleo Chen. Editorial director for the Chicago office of *TrendList*. Sweat prickled on the back of Julia's neck as she watched her boss pull a protein bar from her purse. So much for planning what she was going to say ahead of time. This was punishment. Punishment for procrastinating on keeping her promise.

"I'm doing keto," her boss said, unwrapping the protein bar. "Ever try it?"

"I wrote an article about it once. It wasn't for me." Julia cringed and mentally began compiling a new list entitled "Ten Ways to Fuck Things Up with Your Boss."

Number one. Delay their access to the coffee machine.

Number two. Insult their dietary habits.

Thankfully, Cleo didn't seem insulted. She laughed. "I didn't think it was for me, either, but my doctor has other ideas. He said if I want to see my grandchildren grow up, I need to cut the crap."

"Grandchildren, huh?" Julia dove for the conversational life preserver and clung to it. "How many?"

"Three." Her boss beamed at her. "But it will be four in a few months."

"Congratulations!" Julia returned the smile. So far, so good.

Finishing her protein bar, Cleo waved a hand. "Come with me to my office and I'll show you some pictures."

"Sure." Julia took a quick swig from her mug and followed her boss. She'd been a little shaken after realizing Cleo had been standing right behind her, but maybe instead of a punishment, bumping into her boss unexpectedly was a blessing. A sign that this conversation was meant to be.

Who was she kidding? Murphy's Law on two legs here. Julia didn't do signs. The only thing she could be sure of was something was sure to go wrong.

Inside her office, Cleo gestured to a shelf littered with various sizes of framed photographs. "My grandbabies."

Julia walked over to the shelf and dutifully admired the pictures. "Adorable," she said, stepping back quickly before she managed to spill coffee on anything important.

"Here, let me have that." Cleo took the mug from Julia and set it on her desk next to her own. "Take off your shoes."

"Pardon?"

"Your shoes." Cleo kicked off her heels. "Take them off."

"Um, okay." Julia slipped off her shoes and watched as her boss reached her arms up, stretching them overhead. At a loss to do anything else, she did the same.

"It's Julia, right?" Cleo dropped her arms and twisted her body to the side.

"Yep." Julia twisted too. "Julia Carpenter."

Cleo dropped into a squat.

Julia mimicked the movement. Something in her knee cracked, and she prayed her work pants weren't about to split.

"I find some afternoon stretches really helps get my energy

back up." Cleo gestured toward the coffee mug, still squatting. "And no post-sugar-and-caffeine crash after."

"Totally," Julia agreed, biting her lip as she struggled to hold the squat. Her thighs screamed in protest, reminding her it had been months since her last Pilates class. Andie would be so disappointed. *And she'll really be disappointed if you don't follow through and fight for your job.*

Her boss stood and stepped one leg out, leaning into a lunge. Julia mirrored her.

"Feels good, doesn't it?"

Not the word I'd use to describe it. Julia forced her lips into a smile that she hoped didn't make her look like a gargoyle. "It's funny we ran into each other, because I've been meaning to talk to you."

"We're talking now, aren't we?" Cleo switched legs and smoothly shifted into another lunge.

"Good point." Julia laughed awkwardly, trying to maintain her balance as she lunged forward on her other leg. By the time she managed to pull off the switch without face-planting, her boss was already changing positions again. Julia watched in bemusement as Cleo bent over, palms flat on the office carpet in a downward dog pose.

Okay then.

Julia bit back a sigh and forced her body into a similar position. Her boss's sudden appearance in the break room may have been just a coincidence, but this impromptu yoga session had to be punishment for something.

"What's up?" Cleo asked.

Currently? My ass. Maybe it was all the blood rushing to her head, but Julia decided she might as well go for it. "I heard there's another round of layoffs coming."

"Ah." Cleo met her gaze from between her legs. "And you're worried."

Julia attempted an upside-down nod.

The editorial director rolled to a standing position, and Julia, much less elegantly, followed suit. Going up on her tiptoes, Cleo bobbed up and down. "It's true, there was a memo about staff cuts coming at the end of the month."

Fucking memos. Flexing her calves and hoping she hadn't said that out loud, Julia bobbed too. Popping up and down on her tiptoes, she felt like she was auditioning for a game of Whac-A-Mole. The image was painfully accurate. She needed to stand out from the other moles, do something to avoid getting whacked. She needed to show her worth.

Andie was right. It was time for her TADA moment.

Taking a deep breath, Julia planted her feet on the floor. "I'm one of the best writers you have on staff."

"I know that, Julia."

"Oh." She hadn't been expecting that response. "I didn't think you'd noticed, since I've been writing the same stuff for almost three years."

"I thought you liked writing those lists and quizzes."

"I do." Not a lie.

"And I wouldn't say it's the same. You always deliver fresh, witty, and entertaining content. Your articles get steady traffic on the site. Bring in great ad revenue."

"Not enough, apparently," Julia couldn't help grumbling,

Cleo pressed her lips together.

For a moment, Julia worried she'd gone too far. "I can't lose this job," she blurted.

"I appreciate your honesty." Her boss rested back on her heels. "You were straight with me, so I'll be straight with you. Nothing seems to be enough lately. When these department-wide layoffs come down from the main office, there's not much I can do."

"Is there anything *I* can do? Any extra stories I can pick up?" Julia asked, brain working furiously. "I can switch to another department, write for another column."

"I can probably find a way to keep you on as part time . . ."

Julia shook her head. "I have to be full-time. I need the benefits." Make your ass invaluable. That's what Kat had said. "Give me an assignment, any assignment, any department. I'll make it happen."

"I like your spunk."

Is that what this is? It felt more like desperation. Julia scanned the room, looking for inspiration. Her gaze snagged on a box of key chains on Cleo's desk. Promotional material for the newest *TrendList* segment, a travel adventure log rapidly growing in popularity. Julia pointed to the box. "What about 'Take Me!'?"

"Hm." Cleo tapped her chin thoughtfully. "I couldn't give you much of a travel budget."

"I'll find something local."

"You'd have to come up with an idea fast."

"I'll have a pitch ready for you by Monday."

"Determined, aren't you?" Her boss looked at her, assessing. "Tell you what, Julia. You bring me a pitch on Monday, and I'll consider it."

"Thank you." Julia wanted to collapse with relief.

"You can thank me when I approve your pitch." Cleo slipped back into her heels and handed Julia her coffee mug. "*If* I approve your pitch."

"I'm looking forward to it."

"Excellent!" Cleo pressed her palms together, inhaling and exhaling deeply. "I feel ready to tackle the rest of my day now, don't you?"

"Yep." She grinned at her boss. With her shoes in one hand and Grumpy Cat mug in the other, Julia knew she must look ridiculous, but she didn't care. She'd just been given the chance she needed to save her ass. "So ready."

CHAPTER 3

JULIA

On Friday evening, Julia headed to Andie's place. She was eager to share the results of her meeting with Cleo with her friends, but also nervous. Ever since her bizarre encounter with the editorial director, she'd been a ball of stress. In between meeting her current story deadlines, Julia had spent all her time brainstorming. Despite the confident promise she'd made to her boss, she was worried that she wasn't going to have anything ready on Monday.

She needed a pitch, and that involved coming up with a story idea . . . and in this case, the story needed to be about a place. And not just any place but a freaking cool place. A destination that got readers excited, made them want to shout, "Take me!" But that was also local. Or at least local-ish. So far, nothing she'd come up with had felt unique enough to be worth pursuing.

Julia pushed thoughts about her job to the back burner. Maybe she'd wait until after her next meeting with Cleo to give her friends an update. She was determined to enjoy herself this evening.

Just as Wednesday afternoons were their standing weekly lunch date, Friday nights were their weekly girls' night in. Dick pics aside, Saturdays were for dates, but Fridays were reserved for the three of them and the three Cs: carbs, cocktails, and comedies. They'd eat and drink and watch rom-coms, a tradition begun back when they were all sharing an apartment together, just starting out as grown-ups in the big city.

Well, almost grown-ups. The apartment was an off-campus

place that Andie's parents owned. The three of them had moved in when they were juniors. Now, several years later, the only one still living there was Andie. Kat had left first, taking the condo above the posh flower shop she managed. Julia had moved out a few months after scoring the *TrendList* job, to a matchbook-size loft space downtown. It was tiny but boasted a great view. And was super close to her office.

A perk that wouldn't matter anymore if she didn't come up with an amazing pitch.

Back burner, Julia reminded herself as she unlocked the door. Fun now, worry later.

"Hey," she called out, dumping her purse on the couch.

"Hey." Kat didn't look up from her spot behind the island. Since they both still had keys, Julia wasn't surprised to see Kat at home in the kitchen, cutting triangles of pita bread and spreading them on a plate around a bowl of hummus.

Julia washed her hands in the sink, then reached for a piece of pita and moaned, "Ooh, it's warm."

"I know. I just toasted it." Kat shooed her away from the hummus. "Wait for Andie."

"Where is she?"

"At the store, grabbing some fancy liquor for this new cocktail recipe she wants to try."

Julia made a face. A wannabe mixologist, Andie's creations were hit or miss. She checked the fridge, relieved to see a bottle of white wine chilling. If the latest experiment ended up being a miss, at least they had backup booze.

Kat opened a bag of pretzels and dumped them into a bowl. "What are we watching tonight?"

Swiping a handful of pretzels before Kat could stop her, Julia popped a few in her mouth and walked over to the entertainment center. Grabbing the remote, she clicked to access the streaming service and scrolled until the movie she wanted appeared on the screen.

"*Bridget Jones's Diary*, huh? Going with a classic?"

"I was in the mood for it." Julia polished off the rest of the pretzels in her fist.

"I'm always in the mood for that one." Kat winked, tossing her honey blond braid over her shoulder.

"You're always in the mood for Colin Firth," Julia corrected, tugging on Kat's braid as she walked by.

"Facts," Kat agreed, flopping onto the couch.

"The man has serious BDE."

"Who, Firth?" Julia asked as she inched back toward the kitchen island.

"Well, I'm not talking about Grant. He's got that *Aw, shucks* awkward schtick going for him."

"I kinda like that awkward schtick," Julia admitted.

Kat glanced over her shoulder. "You better not make a move on the pita bread again," she said, shooting Julia a warning look.

Julia held her palms up, proclaiming innocence. "I'm waiting, I'm waiting."

At that moment, a key sounded in the lock and Andie appeared. "Did you bitches start without me?" she asked, face hidden behind the brown paper bag she was carrying.

"Jules tried to," Kat ratted her out. "But I wouldn't let her."

"Well, the gang's all here now, so . . . ." Julia stuck her tongue out at Kat and then grabbed a piece of pita, taking it for a swim in the hummus.

"Very mature, Jules."

"I'm not the one who was talking about Colin Firth's BDE," Julia shot back.

"B. D. *what*?" Andie asked, unscrewing the caps from a couple of liquor bottles.

Julia recognized the vodka label, but she'd never seen the other bottle before. "E," she confirmed, watching with a skeptical eye as Andie measured out shots of the mystery liquid. "Kat is convinced Colin Firth has it."

"Oh, God, it's not some venereal disease, is it?" Andie wrinkled her nose.

"How dare you!" Kat declared, rising from the couch, aghast. "Do not besmirch my Colin that way."

"Hear that?" Julia teased. "No besmirching."

"Got it." Andie added ice to a cocktail shaker and did a little dance around the kitchen, the lithe curve of muscle in her arms bunching as she shook the canister vigorously. A lifelong athlete, she'd have no problem participating in an afternoon stretch session with Cleo. Pouring the mixture into three martini glasses, Andie asked Kat, "So are you going to explain, or do I have to guess?"

"Explain what?"

"BDE." Andie handed Kat a glass.

"Guessing could be fun." Kat grinned wickedly.

"British Devil Eyes?" Andie hazarded, passing a drink to Julia.

"Not a bad guess," Kat acknowledged with a nod. "But nope." Julia caught how Kat surreptitiously lifted the cocktail closer to her nose, giving it the smell test before she raised her glass in a toast. "Na zdrowie," Kat said.

"Sláinte." Julia clinked glasses, but held out a beat longer, watching for signs of gagging. When all seemed fine, she risked a sip.

"Cheers!" Andie chirped, oblivious to their concerns. "What about Boring Dorky Elf?"

"He's not an elf," Kat huffed. "The man is six two!"

"Are we still talking about Colin Firth?" Andie asked. "Because, if so, I'm standing by Boring Dorky Elf."

Laughing midswallow, Julia coughed, spewing her cocktail. "BDE stands for Big Dick Energy."

"Ew," Andie grimaced, turning to Kat. "That man is old enough to be your grandfather."

"He is *not*."

"Your father, then."

"I'm not the one dating guys old enough to be my dad," Kat shot back.

Julia coughed again. That was a low blow.

"Jules?" Kat glanced toward her. "You know I'm right."

"I'm staying out of this one." Julia took another sip of her cocktail, deciding it might be best to change the subject. "What's in this anyway?"

"St. Germain," Andie said, jaw tight, gaze still on Kat.

"The flavor is unique," Julia babbled, over the building tension. "Not bad, just different."

"It's elderflower," Kat explained. "And it's very good." She lifted her glass in salute. "This is an excellent cocktail."

Accepting the compliment for the peace offering it was, Andie relaxed. A sly grin lit her features as she said, "If you want a Colin that has some . . . what was it? Big Dick Energy? Then you gotta go with Colin Farrell."

"Ha!" Kat crowed. "He's shorter than Firth."

"No way." Andie shook her head and reached for her phone.

"You're looking up how tall both the Colins are, aren't you?" Kat demanded.

"Maybe." Andie tapped her screen, brow furrowing.

"Well?" Kat scooted closer. "Was I right?"

"Fine," Andie conceded with a deflated groan. "Farrell is shorter." Hating to lose at anything, she added, "But he's younger. And his BDE is so strong he *seems* taller."

"Five minutes ago, you didn't even know what BDE was," Kat scoffed.

"I'm a quick study," Andie retorted.

Before the battle of the Colins picked up steam, Julia guided her friends toward the couch. "How about we start the movie?" She carried the bowl of pretzels over and hit Play.

Kat set the plate of pita and hummus on the coffee table.

Soon everyone was munching and laughing, sipping and smiling at Bridget's antics. After refilling their glasses with a second round, Andie sat back down next to Kat and said, "Okay, I can see it."

"See what?" Kat wondered.

"Your Colin's big dick."

A giggle-snort escaped Julia. Kat raised an eyebrow.

"I mean the energy, or whatever." Andie waved a hand toward the screen. "The BDE. He's got this confidence. A presence." She licked the side of her cocktail glass. "It's sexy."

"Yeah it is," Julia agreed, raising her glass to clink against her friends. She'd always had a bit of a thing for tall guys.

"Why can't we meet someone like that?" Kat wondered. "You know, have an awkward exchange at a holiday party or something and then it turns into love?"

"Because this is real life." Julia shook her head. "I've had plenty of awkward exchanges at holiday parties. And trust me, it doesn't work that way."

"But what if it did?" Andie insisted. "What if you could stumble across the love of your life wearing a hilariously horrid sweater at a party, or while walking your dog and the leashes get all tangled."

"That's a cartoon, not a rom-com." Julia's mouth quirked. "But either way, you're talking about a fantasy. We don't get meet-cutes with guys with BDE; we get awkward dates with guys who send us unwanted pics of their trouser shrimp."

"Maybe it is fantasy, but that's part of the appeal." Kat tugged on her braid. "I'm with Andie on this one. If we had a chance to meet someone by accident instead of by app, or if life were a little more like a romantic comedy . . ."

On the TV screen, the movie was ending, and the conversation stalled as everyone paused to watch Colin Firth's character kiss Renée Zellweger in the softly falling snow. When he wrapped his coat around them both in the middle of the London street to the tune of a soft, sultry love song, all three girls sighed.

"If life were like a romantic comedy, we'd get more kisses like that," Kat said.

"Total fantasy." Julia shook her head. "I'm as likely to find the wardrobe to Narnia as I am to find my own Mark Darcy. Life isn't like a romantic comedy." As she stared at the melting ice in the dregs of her drink, an idea came to her. "Now *that* would make a great piece for *TrendList*."

"Let me guess." Kat smirked. "'A Dozen Reasons Why Life Isn't Like a Romantic Comedy.'"

"I was thinking ten, but sure, I bet I could come up with a dozen."

"Does this mean you're not getting fired after all?" Andie wondered, collecting their glasses and walking back to the island for refills.

"Laid off," Julia corrected primly. "And that's still a very real possibility, but I've got to keep doing my job while I have one."

"What happened to the asset plan?" Kat asked.

"Yeah, you were supposed to give us an update," Andie reminded her, over the sound of the cocktail shaker.

Julia had intended to keep her pitch problem to herself and focus on enjoying the evening with her friends, but she'd also promised to fill them in. And now that they'd asked . . . She rubbed a hand over her face.

"Well?" Andie pressed. "Did you do the TADA thing?"

"I did."

"And?"

"And this." Julia reached for her purse, pulling out a handful of key chains. She tossed one to Kat.

"What is that?" Andie asked.

"Oh, it's 'Take Me!'"

Andie blinked. "Take you where?"

"No, you daffodil," Kat snapped, her amused tone taking out the sting. She held up the key chain. "It's a new segment on

TrendList." Kat turned her attention back to Julia. "Those videos are all over my social media feed."

"They're all over everyone's social media feed," Julia agreed. "I talked to my boss, and the bottom line is I need to come up with an idea for a place to review by Monday."

"As in *this* Monday?" Andie gasped, handing each of them a fresh cocktail.

Julia resisted the urge to down the whole thing in one gulp. "Yep."

"Ouch." Kat winced.

"Yep." Giving in to temptation, Julia drained her third drink.

"What ideas have you got so far?" Andie wondered.

"Zilch." Julia shook the glass, ice cubes clinking. "And it's only a trial run. Which means I don't get a travel budget, so I need to keep it reasonably local."

"That's good news for you, since you hate traveling anyway," Kat pointed out.

"You would too if you moved around as much as I did when you were a kid." Julia shook her head. Going to college in Chicago was the first time she'd felt grounded. This apartment was the first place to feel like home, and Kat and Andie were the first friends she'd made that she didn't have to pack up and leave after a year or two.

"Not to mention you get carsick all the time," Andie reminded her.

"Not all the time," Julia protested.

Andie and Kat both stared at her, daring her to deny it. The slight downside of having long-term friends: they knew you too well to let you get away with any bullshit. They'd taken too many vacations together for Julia to dismiss the truth. Planes, trains, automobiles . . . it didn't matter what mode of transportation she chose, her motion sickness eventually got the best of her.

Andie frowned, concern creasing her dark brows. "Are you sure this is a good idea?"

"Under other circumstances, the 'Take Me!' segment wouldn't be my top choice, but it's my best chance to keep this job, and I'm willing to do whatever it takes." Julia sighed. "I've got to nail this. I really need to wow my boss with something special. Exciting and new."

"You make it sound like *The Love Boat*," Kat said.

Julia blinked at her.

Kat shrugged. "I've been watching reruns with my babcia again."

"That might actually work," Andie mused.

"You're kidding, right?" Julia swiveled her attention.

"I don't mean the actual Love Boat." Andie laughed. "But maybe there's something like it. A matchmaking cruise ship on Lake Michigan."

"Ooh, sign my babcia up for that," Kat teased.

"Exactly." Julia made a face. "Even if just the thought of a cruise ship didn't make me want to hurl, this sounds like an activity for seniors. Which is fine, but I think the 'Take Me!' target audience veers a little . . ."

"More hip and less hip replacement?" Andie suggested.

"Bingo," Julia said, pointing at Andie.

"Something else my babcia could do on the boat," Kat teased.

Julia ignored that. "Hey, it's only Friday. I've got all weekend for inspiration to strike." She held out her empty glass to Andie. "So how about one more round?"

⁓

Back at work on Monday, the aftereffects of Friday night's four elderflower martinis had faded away, but unfortunately Julia was no closer to deciding on a pitch. She stared at the list of options she'd managed to piece together after a weekend spent scouring the internet. Not a single one felt right.

She glanced at the clock in the corner of her computer screen.

The pitch meeting with Cleo wasn't until this afternoon. Maybe if she focused on something else for a bit, inspiration would strike. Flipping the list over, Julia looked at the title she'd scribbled down for the *TrendList* article, "A Dozen Reasons Why Life Isn't Like a Romantic Comedy."

Using the words *rom-com* and *real life* as her search terms, Julia started poking around for resources. She was scrolling through a list of movie plot summaries when something caught her eye. A resort a little over an hour north of the city, just over the border in Wisconsin, was advertising a grand reopening with a unique twist.

A crackle of energy zinged through her as she read the description. Touted as the "dream destination for fans of romantic comedies," the resort's website promised to make "all your rom-com dreams come true."

WISH YOUR LIFE COULD BE A LITTLE MORE LIKE A ROMANTIC COMEDY? THEN THIS IS THE PLACE FOR YOU.

"There's no way this is for real," Julia muttered. With a snort of skeptical laughter, she couldn't resist clicking to read more about this "destination experience."

COME PLAY IN OUR FULLY IMMERSIVE RESORT, WHERE GUESTS ARE INVITED TO STEP INTO THE WORLD OF ROM-COMS.

She flipped through photos of the picturesque lakefront property, and the more Julia read about what this "rom-com resort" entailed, the more she felt like fate was poking her between the shoulder blades. Her journalistic spidey senses began to hum. For someone who didn't believe in signs, she sure was getting a lot of them lately. The resort was exactly the kind of exciting and new thing she'd been looking for. And it was unquestionably unique. *This is the one.*

Hallelujah, she'd found it. Her perfect "Take Me!" pitch.

Julia leaned forward in her chair and peeked around the side of her laptop. The door to Cleo's office was open. She couldn't just stride over there right now and pitch this idea, could she? Her job—her career—was on the line with this pitch, and she'd done less than fifteen minutes of research, total. Better to wait until this afternoon.

And risk subjecting yourself to more three p.m. stretches?

While Julia appreciated the woman's quest to live a long, happy, grandbaby-filled life, her own hamstrings were still sore from last week. Andie would say it was a symptom of having a sedentary desk job, and her friend was probably right—Julia did spend too much time on her ass. She vowed to get in better shape . . . later. First, she was going to get off her sore behind and nail this pitch.

Wincing only slightly, Julia pushed up from her chair and headed for Cleo's door.

"Julia!" At her knock, Cleo waved her inside. "I thought our meeting was for this afternoon."

"It was, yes," Julia began, immediately wondering whether she'd made a mistake. But she was here now, and the only thing to do was soldier on. "I just couldn't wait to tell you about my idea." Which wasn't a lie.

"There's more of that spunk! I like your enthusiasm." Her boss gestured to a chair. "Please, sit."

Deciding she'd made the right choice, and grateful she wouldn't be fighting for the future of her career while squatting or attempting splits, Julia sat.

"Now then . . ." Cleo clasped her hands together and rested them on her desk. "Where are you taking me?"

———

"Hold up," Kat demanded, waving her chopsticks. "Did you say *rom-com resort?*"

"Uh-huh." Julia fiddled with her own chopsticks, still in their little paper wrapper. She was too worked up to eat. She'd wanted to tell her friends about her pitch right after it happened on Monday but had decided to wait until the assignment was approved. And in the end, the timing worked out perfectly. She'd received the official green light this morning. Just in time to share the news with Kat and Andie at their weekly lunch.

"That's exactly what I said." Julia reached into her purse for her phone and pulled up the resort's website.

"*Come play at our resort perfect for fans of romantic comedies,*" Andie read aloud. She glanced at Julia. "Is this a joke?"

"I know it seems wild. Especially considering we were just talking about this, hypothetically speaking. But it's legit, I swear." Julia bounced in the booth, thrumming with adrenaline. "It's thanks to our conversation Friday night that I found this place."

"The spyware on our phones is really starting to creep me out." Kat shook her head.

"Don't start making tinfoil hats just yet," Julia teased. "This wasn't some spammy pop-up ad. I stumbled across it while working on that story about how real life isn't like a romantic comedy."

"A dozen reasons," Andie added helpfully. "I remember."

"Anyway," Julia pushed on, "I was doing a web search and this place popped up."

"*Make all your rom-com fantasies come true,*" Andie said, reading another line from the website. She raised her eyebrows. "How do they expect to do that?"

"You get to pick from a menu of scenarios popular in romantic comedies." Julia scrolled down. "See?"

"There's paintball!" Andie gasped.

"Uh-huh." Julia pointed at the list. "I think I like karaoke serenade the best."

"But how does this all work?" Kat asked.

"It's a simulation . . . sort of." Julia paused, thinking through her conversation with the resort owner. They'd talked on the phone yesterday, going over the logistics. Maybe it was because she was really enthusiastic about her new venture, but Mrs. Wackyspoon, or whatever her name was, came across as a bit . . .

odd. The woman had babbled on in a bizarre accent Julia suspected was supposed to be British, proclaiming she was delighted to provide a complimentary stay in exchange for promotional coverage with a review of the resort on "Take Me!"

A good thing, too. The lack of expenses was one of the deciding factors in getting her project approved. "Guests are assigned a character, a role to play, they select their activities, and then the games begin."

"Sounds fun." Kat grinned. "Any chance you're looking for some company on this adventure?"

"I was hoping you'd ask." Julia returned the grin. "Here's the best part. I managed to score a complimentary stay for all three of us."

Andie raised her glass in salute. "Impressive."

"When is this grand opening event happening?" Kat asked.

"Week after next." Julia looked at her friends. "I know that's not a lot of warning. Will that work for you?"

"A free stay in a hotel and a chance to spend a week living in a romantic comedy?" Andie whistled. "I'll find a way to make it work. Most of my players will be busy with end-of-school-year stuff anyway."

"It shouldn't be a problem for me, either." Kat fiddled with the end of her braid. "With Mother's Day over and prom season wrapping up, things will be slowing down at the shop til wedding season gets rolling. I'm in."

"So, we're doing this?" Julia asked, excitement bubbling up again.

"Like we could ever say no." Andie grinned.

"Now, show me that list of scenarios," Kat demanded, rubbing her hands together. "Someone told me romantic comedies don't happen in real life, and I'm ready to prove her wrong."

CHAPTER 4

LUKE

Luke O'Neal stood on the balcony overlooking the lobby of the Notting Hill Resort, eyeing the trickle of guests entering the hotel. "We're really doing this."

"Yep." Vijay, his best friend, bobbed his head in agreement. "We're really doing this."

"I can't believe it's finally starting!" Luke's sister declared, her voice brimming with excitement.

"Calm down, Penelope. Things don't kick off 'til tonight." Luke glanced back at the activity below. He shook his head, smiling despite himself. His sister's energy was infectious. "A year ago, if someone had told me this was what I'd be doing, I would have choked with laughter."

"You were at my college graduation party a year ago," Penelope reminded him. "And as I recall, you *did* choke with laughter about this job offer."

"Can you blame him?" Vijay asked. "I thought it was a joke at first, too."

Penelope bristled.

"Oh come on, Pen." Vijay nudged her shoulder with his. "When you told us you'd found some lady who wanted to hire a team to create a romantic-comedy game for her resort—a resort in Wisconsin named Notting Hill—I did wonder if someone was pranking you." Jay shook his head. "Especially when you mentioned how much she was willing to pay."

Luke nodded. "The offer seemed too good to be real."

"Too good to be true, you mean?" Penelope asked.

"No, I mean *real*," Luke insisted. "As in *not fake*."

Penelope rolled her eyes. Luke could hear his sister's mental *Whatever, big bro* as clearly as if she'd said it out loud.

"As for Mrs. Weatherfork," Luke continued, referring to their boss, "the jury is still out." The owner of the resort, Mrs. Miranda Constance Eugenia Weatherfork, was—in a word—eccentric. Luke wasn't sure how much of Mrs. W.'s wild reputation was based on actual exploits and how much was due to outrageous gossip, much of it likely started by the woman herself.

Vijay laughed. "The accent is definitely fake."

"Yeah, but the money is definitely real," Penelope added.

"No arguments there." Despite seeming ridiculous, there were a few facts about his boss that Luke was confident weren't fiction. Fact: she was ridiculously wealthy. Fact: she was spending a ridiculous amount of money on this project. Fact: she had offered them a ridiculously large bonus to be paid once she'd determined that the launch was successful.

In fact, the bonus was so ridiculous one might call it ludicrous. He certainly did. But as Penelope noted, their boss had deep pockets in those weird outfits of hers and could afford it. Luke was determined to earn that bonus. His portion of the funds would provide the seed money he needed to launch his own start-up game company, a dream he'd tucked away for so long that having it within reach now didn't seem possible.

But it was real. *If* this first week proved a success. He rubbed a hand over the back of his neck. "I still think we should have scheduled a practice round first."

"Dude, you gotta let it go." Jay shook his head.

If Luke had been able to do things his way, this week would have been a soft opening with a much smaller guest list, made up of friends and family of the resort employees. A chance to work out any bugs. As a software developer, that's how things were usually done. Teams always tested games and programs in simulation before launch. But his current employer had other plans. "That woman is as impatient as she is eccentric," Luke muttered.

"She's also your boss. This is her resort." Penelope reached up and gave his shoulder an encouraging squeeze. "We need to give the lady what she wants."

"Pen's right," Jay agreed. "Mrs. W. wanted to dive right in with the grand opening. So stop fretting and get ready to make a splash."

Luke shrugged. "I'm just worried the grand opening isn't going to be very . . . grand."

Penelope eyeballed him, another mental *Whatever* stamped on her face. Luke knew she hated when he got pedantic with word choice.

"This is only the beginning," his sister, ever the positive one, promised. "Once word gets out about how much fun this place is, the buzz will build and more people will register for the next session, and the next one, and so on."

"All we've got to do is make sure this first group has a really great time," Vijay added with a wink.

"*Especially* this first group," Penelope winked back.

"All right, what's going on?" Luke demanded.

"Nothing." His sister blinked up at him, her gray eyes, so like his own, beguilingly innocent.

He'd thought she was acting suspicious before, but now he was sure. "I'm not falling for it, Pen."

She blew out a breath. "Fine." Penelope glanced at Vijay. "Tell him."

"I'm not telling him." Vijay shook his head. "You tell him."

"Tell me *what*?"

They both started guiltily as he stared them down.

Vijay broke first. "A reporter is coming,"

"What, like from a local newspaper?" Luke asked. Why would they be afraid to tell him about that? Publicity was Jay's job.

"Not exactly," his friend hedged, gaze shifting to Penelope again.

"Well, then, *what* exactly?" Luke wondered, his voice taking on an edge. Their evasive behavior was making him uneasy.

Jay clasped his hands together and rocked back on his heels. "It's just that, I might have encouraged Mrs. W. to agree to have someone from a website come out and review the resort."

"Okay," he said slowly, still not seeing how this was worrisome. "What site?"

"*TrendList*," Vijay said. "The new 'Take Me!' segment."

"Oh. Wow." His sister sometimes accused Luke of living in a cave, but even he'd heard of the pop culture giant. In fact, he'd recently read an article analyzing the impact of the website's new segment on the travel industry. "Oh, wow," he repeated.

"Don't freak out."

Luke turned to his sister. "Why would I freak out?"

"I don't know. Maybe because, when things aren't in your control you *freak out*."

"It's fine. A big website with international reach is coming to do a story. No problem. We'll show them around, answer their questions." Luke waved his hand dismissively. "Boom. Done."

Again, Vijay and Penelope exchanged glances.

Luke gripped the polished oak balustrade lining the balcony. Despite his assurances to his friend and sister, he felt the twinges of a freak-out starting. "What else aren't you two telling me?"

"They're not here to do a story."

"But Jay just said—"

"They're here to *be* the story."

"Huh?" Luke wasn't being passive-aggressive about word choice this time. He really didn't understand what his sister was saying.

"Let me try, Pen." Vijay stepped between them. "What your sister means is the 'Take Me!' reporter isn't stopping by for a quick interview. They're staying for the week and are going to be part of the game."

"Ah." Luke swallowed.

"Are you freaking out now?" Penelope prodded.

"Maybe." Luke shoved a hand through his hair. "How long have you known about this?"

"Um, a week," Penelope said.

"More like two," Jay admitted sheepishly.

Not this round. Any other round but this one. This first week, he wanted to keep things controlled. Luke pulled his notebook out of the back pocket of his jeans.

"Is he pulling out the notebook?" Vijay asked.

"He's pulling out the notebook," Penelope confirmed with a sigh.

Luke ignored them. Both his sister and his best friend liked to tease him about his ever-present notebook. Vijay said it was Luke's version of a pocket protector, while Penelope insisted it was a security blanket.

They could make fun of him all they wanted. He liked—no, *needed*—to have a place to write his thoughts down.

"I'm going to take a walk," Luke announced. Heading for the door to the terrace, he paused and glanced back at his sister. "Stay out of trouble while I'm gone."

"I'm twenty-three, not three," Penelope reminded him. "When are you going to trust me to handle things?"

"I do trust you, Pen," Luke protested, but even he heard the lack of conviction in his voice. "I just wish you'd be a little less . . . impulsive."

"And I wish you were a little less controlling." She shooed him off. "Go. Make your lists. But don't take too long."

Luke nodded and slipped out the door, hurrying across the terrace and down the stone stairway that led to the beach. He needed some air, a few minutes to breathe, to think. To prepare. At the bottom of the steps, he took the path toward the lake, the sound of crashing waves acting as a salve for his jangled thoughts. After a couple of calming moments, he flipped open his notebook and started a checklist of things he wanted to go over.

They should have told him about the reviewer before. Weatherfork should have told him as soon as she'd arranged it. If his boss had any hope of this project being a success, she needed to give him time to prepare. It was bad enough she'd forced the grand opening.

In his old job, Luke dealt with this sort of thing all the time—stockholders with unrealistic deadline expectations who demanded the product they'd funded be released for sale, whether it was ready or not. As long they kept paying him to fix the inevitable bugs, Luke didn't care. He didn't like it, and he certainly didn't enjoy it, but it didn't bother him.

This, however, bothered him. Luke needed the launch of this project to be perfect. Or at least as perfect as was possible when dealing with the incredibly unpredictable human element. He'd always found code much easier to work with than people, but now this reviewer was thrown into the mix. He'd have to find out who the person was so he could make sure they were having the best time possible, to ensure they would give the best review possible.

Closing his eyes, Luke imagined his problems as a row of dominoes. If he lined them up, he could control how they fell. One after another in a tidy procession. *Click, click, click.*

Eyes still closed, he kept walking. Over the past year, he'd been up and down this path hundreds upon hundreds of times. It was his favorite place on the whole resort. He could walk it blindfolded. Backward. In his sleep. He inhaled the fresh lake breeze, a little calmer now. The dominoes tumbled more slowly. *Click. Click. Cli—*

"Ouch!" A voice, surprised and feminine, collided with Luke's thoughts as his shin made contact with something hard.

What the—

Mental dominoes scattered as Luke stumbled backward, a

warm solid weight falling with him, landing on top of him in the sand.

"*Oof.*"

Had he made that sound? He opened his eyes, his view of the sky above marred by a tangle of bright hair. Not red, not blond, not brown either, but some mix of all three. The strangely colored locks blowing across his face smelled rich and inviting. Like that first breath of freshly brewed coffee when you step inside a café. And it was soft, so silky soft against his cheek.

These details skipped across the surface of his thoughts in rapid succession, like pebbles skipping across a lake, leaving ripples in their wake. Just as things began to settle down, an elbow caught him square in the ribs and sent his thoughts flying again.

"*Oof!*"

This time Luke was sure he'd been the one making that sound. The woman was struggling to get up, and as she tried to stand, she continued to poke and jab him in uncomfortable places. For someone who was so soft, she sure had a lot of sharp, pointy angles. Luke rolled sideways, depositing her in the sand next to him. He stood and offered her his hand.

For a moment, she didn't move, glaring up at him through her veil of not-red-not-brown-not-blond hair. Then she huffed and grabbed on to his hand. If the brush of her hair on his cheek had been soft, the brush of her skin against his was softer still. He was still processing these sensory details when she pulled away from him and began shaking sand from her clothes.

"Do you always walk around with your eyes closed?"

Luke followed suit, brushing off his jeans. "Only when I know where I'm going."

Her mouth dropped open, but no sound came out. She blinked at him. Like her hair, the color of her eyes was mercurial, hard to pin down. Green. Brown. Intelligent. Wary. More pebbles skittered across his thoughts. Who was she? He'd never seen her on this beach before. Was she a guest at the resort? His brain whirred, and he instinctively reached for his notebook.

But it wasn't there. His back pocket was empty. He'd been holding it when he was walking. Holding it when they collided . . .

Luke turned, searching the path. A moment later, he spotted the gleam of the metal spiral in a flash of sunlight, and a moment after that, a seagull swooped down and snatched it up.

"Hey!" Luke yelled, shaking his fist and running after the bird.

Loops of the spiral clipped between its beak, the bird flapped its wings, propelling away from him.

"Give that back you feathered felon!"

"Um, I don't think the bird can speak English," the woman said from behind him, voice dry.

And, if he was not mistaken, amused. At him.

Because he was acting like an imbecile.

Luke glared up at the bird, shaking his fist one more time.

"You better watch out," the woman warned. "Or that seagull is going to—"

Something wet and slimy splattered down the front of Luke's shirt.

"Poop on you," she finished.

Now there was no mistaking it. She was definitely laughing at him. He scowled and dipped his chin, assessing the damage. A zigzag of bird crap decorated his chest. Awesome. And oh, God, the smell. What the heck had that bird been eating for its excrement to smell so bad?

The woman wrinkled her nose.

"It's not me," Luke began. "Well, it *is* me, but it's not . . . It's the bird . . ."

She took a step back.

"Shit," he finished weakly, and attempted to maneuver out of his shirt. He refused to wear what was now basically a seagull diaper. The problem was that Luke also wanted to avoid making contact with the wretched contents of the flying jerk's rectum. Which meant he had to be strategic about where he touched the shirt and how he pulled it off.

"Do you want some help?" the woman offered.

"Do you *want* to help?" he asked, gripping the ends of his shirt between his fingertips and folding the worst of the damage over onto itself.

"Not really."

"Then why did you offer?" Luke grunted, tugging the fabric over his head gingerly, stretching the collar so it didn't touch his face.

"Obligation," she said. "Instinct, maybe."

Luke tossed the shirt on the ground and stared down at her. "Your instinct is to offer help you don't intend to give?"

She raised her chin and met his gaze. "I didn't say I *wouldn't* help, just that I didn't *want* to help."

Luke bit his cheek. He could see why this sort of word game annoyed his sister.

A gust of wind blew in from the lake and the woman's mouth quirked, her attention shifting to his chest. "That's a stiff breeze, huh?"

Heat flushed his skin, and Luke fought the urge to cover himself. "Stop looking at my nipples." Tall, lanky, and more than a tad on the pale side, he'd never been one of those walk-around-shirtless kind of dudes. He was a programmer for chrissake.

"Wow, you're grumpy," she observed.

"You would be too if some woman ran into you, an asshole bird stole your notebook before deciding to take a heinous-smelling dump on you, and then the same woman who knocked you over is now standing there ogling your naked torso."

"I am *not* ogling!"

Luke crossed his arms over his chest, forcing her gaze up to his.

"Okay, fine. Maybe I was ogling. A little," she admitted. "But it's not my fault. You're a giant and it's all, like, right there in my face. How tall are you?" she wondered.

"Six four." He cocked his head. "How short are you?"

"Five four."

Luke narrowed his eyes.

She blew out a breath and rolled her eyes. "Okay, you got me. I'm five three and three-quarters."

His gaze narrowed some more.

"Five three and a half. Almost."

He grinned. Whoever she was, he liked her. All five foot three and almost a half inches of her. Luke was about to ask for her name when a screech assaulted his ears. They both winced. The winged menace had returned. He glanced up, bracing for another poop bomb, and realized his notebook was still in the asshole's beak. What the hell was the bird planning to do with it? Write a manifesto?

"Now do you want my help?" the woman asked.

Luke spread his arms as if to say *Be my guest.*

Jutting her chin in a silent *Okay, buddy, watch me*, she stepped forward and pulled a bag of crackers from her pocket. Shaking the bag, the woman waited until she'd caught the bird's attention.

Luke watched as the airborne weasel circled back.

Once the seagull was close, she tossed the contents of the bag, scattering crackers across the beach. Squawking in excitement, the bird dove, the book dropping from its mouth and landing with a plop in the sand, forgotten as its abductor foraged for the crackers. In a whoosh, several other seagulls joined the fray, beaks snapping in a snacking frenzy.

Luke took advantage of the distraction to scoop up his notebook. He tucked it in his back pocket. "Come on." He reached for her hand and pulled her toward the path. "Now's our chance to escape."

"What about your shirt?" she asked, glancing over her shoulder.

"Leave it," he said, again preoccupied by the sensation of her hand in his. "I'll come back and burn it later."

She laughed.

The bright sound caught him off guard, and he stumbled, sneakers slipping over the sand and pebbles.

Her fingers tightened, warm and soft where they curled against his palm, as she helped him keep his balance.

"Thank you," he muttered, wondering how else he could embarrass himself in the next thirty seconds.

"You weren't walking with your eyes closed again, were you?"

"No, I . . ." he stopped.

She was smiling at him.

That smile. Luke's train of thought derailed, attention rerouting to her mouth. It was a lush mouth, full lips promising to be as warm and soft as everything else.

"Now who's ogling?"

"Huh?" Luke blinked.

"You're staring at my mouth."

"I'm not staring."

Slowly, she licked her lips.

Luke fought the urge to lick his own lips. Or worse, chase the path her tongue just took with his. "Fine." He forced his gaze back to hers. "I'm staring."

At his confession, her smile widened, pulling him in.

He leaned closer.

"Jules!" The voice, deep yet feminine, bounded across the beach, loud enough to rise above the screeching seagulls and crashing waves.

Luke froze. He was bent over his notebook savior, mouth hovering a breath away from hers. If he were an inch shorter, or if she were an inch taller . . .

She stepped back, and he realized she must have been standing on her tiptoes. As he'd been leaning into her, she'd been leaning into him. They'd been about to kiss. And he didn't even know her na—

"Jules!" the voice called again, louder this time.

The woman he'd almost kissed jerked her head in the direction of the sound.

Whoever was calling wasn't visible from where they stood on the beach. But the person sure could yell. "Looking for you?" Luke asked.

"Yeah," she confirmed absently.

"Your name is Jules?"

"Julia, actually."

Jules—Julia—was staring at him with a shell-shocked expression similar to the one he'd bet was stamped on his face.

"Jules!"

They both jumped.

"There you are!" A woman with a trim cap of black hair appeared over the rise. In addition to being loud, she was fast, and in moments she'd reached them. "Feeling better?"

"Much, yeah."

"You weren't feeling well?" The question came out of his mouth before Luke even realized he was asking it.

"Oh." She glanced back at him. The question seemed to surprise her too. "Just a bit of carsickness."

"Ah. That explains the crackers."

She nodded, mouth twitching.

Luke felt a tug in his chest, as if two little strings were tied to the corners of her mouth and had hooked to his heart. When she smiled, the strings pulled tighter.

The grating sound of a throat clearing abruptly clipped those strings, and Luke remembered they were no longer alone on the beach.

"Who's your new friend, Jules?" the dark-haired woman asked. She was staring straight ahead, which meant, Luke realized, belatedly recalling the shirt he'd left in a crumpled, seagull-soiled pile on the sand, that she was staring at his nipples.

"Um, this is . . ." Jules—Julia—paused.

"Luke." He reached out a hand in greeting, resisting the urge to cover his less than impressive *Nothing to see here. Why are you staring?* chest again.

"Hey, Luke. I'm Andie." She shook his hand, at least having the decency to shift her gaze to his face.

"Nice to meet you," he said automatically.

"Same." The girl, Andie, reached into the back pocket of her jean shorts and pulled out a notepad. She held it out to Julia. "You left your precious notepad in Kat's car."

"Oh!" Julia reached for it quickly.

"Precious?" Luke repeated.

"Trust me, she doesn't go anywhere without it," Andie assured him.

"I can understand that," he chuckled. He had to admit, it was rather endearing to discover they shared a habit.

Andie snorted. "I just assume it's one of the hazards of being a r—"

"Writer," Julia said abruptly.

"A writer?" he asked, unable to resist taking a peek at her notepad. "What kind of stuff do you write?"

"Poetry, mostly." She clutched the pad to her chest, casting a cautious glance his way.

"I don't think I've ever met a poet before," Luke said.

"Me neither," her friend Andie added cryptically.

Julia elbowed her.

"Ow!" Andie rubbed her side. "What was that for?"

"For making fun of my poetry," Julia said through clenched teeth. She moved to elbow Andie again, but the dark-haired girl jerked back, a set of keys flying out of her pocket.

Luke could sympathize. He knew from recent firsthand experience how sharp and painful a seemingly delicate elbow could be when thrust into one's rib cage. He bent, digging the keys out of the sand. Something about the key chain caught his eye. He looked closer and realized why it seemed familiar.

It was the "Take Me!" logo. He frowned. This couldn't be a coincidence.

"Thanks." Andie reached out to take the keys back. "For grabbing those," she added, tugging gently when he didn't let go.

Luke shook himself. "No problem." He released his hold on the key chain. "Isn't that from *TrendList?*"

"It is." Julia slid between Luke and Andie and inserted herself into the conversation. "Those are our friend's keys. She's a big fan of all the *Bachelorette* quizzes they do." Julia turned to Andie. "Did you need help bringing in our bags?"

Andie shook her head. "All done. Kat's checking us in now."

They were here for the rom-com week, of course. Questions gathered in the back of his mind. But before he could attempt an interrogation, Andie beat him to it with another question of her own. "Are you staying at Notting Hill, too?"

"Ah . . ." Luke frantically tried to think of a plausible explanation for his presence on the beach. He could lie, but it's not like he could hide from them at the hotel forever. Besides, he was the game master. They'd be meeting him tonight at orientation.

Luke winced internally. He'd been worried about his sister causing trouble, but he was the one potentially screwing things up. Penelope was the event planner. She created the rom-com aesthetic and set the stage. As GM, he was the director. His job was to figure out where to place the characters on the stage, and when. His participation was limited to arranging the guests' experiences, not experiencing them himself.

At least, that was how it was supposed to work.

Luke's brain whirred. Options lined up like dominoes, possibilities spreading out before him in a network of potential scenarios. Swap one element and the web shifted, the path changing. Leading to new options, new possibilities. An idea took shape in his mind, and as Luke surveyed the formation of this new path, his plan clicked into place.

"Ah, yes." He grinned down at them. "Yes, I am."

CHAPTER 5

LUKE

The next few minutes passed in a blur as Luke walked back to the resort with Julia and her friend Andie. Her very chatty friend Andie. He should be grateful. All of Andie's talking saved him from having to say much of anything and risk screwing things up worse than he had already.

He reset the line of dominoes in his head. *Pause. Analyze. Redirect. You can make this work.*

It wasn't a screwup, or at least it didn't have to be. It was a change in plans. And since he was the one in charge of those plans, he could rearrange a few things. He just needed to act fast.

As soon as they reached the steps leading up to the hotel, Luke mumbled something about how nice it had been meeting them both and rushed ahead, scanning the lobby for Penelope. She and Vijay were no longer on the second-floor balcony but had moved to the concierge desk on the main floor. His sister's eyes widened when she caught sight of him making his way toward her.

Without preamble, he grabbed her hand and pulled her behind a decorative screen.

"What are you doing?" Penelope demanded, as Luke crowded into the space behind the screen with her. "And where's your shirt?"

"Yeah, dude," Vijay said, cramming in next to Penelope on the other side of the screen. "What the hell are you doing walking around like that? You're going to blind the guests with your pasty chest."

"Hush," Luke growled, peeking around the screen. The girls

from the beach hadn't made it up the steps to the lobby yet. These long legs of his were good for something.

"What are you doing?" Penelope asked again.

"Trying to be inconspicuous."

Vijay snorted. "Right. A six-and-a-half-foot half-naked pale-ass white guy. Totally not conspicuous."

"That's why we're behind the screen," Luke said quietly between gritted teeth.

"All right, big brother, enough with the cloak-and-dagger. What's going on?"

"A cloak might come in handy right about now," Vijay muttered. "An invisibility cloak."

Penelope silenced Vijay with a baleful glance.

Luke smirked. Pen always could keep Jay in line. He turned his attention back to his sister. "Change in plans."

"You ditch us to take off with your little notebook for almost an hour and come back telling me there's a change in plans?" Penelope stiffened, voice rising. "I thought you don't like sudden changes in plans."

"I don't. Which, if you'll recall, is why I took off with my little notebook in the first place." After another quick glance around the lobby to make sure the coast was clear, Luke tugged on his sister's hand and made a break for the control room.

"Who's the impulsive one now?" Pen grumbled under her breath as she hurried after him, Vijay on her heels.

Luke knew his sister understood him well enough to know that whatever he was doing, no matter how strange it seemed, he had a good reason for it. She trusted him. Now he had to trust her. "I need you to take over as game master."

"*What?*"

"Did you just say you want Pen to be the GM?" Vijay asked, closing the control room door behind him.

"Yeah." Luke caught his friend's eye above his sister's head. "And I want you to help her."

"What are *you* going to be doing?" Pen wondered

"I'm going to be part of the game." Luke slid into his chair and began opening files on the computer.

"You didn't happen to run across any alien pods while out on the beach, did you, Luke?" Vijay asked, sitting down next to him. "Maybe they abducted your brain along with your shirt."

"Hilarious." With a couple more clicks, Luke had created a new character profile, one for himself.

"Jay has a point, dear brother. You never want to play a part in the sims. And putting someone else in charge?" She paused, the sarcastic tilt of her head echoed by her tone. "Did anyone check the temperature in hell today?"

"I ran into a few of the guests on the beach."

"So?"

"So they think I'm a guest too, here for the game, just like they are."

"Why would they think that?"

"Because it's what I told them."

"Why?" his sister repeated, eyeing him.

"I'm getting to that," Luke said, while his character sheet printed. "Has the reporter checked in to the hotel yet?" he asked.

"Just finished up." Vijay pointed at one of the surveillance camera screens for the lobby. He tapped his finger on a trio of women standing together near the bellhop station, confirming Luke's suspicions. "That one. Blond hair. Pink dress."

"Are you sure?" Luke asked, even though he was already sure himself.

"Yep." Jay bobbed his head. "After Mrs. W. had the call with the reviewer to make the arrangements for her stay, I flagged the reservation. Told the front desk to make sure she got one of the best suites."

Luke frowned. "But won't that make it seem like we're pandering to her for a good review?"

"Well, aren't we?" Pen blinked at him. "Isn't that what you were off brainstorming about?"

His sister made a fair point. He had been trying to come up with ways to ensure the reporter had a great time in the hopes of securing a great review. And then he'd stumbled into Julia and everything had gone haywire. He laughed ruefully. This was either a perfect storm of opportunity or a bigger clusterfuck than he'd imagined.

"What's so funny?" Vijay asked.

"Those other two?" Luke flicked a glance at the security screen. "They're the guests I ran into on the beach."

"Ah." Penelope tapped the dimple in her chin. Like their gray eyes, it was another feature they shared. "This could be really good."

"Or really bad," Vijay countered.

"Exactly. We all agree we need to make sure this reporter has a fantastic experience, right? I've already met the two people she arrived with, who I assume are her friends."

"You know what happens when you ass—" Vijay began.

"Don't." Luke held up a hand. "This is more than an assumption. I heard them refer to her as their friend."

"They told you their friend was reviewing the resort?" Penelope blinked. "That seems bold."

"They didn't tell me that part. I made the logical deduction."

"Pardon me, Sherlock," Pen snarked.

"Also, she has a *TrendList* key chain," Luke admitted.

"Way to bury the lede." Jay shook his head. "So what's your plan?"

Luke grabbed the printout of his character sheet and stuffed it into a folder. "I've met these women. I have an in. By inserting myself into the sim, I can use them to cozy up to the reporter, gather intel."

"I don't know about this." His sister wrinkled her nose. "'*Use* them'?" She shook her head. "That's not like you, Luke."

"Bad choice of words," he admitted.

"Take advantage of?" Vijay suggested.

Luke scowled at his friend. "If you mean take advantage of the circumstances, then yes." Guilt nipped at his conscience, but he ignored the unpleasant feeling and focused on what was important. Nailing this opening. Score his bonus. Helping Mrs. W. get what she wanted so she would help him get what he wanted. That was the plan. He was simply making adjustments to ensure the plan worked. "They're here to take part in a role-playing game, right? I'm simply going to be part of that game, too."

"Hm." Penelope made a noise, unconvinced. She opened Luke's folder and scanned his newly created character profile. "You named yourself Lance?"

"Nice. Make sure you pick 'Romantic picnic brunch for two' as your bonus activity," Jay suggested.

"Maybe I will." Luke shot back. "I like brunch."

"Don't make me put you both in time-out," Penelope warned. "Now, let's go over the details of your plan, *Lance*."

"First of all, you need to pretend you don't know who I am." Luke focused on his sister. "When you're running the game, if we happen to cross paths, you have to act like we're meeting for the first time."

"Why should I do that?" Pen wondered.

"I don't want the three of them thinking I work for the resort. They'll question the motives behind everything I do."

"You're going to lie to these women?" His sister's tone made it clear she was still not a fan of this plan.

"It's a game, Pen," Luke soothed, feeling another twinge of guilt at the manipulation he was planning. "It's not lying; it's pretending. The whole thing is made up anyway."

She bit her lip, and he knew she was mulling it over. Pen may have been the one to find this job, but as the developer, Luke was in charge of the simulation. He was the project manager, and in the end he got to call the shots. But he also valued his sister's opinion. She glanced at the monitor where a bellhop was loading the women's bags onto a luggage cart. "This could be a disaster."

"Thanks for the vote of confidence," he grumbled.

She turned to Vijay. "What do you think?"

The fact that Penelope was turning to his best friend for advice shouldn't bother Luke, but it did. He was her big brother. It was his job to look out for her. A job he'd always taken seriously, especially after she'd gotten sick when they were kids. And even though his sister's health had been fine for years, even though he knew Pen was growing up and didn't need his help as much as she used to, Luke still liked being the one she turned to first, the one whose opinion she trusted most.

Jay stroked his chin in contemplation. "I think we should try it Luke's—I mean *Lance's*—way."

Well, at least his best friend was agreeing with him, even if he was giving him shit at the same time. And what the hell was wrong with choosing Lance anyway? It was a perfectly good name.

"Besides," Vijay added, wiggling his eyebrows, "this means *we* get to be in charge, Pen."

That didn't sit too well, either. "Wait a minute." Luke frowned. "Technically, I'm still in charge."

"There's the Luke I know and love." Penelope shook her head, exasperated. "You said you wanted me to be game master." She crossed her arms. "*Technically*," she added in a mocking echo, "that means *I'm* in charge."

"If you insist on getting technical—"

"You started it."

Luke ignored the jab and continued, "As I was saying, yes I want you to take over as GM, but I see it more as you playing a role."

Her gray eyes narrowed to slits. "Playing a role."

"Sure." Luke hastened to explain. "Like I'm going to be pretending to be a guest in the game. Really, I'll still be in charge of all the behind-the-scenes stuff. I don't expect you to actually take charge of everything—"

"Because you don't think I can handle it." She scowled.

"I didn't say that."

"I am not a helpless little kid, Luke!" Penelope stomped her foot.

He raised an eyebrow. At this moment, she looked exactly like a child throwing a tantrum.

She must have gotten the message, because she straightened her shoulders and took a slow, deep breath. Her face relaxed, and when she spoke again her voice was calm and cool. "I have a degree in business with a focus in hospitality. Unlike you, Mr. Programmer, I'm good with people. I can handle this just fine."

"It's more than just that, Pen. And you know it. I've created and led LARPs before. You haven't."

"I helped you create this one," she reasoned. "And you weren't the only one Mrs. W. hired to run this project. She hired me, too. And Jay." She lifted her chin, gaze flinty with challenge. "We've all got a lot riding on this, big brother. If you really believe your plan will help garner a good review and increase the resort's chances for success, you need to go all in. You can't be half-assed about it."

Before Luke could protest, which he was sorely tempted to do, Penelope continued, "If you think this charade of yours will work, I trust you. All I ask is that you do the same for me. At the very least, give me a chance to prove myself."

Luke harrumphed, but he didn't argue.

"So what's the plan, boss?" Vijay asked.

Luke was about to answer when he realized Vijay was asking Penelope. He harrumphed again.

His sister shot Jay a grateful grin before turning back to face him. "We're all in this together, big bro." She patted him on the back. "We make a great team."

Luke relaxed. She had a point. The three of them had been a team well before this venture started. As long as they trusted one another and stuck together, he believed they could succeed.

CHAPTER 6

JULIA

A bellhop pushed the luggage cart down a long hallway, Julia and her friends trailing behind. The hotel turned out to be much larger than she'd expected, and grander too. It reminded her of a resort in Florida that was designed to look like an Italian villa, except this place was built so that the exterior resembled a row of English townhomes smushed together. Something you'd expect to find on a posh street in London, not off the shore of Lake Michigan. Notting Hill in Wisconsin. She smiled to herself as they passed doors to various rooms, all painted a bright, bold blue.

Downstairs, Kat had given each of them a tiny envelope with a key card. Julia had assumed the resort would only spring for one room, meaning the three of them would be rotating on couch duty. But when she got back from her walk along the beach, she'd been pleasantly surprised to discover separate rooms had been assigned to each of them.

At the end of the hall, the bellhop stopped and glanced back at them quizzically. Realizing that he didn't know which of them belonged to which room, Julia and her friends gathered their luggage and handed him a tip. As the squeaking wheels of the cart faded away, they checked the numbers on their envelopes and found the corresponding doors. She and Andie were directly across the hall from each other, while Kat had the room on the wall between, through a set of French doors.

Kat read the sign over the number on her room. "The Princess Suite. Ooh, fancy."

"Hey, how come you get a suite?" Andie wondered, eyes narrowing with suspicion. "Did you pick the good room for yourself?"

Kat shook her head. "I had no idea. I checked in like Julia asked and these were the rooms they assigned each of us." Kat waved her card over the lock. She opened the door and gasped.

"What?" Andie demanded. She craned her neck and looked over Kat's shoulder. "Oh, wow. Jules, you gotta see this."

Curiosity already had Julia following her friends inside. Oh, wow, indeed. "Somebody got an upgrade." Julia whistled. "I see why they call this the Princess Suite."

"Not fair!" Andie pouted, dropping her bags by the door. She eyed Kat again. "What did you do? Flirt with the desk clerk?"

"I'm flattered you think my flirting abilities could manage this," Kat snorted. "I told you, I just did what Julia said and checked us in under the reservation number."

"The hotel had to know that was the *TrendList* reservation." Julia leaned her suitcase against a walnut sideboard. She eyed the basket of fruit and wine resting on top. "I bet they think you're the reporter."

"Me?" Kat gaped. "Why would they think that?"

"Because you were the one to check us in, genius." Andie flounced onto the enormous bed. "Have I ever mentioned I've always wanted a canopy bed?"

"This is the first I'm hearing of it." Kat ignored Andie's not-so-subtle hint and turned to Julia. "This should be your room."

"No." Julia waved a hand.

"If she doesn't want it, I'll take it," Andie declared from among a pile of pillows.

"Really," Kat insisted. "Perk of your new position, right?"

"It's not mine yet," Julia reminded her. "This is only a trial run."

"Even more reason for you to take this room. In case you're out a job soon."

"Kat!" Andie chastised, rolling off the bed. She stood and

patted Julia on the shoulder. "Don't listen to her. You're not going to lose your job."

"Thanks."

"Thank me by letting me have this suite." Andie winked and reached for an apple from the gift basket.

A note card fluttered to the floor and Julia bent to retrieve it. She flicked the card open. *"We're honored you're here. Hope you'll tell everyone about your stay!"* She sighed. "Yep. This suite is for the 'Take Me!' reporter."

"I bet they put those cards in all the rooms," Andie said around a mouthful of apple.

Julia held up the card. "Do they also write *'Can't wait to read your review!'* on all of them too?"

"Possibly," Kat mused.

Julia pursed her lips and narrowed her gaze skeptically. "Really?"

"Okay, you're probably right. But why do you sound upset?" Kat wondered.

"Because it feels like a bribe. I want to write my review based on a *real* experience." She glanced around the room again, gesturing at the luxurious surroundings. "Not some extravagant royal VIP version."

"But you are a VIP," Kat insisted.

Julia fiddled with the card in her hand. "No," she said in a decisive burst of inspiration. *"You* are."

"Excuse me?"

"You can be the reporter."

"No, I can't!"

"Not the real reporter, just my decoy." Julia paced the room, her plan taking shape. "This actually works out perfectly. If the resort thinks you're the reporter and focuses their efforts on catering to you, I'll be free to experience things from a more anonymous angle." She rubbed her hands together. "It will allow me to have the authentic experience I was hoping for."

"Should we pretend we don't know each other?" Kat wondered.

Julia shook her head. "We already checked in together. That would be weird."

"Oh, like any of this isn't weird," Kat snorted, moving to inspect an elaborate bouquet of flowers.

"You two really need to check out this tub." Andie's voice echoed from the depths of the suite. "Forget the bed. I'm sleeping in here."

Kat looked up, mouth quirking. "See what I mean?"

"Hey, if you don't want to play reporter," Andie called, "I'm happy to do it."

"That won't work." Julia followed the sound of her friend's voice into the bathroom. Sure enough, Andie was sprawled inside the enormous Jacuzzi tub, finishing off her apple.

"Can you bring me a pillow?" Andie asked, sitting up.

"You're not sleeping in there." Julia laughed. "And you can't pretend to be the reporter."

"Why not?" Andie stretched her arm out and flicked her wrist. The apple core went sailing overhead, landing squarely in the trash can across the bathroom.

"First, the resort already thinks Kat is." Julia offered Andie a hand and helped hoist her out of the tub. "And second, one of the other guests already met both of us."

"Who?" Kat asked, joining them in the bathroom.

"Luke," Julia replied, unable to resist a smile as she said his name.

"Who's Luke?"

"The guy Jules met on the beach." Andie hopped onto the bathroom counter. "It's not fair. Kat gets to live like a princess for a week, and you're not even here ten minutes and already having a meet-cute."

"I was on a completely empty beach and managed to collide with a guy who had a bird crap on him. It was your typical hot-mess-Julia-walking-disaster scenario, *not* a meet-cute." Julia turned and glanced at her reflection in the vanity mirror. Like everything else in the suite, the mirror was as enormous as it was elegant. She smoothed down her hair, messy from her walk—and tumble—on the beach. An image of Luke flashed in her mind's eye, and heat rose in her cheeks.

"Your blush says otherwise." Andie leaned past Julia to wink at Kat. "It was *totally* a meet-cute."

Julia ignored that. "My point is, we introduced ourselves. He knows who we are."

"But he doesn't know what any of us do for a living," Andie argued.

"That's true," Julia admitted. "No thanks to you." She gave her friend the stink eye.

"What did I do?"

"You dropped Kat's 'Take Me!' key chain and almost blew my cover."

"Oh!" Andie blinked, realization dawning. "That's why you made up that poet shit. I was wondering what the heck you were going on about."

"Poet shit?" Kat asked, moving to stand on the other side of Andie. She reapplied her lipstick, the same perfect shade of rose pink as her dress.

Julia glowered. "It was the best I could come up with in the moment." Recalling the close call with keys, an idea suddenly popped into her brain and she brightened. "Actually, this works out perfectly."

"It does?" Andie paused. "Why? Because I told him the key chain belonged to Kat?"

"Exactly." Julia smiled with smug satisfaction.

"Well, it is my key chain." Kat said. "Did you remember to lock the van?"

"No," Andie said. "And I left the headlights on."

"She's kidding," Julia assured Kat. "You've got nothing to worry about. And neither do I." For once, something was going her way. "If word gets out there's a reviewer from *TrendList* at the resort, we can easily steer the gossip toward you." Julia glanced at her friend. "You don't mind pretending to be me for a week, do you?"

Kat swept an arm around the luxurious bathroom and twirled. "I think I can handle it."

"And if not, I'm happy to play understudy." Andie slid off the counter. "Speaking of, I wonder when we find out what characters we're going to be playing in this game."

"How does that work?" Kat asked. "Do we get to make it up?"

Julia shook her head. "They're assigned. There's probably a packet of information we need to pick up at the front desk, or maybe at the concierge. I should have checked . . ."

"Oh!" Kat dropped her lipstick and ran from the bathroom.

Julia glanced at Andie, who shrugged and picked up the lipstick tube and began outlining her lips in pink.

Kat returned in a rush and plopped three folders on the bathroom counter. "They gave me these when I checked in."

"Why didn't you hand them to us with our room keys?" Andie asked, capping the lipstick and passing it back to Kat.

"I assumed it was the usual hotel junk. Maps, room service menus, spa coupons . . . Our names aren't on them, just the room information."

Andie picked up a folder. "Well, this one's for you, Your Highness," she said, giving Kat the folder labeled "Princess Suite."

She held up the other two folders and offered them to Julia. "Which one?"

Julia glanced at the labels. "I'll take the Trendy Coffee Shop room."

"I could have guessed, caffeine junkie." Andie grinned and handed over the folder before glancing at the last one. "That leaves me with Posh Manhattan Apartment." Andie raised an eyebrow, considering. "That doesn't seem so bad. I mean, it's not the royal treatment, but . . ."

"Are all the players resort guests?" Kat wondered, changing the subject.

Julia shook her head. "The hotel website mentioned professional performers also playing parts. I think it's going to be kind of like one of those murder mystery dinners, where guests are given a role to play but actors control the flow of the game."

"This sounds like LARPing," Andie mused.

"Like what now?" Kat cocked her head.

"Live action role-playing." Andie shrugged. "I've done a few."

Kat turned to Julia. "Did you know about this secret nerd life she's been hiding from us?"

"Shut up," Andie grumbled. "It's fun," she added, turning around to face the mirror.

"I'm not disagreeing with you," Kat said.

"Yikes," Andie said to her reflection. "This color looks terrible on me."

"I'm not disagreeing with you," Kat repeated, smirking as she handed Andie a tissue. "Rose is a summer flower and a summer color. I'm a summer. Jules is an autumn. You're a winter."

"If you say so." Andie wiped her mouth. "How about we move this riveting conversation out of the bathroom?"

"You're the one who wanted to sleep in the bathtub," Kat teased.

"Yeah, but I've got a posh apartment in Manhattan now," Andie teased back, patting Kat on the cheek.

For a brief moment, as Julia settled onto one of the plush chairs in the suite's decadent parlor, she regretted insisting that Kat take this room. But she quickly dismissed the thought and scanned the contents of her folder. "There isn't much here," she said, looking over the information, which included a name, occupation, and basic backstory.

"That's standard," Andie said flopping onto the sofa. "Leaves room for you to get creative and fill in the details."

"There's an itinerary." Kat joined Andie on the couch. "Dinner tonight is at seven."

"Oh, thank God, they're going to feed us." Andie exhaled with relief.

"Did you think you weren't going to eat for an entire week?" Kat wondered.

"No." Andie shrugged. "I just figured we'd be on our own."

"All meals are included," Julia explained. "It's part of the experience."

"Oh, and it says there's a Mix and Mingle Cocktail Hour at six," Kat added, reading from the itinerary again. "I like the sound of that."

"They're probably doing that instead of a hot seat session."

Julia turned to Andie for clarification. "Hot seat?"

"It's a LARPing activity where the players break into groups and grill each other."

"About what?" Kat asked.

"Basic stuff." Andie shrugged. "Favorite color, favorite food, biggest fear . . . You know, things to help develop your character."

"Like speed dating." Kat grinned.

"Kind of, yeah." Andie winked. "But with yourself."

"Should we figure some of this out now?" Kat wondered. "We can do it together." She pulled out her sheet and read, "*Bridget Johnson, sales executive from London.* Aw, do you think that's supposed to be like Bridget Jones?"

"I think that's a safe assumption, yes." Julia laughed. "I'll go next. I'm Meg Bryant."

"Subtle," Andie snorted.

Julia nodded. Yes, she'd gotten the obvious nod to rom-com royalty Meg Ryan. "*Occupation: bookstore owner from Seattle.*" She rolled her eyes. "It's a tad twee, but I can work with it."

"What about you, Andie?" Kat asked.

Andie pulled out her sheet and scanned the page. "You have got to be shitting me."

"What?" Kat tried to read over Andie's shoulder.

"Back off, Bridget." Andie wiggled out of reach and read her sheet out loud: "*Carrie Day, fashion designer from NYC.*"

Julia and Kat burst into giggles.

"What's so amusing?" Andie groused.

"*You* as a fashion designer?" Kat shook her head vigorously. "It's hilarious."

"Tell me, what's your biggest fear, Carrie?" Julia asked, struggling to keep a straight face.

"Outlet malls," Andie replied, deadpan.

Kat collapsed onto the couch cushions in another fit of giggles.

"We should get changed before dinner." Julia grinned. "Too bad we probably won't need costumes."

"It'd be fun," Andie agreed, "to dress up in a famous costume from a romantic comedy. I'd love to wear the red dress from *Pretty Woman*." She gathered up her stuff. "Even though I don't have the legs to pull it off."

"You've got great legs."

"I didn't say my legs weren't great." Andie glanced down, patting one thickly muscled thigh. "But they are short and stumpy. And that dress is made for someone tall and willowy." She hoisted her duffel bag over her shoulder. "You could make it work, Kat."

"Not my style." Kat shook her head. "I'd want to wear the outfit Molly Ringwald's character makes for herself in *Pretty in Pink*."

"Of course," Andie and Julia replied in stereo, sharing a knowing grin.

Julia retrieved her luggage. "I suppose I'd pick the dress Meg Ryan wears in the New Year's Eve scene from *When Harry Met Sally*."

"Good choice." Andie nodded.

"Ooh, yeah," Kat cooed. "Sexy off-the-shoulder gown in that gorgeous blue."

"And those long fancy gloves," Julia added.

"They weren't gloves," Kat insisted.

"They weren't?" Julia glanced at Kat. "Are you sure?

"Jules, please. I know my rom-com outfits. They were detached sleeve things."

Andie snickered. "Is that a technical term?"

"What would you call them, Miss Fashion Designer?"

"I don't know—odd? Besides, who really cares about the dress?" Andie argued. "The most important thing about that scene is what Harry says to Sally."

"Agreed." A wistful sigh escaped Kat. "When he lists all the things he loves about her . . ."

"And how he wants the rest of his life to start now . . ." Andie echoed Kat's sigh. "To have someone say that to you."

"It would be wonderful." Julia couldn't help it, she sighed too. "But it's pure fantasy."

"Oh, come on, Jules," Kat groaned. "It's romantic."

"It is," Julia agreed. "But have you ever met someone you can picture saying those things to you in real life?"

Their silence made her point. After a beat, Andie shifted her bag on her shoulder and grabbed another piece of fruit from the gift basket. "Well, that's why we're here, right? To live the fantasy." She pointed at Julia. "And *you* need stop being so negative."

"Yeah," Kat chimed in. "You need to be open to the idea of this being real—or at least *feeling* real. Otherwise it's going to be a very long week resulting in one very crappy review."

"See, that's where you're wrong." Julia shook her head. "My attitude makes me the perfect person to write this review."

"Because you're going to hate this place?" Andie wondered, opening the door to the suite.

"No." Julia rolled her suitcase into the hall. "Because," she jabbed a thumb at herself, "if they can manage to make this skeptic feel like she's living in a rom-com, they can make anyone."

CHAPTER 7

LUKE

After grilling Luke on the details of his plan, his sister had sent him to his room to change—accompanied, also at Penelope's insistence, by Vijay. He'd intended to just rinse off and put on a clean shirt, but Pen had laughed and told him if he was going to go forward with this charade, he needed to follow her rules. And one of those rules was that he "dress appropriately for the part."

Luke never should have told his sister she was in charge. The power was already going to her head. But after a few minutes of arguing when they were already pressed for time, he finally agreed to go upstairs with Vijay so he could, according to Penelope, "look like a love interest."

What was that even supposed to mean? Was there some secret rom-com hero dress code he was unaware of?

Apparently, there was. And it consisted of crisp dress shirts in colors the exact shade of gray as his eyes and fisherman sweaters and those knit shirts with the buttons at the neck that Vijay informed him were called Henleys.

"You sound like a Macy's ad. How do you know all this stuff?" Luke wondered.

"How do you *not*?" Vijay glanced over his shoulder from his spot in front of Luke's closet. "You've watched even more of those movies with your sister than I have. Didn't you ever notice what the characters were wearing?"

"Um, this is *me* we're talking about. On any given day, I hardly notice what *I'm* wearing."

"Good point." Vijay turned back to the closet and frowned. "Is this everything?"

"I've got a few things in the dresser." Luke moved to open a drawer, pulling out a hoodie.

"A sweatshirt? No way." Vijay shook his head. "Pen would kill me." He pulled a few shirts from the closet and tossed them on the bed. "I can't believe we've been living here for almost a year and these are all the clothes you own."

"Yes, you can."

"You're right," Vijay sighed. "Unfortunately, I can."

He and Vijay had been best friends since grade school. And Luke's fashion sense, or lack thereof, hadn't changed in more than twenty years. Jeans. Sneakers. T-shirt. Nicer dress shirt when the occasion called for it. Lucky for him, in his line of work, the occasion rarely called for it.

Vijay stared at the clothes strewn across the bed. "This is hopeless." He headed for the door. "Come with me."

"We don't have time to go shopping."

"I know." Vijay held the door to Luke's room open. "We're going to my room."

Jay, Luke, and Penelope all had suites on a floor of the hotel reserved for staff. Vijay was just a few doors down and Pen's room was in the opposite wing, near Mrs. W.'s suite. The contract to create the rom-com sim for the resort included room and board at the hotel. A great perk, and one of the reasons Luke had been so quick to agree to Penelope's suggestion and apply for this programming position.

She'd been the one to find Mrs. W.'s bonkers job posting last spring, during a frantic about-to-graduate-college search on LinkUp. From the beginning, he'd thought the listing was too good to be real. The Notting Hill post had included a call for a game developer, an event planner, and a marketing director. It was as if someone had tailor-made a job opportunity for the three of them. He was in charge of creating the sim and integrating it with the hotel's management system, Penelope oversaw plans for the guests' dining and lodging experience, and Jay was responsible for handling marketing and designing a publicity campaign. As Pen had said, they made a great team.

Inside Jay's room, Luke was impressed as ever by his friend's organizational skills. The closet was filled with neatly hung shirts and pants. *Who hangs up pants?* All arranged by color. Jay slipped an impeccably pressed shirt from a hanger and thrust it at Luke.

"This will never work, Jay." Luke eyed the shirt his friend held up. "I'm at least six inches taller than you."

"Seven inches. And thanks for rubbing it in," Vijay grumbled, throwing the shirt at Luke's head. "It's not my fault you're the Jolly Green Giant."

Luke shook his head, grinning as he recalled a similar comment made by a certain hazel-eyed girl on the beach.

"It's not funny."

"I'm not laughing at you."

"Then what are you smiling about?"

"The woman I met on the beach."

"The one who got us into this mess?" Vijay wondered.

"Yeah. She called me a giant too."

"I change my mind." Jay frowned, giving Luke a once-over. "You're too scrawny to be a giant."

"Ouch. Now who's rubbing things in?" Luke finished doing up the buttons and held out his arms. The sleeves were too short, flapping awkwardly above his wrists. "I told you this wouldn't work."

"What are you talking about?" Vijay rolled the cuffs midway up Luke's forearms. "This is perfect."

"Are you sure I can't wear one of my own T-shirts?"

"Absolutely not. T-shirts in romantic comedies are only for guys who look like their muscles are about to bust the seams. Think Ryan Reynolds or Ben Affleck."

"Ben Affleck sucks in rom-coms."

"Fair point." Vijay bobbed his head. "But *my* point is these are guys who also play superheroes. And as we've already established"—he poked Luke in the chest—"you don't have the goods."

"Dude. Harsh."

"Besides," his best friend continued, ignoring him, "if you're going to wear a T-shirt, it should be a V-neck, and preferably black. All yours have video game characters on them."

"Not all of them."

"Fine. Most of them."

"Some of those are vintage, you know."

"Is that what we're calling it?" Jay snorted. "It doesn't matter, because you're wearing this."

"I don't know." Luke eyed himself in the mirror over Vijay's dresser, identical to the one in his own room.

"You look great, trust me." Vijay glanced at the clock on the bedside table. "I'm done giving you compliments. Now sit down so I can do something with your hair."

By the time Jay was finished, the cocktail hour was already in full swing. Feeling like Frogger making that first jump onto the busy highway, Luke squared his shoulders and entered the fray. All around him, people were laughing and chatting, pointing to their name tags and introducing themselves to each other as their characters.

Shit. He was late and had missed getting his name tag. Luke ran a hand through his hair and regretted it immediately. What the hell had Jay put in there? This whole thing was a disaster. He never should have attempted to make changes so late. He should have left things alone and stayed behind the scenes, where he belonged. Pen was right. Luke developed the sims. He organized them. He didn't play in them. He should turn around, walk back out, and admit to his sister he'd made a mistake. Apologize for freaking out on her and suggest they stick with the original plan.

So what if there was a reviewer for one of the most influential pop culture websites in the country at the resort? He could figure out how to make sure she had a rave-worthy experience without getting directly involved. This secret-spy-mode shit was a ridiculous idea. What had he been thinking?

He was about to abandon the scheme and make his escape when a pair of hazel eyes met his from across the room.

And just like that, Luke knew he wasn't going anywhere.

CHAPTER 8

JULIA

A little before six that evening, unpacked and refreshed, the girls gathered in the hall outside their rooms.

"Shall we head downstairs?" Kat asked in an exaggerated clipped British accent.

"What's wrong with your voice?" Andie wondered.

"I think she's pretending to be Bridget," Julia hazarded a guess.

"Precisely, dear gel," Kat confirmed regally.

"You do know 'Bridget Jones' took place in the twenty-first century, right?" Andie asked. "Very early in the century, I admit. But still."

Kat lifted her chin like a haughty English aristocrat. "I fail to see your point."

"Well that's obvious." Andie rolled her eyes. "You sound like someone from a BBC costume drama."

"Move along, you two. That's enough." Julia marched them down the hall to the elevators. "It's time to mix and mingle." Downstairs in the lobby they followed signs for the Rom-Com Reception and joined the line in front of a small table outside the door to one of the hotel's ballrooms. A pretty girl who looked to be in her early twenties was checking people in.

Something about her face seemed familiar. It niggled at Julia enough that when she reached the front of the line she couldn't resist asking. "I'm sorry," she smiled politely, "but have we met before?"

"I don't think so." The girl returned the smile. "It's nice to meet you, though. I'm Penelope, I'll be your GM."

Julia glanced at Andie.

"Game master," Andie whispered.

Ah. "Hi, Penelope. I'm—"

The girl put her finger to her lips. "Shh, don't tell me your name." She winked. "Not your real one, anyway. Who are you supposed to be for the week?"

"Oh." Julia hesitated, mind going blank. "Um. I'm Bridget."

Kat moved closer. "No, I'm Bridget."

"Right." Julia winced.

"It can be a bit confusing at first." Penelope smiled in understanding.

Andie jumped in, saving her. "She's Meg. And I'm Carrie."

"Got it." Penelope pulled three name tags from a file box in front of her. "Before I can give you these, I need to ask you to please hand over your cell phones."

"You want me to do what now?" Andie wondered.

"All players must turn in their mobile devices before they will be allowed to participate in the game. Don't worry . . ." Penelope calmly reassured them. "The hotel will keep them safe and secure in a lockbox."

Julia couldn't resist checking her messages one last time before giving her phone up. She wasn't expecting any updates from *TrendList*, but if her boss happened to reach out, she wanted to make sure she responded.

"Anything important?" Andie asked.

"Nope." She shook her head. "It's just weird to think I'll be without my phone for the entire week."

"Amazing how attached we become to these things, huh?" Kat turned to Penelope. "Hey, um, what if we promise to leave our 'mobile devices' in our hotel room?"

"How good are you at resisting temptation?" Penelope asked, gray eyes twinkling.

"Not great," Kat admitted, reluctantly handing over her phone.

"Thank you." Penelope smiled kindly. "If it helps, you're

allowed to check your devices at any time. Players who wish to use their phone may request to access it from the lockbox, but they will be asked to remain in a secure location and to return the phone to the box when finished."

"Whoa," Julia exhaled in surprise.

"I know it seems a little extreme," Penelope continued.

"A little?" Kat muttered.

"Personally, I love the idea of spending time meeting people without the distraction of phones," Andie said as she turned hers in.

"Exactly." Penelope leaned forward, as if sharing a secret. "There is some rhyme to our reason here. One of the main benefits of this experience is the chance to take a break from regular daily life. Without the constant distraction of their phones, players will be more present, live in the moment. Have real interactions with each other."

"And hey," Andie said, "as an added bonus, no phones means no dick pics for a week!"

"Imagine that." Julia grinned.

"I'll add that to the list of perks." Penelope laughed. "And remember, should you need your phone for any reason, all you have to do is visit the concierge desk and they will set you up." Penelope handed each of them their name tag. "Here you go."

"Thanks." Again, Julia had the impression they'd met before, but she brushed it aside and took the name tag the girl handed her. She waited for Andie and Kat to get theirs, too, and once they all had them pinned on, they headed into the reception together.

Julia glanced around the room, relieved to see it had already started to fill with a variety of people. She hadn't known what to expect, wasn't really sure what kind of people would be interested in a resort that promised an immersive rom-com experience. She'd had a vague sense it would be mostly women in their late twenties to early forties.

But now she realized that had been narrow-minded of her.

And shortsighted. It was a good thing her initial expectations had been wrong, since the best location choice for a "Take Me!" piece would be a place that appealed to the interests of as many people as possible.

With that thought fresh in her mind, Julia began taking mental notes as people of a variety of ages and genders milled around the room—some alone, some in groups. Her attention snagged on a woman in an outfit that defied description. "Whoa." Julia swiveled her head toward the front of the room. "You two need to check this out."

Andie and Kat turned to follow the direction of her gaze.

"Whoa!" Kat's eyes widened, mouth dropping open. "That's a lot of pink . . . even for me." She leaned closer and whispered, "I thought we weren't supposed to be wearing costumes."

"Maybe it's not a costume," Andie whispered back, unable to stop staring.

"You know, I'm guessing it's the owner," Julia mused. "Mrs. Wackyspoon or something . . ."

"Greetings, gentle guests!" they heard the woman declare in an overblown British accent that rivaled Kat's. "I'm Mrs. Weatherfork."

"Close enough," Julia mumbled.

"And her outfit certainly is wacky," Andie added, while Kat tittered.

"Quiet," Julia ordered under her breath. "She's the one responsible for comping our stay."

That shut them up. They watched as Mrs. Weatherfork continued meandering through the crowd, greeting people as she went. Julia was still absorbing the impact of the resort owner's bizarre costume when she realized several dogs were scampering around the woman's feet. "Where did those corgis come from?"

"Under her skirt?" Andie suggested. "There's so much material, she looks like she could keep a whole kennel up there."

"Andie!" Julia chided. But she couldn't keep a giggle from

escaping. It was true. The woman was wearing an impressively voluminous gown, frothy folds of bright pink floating all around her as she approached them.

"Ah, ladies. Good evening." The woman bowed her head and did an elaborate curtsy.

Julia glanced at her friends. They looked as bewildered as she felt. Nothing to do but wing it. She pasted a polite smile on her face. "Good evening," she replied, and tried to copy whatever that bow/curtsy thing was. Beside her, Andie and Kat attempted to do the same. It was a miracle they avoided poking someone's eye out. Good thing this wasn't one of those Jane Austen reenactments or they'd be hopelessly lost.

"Mrs. Miranda Constance Eugenia Weatherfork. At your service. I'm the owner of this fine abode." She waved her hand, indicating the resort at large.

"It's absolutely charming," Kat cooed, her accent so thick now it seemed to drag each vowel into its own syllable.

Julia and Andie shared a glance, silently daring each other not to laugh.

"How are you enjoying yourselves so far?" Mrs. Weatherfork asked.

"Um, so far, so good." Julia pressed her lips together, turning her attention away from Andie before she broke first.

"And your lodgings. Are they to your satisfaction?"

"Quite satisfactory, indeed," Kat replied regally. "Thank you." For some inexplicable reason she curtsied again.

"I'm curious," Julia asked, careful to keep her voice casual, "what inspired you to develop a resort theme based on romantic comedies?"

"My husband."

"That's sweet." Julia smiled.

"The buffoon is always making fun of them."

"Oh." Her smile faded.

"I adore romantic comedies. They bring me such joy." She

clutched at her silk-covered bosom. "It was my greatest wish to experience what it was like to be in one."

"Understandable," Andie said.

"Well, my Harold doesn't understand. Thought I was a ninny for wanting to live in a fantasyland. I decided then and there I would find a way to prove to him and the world that it's possible."

"Bully for you!" Kat cheered, clapping her hands like she was at a golf tournament.

"Thank you, my dear." The woman nodded graciously. "I hope you all enjoy your stay here at Notting Hill."

"We plan to," Andie said.

"Oh, and one more thing," Mrs. Weatherfork added, lowering her voice conspiratorially. "Of course I want you to have fun, but remember to respect the boundaries of the game."

"Of course." Kat empathized solemnly. After a beat she asked, "What does that mean, exactly?"

"It means no engaging in hanky-panky with my employees," Mrs. Weatherfork warned. "I'm not running that type of establishment." She sighed wistfully. "Unfortunately, my lawyer told me I couldn't." Gathering her voluminous skirt, she bade them good evening and sailed on to greet the next cluster of guests.

"That woman is officially my hero." Andie chuckled in admiration as Mrs. Weatherfork swept past them, gown fluttering behind her, fluffy-butted corgis in tow.

"She is quite the character," Julia remarked, taking out her notepad and summarizing her observations about the resort's colorful owner.

"She's definitely life goals," Kat agreed. "Put that thing away." She smacked at Julia's notepad. "This is supposed to be a cocktail hour, and for some reason I don't have a drink in my hand." She tilted her chin toward the bar. "Let's fix that, shall we?"

While the bartender filled their order, Julia took a moment to scan the room.

"Looking for your shirtless man from the beach?" Andie whispered.

"What? No," Julia sputtered. She hadn't been. But now that Andie mentioned it, Julia couldn't resist scanning the room once more.

"You probably won't recognize him with his shirt on," Andie teased.

"He was wearing a shirt when I first saw him."

"Was he now?" Andie purred. "Then how did his shirt come off?"

"Whose shirt is off?" Kat asked. "What are we talking about?"

"Julia's meet-cute mystery man."

"He's not a mystery man. He said his name is Luke."

"Is he part of this thing?" Kat studied the crowd. As if she'd be able to recognize someone she'd never seen before.

"I think so. He said he was staying at the resort."

"Did he?" Andie challenged. "You asked, but I don't recall him answering,"

"He walked back to the hotel with us."

"Yeah, and then took off like a bat out of hell as soon as we got here." Andie dropped her voice. "Maybe he's a fugitive or something."

"Don't be ridiculous." Julia snorted. "Wrong movie genre."

Andie leaned toward Kat, hand cupped over her mouth as she whispered in an exaggerated tone, "When I found them together, Jules looked like she was just about to kiss him."

"I was *not* just about to kiss him." *Had I been about to kiss him?* Julia replayed that moment on the beach, the way his gaze had drifted to her lips, gray eyes focused, so intense that a shiver had run down her spine. She swallowed. "Okay, *maybe* I was *thinking* about kissing him."

"And I did mention he was half-naked, right?" Andie added.

"Oh my God, he wasn't naked. He just had his shirt off," Julia corrected, exasperated.

"Sounds very romantic to me," Kat cooed. She placed her elbows on the bar, chin in her hands, lashes fluttering up at Julia in feigned flirtation.

"His shirt was off because a bird had just taken a crap on it."

"Oh." Kat wrinkled her nose and straightened. "That's not so romantic."

"It wasn't romantic." Julia pictured the moment with Luke on the beach. "It was funny, and a little strange." A smile tugged at the corner of her mouth. "Though there was something sweet about it too," she admitted.

"Aw!" Kat cooed. "Andie's right. This really does sound like a meet-cute straight out of a movie."

"Maybe he's not a guest but one of the actors," Andie suggested.

"That would make sense, I guess." Julia digested the idea, heart sinking. It figures. For the first time in her life she had unexpectedly met someone in a weird but delightful way that felt exactly like she'd imagined it would in a romantic comedy, and it would be just her Murphy's Law brand of bad luck if the whole thing turned out not to be real after all.

The unwelcome notion hovered like a dark cloud over her thoughts. What if their encounter today wasn't unexpected? She was at a place that promised to provide exactly that kind of experience, after all.

If so, they were doing an A-plus job so far.

But how would anyone have known ahead of time that she was going to get carsick on the drive and go for a walk by the lake the moment she arrived? Luke had definitely been on the beach before her. And the whole thing with the seagull—that couldn't have been planned . . . could it?

"Can you train a seagull?"

Andie and Kat gaped at her.

"Never mind." Julia picked up her glass and turned, resting her back against the bar as she sucked down half her espresso martini, irritated with herself for fixating on some guy who probably wasn't even who he said he was. The depressing thought had barely wormed its way into her thoughts when she glanced up.

And up.

Straight into the pair of gray eyes she'd been fixating on.

CHAPTER 9

JULIA

The great thing about cocktail hour was that there were cocktails.

Delicious, distracting cocktails.

Slightly past tipsy but still a long way from drunk, Julia nursed what was left of her second espresso martini in one hand while she tried to smooth the curling edge of her name tag down with the other. All while dutifully ignoring the tall guy in the corner.

Thanks to his height, Luke had been impossible to miss since the second he'd entered the room. Their eyes had locked, and Julia had one of those moments she always laughed at when reading it in a book or watching it on a screen. The kind where a character is so caught up in her feelings that she forgets how to breathe.

She didn't forget how to breathe, exactly. She knew *how*, she just forgot to do it. It was as if every bit of her brain was so focused on him, it didn't have the energy or attention span left to maintain the most basic of bodily functions, even though they weren't supposed to require thought in the first place.

Julia had been sure he'd walk over to her. She'd even begun to imagine it happening in slow motion, picturing his long legs devouring the space between them.

Instead, his long legs had carried him in the opposite direction as far and as fast as possible. *Ouch.*

So she'd done what any self-respecting woman who'd just been dissed would do: she ordered another drink and huddled closer to her friends. For a while, the three of them had stuck together like a trio of nesting dolls, one on top of the other, as they inched through the crowd, introducing themselves—that is, the character version of themselves—to the other players. It wasn't long before a very good-looking guy with striking blue eyes and a perfect shadow-beard had swept Kat, er Bridget, off to a quiet corner.

"Our Bridget sure is having a good time," Andie observed.

"To be honest," Julia confessed, "I'm a little jealous."

"Don't be. He's an NPC."

"A what?"

"It's a LARPing thing." Andie twirled the cocktail stirrer in her drink. In her role of NYC fashion designer Carrie, she'd been ordering cosmos all evening.

"Spell that out please, nerd girl." The affection in Julia's tone turned the word into more of a compliment than a tease.

"NPCs are nonplaying characters. In this case, actors the resort hired to help create the immersive world for the guests. Mr. Blue Eyes is definitely one of them."

"How can you tell?"

"Besides the perfection of his jawline?" Andie jerked her chin in the couple's direction. "See that little button he's wearing?"

Julia glanced back over at the guy Kat was with, trying to be discreet as she examined him. *Bingo*. "I see it." Over one firm pec perfectly showcased inside a tight black V-neck T-shirt was a little blue button. "Is there something significant about it?"

"For a game to feel immersive, the actors will blend in with the players. But it's protocol for nonplaying characters to indicate their status with some kind of token. Something simple like a wristband, or a scarf . . ." Andie fixed her gaze. "Or a button."

"Interesting." Julia observed the room for a moment, and sure enough, she began to spot buttons on several other guests chatting and laughing. Of the fifty or so people in the room, she estimated around a dozen were wearing the blue buttons. "Think anyone would notice if I got out my notepad again and wrote all this down? It would be great background info for the 'Take Me!' piece."

"And risk blowing your cover?" Andie teased. "Maybe you can convince Kat to walk around with it for you." She turned back to the couple. "Though she is a little busy at the moment." Andie whistled. "That man is almost too pretty. He's got that *I'm not a doctor but I play one on TV* vibe."

Julia laughed. Andie was right. He was a very specific, almost too perfect, brand of gorgeous. A thought occurred to her. "I think this is further proof that the powers that be definitely think Kat is the *TrendList* reporter."

"How do you figure?" Andie asked.

"Well, look at Dr. Hottie. They've obviously assigned their top . . . What did you call it?"

"NPC."

"Top NPC to keep her entertained." Julia paused. "Not that Kat couldn't attract the attention on her own." It was true. Her friend was funny and easygoing and gorgeous.

"If they did, it seems to be working. She looks pretty entertained right now." Andie chuckled. "And she's gotten *really* into character."

Julia eyeballed Andie's cosmo. "As have you."

"I'm hoping it leads to some sex in the city." Andie raised her glass and clinked it against Julia's. "Figuratively speaking. About the city, I mean. I'm being totally literal about the sex."

"Understood, Carrie." Julia laughed. "Meet any potential Mr. Bigs yet?"

"Nah." Andie shook her head. "A lot of the people here came as couples. I don't get it. They're married. They've already found their one. What are they doing at a place like this?"

"Maybe marriage doesn't always mean you've found the one," Julia said, thinking of her parents. "Maybe they're here to relight the spark. Or maybe they just really like rom-coms."

"Maybe." Andie shrugged. "How about you, Meg? How are you holding up?"

"Honestly? I suck at this," Julia admitted. "I have to keep pausing to remember to introduce myself as Meg. And more than once, when someone asked me what I liked best about where I was from, I caught myself talking about my favorite places in Chicago. What do I know about stuff in Seattle?" Amazingly, it was one of the few places in the contiguous forty-eight states where she *hadn't* lived.

"There's that tower thing—the needle? And Starbucks," Andie suggested. "You love Starbucks. Stick to the truth as much as possible. Stop overthinking things." She tipped her head back and finished off her drink. "Ready for another?"

"Why not." Julia downed the rest and handed her glass to Andie. "Nothing too bizarre, please," she warned. Andie's mixology interests extended to ordering creative drinks as well as making them.

"No promises." Andie winked.

As she watched her friend disappear into the crowd, Julia considered Andie's advice. Stick to the truth. Ha. Easier said than done when she was already pretending to be a character—on top of pretending to be somebody else even before the game even got started.

Well, not somebody else. Just not herself. Not the reporter who was here to do a story on the resort. She turned to check on Kat and Dr. Five O'Clock Shadow. They appeared deep in conversation, foreheads almost touching as they stared into each other's eyes, fingers entwined over the top of the little table where they stood. Julia frowned.

"What's wrong?" Andie asked as she returned with their drinks. She passed one to Julia and took a sip of the other, following her gaze to the corner. "Oh, *now* you regret asking Kat to take your place." Andie laughed. "I see how it is."

"It's not that," Julia mumbled into her glass. "I just hope she's careful."

"Something worrying you?"

"If we're right and that guy is an actor, one the resort has purposely told to pay attention to Kat, I don't want her getting the wrong idea." Her friend was so hungry for love, she often jumped into relationships that weren't good for her. "I don't want her to get hurt."

"As long as she remembers it's a game, she'll be fine. Kat can take care of herself." Andie squeezed Julia's shoulder. "She's doing what she's supposed to be doing—meeting and mingling. Which is what we should be doing, too. You know what? I'm going to spend the rest of the evening with the next guy that flirts with me."

"What, like *all* night?" Julia wondered.

"Slow down, you fast woman!" Andie gasped in mock outrage. "I know what I said about sex earlier, but let's start with dinner first." She crossed her arms. "I want you to promise to do the same."

"No way. I'm not promising to pick up the next guy who tries to talk to me." Not that many guys had tried this evening. There'd been a few friendly exchanges, but as Andie had said, a lot of people were here as couples. That limited her options.

"What if I pick him for you?" Andie smiled sweetly. "I promise to choose a good one."

"Fine." Julia sighed. What did she have to lose? It was just dinner. In a group. "But only if you hold up your end of the deal first."

"You're on."

No sooner had the words left Andie's mouth than a standard-issue Midwestern dude-bro appeared before them, beer in hand. "Evening, ladies."

"Good evening." Andie smiled invitingly.

Julia had to hand it to her friend. When Andie decided to do something, she committed.

The guy took a sip of his beer while giving Andie the once-over. "Usually when I see a pretty girl like you, I wanna ask for her number."

Not the sexiest opening in the history of pickup lines, Julia thought, wondering where he was heading with this.

"But can you believe they took our cell phones for the week?"

"I think not having phones is a great idea," Andie said. "It allows us to get to know each other better . . ." She paused and leaned closer to check out his name tag. "Burt."

"Who's Burt?" he wondered.

"I keep forgetting too," Julia admitted, taking pity on him and pointing at the label stuck to his Green Bay Packers jersey.

"Oh, yeah." He glanced at it. "But that's not my real name." He wiggled his eyebrows. "I bet you can't guess what is."

"Ernie?" Andie suggested.

"Huh? No." Burt shook his head. "Wait." He huffed out a laugh. "I get it. Burt. Ernie." He grinned at Andie and sidled up to her. "That's good. You're very funny."

"I'm a riot," Andie agreed, deadpan.

"I'll give you a clue," he continued, either missing or ignoring Andie's sarcasm. "My real name rhymes with my fake name."

"Ooh, a brain teaser," Andie said, still poker-faced. "Is it Dirt?"

"Why would someone name their kid Dirt?" Not-Burt seemed exceedingly concerned at the prospect.

"They really love the earth?" Julia offered.

Andie snorted with laughter. "I give up. What's your name, Rhymes with Burt?"

"It's Curt. Actually, it's Curtis, but only my mom calls me that." He put a hand up to his mouth and pretended to yell in what Julia assumed was a shrill imitation of his mother. "Curtis! Turn off that video game and come take the garbage out!"

"You still live at home, huh?" Andie asked, smile plastered to her face.

"Temporary situation only," Burt-actually-Curt-only-my-mom-calls-me-Curtis assured her.

"If you'll excuse us one moment." Andie grabbed Julia's arm and stepped away.

"What's the matter?" Julia whispered. "Do you want to abandon the Curtis ship? I won't blame you if you do."

"Nah." Andie shook her head. "I'll ride this one out." A gleam appeared in her dark eyes. "Which means it's your turn." She flicked her chin at someone behind Julia. "I pick *him*."

Instinctively, Julia knew exactly who her friend had chosen. She glanced over her shoulder for confirmation. Yep. It was Luke. He was leaning against the wall, arms crossed as he surveyed the room. "This was your plan all along, wasn't it?" Julia hissed.

"And if it was? A deal is a deal. Now pull up your big girl britches and go talk to him already," Andie ordered.

"Excuse me?"

"You and your guy from the beach have been making eyes at each other ever since he walked in tonight."

"I don't know what you're talking about," Julia lied.

"Uh-huh," Andie drawled, dragging the word out in a way that emphasized her mountain of doubt. "Did you really think I didn't notice you notice him?"

"Fine," Julia admitted in a rush. "I noticed him. But it doesn't matter, since he's been ignoring me."

"You're kidding, right?" Andie rolled her eyes heavenward. "He's been checking you out whenever he thinks you're not looking. I swear, it's like a junior high dance up in here." Andie nudged Julia forward. "Now stop being a ninny and go talk to him."

This *was* just like junior high. A flashback to a school dance, sixth grade. Julia had been wearing a peach sweater. She remembered because she'd associated the color with shame ever since. The boy she liked, Jimmy, was wearing a striped button-down shirt. He'd been leaning against the wall too. Slouching in the back of the gym with some of his friends, hands in his pockets, too cool to join in dancing.

And that's how he'd always seemed to Julia. Cool. Definitely too cool for someone like her. But in a moment of weakness, probably brought on by hair spray fumes and the sugar high from too much cheap fruit punch, Julia had made the mistake of telling her friends that she thought Jimmy was cute. And before she knew it, she was getting pushed across the gym floor. A crowd of people seemed to grow around her, the closer she got to Jimmy.

By this point, his friends had picked up on the situation, dropping their veil of indifference long enough to join in the fun, grabbing Jimmy's arms and yanking him toward her. They met in the middle of the dance floor, still more people crowding around, forming a circle. Jimmy glanced at his friends, shrugging them off before turning to face her.

In that moment, the music changed. A slow song came on. Oh, God, was the DJ in on this too?

And even as she stood there, hot and itchy in her peach sweater and wishing she was anywhere else, Julia couldn't help hoping it would happen. That Jimmy would notice her. *Notice her.* See her in that magical way it happened in the movies. He'd see the real Julia hiding inside this horrible peach sweater, recognize her as the one meant for him, and then he'd ask her to dance.

But he didn't. He just stood there.

Seconds ticked by. People began to whisper.

Unable to handle the awkwardness a moment longer, Julia cleared the gravel from her throat and decided to do the unthinkable. She'd ask *him* to dance. She'd be the rebel girl who flouted tradition and wowed him with her confidence and daring. And then he'd see her. *Really* see her.

She did it. In front of everyone. She asked Jimmy to dance.

And he said no.

"No thanks," were his actual words. The casual, offhand

politeness was somehow worse than open disdain. As if she wasn't worth that much energy.

And Julia had known with a searing certainty that the movies she loved were full of lies. Nothing but empty promises woven by Hollywood myths.

The memory of that moment on the dance floor with Jimmy in sixth grade played out in Julia's mind in a flash, humiliation churning in her gut as if it had happened yesterday rather than more than half her lifetime ago. She tried to remind herself that it *had* been a long time ago. This wasn't junior high, and she wasn't an embarrassed preteen who was more sweating in peach than pretty in pink.

Pushing the memories aside, she glanced behind her. Andie had already returned to Not-Burt/Curt. In front of Julia, *he* still hadn't moved from his spot against the wall. She stepped forward slowly. Giving Luke time to bolt. There were no sidekicks here to grab his arms and force him to talk to her.

Too much of a coward to keep her eyes on his face while she moved closer, her attention shifted, and Julia swallowed hard when she caught sight of rolled sleeves revealing long lean forearms dusted with hair. He wasn't bulging with muscle—far from it—but there was something very masculine about the way he stood there, leaning against the wall, arms crossed.

She took a deep breath and stepped closer, shifting her gaze back to his. "Hey."

"Hey."

Okay, so far so good. It was only a monosyllabic exchange, but he hadn't tried to escape. Wasn't desperately looking around for the nearest exit. She moved to lean against the wall next to him. "I see you found a new shirt."

"Uh, yeah." He glanced down in surprise, as if he'd forgotten what he was wearing.

"It looks nice." She let her gaze travel over the soft gray fabric. "It matches your eyes."

"Thanks."

"As a bonus, there's no bird crap on it." Julia cringed. Had that been too much?

He cracked a smile, little crinkles appearing at the corners of his eyes, which made Julia's insides go all warm and mushy.

Great. He smiled at her, and she turned into oatmeal.

"You look nice too." He eyed her up and down. "Very nice."

Julia flushed. Not because of what he said, but *how* he said it. Like he wasn't just politely returning the compliment but really thought it. And suddenly the word *nice* had never felt so, well . . . *nice*.

She turned her attention to the other guests milling around and chatting, introducing themselves. "I'm not sure how this is supposed to work," she admitted. "Seeing as how we've kind of met already."

Now it was his turn to cringe. "We could pretend that never happened," he suggested.

"And miss out on one of the most entertaining moments I've had in recent memory?"

He grimaced.

She grinned. It was fun to tease him. From the corner of her eye, she inspected his shirt again, searching for a blue button like the one on Kat's guy. Nope. But he wasn't wearing a name tag, either, so what did that mean? "If it makes you feel better, we can pretend to start over," Julia offered.

"You sure?" he asked.

"Yeah. I mean, it's all supposed to be pretend anyways, right?" she said, as much a reminder to herself as anyone else.

"Right," he agreed. "Pretend." He pushed off the wall and held his hand out to her.

Julia shook his hand, her skin tingling at the contact.

"I'm Lance."

"Lance?" She made a face. "Really?"

"You don't like the name?"

"Luke fits you much better."

"Guess that's a good thing." He grinned.

Oh, there were those little eye crinkles again.

And now she was tingling in other places. Julia guessed he was a few years older than her. Around thirty. "Can I just call you Luke?"

"That isn't part of the game."

"It can be our little secret," she whispered. For some reason, it was important to her to be able to call him by his real name.

"What should I call you, then?" He raised one sandy brow. "Jules?"

"Julia is fine." She tried to ignore the tickle of pleasure at hearing him use her nickname. She should be annoyed, not pleased. There were very few people in her life she allowed to call her Jules.

"Okay, *Julia*. We can use our real names, but only when it's just the two of us. Agreed?"

"Agreed." She nodded, enjoying the sound of her name on his lips and the idea of this little shared secret between them way too much.

"But when we're around the other players, what am I *supposed* to call you?" he asked, bending down so he could speak quietly in her ear.

"Oh, um . . ." Julia inhaled, mind going blank. He was so close. And he smelled so good. She'd noted it briefly on the beach earlier when she'd face-planted on top of him. It had been subtle, hidden within all the outdoor scents of the lake. But even then, she'd wanted to bury her face into his neck and breathe him in.

"My name?" She exhaled, letting out a shaky laugh, her brain still on hiatus. "Shit."

"That's the name they gave you?" He stepped back, mouth curved in a teasing grin. "No wonder you want to use your real name."

"You know that's not what I mean." She pointed to her name tag. "Meg. Meg Bryant."

"I think your tag's coming off, Meg." He reached out and smoothed the corner with the tip of his finger. "That's better."

"Thanks," she croaked.

"No problem."

Was it her imagination or did his voice seem a bit huskier?

"So." He cleared his throat. "Meg Bryant, huh? That makes sense."

"What do you mean?" She cocked her head at him.

"It's just, uh, obvious what they were going for." He spoke quickly, almost nervously. "It's a good movie reference."

Was he embarrassed about being into romantic comedies? "Why are you here?" she asked abruptly. The question had tumbled out of her mouth as soon as it popped into her head. *Ah, alcohol.* She shouldn't have agreed to that third cocktail, especially since she was supposed to be working.

But it was out there now, so she might as well forge ahead. Besides, discovering why a single guy would choose to spend a week at a rom-com resort would be great for her article. "Why did you sign up for this"—she waved her hand, indicating the room at large—"game, or whatever you want to call it?"

"Why did *you*?" he countered.

"Hey, I asked first." Julia stared at him. She knew that trick. Classic deflection; answer a question with a question. Again, she wondered if he was one of the actors. Julia thought back to when they met. Had Luke been wearing a button then? Possibly. She didn't remember seeing one, though his shirt had been off during much of their conversation.

"Good evening, everyone!" A voice carried across the room, derailing her thoughts. Julia turned toward the sound. Penelope, the game master, was standing by the bar, wireless microphone in hand. "I hope you've all enjoyed getting to know each other." Penelope glanced around the room, smiling as she paused, her attention on a couple in the corner. "Apparently some of us are getting to know each other a little more than others."

Julia realized the comment was directed toward the spot where Kat was all but in Dr. Shadowbeard's lap now.

Luke must have made the same connection. "They seem to be having fun." He observed drily. "You know her, right?"

"What?" Julia was surprised at the irritable sensation prickling in her chest. Not jealousy, but perhaps a distant cousin to it. An urge to hoard his attention for herself.

"I saw you making the rounds together earlier, along with your other friend . . . the one I met this afternoon."

"Oh, um, yeah." Julia turned into oatmeal again. Warm, mushy oatmeal. Andie was right. He *had* been watching her.

"Just a quick announcement that dinner is about to begin," Penelope continued.

"Has it really been an hour already?" Luke wondered.

"Apparently." Julia shook her head, glad she wasn't the only one who felt like the time had flown by.

"If everyone will please follow our gracious hostess . . ." Penelope stretched an arm out, indicating where the glowing pink orb of Mrs. Weatherwhatever stood waiting in front of a pair of French doors, a corgi in each arm. "You'll all get a chance to continue your conversations at dinner."

"Do you think the dogs get their own seats at the table?" Julia wondered.

"I think they probably get their own table."

Julia laughed. But then Luke's hand was at the small of her back, leading her forward, and she forgot about dogs and dinner and anything and everything else except how it felt to have him touch her like that, the warmth of his skin seeping through the thin cotton of her dress, palm pressed against the base of her spine. Cocktail hour may have flown by, but Julia had a feeling this was going to be a very long week.

CHAPTER 10

LUKE

Luke kept his hand on Julia's back as they made their way into the dining room. At first, the gesture had been merely polite, done more out of habit than anything else. But as they maneuvered around tables, he became aware of the intimacy of their contact. Acutely aware. His fingers splayed against the base of her spine, his brain whirring, processing the sensory overload. The heat of her skin, the sway of her hips, the soft fabric of her dress, and beneath that—the unmistakable outline of her panties.

In an instant, Luke was picturing her in that one item of clothing and nothing else. He flattened his palm against her back, fighting the urge to trace the delicate edge lower. He was saved from himself when she shifted away from him, moving toward a table where her friend stood waving.

The blond one. The reviewer. The reason he was supposed to be participating in this charade in the first place. Luke sucked in a breath and hurried to catch up. He needed to remember what was on the line. Keep his eyes on the prize and get his head out from under Julia's dress and into the game. Fantasizing about panties . . . What the hell was wrong with him?

He held out a chair for Julia before taking the seat next to her, nodding as more people joined their table. Two men in their early thirties, who had clearly come together, and Julia's other friend, the dark-haired one he'd met on the beach, accompanied by a guy in a Green Bay Packers jersey. A football jersey. Luke scowled.

And he wasn't allowed to wear a classic video game shirt? The injustice.

The dude sat down and immediately reached for the breadbasket.

"Where's your name tag?" Packers jersey asked, offering the basket to Luke.

"Oh." Luke glanced down and feigned surprise. "It must have fallen off."

Jersey guy pointed to his own name tag. "Burt. But my real name is Curt, which rhymes with Burt, so you can call me either one."

"Good to know." Luke laughed. "Um, you can call me Lance." It took him a second to recall his character name. After spending most of the last hour chatting with Julia, the information had gotten lost behind more important details. Such as the fact that she liked his real name. He smiled to himself, mouth curving in a goofy grin.

"How about you?" Curt asked the couple across the table, as he slathered butter on a roll. "What're your names?"

"I'm Patrick. And this is my husband, David."

"That's me." David reached for Patrick's hand and squeezed. "The names are obviously fake, but the relationship is real." He grinned. "And no, we're not here to role-play as the sassy gay best friend."

"Don't get us wrong," Patrick said. "We love a good rom-com trope."

"But that tired trend belongs in the past," David declared, reaching for his glass of wine. "Along with mullets and shoulder pads."

"I most certainly agree," the blond said, in that exaggerated accent. "I'm Bridget, by the way." She wiggled her fingers in a cheeky wave. "A pleasure to meet you."

"The pleasure is all mine." Patrick bowed politely. "The

accent is a nice touch," he added, maintaining an impressively straight face.

"And who's the devilishly handsome fellow glued to your side?" David asked, resting his chin on his fist.

"The name's Zach," he said, easing back and slinging a casual arm over the top of Bridget's chair.

Luke noted the way she immediately leaned in to his touch. The reviewer certainly seemed to be enjoying her interaction with the actor. Annoying as it was, he shouldn't be surprised Zach was the one she'd gravitated to.

Zachary Brennan was a living, breathing, walking checklist of rom-com hero attributes. Bright blue eyes? Check. Charming grin? Check. Perfectly groomed scruff? Check. Luke honestly wasn't sure how the dude managed that last one. Maybe he got up to shave in the middle of the night so the five o'clock shadow would start to appear around noon.

It wasn't outside the realm of possibility. An actor with a capital A, the man was dedicated to his craft. Luke could respect that, even if he didn't like the guy. And he really, really didn't like the guy.

The feeling was mutual. From the first time they'd met, during the job interview for Notting Hill, Luke and Zach had butted heads, barely tolerating each other's presence. Zach wasn't great about following instructions, and more than once during the weeks of prep leading up to this week's opening, Luke had considered firing him.

He might have, too, if he wasn't worried the other actors would quit in protest. Luke had hired most of them based on Zach's personal recommendation, and he was well aware they looked up to Brennan as their unofficial leader—a fact that Zach exploited to his advantage, flouting Luke's authority at every opportunity.

Luke even took the man's clothing choices as a personal affront. Zach was wearing a tight, black V-neck T-shirt—and yes, he had the muscles to fill it out. Jay had called that one.

Whatever. Luke tugged at the sleeves of his too-short dress shirt, rolled just below his elbows. Julia had commented on the shirt. Said she liked it. She'd even mentioned how it matched his eyes. Pleasure rippled through him, and he had to admit, Jay might be onto something with the dressing up thing.

"What are some of your favorite rom-coms?" Julia asked, pulling his attention back to the conversation.

Luke hesitated, surprised to realize he didn't have a ready answer. Did he have a favorite? He'd never really thought about it. Over the years, he'd watched a metric ton of romantic comedies with Penelope. Many of them multiple times. He watched them because they made Pen happy. He liked the movies well enough, sure, but he didn't love them like Pen did. "Honestly, I'm not sure I can pick one."

"Really?" She quirked a dubious brow. "I would have thought anyone participating in this game must have at least one favorite."

"Not necessarily," Curt said, shaking his head and butting into the conversation.

Julia shifted her gaze. "Why are you here, then?"

"A wedding."

"What?" She squinted at him in disbelief. "Is that your cover story, or backstory or whatever?"

"Nah, I can't remember what that sheet they gave me said. My buddy is getting married here this weekend. For real. On Sunday." Curt gestured with his butter knife toward another table. "That's him over there with his finacée. This whole thing was her idea. Thought it would be *romantic* to act out some movie shit. Invited the whole group of us, all the bridesmaids and groomsmen, to get here a week early."

"The entire wedding party?" Julia asked.

"Except the maid of honor." Curt brushed bread crumbs from his jersey. "She's the bride's sister and is kind of a pain in the ass."

Luke bit back a laugh. This guy was a character and they weren't even paying him.

"Well, now that we know why Curt is here, anybody else care to share why they chose to come here this week?" Julia wondered.

Luke spared a glance across the table again. Currently, Zach was nuzzling the blond woman's neck. And she didn't seem to mind at all. He supposed he should be glad to see her enjoying herself, but he thought the reviewer would be eager to gather this kind of information, learn why people chose to participate in this game, what they were hoping to get out of the experience and all that. At the moment, she seemed interested in only one experience. Luke cleared his throat.

Zach lifted his head and met Luke's eyes. There was a challenge in Mr. Rom-Com Hero's face. A *What are you gonna do about it, boss?* look.

And what *could* he do? Luke was supposed to be just another player in the game. He'd already come close to screwing things up a few times tonight by being too aware of specific details, like who Julia's friends were. Luckily, Julia had accepted his excuses, but he needed to be more careful. Right now, best to take a step back. He'd deal with Zach's behavior later.

While he'd been distracted, the subject of live action role-playing had come up. Luke caught the thread of the discussion as Patrick and David were explaining how Notting Hill was the latest of many role-playing adventures they'd done.

"Are you both professional LARPers?" Carrie, the dark-haired girl, asked.

"I wouldn't say we're professional." Patrick shook his head. "Nobody is paying us to do this."

David grinned. "At least not yet, anyway."

"I didn't know this kind of thing existed until a few weeks ago," Julia admitted. "This is my first one."

"Are you all first-timers?" Patrick asked, glancing around the table.

"Not me," Carrie—what was her real name? Andie?—said. "I've done a few on the weekend, like at a campground or something. Nothing too elaborate." She leaned forward. "How many games have you participated in?"

"Let's see . . ." Patrick tapped his fingers on the table. "There was the manor estate in Poland, that castle in Romania—"

"Really?" Bridget asked. "Romania?"

"Yep." David lowered his voice dramatically. "That one was vampire themed."

"Cool." Carrie's eyes were glittering with excitement.

"It was," Patrick agreed.

"It was scary as fuck is what it was." David shivered. "I still have nightmares."

"What else . . ." Patrick wrinkled his brow in thought. "Oh, the pirate one in Bermuda was fun." He winked. "Lots of rum."

"I can't believe there are so many." Julia shook her head, her face awestruck.

"What was your favorite?" Bridget asked.

"Ooh, good question." David rubbed his jaw. "I'd say it was a tie between the court of King Henry VIII we did outside of London and the Camelot one. The costumes were incredible."

"Not like this one, huh?" Julia added.

"I don't mind the simplicity, actually." David shrugged. "It's much more comfortable getting to wear your own clothes. Easier to pack, too."

"Is that so?" Patrick teased good-naturedly. "Then how do you explain the three suitcases you insisted on bringing?"

"What about you?" Julia turned to Patrick. "Which was your favorite?"

"My favorite was the first one we ever did together." Patrick reached for David's hand and squeezed. "Just a little group, about half a dozen of us or so."

"What was the theme?" Luke asked, genuinely curious. He'd like to have a chance to talk with these two some more and pick their brains on a few things.

"Dragons," Patrick said in a dramatic whisper.

"Ooh," Andie breathed. "I've always wanted to do one that was based on Tolkien."

"Oh, yeah?" Curt asked. "You mean like hobbits and elves and that kind of shit?"

"Yes." She narrowed her eyes. "That kind of shit."

Curt must have realized he'd stepped in it, because he raised his hands, palms out, and said, "It's totally cool if it is. I love me some *Game of Thrones* action."

"Really?"

"Oh yeah, and not just because of all the T and A. Though I'm not complaining about that."

"Of course not," Andie said stiffly, sable eyes flaring as if she were about to roast her companion Mother of Dragons style.

"How are things going here?" Pen asked cheerfully, sidling up to their table in a *whoosh* of positive energy. Luke hid a grin behind his water glass. His sister had perfect timing. He'd noted how she'd been making her way around the room, stopping to chat at each table, and he was impressed.

As game master, it wasn't something he would have thought to do. He considered his role as more like an overseer. "God looking down on his minions," was how Pen had once snarkily phrased it.

But watching his sister now, Luke realized the advantage in taking time to meet the players in smaller groups. It allowed her a chance to connect with them as individuals and evaluate how the game was progressing in real time. As Penelope engaged the table in a few minutes of friendly chatter, Luke was impressed again. She was gregarious and professional and seemed to put everyone at ease.

He knew Pen accused him of still seeing her as a helpless kid, and maybe she had a point. Over the past year, while planning this project together, his sister had often reminded him of the degree she'd earned. Whenever they'd gotten into an argument over a detail, she'd trot out her credentials, listing all the ways she was qualified to have an opinion. In his usual big brother manner, Luke had listened but not heard.

He'd made her GM and had agreed to trust her to do the job on her own, but until he saw her in action tonight, he hadn't pictured her actually taking control, let alone doing it in a manner that was so uniquely her. She was doing more than simply filling in for him as leader . . . She was leading. And if Luke had bothered to pay closer attention to his sister, he wouldn't have been so surprised. The realization was a punch to the gut.

Luke had the sudden urge to jump out of his chair and hug her. He might have, too, if they weren't supposed to be acting like they didn't know each other. He forced his attention to the servers as they arrived with the meal.

Penelope reminded the group to look over their activity options for the week. "Don't worry, you don't have to make your selections this minute. Everyone starts tomorrow with the first big kickoff activity."

"Breakfast?" the dark-haired girl asked, unrolling her silverware and placing her napkin on her lap.

"Breakfast first, of course," Penelope agreed. "Followed by a walking tour of the hotel and grounds led by the resort owner herself. She is looking forward to showing off everything Notting Hill has to offer."

"I saw you had paintball on the itinerary," Carrie said, a feral gleam in her dark eyes.

"We most certainly do," Penelope confirmed.

"Uh-oh," Julia muttered under her breath.

Luke glanced at her and leaned closer. "What?" he whispered.

"Andie"—she tipped her chin toward her friend—"I mean Carrie, is rather, um, competitive."

"That's a good thing, right?" he asked, making a mental note that he'd correctly recalled her friend's name was Andie.

"It is, as long as she wins."

Luke chuckled.

"Oh, you laugh now. Just wait."

"Not that I'm complaining," Curt said, cutting into his chicken marsala, "but what's paintball got to do with romantic stuff?"

"Paintball is a staple of many romantic comedies," Penelope assured him.

"I never thought about it before, but that's true," the blond one, Bridget, whose real name he suspected was Kat, piped up.

Nice of her to join the conversation. Luke was being uncharitable, but knowing that she was here to judge everything he'd created, knowing that her opinion, and how she expressed that opinion on a very influential website, could have a significant impact on the success of this launch—not to mention his future— was gnawing at him.

"Oh, yeah?" Curt asked.

Luke was beginning to think that particular phrase made up ninety percent of this dude's conversational skills. "Yeah," he said, unable to stop himself.

"Like what?"

"Uh . . ." Luke regretted opening his mouth, and he felt his sister's attention turn to him while he fumbled for an answer. "There's the one with the guy who still lives with his parents."

"*Failure to Launch*." Julia supplied, saving him.

"Right!" Carrie/Andie laughed. "Sarah Jessica Parker kicked everybody's ass in that."

"And there's my personal favorite," Julia added, "*10 Things I Hate About You*."

"Good one." Bridget sighed wistfully. "Oh, Heath."

"One of the greats, gone too soon," Zach agreed solemnly, wrapping a comforting arm around her. She melted against him, her head resting on his shoulder.

Luke watched the exchange with annoyed curiosity. How had Romeo in skinny jeans established such an easy connection with her so quickly? The guy was *good*. He should be pleased. It made his job easier. He wanted to make sure the reviewer enjoyed her experience. Mission accomplished.

Still. Maybe it was just his natural pessimism, but Luke couldn't shake the kernel of worry lodging in his gut.

Bridget had moved on from movies to naming rom-com novels that included paintball scenes.

"Well, then, it sounds like I'll be seeing all of you at paintball for sure!" With an easy, polished smile—one that didn't hold even the slightest hint that the two of them knew each other, let alone that they were siblings—Penelope nodded at Luke and said goodbye to the group before moving on to the next table.

"*This Means War!*" Andie exclaimed suddenly, pounding the table, rattling silverware.

Luke bent his head to Julia again. "You're right, she *is* competitive."

Julia giggled. "She's talking about the movie."

"Huh?"

"The rom-com with Chris Pine and Tom Hardy?"

"Uh, right." If Penelope had still been at their table, she'd be gloating right now. Luke was notoriously bad at remembering titles.

"Tom Hardy," Andie purred. "Now there's some Mr. Big potential."

"Excuse me?" Bridget huffed, accent wavering. "Are you dissing Chris Pine? You know he's my number one Chris."

"Oh, I know all about your Chris rating system," Andie snorted.

"Rating system?" Patrick asked, eyebrows raised.

"It's a little inside joke of ours." Bridget smiled wickedly. "Pine." She held up her index finger. "Hemsworth." She held up her middle finger. "Evans." She held up her ring finger.

"What about Pratt?" Zach wondered. "He's a Chris too, right?"

"Barely." David *tsk*ed.

"Sure." Bridget held up her pinkie. "Pratt."

Julia giggled.

"You can have all the Chrises you want." Carrie shrugged smugly. "One Tom Hardy still beats your whole hand."

Beside Luke, Julia squirmed, lips pinched with barely contained laughter.

He watched her, bemused. "Are they talking about what I think they're talking about?"

"Possibly." She gave him a coy smile, glancing sideways at him from beneath her lashes. "Depends on what you think they're talking about."

"I think," he said, lowering his voice so only she could hear, "you have some very creative friends."

A pretty pink blush rose in her cheeks, but she lifted her chin and met his gaze, eyes sparkling with excitement and a hint of wariness. "Is that a bad thing?" she whispered.

"No, I don't think it's bad." He brushed his index finger over the top of hers and she shivered. "Do you?"

She swallowed and shook her head, watching his hand move over hers.

Her reaction made his breath hitch. A wave of boldness swept through him. He shifted their hands beneath the table, stroking his middle finger over hers and then repeating the movement with their ring fingers.

"Yay, dessert!" Andie announced gleefully, startling Luke into dropping Julia's hand, shattering the moment. A server slipped between them and plunked down plates of pie and ice cream.

Luke blinked. His brain felt thick inside his skull, thoughts fuzzy as if he'd done a round of shots.

Lust. He was drunk on lust.

He glanced over at Julia. She also seemed disoriented. Maybe she'd felt it too.

Julia wiped a hand across her face and stared down at her plate. "Wait a minute," she mumbled, picking up her fork and prodding the pastry crust. A smile dawned. "This is Sally's pie."

"Aw, you're right." Andie chuckled, pulling her plate closer. "That's a clever touch."

"Who's Sally?" Curt wondered.

"From *When Harry Met Sally*," Andie explained. "Sally orders an—"

The other two girls chimed in and together all three recited, "'Apple pie, heated, with strawberry ice cream on the side.'"

Luke felt a burst of pride for his sister, recalling how Penelope had insisted that this should be the dessert at the first night's meal. He knew she'd be delighted to hear how quickly the players had made the connection.

"Oh, yeah?" Curt poked at his plate.

Well, not all the players. Luke's happy balloon deflated a little. One more, *Oh, yeah* and he might not be able to resist stuffing that Packer's jersey in Curt's pie hole.

Oblivious to the violence being contemplated against him, Curt continued to poke at his ice cream. "I was wondering why it was strawberry instead of vanilla. Who ever heard of serving apple pie with strawberry ice cream instead of vanilla? It's weird."

"That's the point," Andie gritted out.

If Curt didn't watch it, Andie was going to be the one to do the jersey throat stuffing. Luke bet when he told his sister about the antics of these two, Penelope would declare it was an opposites-attract romance and only a matter of time before tension led to passion and they were falling in love.

He glanced at Julia, wondering what Pen would have to say about the two of them.

Not wanting to follow that train of thought too far, Luke focused on his pie. His sister wouldn't have anything to say, because nothing was going to happen between him and Julia.

Nothing other than what had happened already.

Nothing other than what he wanted to happen.

Other than that, nothing at all.

CHAPTER 11

LUKE

Five a.m. arrived with the usual canine cacophony of yapping corgis parading past Luke's door. Mrs. W. took them out for their morning constitutional at the same godawful time every morning. He hadn't needed an alarm clock since he'd arrived at the resort.

He blinked and stared at the ceiling, waiting for the synapses in his brain to start firing. The mental fog seemed to take longer than usual to dissipate today. Not surprising. Last night, simultaneously riding the contact high of spending time with Julia and worrying about Zach messing things up with the reviewer, he hadn't gotten much sleep.

What could have been ten minutes or an hour later, Luke groaned and rolled out of bed. He opened a few drawers in his dresser, pulled on a pair of jeans and, as he did every day, grabbed the first shirt he saw. He was about to tug it over his head when he stopped and actually *looked* at the shirt. It was, like almost all the T-shirts he owned, a video game shirt.

This particular tee had an image from a space alien shooter that had been popular in the eighties. He loved that game. He loved the eighties. He loved this shirt. But Jay had a point. Perhaps Luke's closet could do with a refresh. Nothing major, though. He didn't care how much his friend made fun of him, he was not getting rid of his collection. But he could add a few new things. Maybe some shirts like the one he wore last night.

The one Julia had liked.

Luke shook himself and put on the shirt. Eighties space aliens would have to do for now. He rushed through the rest of his morning routine, his mind on Julia the entire time. She'd said she liked his shirt because it matched his eyes. Warmth tickled in his belly at the memory. He caught the goofy grin spreading across his half-shaved face and raised a mocking brow at his reflection. Enough nonsense. He was going to be late.

Meetings were held in the employee rec center located on the far southwest side of the floor reserved for staff. The space had turned out to be another unexpected perk of the job. There was an indoor pool, a small kitchen stocked with snacks and drinks, and best of all, a game room furnished with plenty of seating areas and a giant flat screen for video presentations.

He stopped to grab a bottle of high-octane cold brew from the staff fridge and chugged half of it right there. It was the closest he could get to injecting caffeine directly into his veins. Feeling more alert already, Luke found a spot on one of the many couches scattered about the game room and greeted the other employees as they trickled in. He took a quick head count, pleased to note that most of the actors participating in the sim were already in attendance.

Good. Following the morning briefing, they were supposed to head down for breakfast with the guest players at eight. One face, however, was absent. Zach. Figures. Captain Romance Hero probably needed to catch up on his beauty sleep. Luke gritted his teeth. Maybe he could arrange a drive-by yapping of the corgi parade.

At precisely seven a.m., Mrs. W. swept into the room in a swish of purple satin, said parade of corgis at her heels. Penelope brought up the rear, face wreathed in smiles as she dodged the little fur balls.

His sister had always wanted a dog. She would have been happy with any pet, really. But their parents had never allowed it. When he was younger, Luke assumed it had something to do with keeping Pen safe. Her immune system had been so fragile then, there was a lot of stuff that wasn't allowed. Eventually, he realized the truth. His parents simply didn't feel like dealing with it.

Luke shoved the unpleasant memories away and tried to focus on the meeting. But as his boss waxed on about how this resort was her passion project, Luke's thoughts drifted. Pen's birthday was next month. He should see what kind of dog she might like. Something small. Maybe like one of Mrs. W.'s corgis. A burst of applause sent the pack into another yapping frenzy. He grimaced. Maybe not.

Mrs. W. stepped aside to let Penelope take over. Unlike the rambling jumbled word soup of their boss's speech, Pen was brief and concise. She'd often run morning meetings with the staff before, but this time his tech-averse sister even had a PowerPoint review of the daily schedule of activities. She was wrapping up the meeting with a reminder about performer expectations when Luke spotted a thatch of artfully mussed dark hair in the back of the room.

Speak of the manscaped devil.

Luke slipped past the clumps of actors lingering to chat and cornered Zach in the employee kitchen. "Brennan."

"O'Neal." Zach parroted Luke's serious tone.

"You're late."

"I'm here now, aren't I?" he asked, filling a sports bottle from the water cooler.

"You missed the meeting."

"A tragedy. Whatever shall we do?"

Luke clenched his jaw, working to keep his temper in check. "Where were you?"

Zach took his time squirting water into his mouth before replying, "Around."

"'Around,' huh?" Luke leaned back against the counter. "Could you be a little more specific?"

"Relax. I was at the gym. Never miss a Monday," Zach said, a douchey grin accompanying that douchey expression. He passed an assessing glance over Luke. "I'm guessing you've missed a few, though."

Zach lifted his arm to chug some more water, and Luke swore the guy was flexing on purpose. He crossed his own admittedly much less impressive arms and considered giving the bulkier but shorter man a demonstration of Newton's second law of motion. He might not have the power, but he had the reach.

"What's going on in here?" Penelope demanded, appearing in the kitchen. "Is something wrong?"

"Nope." Zach flashed her an easy grin.

She turned to Luke, crossing her arms and mirroring his stance.

"Nothing's wrong," he agreed, relaxing. "Zach was just leaving. Weren't you, Zach?"

"Yep. Gotta get downstairs." He wiggled his eyebrows and did something debatably obscene with the water bottle. "I have a breakfast date with my new friend, Bridget."

"I can't stand that guy," Luke muttered as he watched the actor saunter off.

"Well, get over yourself, because he's the best performer we have," Penelope said, her tone completely unsympathetic. "Which is why I paired him up with the reviewer."

"*You* did that?" Luke turned to his sister. "On purpose?"

"I just said I did." Penelope set the stack of papers she was holding on the counter. "Go on." She fisted her hands on her hips and looked at him expectantly. "Tell me why that was a bad idea."

He smashed his lips together, trapping his response before it escaped.

"You made me the game master," she reminded him.

"I know I did."

"And you said you were going to trust me to handle it."

"You're right." Luke tried to rein in his concerns. "I'm sorry,

Pen. You've barely had a chance to step into the job and here I am second-guessing your first move."

Her face softened. "I understand why you're worried about Zach. He can take things too far." Before Luke could respond she continued, "But that's also what makes him so good at this. He commits to his role one hundred percent. You saw him with the reviewer last night; they were having a great time together."

"They were," Luke agreed, careful to keep his tone light. He seemed to be back on neutral ground with his sister and he didn't want to lose that. He hated arguing with her. They teased each other all the time, but serious disagreements didn't happen often, even when they'd been kids. They were too busy navigating the minefield of their parents' fights. "I just don't want anything to backfire."

She smiled. "I guess it's a good thing you've decided to be a part of the game, then. You can keep an eye on him." She paused to poke him in the ribs. "But if there's a problem, let me handle it. Deal?"

He nodded. "Deal."

"We're in this together, right?" Pen reached up on her tiptoes to give him a hug.

Luke bent and met her halfway, wrapping his arms around her and lifting her off her feet. "Right."

"We're a team. You and me." She gave him a tight squeeze. "And Jay."

"We are," he agreed, setting her down. A little sting pierced his heart. It was stupid and selfish and small of him, but he couldn't seem to help it.

"Speaking of the third pea in our pod, Jay's waiting for me downstairs." Penelope gathered her papers from the counter. "Oh, and Mrs. W. wants to see you in her office. That's what I was coming to tell you, before I got distracted with having to break up the playground pissing contest."

"It was not a—"

"Save your breath." Penelope shook her head. "And no punching Zach. We need to keep that pretty boy's face intact."

"What about below the belt?" Luke asked. "Mrs. W. was pretty clear he won't be needing that while on the clock." Luke dodged the pencil missile his sister torpedoed at him. "I'm kidding. Go help Vijay. I'll be down in a bit."

He waved his sister off and grabbed another bottle of cold brew. It wasn't even eight o'clock yet and he was exhausted. Mrs. W.'s office was directly across the hall from the staff rec center. He raised his hand to knock on the door, but the corgi coalition announced his arrival before he got close enough to bother.

"Enter."

Luke opened the door. Thankfully, the noisy fur balls recognized him and settled their overfluffed bottoms onto their custom-made doggie divans, resuming the other half of their very difficult lives of napping and yapping. "You wanted to see me?"

"Ah, Luke. Yes." She gestured to a chair. "Please. Sit." Mrs. W.'s British accent was always toned down when she was one-on-one. It was one of many eccentricities he'd noticed about the woman. After their first project consultation, almost a year ago, Luke had started a running list in his notebook. Out of habit, he patted his back pocket, relieved to discover it tucked safely inside. He'd been so out of it this morning he couldn't remember grabbing it before leaving his room.

"I know you need to get downstairs to join the others, so I won't keep you long." Mrs. W. pulled one of the dogs into her lap, scratching the spoiled beast beneath its little fox-face snout. "I see you've joined the game in a more active role. Maybe I missed something during our earlier conversations, but was that always part of the plan?"

"Um, no. That was a recent development." Luke squirmed, resisting the urge to pull out his notebook. Not because he needed to check his notes but because he wanted to hold it. Maybe Pen and Vijay had a point about it being his security blanket. "I decided I could do a better job making sure the players are having an optimum experience by getting involved directly."

"Ah. See the lay of the land." Her mouth pinched thoughtfully. "This leaves your sister with the bird's-eye view, then?"

"She has taken over control of that aspect of the game, yes," Luke said slowly, trying to gauge his boss's reaction. Was she upset he hadn't cleared the change with her first? There wasn't anything in their agreement that would require him to. For all intents and purposes, Luke had complete creative control. "I trust Penelope to handle any situations that come up."

"Oh, I know she is quite capable. I have no concerns there. I wouldn't have hired her otherwise." Mrs. W. scooted the dog off her lap and stood, walking to the window and looking out across the Lake Michigan shoreline. "I've had a good feeling about all of you ever since you first replied to my job posting for this project. The three of you together were exactly what I'd been looking for. Serendipity, one might say."

"I was thinking the same thing this morning myself," Luke admitted.

"I commend you on your commitment to the success of this project." Mrs. W. waved a hand, indicating he should join her at the window. "In fact, I've been so impressed by your dedication throughout the development process that I've been thinking . . . maybe I should increase the bonus I promised."

"It's already very generous," Luke said. He hesitated, gathering his thoughts as he watched the morning sunlight glitter on the water. Aside from getting to live and work with his sister and Jay, Luke had accepted Mrs. W.'s job offer because of that bonus. It would provide security for his sister and allow him the opportunity to go after his own dreams. Dreams he'd put on hold since . . . well, since forever.

He'd always wanted to run his own game company, but establishing a start-up came with a lot of risks—risks he'd been unwilling to take. If it was just himself, if it was only his life and his future on the line, Luke would have gone for it right out of college.

But he had Pen to think about, her life and future to consider. His sister graduated high school the same year Luke earned his masters in computer science. When she decided to get her business degree from the University of Wisconsin in Madison, he'd set his dreams aside and had gone to work as a developer for a software firm in the same city. It was boring as hell, but it paid the bills and allowed him to be nearby in case Pen ever needed him. He'd told himself it had been enough.

And he'd even managed to convince himself that was true, until Mrs. W. came along with her wild offer. Suddenly the possibility of *more* was within his reach, and Luke finally admitted to himself how much he wanted to chase that dream.

However, Luke had concerns about the details. He knew his boss was good for the money. He knew she would honor their bargain and pay the bonus if her expectations were met. The problem was, he was still unclear on the precise parameters of those expectations.

The contract only stipulated that the bonus would be triggered if—and only if—Mrs. W. decided she was satisfied with the results of the romantic-comedy experience they created. At the time, he'd been unconcerned about the vague language.

Frankly, he would have signed that contract regardless. It took care of his immediate interests. Luke had been worried about what would happen after Penelope finished school. He knew he was protective—overprotective, according to Pen—but he had good reason to be. It meant a lot to him that he'd been able to keep his sister close. Earning the bonus was a bridge he'd cross later, a problem for tomorrow.

Well, tomorrow was now, and Luke had to figure out what steps he needed to take to cross that bridge. Dealing with Mrs.

Weatherfork was tricky. Yes, she was eccentric, but he'd also seen evidence of a brilliant mind beneath the oddities. She reminded him of a steel trap with a faulty lock mechanism.

"Since you brought up the subject," he finally said, setting aside his musings and turning away from the window, "I had a few questions pertaining to the bonus."

"Oh?" She folded her hands and encouraged him to continue.

"I was hoping you might provide more concrete guidelines."

"Concrete," she repeated.

"For how you plan to evaluate the game's success," Luke elaborated.

"The game's a success if I say it is."

"Yes," he agreed, struggling to keep the irritation from his voice. "But what factors will you be basing your decision on?" Unable to resist, he grabbed his notebook and flipped it open. "Are you looking at registration numbers? Hotel revenue?"

"I don't give a fig about the money."

How nice for you. "What about notoriety? I know about the reviewer who's here to cover the grand opening. Are you looking to build public interest?"

"Not exactly." Mrs. Weatherfork returned to her desk chair. She patted her lap.

For a horrified second, Luke thought she was inviting him to sit there.

"Young man . . ." She waited until the ball of fur that had jumped up settled down, little black nose tucked into her arm. "You know I started this venture to make a point to my husband."

He shifted uneasily. Luke had yet to meet the infamous Harold Weatherfork, but by all accounts, the goose was as goofy as the gander.

"Of course, I want the project to meet all standard benchmarks of success in terms of revenue and registration." She stroked her hand along the back of the dog in her lap, smoothing down the tufts of fur. "But I also consider success to be based on what I'm trying to prove."

There was that steel trap. "Which is . . . ?"

"That romance is real, of course."

Snap. And there went that faulty lever he was worried about.

"I want to show Harold that people are coming to this little rom-com world you've created because they believe—like I do—in the magic of two people falling in love against all odds."

"True love." Luke blinked. "That's what you're expecting me to deliver?"

"Don't look so concerned." She chuckled. "I'm expecting you to deliver the romantic *experience.* I want to prove to my husband that it's possible to create a place where people believe, at least for a little while, they really are part of a romantic comedy. If I'm satisfied you've done that, you'll have your bonus." She met his eye with a shrewd little wink. "Understand?"

"I think so." Luke scribbled down some notes, dominoes lining up in his mind. His boss was an eccentric entrepreneur, but crafty too. Grandiose claims of proving to her husband some intangible concept about romance aside, her concept for the resort was rather brilliant.

What she was asking for was abstract, yes, but he'd seen it in action plenty of times before. Every time he watched a rom-com with his sister, in fact. With each movie, Pen went on an emotional journey with the characters, experiencing the highs and lows, laughing and crying . . . falling in love.

As for himself, Luke wasn't sure what it felt like to fall in love. He'd never been in love before, not romantically. And after watching the way his parents had eviscerated each other, Luke wasn't sure he was all that interested in experiencing that kind of love. He loved his sister. He even loved Jay. But he wasn't so obtuse as to think that was the same thing as wanting to ride off into the sunset with someone. So while he couldn't fully appreciate what

Mrs. W. wanted her guests to experience, he understood the concept in theory.

What his boss described was intangible, but not impossible. And not immeasurable, either. Difficult to extrapolate, but if he had the guests fill out evaluation forms at the end of the week, rating and describing their experiences, their responses would provide concrete data points he could interpolate.

Technical details aside, in the end, Luke knew that, ironically, his real shot at that bonus hinged on his ability to create exactly what Vijay promised in the hotel's website promo.

For the chance to achieve his dreams, Luke had to do one thing.

Make the fantasy real.

CHAPTER 12

JULIA

Julia snuggled deeper into the plush pillows, drifting in and out of a very pleasant dream involving gray eyes and great hands. She stretched luxuriously, spreading her arms and legs out as far as they could go, relishing the decadent freedom of a king-size bed. When had she ever had a king-size bed all to herself?

Never, that's when. Kat could have the fancy suite. This was all the luxury Julia needed. The mattress in her place was barely bigger than a toddler bed . . . She swore she could buy crib sheets and they'd probably fit. But it was the only thing that worked in what passed for a bedroom in her tiny apartment. But oh, to be able to roll over and over and—she rolled again—yep, over, and not fall off the bed? Heaven.

There were times Julia wished she'd never moved out of the place she'd shared with Kat and Andie, but it was a step she'd always believed she needed to take. Part of the ladder to full-fledged adulthood that had been drilled into her since childhood. A ladder lined with rungs of responsibility, like living on her own, establishing job security, and maintaining a long-term relationship. She'd managed the first, was working on the second, and the third . . . well, she wasn't even sure she wanted the third to happen.

Maybe she'd change her mind. When she was ready. When the right person came along.

But part of her worried she'd never be ready. Or that the right person would never come along and she'd finally give up and just settle, commit to a long-term relationship with someone not because she couldn't imagine spending the rest of her life without them but because it was better than being alone. And wasn't that worse? After having a front-row seat to her parents' relationship, she thought so.

She knew that, for some people, being alone was the happy ending they wanted. They lived full, contented lives, and that was great. But she also knew she wasn't one of those people. She wasn't built that way. On some fundamental level, Julia craved a life partner. A soul mate.

Deep down lurked doubts that scared her, fears drifting in the darkest parts of her heart that she didn't want to study too closely in the light. But here, in this giant bed, those doubts crept out of hiding. Maybe it was being alone in such a big bed, surrounded by so much empty space. Maybe it was all the feelings stirred up last night as she'd stared into a certain pair of gray eyes and talked and laughed.

And wanted.

And dreamed.

Tendrils of the dream she'd been having drifted to the surface, curling around her thoughts. Julia flopped onto her back, trying to make sense of the vague images and lingering sensations. Her head was hazy . . . and she was horny as hell.

She was having a feelings hangover. Last night, she'd gotten drunk on the heady cocktail of easy conversation, warm smiles, and meaningful glances. Not to mention all that "accidental" touching they'd been doing. What she was experiencing now was simply a reaction to the buildup of endorphins from spending all that time with Luke.

They hadn't even kissed. Not even an almost-kiss like when they first met. Despite what she told her friends, that had *definitely* been an almost-kiss. And Julia hadn't stopped thinking about it since. What would have happened on the beach if Andie hadn't come along and interrupted the moment?

In her dreams last night, she'd gotten her answer.

Julia closed her eyes, remembering. Alone on the beach, they'd kissed. Hell, they'd done a lot more than kiss. Her body grew warmer, a pulsing ache building inside. She sifted through her mind for details of the dream while her hand drifted lower, fingers stroking the source of that throbbing heat. Her legs grew heavy and she let them fall open, relishing the slide of smooth sheets against her bare skin, reveling in the freedom to spread her thighs as wide apart as she desired, stretch her legs out as far as she wanted.

She pointed then flexed her toes. Imagined she was lying in the sand. Digging her heels into the mattress, she lifted her hips and rocked against her fingers. Back and forth, slow and easy, the friction sending a ripple of pleasure through her. Like the tide outside her window, gently rolling in and out. She increased the pressure, sensations building in intensity. When her fingers dipped inside, she imagined *his* fingers there.

Fuck, what he could do to her with those hands. Ever since the Chris conversation at dinner, Julia had thought about Luke's hands. She shivered, recalling how his long, elegant fingers had stroked over hers, one at a time. By the time the pie had arrived, she was ready to be his dessert.

Eyes still closed, she pictured his gray gaze, and her body lit up with awareness, the way it did every time he looked at her. *Yes.*

"Julia."

He was calling her name.

"Julia."

"Yes." She turned her head and moaned into the pillow. So close now.

She bit her lip. *Yes.* Her hips and hand began to move faster. *Yes. Yes. Yes.*

"Julia!" A knock sounded at her door.

Julia's eyes snapped open and she froze.

"Jules?" a voice called, louder now. Andie's voice. "Are you awake?"

"Yes," she croaked. With a sigh of frustration, Julia rolled across the bed. "Coming!" She struggled to untangle herself from the sheets, now wrapped around her in a strangled mass from all her excessive thrashing about.

The knock came again.

"I'm coming," she repeated, peevishly wishing she actually was. Ugh. This was just like watching a rom-com fade to black. A disappointing interruption right before the good stuff happened.

Giving up on the detangling efforts, Julia bundled up armfuls of bedding and bunny-hopped her way to the door.

Andie stood there, freshly showered and wide awake. "Are you feeling well? You didn't forget to pack your meds, did you?"

"Yes, I'm feeling fine. And no, I didn't forget my prescription. But thanks, Mom."

"Excuse me for caring. It's not like you haven't forgotten before," Andie sniped. "You're not dressed yet."

"I decided to sign up for the toga party." Julia held the door open with one hand and tugged the sheet higher with the other. "You didn't see it on the itinerary?"

"Nope, not on here." Andie held up the sheet with the list of activities. "We're supposed to turn these in at breakfast." She slipped past Julia, into the room. "Which we're going to miss if you don't hurry up and get ready." She paused, cocking her head. "Jules—are you naked under there?"

"You're supposed to call me Meg." Julia let the door swing shut and hopped into the bathroom. She flipped on the faucet. "Remember, Carrie?"

"Not when it's just us." Andie glanced around, taking in Julia's disheveled appearance before eyeing the rumpled bed. "And it *is* just us in here, right?"

"Yes, it's just us," Julia snapped. "Who else would be in here?"

"I have a few ideas." Andie smirked. She pointedly watched Julia dry her hands. "Were you playing with the Chrises?"

"That's Kat's thing, not mine." Julia flushed and clutched at the sheets still draped around her, trying to keep them from slithering to the floor. "But yes," she admitted. "I was."

"Good for you." Andie laughed. "Now hurry up and get some clothes on." She checked her smartwatch. "Breakfast starts in fourteen minutes and twenty-seven seconds."

"Great. I only need fourteen minutes and twenty-five seconds," Julia promised.

Fourteen minutes and twenty-one seconds later, Julia made it to the breakfast room in time to snag a cup of coffee before Andie flagged her down. She was sitting at one of the banquet tables, along with David and Patrick, the couple they'd had dinner with last night. And, in an interesting development, seated next to Andie was the football jersey guy from last night.

"Where's Kat?" she asked, when she reached the table.

"You mean Bridget?" a chipper faux-British voice called from behind her. "Right here."

Julia turned, smiling at her friend. "Yes. Bridget."

Kat/Bridget yawned. "Remind me again, why are we up so early?"

"Food." Andie jabbed a finger at the breakfast buffet.

"Uh-oh," Kat murmured, as she and Julia hurried over to the buffet. "She's got her game face on."

"You didn't notice it when she came to your room to check if you were awake?" Julia asked, filling a bowl with yogurt and granola.

Kat scooped some scrambled eggs and a few sausages onto a plate. "I refused to open the door."

"Smart," Julia said, topping her bowl off with slices of fresh fruit, wishing she'd thought to do the same.

Back at the table, she slid into the empty seat on the other side of Andie, who was busy smothering a bagel with cream cheese. "What are we carb loading for, anyway?"

"Did you forget?" Andie asked, biting into the bagel. "We have the walking tour of the resort this morning."

"I thought we were doing paintball." Kat took a seat across from them.

"That's tomorrow." Andie held up her itinerary. "I hope you two remembered to bring these down with you. We need to finish filling them out."

"Hard to forget when someone yells a reminder through your door at seven forty-five in the morning," Kat grumbled. Her face brightened as she began to read off the list of activities. "Ooh, they have cookie baking! And a wine and paint night."

"You're not going to want to miss that one," Zach announced. He bent to kiss Kat's cheek. "Morning, gorgeous."

"You're not looking so bad yourself," Kat observed, blatantly checking out his backside as he sat down next to her. "Does this mean you plan on doing the wine and paint night too?"

"I guess you could say that." White teeth flashed. "I'm going to be posing."

"In the classic style?" Patrick asked.

"By which he means 'naked,'" David clarified.

"Sign up and find out." Zach grabbed a sausage off Kat's plate and winked.

"You're on." David's lip curled in a playful smirk. He and Patrick took out their schedules and began filling it in, laughing softly together.

"What's so funny over here?" a voice asked from behind Julia. *Luke.*

"Is this seat taken?" He nodded at the one next to her.

She shook her head, flushing. She was supposed to call him Lance. But it was no good. Even though she had known him for less than twenty-four hours, in her mind, he was Luke. And in her mind, Luke had been about to get her off this morning. Julia gulped her coffee, not caring that the hot liquid seared her throat. She needed the caffeine to jolt her back to reality.

"Hey." Luke waved a hand in front of her. "Everything okay?"

"Sorry." Julia blinked, realizing he'd been talking to her while she was thinking about—"I was just thinking."

"About what?"

Her gaze snagged on his hand and her belly clenched. She winced internally. Of course he would ask that question; it was a perfectly logical response to her statement. "Oh, about the week ahead." There. That was honest enough.

"Have you finished filling out your itinerary yet?" he asked.

"Not yet." Unable to stop herself, her gaze drifted to Luke's hands again. They were big hands. Long fingers wrapped around a bottle of iced coffee, thumb lazily moving back and forth, wiping at the condensation on the glass. Julia swallowed. She doubted the activity she'd been considering was listed. "What about you?" she asked. "What are you interested in doing?"

"I'm curious about these bonus choices," Kat chimed in. "It looks like we get to pick one personalized activity."

"See anything you like?" Zach purred.

"Everything looks good," Kat replied, voice equally throaty. Her eyes were not on her paper.

Julia exchanged glances with Andie. Zach might be one of the actors, but their friend seemed to be enjoying his particular brand of charm.

"Stuck in an elevator?" Curt asked, biting into a muffin with gusto. "What's that?"

"I'm guessing it's just what it says," Andie remarked, watching him with less gusto. "You get stuck in an elevator."

"Why would anyone *choose* to do that?" Curt waved the muffin around, sending crumbs flying across the table. "You explained the paintball thing last night. I'm good with that. But how is *this* romantic?"

"I suppose it depends on who you're stuck with," Andie mused.

"You don't even have to actually get stuck." Kat shot Zach a meaningful look. "As long as there's enough time for some hot kissing to happen."

"Characters getting trapped in an elevator is a rom-com staple." Julia tapped her chin thoughtfully. "There's a great stuck-in-the-elevator scene in *Set It Up*, but no kissing."

"Right." Andie snickered. "Just some peeing."

"Peeing?" Curt's mouth fell open. Luckily for everyone else at the table, he'd finished his muffin. "Look, no offense, but if I was stuck in an elevator and pee was involved . . . well, romance would not be the first thing on my mind."

"I think getting stuck in an elevator could be very romantic," Kat murmured, leaning into Zach.

"Minus the peeing part, of course," Julia added.

Beside her, Luke smothered a laugh.

"Hey now, don't yuck someone else's yum," David chided.

"He's teasing." Patrick paused. "I think." He grinned at Julia. "What bonus activity are you picking?"

She glanced at her paper, nibbling her bottom lip, working it back and forth in contemplation. "I can't decide."

Andie nudged her. "Well hurry up."

"What's your rush?" Julia wondered. "You need to go pee in an elevator or something?"

"I was planning to do that in your shower," Andie countered.

"You're such a jock." Julia rolled her eyes, shaking her head.

"Seriously, Jules. Hurry up. I don't know if slots fill up for certain activities."

"They don't," Luke said. "That's not how it works."

She and Andie both turned to look at him.

"I don't think so, anyway," he clarified, shifting on his chair.

"You still need to hurry up." Andie finished off her bagel.

"Fine. Karaoke serenade." Julia circled her choices and handed her sheet to Andie.

"Classic," Zach agreed, nodding enthusiastically. "And another memorable Heath moment from *10 Things*."

"That scene is one of my personal favorites," Julia admitted.

Even her cynical heart had melted during that sweet scene. "I've never had anyone serenade me before."

"But what if the person doing the serenading isn't a good singer?" Luke asked.

"Even better!" Julia laughed. "That's rom-com gold. Think Cameron Diaz in *My Best Friend's Wedding*."

"Or Joseph Gordon-Levitt in *(500) Days of Summer*." Andie placed a hand over her heart. "So terrible, but so wonderful at the same time."

"He was drunk off his ass in that scene, right?" Julia asked.

"Adorably so." Bridget smiled wickedly and pointed to herself. "While we are on the topic of adorable drunken karaoke . . ."

"*Bridget Jones's Diary!*" Andie crowed. "Oh, she was so smashed."

"Oh, yeah?" Curt grinned. "I admit I've done some drunk singing myself."

"And I bet it was charming," Andie remarked.

Despite her caustic tone, Julia thought she caught a note of fondness in her friend's voice. She glanced at Andie, considering. Perhaps Curt was growing on her. Which was wild, because they were total opposites.

Though now that she thought about it, the possibility was actually hilarious, especially considering how "opposites attract" was a standard rom-com trope. A thrill ran down Julia's spine and she had to remind herself that this was a game. None of it was real.

CHAPTER 13

JULIA

After breakfast, Julia and her friends joined the large crowd of guests gathered in the lobby, where Mrs. Weatherfork welcomed them again. Today the resort owner was decked out in a lime-colored wrap dress topped by a creamy pale green scarf.

"She looks like a piece of key lime pie," Andie muttered.

Julia swallowed a giggle as the outlandishly attired woman proceeded to launch into a lengthy history lesson of the hotel, including a detailed description of the original oak balustrades lining the foyer staircase and balcony, courtesy of some nineteenth-century lumber baron who made all his money chopping down half the forests of Wisconsin. Then it was on to the terrace, for more detailed description of the brickwork patio and stone steps. The speeches continued at the gazebo, the tennis and croquet courts, and the garden conservatory.

After viewing the resort's private pond, outfitted with several canoes and paddle boats, they were now making their way up a winding gravel trail. Julia tapped her notepad irritably. She'd been planning to take some notes for her review, but so far, the "tour" had been one endless, boring lecture.

Boring and exhausting. Before hitting the trail, Mrs. Weatherfork had commandeered a golf cart for herself and her contingent of corgis. The woman even had little car seats for each of them. Meanwhile, the guests were forced to trudge along on foot.

"How long is this tour supposed to last?" Julia asked, pushing back the heavy curtain of her hair, which had been getting wilder and frizzier by the moment in the growing humidity. Soon she'd be fluffier than Mrs. Whackadoodle's pampered pets. Julia glanced up at the golf cart, envious of the four fur balls bouncing along in contented comfort, their owner's long silk scarf flapping in a breeze Julia had yet to feel. "We've been walking for hours," she whined.

"It's only been seventy-five minutes." Andie laughed, checking her Fitbit. "That's barely even one hour."

"Well, it feels like ten," Julia grumbled, as she paused to rest in the shade of a massive pine tree.

"You should have eaten more at breakfast," Andie chided, adding, "and that sedentary lifestyle of yours isn't helping." Andie kept walking, short legs eating up the path with brisk efficiency. "I've been telling you for years to get out and move more."

"If I strangled her right now, would that be considered murder or self-defense?" Julia wondered aloud, watching as her sporty friend outpaced the corgi caravan and disappeared around another curve in the trail.

Kat snorted. "You'd have to catch her first."

"Good point." Julia sighed and let Kat pull her forward. "What happened to your Bridget accent?"

"I got tired of it." Kat shrugged. "Besides, it doesn't matter, since Bridget's boy toy isn't around anyway. I haven't seen Zach since breakfast."

"Maybe he's not fond of nature," Julia suggested.

"Maybe he's not fond of me," Kat countered.

"Please. He was all over you last night." Julia swatted at a mosquito attempting to make her its next victim. "Ack! Why are we even out in the woods? The first part of the tour made sense. Even though we were getting buried in details, I get seeing all the great stuff the resort has to offer. But I don't understand how a nature walk can be considered part of the rom-com experience."

"Are you kidding?" Kat shook her head. "Think of all the romantic comedies that have characters taking a walk around Central Park, or going on hikes, or strolling through a garden."

"Yeah, but aren't those romantic walks supposed to happen with, oh, I don't know . . ." Julia upped the snark ratio in her voice. "Someone you want to get romantic with?"

"Not always." Kat sidled up next to Julia and put an arm around her waist. "Sometimes it's a chance for a group of friends to catch up and *talk* about who they're interested in getting romantic with."

"Well, I don't see anyone around here who matches that description, so . . ."

"Come on. We both know who you want to get romantic with," Kat teased.

"I'm not here looking for my soul mate." Julia's face scrunched into a stubborn pout as she stared down at her notepad. "I'm here to do a job."

"If you say so," Kat muttered.

"What was that?" Julia asked, her voice sharp.

"Nothing." Kat shrugged.

"I know you, Kat. That little comment was not nothing." Julia was too crabby to let this slide. "Tell me what you're thinking."

"Fine." Kat took a breath. "I know you're hoping for the same thing I am."

"You do, huh?" Julia stopped walking and put her hands on her hips. "And what's that?"

"To experience all the over-the-top, wonderfully cheesy, cute, and adorable moments we see in rom-coms. We want to live the fantasy." Kat clasped her hands together. "To have a real meet-cute. To stumble into love. To find *the one*."

"Yeah, but it's still a fantasy." Julia snorted. "I don't expect to actually find 'the one' here."

"Don't you hope you might, though?" Kat pressed. "Even just a little? It's okay to admit it."

At first, Julia didn't answer. She started walking again in silence. Yesterday, she would have vehemently denied the possibility, but now, after meeting Luke . . .

"Fine," she admitted. "Maybe a little."

To her credit, Kat was gracious in her victory. She didn't gloat; she simply gave Julia a small, knowing smile.

"What are you two whispering about back there?" Andie called from where she'd stopped to wait for them.

"I was just telling our girl Jules here she can still have some fun while working on her review."

"I'm not saying I don't think I should be having fun," Julia protested. "I just don't agree with some of Kat's suggestions for what qualifies as fun. Not under these circumstances, anyway."

"Under what circumstances, then?" Andie asked.

"Huh?"

Andie popped open the sports bottle she was carrying. "I'm assuming the circumstances being discussed involve a certain someone?"

"You know they do," Kat agreed. "What's in there?" She pointed at the bottle Andie was chugging.

"Vodka."

"Really?" Kat grabbed it and took a swig. "Tease! This is just water."

"You honestly thought I could chug vodka like that?" Andie shook her head. "I don't know if I should be insulted or proud." She grabbed her bottle back and turned to Julia. "What I'm hearing is that you feel weird about engaging in any . . . What's the word I'm looking for?"

"*Hanky-panky?*" Kat suggested.

"That works." Andie grinned. "You want to avoid any hanky-panky because you feel it would be inappropriate, given the circumstances of who you are and why you're here."

"Exactly." Julia exhaled. "I'm glad you understand."

"Yeah, but here's the thing. I don't." Andie took another sip of water and shook her head. "I mean I *would* understand, except that I watched the two of you together last night and he was giving you the look."

"What look?"

"You know the one. The one when he looks at you, he *looks* at you."

Julia stopped walking, hands on her hips. "What are you talking about?"

"Kat, you know what I'm talking about, right?"

"Yep." Kat promptly confirmed. "Everyone knows the look."

"Apparently not everyone," Julia snapped. She was hot and irritable and didn't want to have this conversation. "Are you sure that isn't vodka in there?"

Both of her friends stared at her with another kind of look. One Julia definitely knew and didn't like. It was a look that said, *You know exactly what we're talking about but you're pretending you don't because you want to avoid facing the feelings that come with acknowledging you know what we are talking about.*

Because she *did* know.

As if reading her mind, Andie stepped closer. "This is not vodka, I am not drunk, and you know exactly what look we're talking about." She glanced behind Julia and lowered her voice. "I know you know because he's giving you the look right now. But I don't have to tell you that, because I bet you can feel it."

"That's ridiculous. I have no idea what you mean." But even as Julia denied it, she knew. Because she *did* feel it. A tingling awareness. Luke had joined the group taking the walking tour. Unable to resist, she glanced over her shoulder. Yep. There he was. Quite a distance back but easy to spot. His long legs loping lazily along. Gray gaze on her.

"He's staring because he's probably wondering what the hell the three of us are doing, standing here in the middle of the trail," she deflected. "Or maybe he's horrified by the circus act my hair is becoming in this freaking humidity. It's like a car wreck. He can't look away." Julia fanned herself with her notepad, trying to circulate some cooler air. "We're at a lakefront resort. Where's that legendary Lake Michigan breeze?"

"I'd say someone is getting worked up," Kat observed.

"Yes, she does seem a bit hot and bothered," Andie agreed. "You'd never guess what I caught her doing this morning." She turned to Julia, gaze speculative. "I thought you were hangry, but maybe you're horn—"

"You know what? I *am* hot. And *you're* bothering me. Why don't you two go on without me." Julia waved to her friends. "I think I'm going to head back to the hotel."

"But—" Kat began.

Andie tugged on Kat's arm. "It's fine. Let her go." She waved at Julia. "Go ahead. We'll see you later."

Julia felt like an ass for blowing up. Part of her wanted to take back her words and stick with her friends. Not to mention do her job and participate in the scheduled resort activities, no matter how boring or irritating they turned out to be. But she'd made too big a stink to change her mind now, so she turned around and began retracing her steps, nodding and sharing an awkward smile as she passed other guests on the trail.

She couldn't blame her attitude on the weather. Or not eating enough at breakfast. Or even the frustrating interruption this morning. No, she knew much of her reaction was driven by the desire to prove to them that she was right and they were wrong.

Lurking beneath that urge was fear. Fear that her friends were the ones who were right. That it wasn't just Andie and Kat who held the outlandish belief that it might be possible to find true love at this rom-com fantasyland. That maybe she did, too.

Deeper still was hope. Hope that not only could true love happen in a place like this but that it could happen anywhere. That it was real. Julia twisted the map in her hands. That was the scariest part of all of this. To discover that despite everything she thought she knew about herself, this hope existed when she thought it never could.

"Hey," Luke called. "What's wrong?"

"Nothing," she growled.

"If nothing is wrong, then why are you ditching your friends?" he asked, reaching an arm out to stop her as she was about to pass him on the trail. "Did something happen? Are you not having fun?"

"I didn't ditch my friends," she argued, tugging her arm out of his grip. She stuttered to a halt. "Well, I did. But nothing's wrong. They're fine."

"Are you fine?" he asked gently, eyes searching hers.

Julia shook her head. The way he was looking at her turned her thoughts fuzzy, made it hard to think. "I'm a little tired, that's all. I'm going back to the hotel."

"But—" he began, glancing up ahead toward the others.

"You too?" she snapped. "What is up with everyone and their *buts*?"

"Um . . ."

"Sorry," she groaned. "That didn't come out right."

He chuckled. "Mind if I join you?"

"Do you mind walking with a harpy who might shred your face if you say the wrong thing?" Julia countered.

He blinked.

Julia shoved her notepad in her pocket. The urge to be alone and stew in her little pot of grumpy angst was strong. It was a safe shadow she could go hide in. But the thought of spending time with Luke was like a candle in that shadow. A welcome, cozy light that she wanted to cuddle up with.

"What if I promise not to say anything?" he asked. "Is my face safe?"

"I suppose." A reluctant smile pulled at the corners of her mouth. The candle burned brighter.

They continued down the path in comfortable silence, the quiet broken only by occasional birdsong and the crunch of their shoes on the gravel trail. Again, she noted how his long, lean legs stretched lazily; his pace could at best be described as a causal stroll. Julia shook her head. "How does someone so tall walk so slowly?"

"Am I allowed to answer?"

"Shut up." She smacked his arm.

"Okay." He walked on in silence.

"No." Julia swatted him again. "I meant 'Shut up' as in 'Shut up, yes, you can talk to me.'"

"Hm. No clue why that response might be confusing." He dodged a third smack and grinned. "I think the question should be: How does someone so short walk so fast? The three of you were way ahead of everyone else."

"Hey, I was just trying to keep up with my friend."

"My point exactly. Her legs are even shorter than yours."

Julia giggled.

"I like it when you laugh."

His abrupt confession caught her off guard. Julia's chest tightened, heart rattling against her ribs. She stared at the ground, trying to get a handle on the sudden burst of light that bloomed inside her at his words. The candle had become a bonfire.

"I'm sorry." He hesitated. "Is it weird that I told you that?"

"It's fine. It's not weird." It wasn't weird, and it was more than fine. It was wonderful. It was simple and honest and . . . real. She kept her gaze trained on their feet, her shorter legs seeming to take two steps for every one of his. She laughed again and could sense more than see the grin that spread across his face in response. The bright, toasty-warm feeling expanded.

Meanwhile, the trail ahead dimmed. Julia glanced up. "Uh-oh." The sky was turning an ominous color, the summer sun swallowed by a swath of dark clouds. "That can't be good." Abruptly, the cool breeze Julia had been longing for swept over her, the wind kicking up and making the trees lining the path shudder.

Luke cursed and reached for her hand. "There's a storm blowing in from the lake. We better pick up the pace."

If it had taken two of Julia's steps for every one of his before, it took at least double that now, maybe triple. But he kept a firm grip on her hand as they raced along the trail. They were running into the wind, the force of it stinging Julia's cheeks and sending her hair into a frenzy.

It felt good. And when the skies opened and a torrent of rain spilled down, drenching her instantly, that felt good, too. Fresh and clean and cool. Julia inhaled deeply, wanting to absorb the cleansing newness deep inside.

"You're enjoying this, aren't you?" Luke muttered

"I am." She gulped more air. "But I gotta slow down."

"Oh, thank God." He slowed his pace. Beneath the thin cotton of his shirt, his chest heaved. "Man, I'm out of shape."

"You're not the only one," Julia admitted, bending over, hands on her knees as she tried to force her heart to shift from a gallop to a trot. By the time she got her breath back and her pulse down, the initial fury of the storm had passed, taking the fierce wind and heavy rains and leaving a soft, steady drizzle in its wake.

"Oh, I'll be feeling the effects of that for the next month at least," he assured her. "It was kind of fun, though." Luke smiled, pushing rain-slicked hair back from his face.

"Yeah." Julia straightened. "It *was* fun." And even though her lungs were once again at full capacity, she was still finding it hard to breathe when he was smiling at her like that.

Maybe her friends had a point.

Maybe she should allow herself some fun.

Maybe even a little hanky-panky.

She peered into the forest lining the trail. "Do you think we should look for a spot to get out of the rain?"

"I'm pretty sure the worst of it is over. Besides . . ." He glanced down at his soaked clothes. "It's not like we've got anything left to keep dry."

"I wouldn't be so sure about that." She kicked out a leg and wiggled her foot. "I think one toe is still pretty dry."

"You want to seek shelter in the woods for one toe?"

"Um . . ." Okay, so the guy wasn't very good at taking a hint. Or she wasn't very good at flirting. Probably a bit of both.

"Oh." A beat later, his eyes lit with understanding. "Oh, right. Your toe."

Julia almost laughed, he looked so much like an actual light-bulb had clicked on inside his head.

"Yes, of course." He reached for her hand. "We must do what we can to keep that toe dry." Luke stepped off the path and slipped. "Whoops-a-daisies." He straightened and glanced over his shoulder at her. "Careful. The grass is slick."

"Did you just say 'Whoops-a-daisies'?"

"Definitely not." Luke cleared his throat, squinting into the woods. "I think I see a fallen log near that evergreen." He pointed out the spot. "Will that do?"

"Sure." Julia suppressed a grin.

They walked together, moving gingerly across the damp forest floor. Once they were both settled, Luke asked, "Well, was our mission to protect your toe from the elements successful?"

"Um . . ." Julia wiggled her foot again. "Yes. Thank you."

An awkward silence descended. She glanced around, taking in their impromptu sanctuary. Despite the recent downpour, the log was mostly dry, nestled as it was beneath a big pine tree, its branches thick with needles.

"It's very cozy here."

"It is," Luke agreed.

"Smells like Christmas."

"It does."

More awkward silence.

Between the soft thrum of the rain around them and the warm, quiet closeness of their shelter, the moment had the potential to be incredibly romantic. *If this were a movie.* But it's not, Julia reminded herself. So, instead, the moment was awkward and uncomfortable and why did she think she could do this?

At some point in the middle of her internal wallowing about all the ways this moment could be romantic and wasn't, Julia realized Luke was looking at her.

And it was *that* look.

Like Andie said, she could *feel* it.

Julia pretended to be fascinated with the texture of the bark on the log, the pattern of fallen pine needles on the ground—anything and everything that allowed her to avoid looking at Luke—because she was afraid that if she looked at him, he would stop looking at her. And she didn't want him to stop looking at her the way he was right now, because she liked the way it felt too much.

"Is something wrong?" Luke asked.

"Huh?"

"You won't look at me."

"I'm fine." Julia winced. She was so bad at this. "I was just looking at the, um, log. It's a very nice log. Very sturdy. Makes a very nice place to sit."

Oh, God, she had verbal diarrhea. She cringed inwardly. Why was she thinking about diarrhea right now? "And the trees. I've never seen such pine trees. The branches are so big and thick and—"

"Can I kiss you?"

Julia froze. She met his gaze. And now she was looking at him and he was looking at her and yes it was with *that* look. The one that made her feel beautiful and perfect and precious and amazing and oh shit she didn't answer him yet, did she?

"Um, okay."

He leaned closer, and for a split second, Julia wished he wouldn't kiss her, because she wanted to hold on to this moment, this perfect moment, before it was ruined by a kiss that couldn't possibly live up to the romantic promise currently vibrating between them.

But then his lips brushed hers and it was . . . She closed her eyes. It was . . . *magic*.

Julia had been kissed before. She'd kissed and been kissed. She'd had some bad kisses, a lot of okay kisses, and even a few good kisses, but she'd never had a magic kiss. One that she felt all the way through her, from lips to toes and back up again. And he hadn't even actually really kissed her yet, just touched his lips to hers.

When he finally did kiss her, it was soft, and slow, and sweet. He kissed her over and over, brief, delicious sips of contact. Gradually, his kisses became longer, his mouth pressing firmer to hers, lingering, the tip of his tongue gliding along the curve of her lower lip as if learning its shape. Julia was intensely aware of each shift in movement, mentally cataloguing every detail of their kiss.

I am having a hyper-romantic super-hot kiss in the freaking rain!

And it only got hotter. When his mouth opened over hers, tongue slipping inside, all coherent thought evaporated. *Poof.* Gone. Julia no longer had a brain, just a body. A body that was tingling and aching and yearning. She moaned and gripped his shoulders, chasing his tongue with hers. His fingers sifted through her still-wet hair, palm cradling the back of her neck, while his other hand wrapped around her waist and pulled her closer.

His hand moved from her neck down her back, fingers stroking her spine. Julia shivered.

"Cold?" Luke's voice was a husky whisper.

Which was more sound than Julia could produce right now. She shook her head.

His lips grazed her throat and she shivered again.

"You sure?" he asked, his breath a warm caress on her neck.

She moaned. Her vocal cords seemed to have forgotten how to do anything but make incoherent noises.

Luke smiled. She could feel the curve of his mouth against her skin. He leaned back and gazed down at her. "Not in the mood to talk, huh?"

She might have tried to respond to that, but he gripped her

hips and pulled her onto his lap, her thighs spreading, pressing against his. Her position on top of him put them almost at eye level with each other. Julia took the lead this time, controlling the kiss. As her mouth moved over his, a wordless groan of pleasure escaped him, sending power and excitement surging inside her.

Hands braced on his shoulders, she rose up, her knees pressing into the bark. Straddling him on the log in her shorts should have been uncomfortable as hell, and maybe it was, but she was too busy enjoying herself to notice. She deepened the kiss, losing herself in the feel of her mouth on his, of his hands on her skin, cocooned by the cool scent of pine and the warm, soft patter of summer rain.

His fingers dug into her hips, and they both moaned, tension spiraling between them. *Hell yes.* This had to be the hottest thing she'd ever done in her life. Wanting more, Julia leaned into him. She realized her mistake a moment too late as their center of balance shifted on the log, causing them both to slide backward.

Oh shit, we're going over.

"Whoops-a-daisies!" Luke yelped.

He hit the ground first, back landing with a thud, Julia crashing down face-first on top of him. They lay there, stunned, staring at each other in openmouthed silence as the details of the moment slowly registered.

A giggle bubbled up inside her, quickly turning into a full-blown belly laugh. "I *knew* you said, 'Whoops-a-daisies'!"

From beneath her, Luke heaved an aggrieved sigh. But when her laughter finally tapered off so she could take a breath, he said, eyes twinkling, "Good thing I like your laugh so much."

"Good thing you're so funny."

He grimaced and she tittered. "I'm sorry," she said, swallowing another giggle and rolling off him. "Are you hurt?"

"Aside from my pride?" He sat up. "I don't think so." He patted the ground. "Luckily, the rain softened things up a bit." Luke got to his feet and offered her a hand.

Julia stood and wiped at the dirt and pine needles clinging to her. She realized her notepad had fallen out of her pocket and glanced around frantically. She caught a glimpse of paper amid the detritus on the forest floor and dove.

At the same time, Luke bent and reached for something on the ground. They narrowly missed colliding again. Julia stood and then realized she'd grabbed his notebook. She recognized it from the seagull encounter yesterday. "I believe this is yours?" She held it out to him.

"And this must be yours," he said, eyes twinkling with mischief as he held up her notepad.

Julia controlled the instinct to snatch it out of his hand, managing to nod calmly as she traded with him.

He watched as she tucked her notepad away, mouth twitching. "I'd say this makes us even."

"Excuse me?"

"I knocked you over once, now you've knocked me over. We're even," Luke explained, sliding his notebook back into his pocket.

"Aha! You admit that first fall on the beach was your fault," Julia teased, crossing her arms.

"I do. And I am sorry," he said, rubbing the base of his spine. "Even though I seem to be the one taking the brunt of these falls."

Julia snorted and followed him as he made his way around the log and back to the trail.

"That didn't sound like a very sympathetic snort," Luke observed. He'd reached the path but began walking the direction opposite to the way they'd been headed when the storm hit.

"Where are you going?"

"Back to the hotel." He blinked at her. "Isn't that where you want to go?"

"Yeah, but—"

"The trail is a loop." He pointed at the bend ahead. "You were almost back at the resort when you decided to turn around earlier."

"What?" In a matter of minutes, the trees began to thin and

Julia could see the bright shingles of the resort's roof shining in the late morning sun. Yep, the trail made a loop through the forest. Between the thick line of trees and the way the path curved, it had been impossible to tell. She supposed it served her right for throwing a temper tantrum. She sighed. "Why didn't you say something before?"

"I started to." He shrugged. "But you seemed pretty determined you knew where you were going."

Julia bit her lip. She did tend to think she was right and everyone else was wrong.

"The thing is," he began, "I apologized for running into you on the beach, but I won't apologize for not telling you about the trail." Luke stepped closer, chest rising as he took a deep breath. "I don't regret where this change in direction ended up." He smiled at her, mouth curving with wicked unrepentance.

"I'm sorry for knocking you off the log." Julia returned his smile. "But you're right." She acknowledged the truth in his words. "I don't mind where we ended up, either."

She'd been wrong about the path, and maybe she'd been wrong about Luke, too. That's what Andie and Kat had been trying to tell her, and they were right. Why shouldn't she have fun while she was here? Like her friends said, that's what this whole experience was supposed to be about.

"No regrets?" he asked, entwining his fingers with hers.

"No regrets," she agreed, enjoying the feel of her hand in his entirely too much.

Not yet, anyway.

Julia couldn't stop that thought from entering her brain.

She'd been willing to admit her friends might be right about embracing her time here, allowing herself to have fun with Luke and truly experience the place she was supposed to be reviewing . . . but she still wasn't sure about the rest of it.

How could she be? It all seemed too good to be real.

CHAPTER 14

LUKE

After his escapade in the rain, Luke needed a hot shower. Or maybe a cold one, since he couldn't seem to stop replaying what he'd been doing in the rain. A smile crept across his face. Despite muscles cramping from his race through the woods and a bruised backside from the tumble off the log, Luke would relive those few minutes alone in the woods with Julia in a heartbeat.

The way she'd looked at him, the swirling colors in her eyes, even more chimerical in the shadowy light beneath the trees, her storm-drenched hair hanging down her back in thick waves of amber and honey, mahogany and chestnut. He still couldn't decide what shade her hair was. If Luke was writing her character description for a role-playing game, he'd probably say auburn, her eyes hazel. But neither of those words did justice to the real thing.

That had not gone at all like he'd expected, and yet Luke wasn't sorry his plans had been derailed. Like he'd told Julia, no regrets. Not about that, anyway. He couldn't help wondering if he'd regret his decision to step back from his responsibilities by stepping into the game. The whole point of doing so, at least he kept telling himself, was to ingratiate himself with the reviewer. How he was planning to manage that when he kept getting side-tracked by Julia, Luke wasn't sure.

It wasn't like him to act so impetuously. He never made a change of plans without carefully thinking things through and analyzing the options. But in this case there hadn't been time.

More significantly, he'd allowed logic to take a backseat to impulse. He frowned, trepidation clouding his mind like mist rising off the lake.

"What's your problem?" Vijay demanded.

Luke's head snapped up. "Huh?" While his thoughts had been otherwise occupied, his feet had gone on autopilot and taken him to the control room.

Vijay eyed him. "And why are you hovering in the doorway?"

"I'm not hovering." Luke crossed his arms, chagrined to realize he was indeed hovering.

"Do you think it's a good idea for you to be in here right now?" Jay asked.

"Depends." Pulling the door closed, he grabbed the seat next to Jay. "Where's my sister?"

"She'll be here soon. She's dealing with a last-minute request from Mrs. W."

"What kind of request?" Luke asked warily.

"Nothing you need to worry about. Don't get your Mario underwear in a twist."

"I haven't worn Super Mario Brothers underwear since I was a kid."

"Dude. I distinctly recall you wearing a pair in high school."

"It was *junior* high. And it was only that one time." Sometimes it sucked having a best friend who'd known you forever.

"Whatever you say, man." Vijay leaned back in his chair, stretching his arms overhead.

Luke was only too happy to drop the subject. He sifted through the stack of papers on the desk. "Are these the completed itineraries?"

"They are. And the bonus lists, too."

Craving a return to a sense of normalcy, Luke logged in to the resort's management system he'd created and opened the program he'd developed to organize the data for the rom-com sim. He pulled the first page off the stack and began entering the information.

"Pen and I can take care of that, you know."

"I know," Luke acknowledged as he continued typing, soothed by the simple, straightforward task. He handed Jay the page he'd finished entering and grabbed another.

Vijay fiddled with the edge of the paper. "What's up with you?"

"Nothing," Luke insisted. A blatant lie. The second page done, Luke handed it off and picked up a third. He'd designed the programs to work symbiotically but hadn't had a chance to test the applications in real time. "I still think we should have had a trial run before the grand opening." Luke shoved another finished page at his friend.

"And I still think we should have created an online entry form for the guests instead." Vijay tapped the pages against the desk, straightening them. "I could link it on the hotel's website so people could fill it out before they arrived."

"I told you, I don't want to do it that way," Penelope snapped from the doorway.

Luke and Jay froze, exchanging guilty looks. It didn't matter if what they'd been doing was wrong or not. It didn't matter that Penelope was six years their junior. She'd always had the ability to make them feel like they'd been caught stealing from the cookie jar.

"Why not?" Jay asked, standing up and offering his chair.

Penelope ignored the offer. "Because it's too much like filling out a dating app."

"How many dating apps have you filled out?" Jay demanded.

"None of your business." She sniffed, wrinkling her nose as she stepped closer to Luke. "Ugh, you smell like a soggy picnic blanket."

"That's you?" Vijay flapped the pages he was holding at Luke, as if to air him out. "I've been wondering what that stench was."

"It's because of the walking tour." Luke shrugged. "I, uh, got caught in the rain."

"Most of the stragglers arrived back in the lobby a few minutes before the storm started," Penelope said, brows furrowing. "What were you doing out there for so long?"

He flushed under his sister's suspicious gaze.

"And what are you doing in here?" Her eyes narrowed. "You came to check up on me, didn't you?"

"Would you believe me if I told you I didn't plan to stop by?"

"No," Penelope said flatly. "That doesn't sound like you at all."

"It's true," Luke insisted, still freaked out by the recent glitch in his brain. "I was on my way to take a shower and somehow ended up here." He held his breath, waiting for his sister to call BS.

Instead, she glanced over his shoulder at the computer screen and bristled. "Are you entering the itinerary data?"

He smiled feebly. "I figured since I was here I might as well help."

"Luke! Stop micromanaging things! I can handle this. Why won't you trust me?"

"I *do* trust you."

Her face puckered in doubt.

"Really." He made a show of standing up and slowly backing away from the computer.

Gloating, Vijay met Luke's eyes and silently mouthed, "I told you so."

Pen huffed and slid into the chair, picking up where he'd left off entering responses. Her fingers attacked the keyboard with rapid, angry clicks. "You should have seen some of the dirty looks I got last night when I told people we'd be keeping their phones for the week," Penelope pouted. "Technology ruins everything."

"Says the person currently entering data into a computer," Vijay teased.

Only Jay would risk taunting Pen when she was in one of her moods.

"Shut it," Penelope sniffed. "I could figure out the schedules by hand if I wanted."

"You could," Luke agreed. "But without my program, it would take you most of the week."

"Your brother's right." Jay dropped back into his chair and rolled closer to Penelope. "By the time you had all of this organized, it would be time for everyone to pack their bags and go home."

"I know he's right," Penelope grumbled, handing Jay a sheet and moving on to the next. "That doesn't mean I have to like it."

Luke grinned, heart aching with bittersweet tenderness for his sister. Maybe it was because of all the years she'd spent hooked up to machines as a kid, gadgets and gizmos monitoring her every breath, heartbeat, and a host of other bodily functions, but she'd never been a fan of tech stuff. "While you're at it, can you make sure to match up my schedule with the reviewer's friend?"

"Your plan to get in her good graces is going that well, then?" Penelope asked, flipping through the files. "Did you two enjoy yourselves on the trail?"

"Why?" Luke asked, suddenly nervous. "Did someone say something?"

"Say something about what?" His sister swiveled on her chair to look at him. "What happened?"

"Why do you think something happened?" Luke hedged. Nobody could have seen him with Julia in the woods. They'd been completely alone . . . at least he'd thought so. The fact that he was worried he'd been seen concerned him on several levels. He was supposed to be doing a job and had crossed a line. Luke wasn't sure whether the fact that he'd completely forgotten there'd been any lines in the first place was a point in his favor or a strike against him.

"I didn't think something happened until you started acting like something did." Penelope scowled.

Despite the storm clouds gathering in his sister's gray eyes, Luke relaxed a fraction. She didn't know about the kiss. He mentally scrambled for an escape route. "I know something that *didn't* happen . . ." he improvised.

"And what's that?" She cocked her head at him.

"Zach didn't show up for the tour today."

"What do you mean he didn't show up?" Penelope frowned. "He was with the reviewer at breakfast." She tapped her chin. "We both saw them together there."

"Right. And he should have been with her on the tour." Irritation crept into his voice. "He's an actor. He's getting *paid* to be here. He needs to show up on time, when and where he's supposed to." Luke sighed. "This is exactly what I was worried about. I'll deal with him."

"How many times are we going to have this conversation?" his sister asked, throwing up her hands. "You put me in charge. That was your decision." Penelope stood and faced him, spine stiff. "Which means now I get to make the decisions," she declared. "I chose to pair Zach with the reporter. *I'll* deal with him."

Luke was about to protest, when a look from Jay stopped him. He sighed. His friend was right. The middle pea in the pod, keeping the peace.

"That reminds me," Pen said, settling back into the chair and shifting her attention to Jay. "Were you able to deal with that thing I asked you about?"

Jay nodded "All set."

"Perfect."

"What thing?" While Luke was glad his sister was no longer glaring at him like she wanted to remove his stubborn head from his body, he didn't like the vibe he was picking up. Something was going on, and he hated being out of the loop. "What did she ask you to deal with? What's all set?" he demanded. "What's perfect?"

"You." Penelope grinned up at him. But it was the evil kind of grin shared between siblings when one was about to do something unpleasant to the other. "Or, you will be as close to perfect as we can make you."

"Does not compute." Luke shook his head. "Need more data."

"Your sister sent me on a little shopping spree for a new wardrobe."

"No," Luke said.

"For you," Jay elaborated.

"I figured that part out, thanks," Luke growled, not about to admit that, this morning, he'd been thinking about doing the same thing himself. "No," he reiterated.

"Yes," Jay countered, his grin almost as evil as Penelope's.

"Go take your shower," Penelope said. "We'll meet you upstairs in an hour."

"What's happening in an hour?" Luke wondered, not sure he wanted to know the answer.

"A new activity has been added to your itinerary, Lance." His sister held up Luke's form. "Makeover montage."

"You're joking."

"Your T-shirt is a joke," Jay neatly rejoined.

"It'll be fun," Pen said. "Ooh!" she chirped, turning to Vijay. "We can have him do one of those mini fashion shows for us, like in the movies."

Luke grimaced. "Absolutely no—"

"Great idea, Pen." Jay clapped Luke on the back, cutting him off. "Come on. Let's take you from a *Before* to an *After*."

⁓

True to their word, minutes after Luke got out of the shower, Pen and Jay appeared at his door, loaded down with shopping bags. By the time they'd finally finished with him, he could wear a new article of clothing every day for the rest of the month.

Luke adjusted a sleeve on the shirt Penelope had picked for him to wear tonight. Unlike the one he'd borrowed from Vijay, this one was his actual size. But it still didn't fit right; shirts rarely did. He tugged at the cuff again. Jay suggested Luke should get some custom made by a tailor and he'd snorted with laughter at the idea. "Modeling" outfits for the two of them had been insufferable enough.

Even after a solid hour of that torture, there were still a few hours to go before dinner, and Luke was starving. He headed to the staff kitchen for a snack. Scrounging up a box of crackers, Luke wandered into the game room. A handful of employees were scattered about the space, eating a late lunch and chatting or watching TV. Over in one corner, reading a magazine with his feet propped on the seat next to him, was Zach.

Temper flaring, Luke knocked the magazine out of the actor's hands.

"Something on your mind?" Zach leaned back in his chair and crossed his arms, the sleeves of his T-shirt straining against his biceps.

Grabbing the back of the chair holding Zach's feet, Luke yanked. "You missed the walking tour." He took a seat in the now empty chair and folded his hands. He would keep his promise to Penelope and wouldn't touch pretty boy's face, but Luke couldn't resist putting him in his place. "I don't care what you do on your free time, but right now, you're on *my* time. The resort's time. You're not a player, you're a performer. Participation is not optional."

"I did you a favor."

"Pardon?"

"By skipping that whole traipsing-through-the-forest thing." Zach leaned forward. "Look, I'm supposed to be charming the blond one. Bridget, right?"

"Something like that."

"How well is that going to go if we start by spending an entire day together?"

"Your charm runs out that fast, does it?" Luke smirked.

"Hardly." Zach smirked right back. "I don't want to overpower her. She got her first taste of Zach cake last night at the cocktail party. And a second helping this morning at breakfast. I bet she's been thinking of me all day. And now, I bet she can't wait to see me again."

He can't be serious. Luke's lip curled in distaste "Please don't ever use the term *Zach cake* ever again."

"This is basic stuff, man. Romance one oh one. Whet their appetite, then leave them hungry for more."

"Romance one oh one, huh?" Luke sneered. "That sounds more like Introduction to Being an Asshole to me." Even though the concept seemed crude to him, Luke couldn't help thinking about all the time he'd spent with Julia in the past twenty-four hours. If anything, the more he was with her, the more he wanted to be with her.

But what about her? a voice buzzed inside his head. *How long before she gets tired of spending time with me?*

Earlier, he'd asked Penelope to align his itinerary with Julia's, telling himself it made sense to do so because it would match up with the reviewer's schedule as well. At breakfast this morning, all three friends had selected the same group activities. The only differences had been their choice of bonus experiences.

Had it been a mistake to plan so much time with her? Maybe he should skip dinner tonight. Give her some space before she started to get annoyed by his company. Luke was aware of his own flaws. He knew he could be aggravating. He tended to talk too much and for too long about stuff most people weren't interested in. The point of joining the sim was to make sure she and her friends had a fantastic time, not to bother them or bore them out of their minds.

As much as he hated to admit it, Zach might be onto something.

"Fine," Luke said. "But I expect to see you charming the pants off her tomorrow." He paused, frowning. "I did not mean that literally."

"Why are you so focused on what I'm doing with her, anyway?" Zach asked.

"We want to make sure all our guests have an enjoyable experience."

"Yeah, but why did Penelope make a point of assigning her to *me*? Why are you two so focused on this one *particular* guest?" Zach narrowed his eyes, cool blue gaze assessing. "What's going on? Is she like Mrs. W.'s niece or something?"

"That's not your concern." Luke leaned forward. "Just make sure she has a good time."

Another smirk. "Oh, don't you worry about that."

Luke ignored the blatant innuendo. The actor was testing how far he could push him. He was going to find it was a very short leash. "You're on the schedule for paintball tomorrow." Luke stood. "Don't be late."

CHAPTER 15

JULIA

Retreating to her room at the hotel, Julia shucked her rain-soaked clothes. She jumped in the shower, intending to be quick, but thoughts involving gray eyes and great hands—and a great mouth, now that she knew what kind of kisser he was—led to a longer— and hotter—shower than she'd anticipated. By the time she reluctantly dragged herself out of the shower and got dressed, she'd missed the next activity on the schedule—an afternoon spent canoeing on the resort's private pond.

Guilt poked holes in her good mood and she deflated a little. She had ditched her friends while out on the trail, and now she'd skipped spending time with them this afternoon, too. Not to mention the fact that she was supposed to be taking in as much of the resort's rom-com experience as possible for her "Take Me!" article.

She'd had quite the experience today, just not exactly something she could include in a review. Having a bit of fun was one thing; the point of this place was to indulge in romantic fantasies, after all . . . But how far was too far?

It was time to clear her head and regroup. After the canoe excursion, the plan had been to retreat to their rooms to freshen up, then meet in the lobby so they could go in to dinner together. Since she'd already showered and changed and was now ahead of schedule, Julia decided to head downstairs. She'd get there early and take a few notes while waiting for her friends.

Finding a comfy spot on one of the lobby sofas, Julia pulled out
her notepad and settled in. Instinctively, she reached for her
phone before remembering it was still in the hotel lockbox. She
had to admit, it was rather nice to spend a day without constantly
checking emails and social media updates, free from the general
chaotic noise of the constant stream of information and expectation that was usually within arm's reach at all times. An unexpected perk of living in fantasyland for a week.

Without the distraction of her phone to occupy her, Julia
lounged on the cushions and did a bit of people watching instead.
From what she'd seen at the cocktail hour last night, there were
about fifty to sixty people participating in the role-playing game.
Adding in the performers, the total was closer to seventy-five.

She wondered whether the hotel was booking guests other
than those involved in the rom-com simulation. She added a note
to look into that, as well as to find out more about the resort's plans
for expanding the program. Did they intend to run it on a weekly
basis? Monthly?

"Hey." Andie flopped down onto the sofa next to her.

"Hi." Julia blinked. "I didn't see you come in."

"I know. You were tuned out." Andie grinned. "You had your
reporter face on."

"What's my reporter face look like?"

"Like my game face. Focused. Intense."

"Sorry I missed canoeing," Julia apologized. "How was it?"

"Wet."

Julia's eyes widened, "Someone fall in?"

"Several someones. Including this someone." Andie jabbed a
thumb at herself. "Thanks to a certain Cheesehead who doesn't
know how to steer a canoe."

"Curt?"

"The one and only."

"Please tell me he recited some bawdy limericks."

"No." Andie's mouth quirked. "But I did."

A snort of laughter escaped Julia. Having watched *Bridget Jones's Diary* so recently, that scene was obviously still fresh in both their minds.

"What about you?" Andie eyed Julia. "How was your walk back?"

"Also wet."

Andie coughed.

"Because of the rain," Julia clarified, cheeks heating,

"Ri-i-ight," Andie drawled, but she didn't press for more details. Her gaze shifted to Julia's notebook. "Making any progress?"

"Some." Julia tapped her pen against her chin. "I'd like to interview the owner, but I don't want to blow my cover."

"So have Kat do it."

"Have me do what?" Kat asked.

Andie glanced up. "There's our third musketeer."

Julia made room on the couch for Kat. "I was just telling Andie I have some questions I'd like to run by the owner."

"And since I'm supposed to be you, you want me to do it," Kat summarized, sliding in next to Julia. "Sure."

"Really?"

"Yeah, why not?" Kat smiled. "Just don't expect me to memorize the questions, okay? Send them to my phone—wait, you can't do that."

"I'll give you my little notepad," Julia decided, wondering why she hadn't thought of it sooner. "I'll write all my questions down and you can record the answers and give it back to me." She started scribbling.

"What are you doing?" Andie demanded.

"Writing down my list of questions." Julia cocked her head. "Weren't you listening?"

"Put that away." Andie waved a hand at the notebook. "Dinner first. Reporter stuff later."

Julia and Kat shared a look before following Andie into the dining room. They both knew better than to argue with their friend when she was hungry.

"Where should we sit?" Andie asked.

"Depends." Julia hesitated. "Are either of you expecting someone to join you?"

"I'm not, no." Andie's mouth pinched. "But that doesn't mean a certain Packers fan won't show up and try to tailgate at our table."

Julia laughed. "What about you, Kat?"

"I haven't seen Zach since breakfast," she admitted, shoulders drooping.

Julia frowned in sympathy. "I'm sure he'll turn up at some point." She glanced around the room. She hadn't made specific plans to see Luke, either, but she couldn't help the twinge of disappointment when she didn't catch sight of a head of tousled sandy hair rising above the crowd sitting down to dinner.

"It'll be good to sit with some new people, meet other guests." Some of the tables had already filled, but there were still plenty of open seats left. Julia pointed to an empty table off to the side. "How about over there?"

"Done," Andie said.

By the time they reached the table, a pleasant-looking couple that Julia guessed to be in their early fifties had found their way to the same spot. "Mind if we share?" she asked.

"Please, join us." The woman smiled and gestured to the open seats.

As they settled around the table, Julia remembered to introduce herself as Meg, and her friends followed suit.

Kat's greeting as Bridget was wan, and Julia hoped her friend cheered up soon. She hated seeing her upset and hoped Kat's mood wasn't a sign she'd already gotten emotionally invested in Zach. This was exactly the kind of thing Julia had been worried about.

Like you're one to talk, Miss Make Out on a Log. That was different. It was just a kiss. One epic kiss in the rain.

And a dozen more imagined in the shower. Julia grimaced. She couldn't escape her own BS detector.

One of the flaws in her plan to "just have fun" was that she tended to get too serious too fast. Physical intimacy always seemed to carry more weight for her than the person she was intimate with, ever since her first real kiss.

In high school, Julia had been thrilled when she'd been asked out on her first official date. Ben. That had been his name. The evening had started out with the typical dinner and a movie. But then she and Ben had taken a walk in the park after. She could still remember how the gravel trail glowed in the moonlight, the night sounds of insects humming softly in the background as her date had pulled her close in the shadow of a giant oak and kissed her. A *kiss* kiss, with tongue.

At the time, Julia could have died from the romance of it all. She'd been so wrapped up in that kiss and the feelings it inspired in her that she'd assumed the intimate moment was the start of something serious. She was so sure of it, in fact, that Ben's reaction the next day had caught her completely off guard. Instead of asking her to be his girlfriend, or even asking her on another date, he'd given her the cold shoulder, as if what they'd shared had been no big deal.

Like the awkward encounter at the junior high dance, her heart still bore scar tissue from that experience. It had been a painful lesson . . . one she apparently had yet to learn. In retrospect, she thought cynically, considering her first kiss in the forest and her make-out session in the woods today, maybe her problem was that she had a tree fetish.

Pasting on a smile, Julia turned her attention to the couple, who had introduced themselves as Harry and Sally. "You must have gotten a kick out of the dessert last night, huh?" she asked.

"It was perfect," the woman gushed.

"She kept shouting, 'It's my pie! They're serving my pie!'" Harry raised his voice, mimicking his wife, before turning to smile at her indulgently. "I think she scared a few of the people at our table."

"I do have a tendency to get carried away."

"Nothing wrong with a bit of enthusiasm." Andie grinned. "I say if you're going to do something, might as well go all in."

"Ooh, I like that." The older woman clasped her hands.

"Truth is, we don't get out much," Harry admitted. "This is the first time in years we've had a chance to let our hair down. Well, I don't have any hair to let down." He chuckled and rubbed his bald head, warm brown skin gleaming in the light of the banquet hall's chandeliers. "But you know what I mean."

Julia laughed. "I do." She liked these two and was glad they'd ended up sitting together.

"Our youngest will be going off to college this fall," Sally explained. "And we'll be empty nesters."

"For years, all we seemed to focus on was the kids," Harry chimed in. "And now, it's like we have nothing to talk about."

"We've always enjoyed watching romantic comedies together, so we thought this might be fun." Sally squeezed her husband's arm. "A way to rediscover each other."

"That's so sweet," Julia gushed. "What a great reason to come here." She fought the urge to take out her notepad and launch into a full interview on the spot. From newlywed couples just starting out to those looking to rekindle the spark, there was so much more to this experience than she'd ever imagined.

"May I have everyone's attention for a moment, please," Penelope, the game master, announced from the front of the room. Once the conversations had died down, she continued. "I hope you've all enjoyed your first full day at Notting Hill. Now that everyone has had a chance to tour the resort and itineraries have been filled out and schedules assigned, we're ready to shift into full swing! It's time to experience what it's like to become a part of the blissful, sometimes bananas fantasy world of romantic comedies!"

A smattering of laughter and applause filled the room. "With that in mind, we thought it would be fun to start things out with a bang. So how about a little rom-com-related contest?"

More cheers.

"Do you think she means a trivia game?" Sally wondered.

Andie clapped her hands. "Bring it on."

"Now then, for this contest, you simply have to do something that—and this is a direct quote—'most women at one time or another' have done."

"*Oh*," Andie breathed, eyes widening.

"Oh, indeed." Kat leered. "A very big O."

"Wait." Julia glanced uneasily between her friends. "You don't think we're supposed to . . ."

"However, faking it is not relegated to any one gender, so I want to clarify that this contest is open to all players."

Appreciative chuckles mixed with another round of applause.

"Does that answer your question?" Andie asked, dark eyes twinkling. "Yeah, I think that's *exactly* what we're supposed to do."

"Here?" Julia looked around the room. "In front of everybody?"

"That's how she does it in the movie," Sally reasoned.

"We're not *all* supposed to do it, are we?" Harry asked.

"She did say all genders. Why?" his wife teased. "Having some performance anxiety?"

"Participation is completely optional," Penelope continued, "but I do want to mention there will be a prize. A certificate for a couple's massage in our spa." She gestured toward a table in the center of the room. "The winner will be chosen by our charming hostess, the lovely owner of Notting Hill Resort, Mrs. Weatherfork!"

Applause once again filled the room as the charming hostess got to her lilac-slippered feet, waving her bejeweled hand in the

air like she was on a parade float. Gone was the key lime pie ensemble of this morning. Tonight, the eccentric lady was dressed
head to toe in a cloud of purples.

"Do you think her closet looks like a bag of Skittles exploded?"
Julia wondered.

"I'm more curious about her lingerie drawer," Kat admitted,
mood perking up.

"You want to see her underwear?" Julia stared at her friend.

"Her pajamas, you freak. If she dresses that absurdly during
the day, imagine what her nightwear looks like!" Kat grinned. "All
right. Who's ready to fake some fireworks?"

Andie straightened in her seat. "I'm game."

Julia bit her lip. No surprise there.

"Me too," Kat confessed. "I've always wanted to try something
like this."

"You've always wanted to be an exhibitionist?" Julia asked.
Though, knowing Kat, this was also not a surprise.

"Count me in." Sally waved her hand.

"Are you sure?" her husband asked.

"Yes, I'm sure." A shy titter escaped her. "I'm Sally, aren't I?
This is my moment to shine!" She patted her husband's hand.
"You sit back and let me do all the work." She turned to the group
and winked. "It will be just like at home."

Julia swallowed a bubble of nervous laughter. "Well, I guess if
you're all doing it, I can try and join in."

"'Do. Or do not. There is no try.'" Andie winked.

"Is that one of your coaching slogans?" Julia wondered.

Andie gasped in mock outrage. "Excuse me, that is Master
Yoda."

"Your nerd is showing again," Kat teased. "Now then, should
we all go at once?"

"Wait, *right now*?" Julia asked. "Actually, I don't think I . . ."

But Andie and Kat had already closed their eyes and started
to moan.

On her left, Sally was breathing heavily, fingers stroking over her face and down her neck in a very accurate rendition of Meg Ryan's performance.

Okay, this was getting awkward. Julia glanced around the rest of the dining room, where others were joining in, picking up the pace, a chorus of ecstatic shouts mixing with the sound of hands slapping against tables. "Yes. Yes. Yes!"

It was one thing to watch someone fake an orgasm in a movie, it was another to witness dozens of people do it firsthand. But it was when the pack of corgis joined in, barking and howling, that Julia truly lost it. She wondered if she could slither off her chair and hide under the table from the group orgy in which she suddenly found herself.

After a few more uncomfortable seconds, Andie and Kat started to taper off. Soon they had stopped completely, their full attention on Sally. The woman had an impressive set of lungs . . . and stamina. The rest of the room quieted while Sally continued to yell and moan, climax ebbing and flowing.

Kat had mentioned fireworks, and that's exactly what this was—like watching a fireworks show. Sally would start to really gather some steam, to the point that Julia was sure the grand finale was about to happen, but then she would ease off, shifting into a series of slower, more sensual noises. And then she'd increase the tempo again, louder and faster, until Julia was once again convinced the climactic end of the show was approaching.

Finally, the big O arrived. Like her movie predecessor, Sally came. And came and came and came. In the immediate aftermath of the orgasmic explosion, the dining room felt obscenely quiet. No murmur of conversation. No clatter of plates or clank of silverware. Even the dogs had gone completely silent. Several people were gaping, their mouths wide open.

Should she clap? Julia felt like she should clap. A performance that epic deserved some applause. The rustling of lavender silk abruptly broke the silence as Mrs. Weatherfork stood. The entire dining room turned toward their brightly dressed hostess. She cleared her throat and coyly announced, "I'll have what she's having."

Laughter burst across the room, followed by thunderous applause. The owner of the resort approached their table. "Well done." She handed Sally an envelope. "Enjoy." She waggled her artistically arched eyebrows. "I'd say you've earned it." With a wink, the woman returned to her seat, ever-present entourage of corgis in tow.

"Take a bow honey, they're clapping for you," Harry said.

"Oh, stop," Sally demurred with a bashful grin.

"It was a spectacular performance," Kat chimed in.

"Very impressive," Andie agreed. "You definitely went all in."

Sally ducked her head shyly but managed to stand up and take a bow. Growing bolder, she began blowing kisses to the crowd.

"I don't know whether to be impressed or concerned," Harry admitted. But his voice was playful, and his smile was warm and genuine as he pulled his wife onto his lap and gave her a kiss.

Their banter had the easy, affectionate teasing of two people who had known and loved each other a long time. Would Julia ever have that? Ever have that kind of relationship? Her parents didn't. Part of it was probably due to the fact that although they'd been married almost thirty years, thanks to all the work travel, her mom and dad had rarely been together in the same place long enough to develop such a bond.

But that was an excuse. Julia sighed. Ever since she could remember, she'd known her parents had both been faking it. Faking love. Faking happiness. Faking marriage.

She refused to do the same. If she was going to be with someone, Julia promised herself, what she had would be real.

CHAPTER 16

LUKE

After eating dinner alone in his room, Luke spent another restless night, thoughts fluctuating between anticipation of seeing Julia again and dread that he may have somehow screwed things up. His impulsive behavior continued to risk making a mess of things with her, with the sim, possibly with both. He was wide awake and irritable as hell when the corgi alarm system scampered by, and he uncharitably imagined drop-kicking one or two of the fluff balls.

What if, after their kiss in the woods yesterday, she'd been upset when he didn't show last night? They hadn't discussed dinner. Hadn't made plans of any kind. But if Julia had been thinking about him even half as much as his thoughts had been focused on her, she'd have noticed his absence. Would she be mad at him? Or, as Zach had predicted, even more interested in seeing him again?

He wasn't going to get any answers lying in bed. And he certainly wasn't going to get any sleep. Luke got dressed, pulling on one of his old shirts. He was so out of sorts right now; he needed something that felt normal. Besides, they were playing paintball today, not the best time to try out a fancy new wardrobe.

Thinking about the day ahead, Luke bypassed breakfast, grabbing a coffee and heading outside. He needed to gather his thoughts, get some fresh air. But taking his usual walk on the beach wasn't an option. Simply considering it was enough to stir up thoughts of Julia. He needed to clear his mind, not cloud it.

He decided to head out to the paintball field and see how the final setup was coming along. Luke reached the edge of the south lawn and finished his coffee, looking over the capture-the-flag-style obstacle course. Towering stacks of hay bales created a variety of strategic hiding places for players to ambush each other. Twin wooden observation decks faced off from opposite sides of the field; a brightly colored flag, one red, one blue, waved tauntingly from each. Glancing at the flags, Luke felt a rush of anticipation.

"You're excited about getting to play today, aren't you?"

He turned to see Vijay crossing the field. "What makes you say that?"

"You're making the same face you did when you found that Atari system at a yard sale."

"It was a boxed fifty-two hundred. In mint condition."

"You're right." Vijay grinned. "It was pretty sweet." His smile faded as he took in Luke's clothes. "Dude. What was the point of doing a makeover montage if you're just going to keep wearing your old shit?"

"No one is going to see my 'old shit' underneath the paintball stuff," Luke argued.

"Oh. My bad. I didn't realize you were planning to spend the entire day in those coveralls like some serial killer," Jay snarked, his tone indicating that he considered Luke to be a lost cause. "A Pac-Man shirt. Really?"

"Pac-Man is a legend," Luke declared haughtily.

Jay groaned. "At least I know what to bury you in."

"What's that supposed to mean?"

"Your sister is ready to kill you." Jay shook his head. "Pen guessed you'd be out here. She told me to tell you to get your bossy ass back to the hotel."

Luke's stomach dropped. "What'd I do this time?" Immediately, his thoughts turned to Julia. Had Penelope found out about their little woodland tryst after all? Guilt prickled in his chest. He'd let things go too far.

"You got into it with Zach. Again." Jay *tsk*ed. "After Pen explicitly said she was going to handle him. And she can, you know."

"I know she can."

"Then give her a chance." His friend's reproach was mild, but Luke detected the undercurrent of frustration. And disappointment.

"I'm trying to let go of being in charge." Luke shifted uncomfortably under Jay's doubtful gaze, the back of his neck hot with shame. It was true, he hated not being in control. It was a constant struggle to resist double-checking everything Penelope did. But he'd made his sister game master, and more than that, he'd promised to respect her position. He'd already bent that promise multiple times. "I'll do better."

"I hope so, for Pen's sake," Jay said. "And for yours," he added, mouth curving in a sardonic grin. "You need to learn how to loosen up. Stop trying to control everything all the time."

"Funny you should say that." Luke observed sarcastically. "Lately I feel like nothing is in my control." Maybe that was his problem. Ever since he'd rashly decided to put Pen in charge, it was as if a seal had been broken. That one impulsive choice to jump into the game had been the first domino, setting off a chain reaction of other impulsive acts. Like yesterday in the woods with Julia. "Have you ever met someone who made it impossible to think straight?"

His friend cocked his head, studying him. "I'm guessing you have?"

Luke winced. Again, he'd acted without thinking, the question spilling out of his mouth before he could stop it. But he realized he didn't regret it. Despite his discomfort and the potential for embarrassment, he wanted to know Jay's answer. "Obviously, since I'm asking."

Jay was silent for a moment. "Yeah, I have." His mouth quirked. "Your sister."

Luke laughed. There was no question Pen got under his

friend's skin and scrambled his brain. She could do that to him, too. But that was a sibling thing. Not at all like what he felt around Julia. Clearly, Jay had misunderstood his meaning. Luke shook his head, deciding it was best to change the subject. "Where is she, anyway?"

"Checking on the thing Mrs. W. asked for."

"Right." Luke eyed his friend. "I remember you saying something about that yesterday. What is this *thing*?"

"Oh, you'll see," Jay hedged.

"Not even a little hint?" Luke wheedled.

"Nope," Jay said breezily, blatantly enjoying taunting him. "Now stop fretting and get moving. The teams are supposed to meet in the lobby in less than an hour."

Not long after he arrived back at the hotel, the lobby began to fill with players. Luke noted with satisfaction that Zach was among the first to arrive. The actor had changed from his rom-com hero uniform of V-neck, jeans, and boots into sweats and sneakers, but somehow the dude still looked like a cologne ad. He'd probably look good even in the paintball coveralls they were all forced to wear.

Sure enough, once everyone had checked in, signed their waivers, and zipped up their coveralls, Zach managed to look like a superhero while Luke was a scarecrow, arms and legs sticking out awkwardly from his ill-fitting uniform. Glancing around the room, he noticed Julia and her dark-haired friend putting on their uniforms while chatting with an older couple. He tried to casually make his way over to where they stood.

His attempt at subtlety was blown when the man glanced over at Luke and guffawed. "So much 'for one size fits all,' eh?" He chortled, tugging at the zipper on his coveralls, where it strained over his generous middle. "Doesn't work so well for us big and tall fellas."

The woman next to the man patted his belly affectionately. "We know you're the *big* part of that equation." She turned to

Luke. "And you're definitely the *tall* part." She smiled up at him. "I'm Sally. This is my husband, Harry."

Luke returned the smile and was debating whether to introduce himself as Lance or Luke when Julia made that decision for him.

"Luke!" Julia beamed and reached for him, then abruptly drew back, smile fading and arms dropping to her sides.

Luke's gut tightened. He offered her an awkward, apologetic grin, noticing how her sleeves were dangling past her fingers. "Can I help?"

"Um, sure." She held her arm out to him.

"You two know each other?" Sally asked.

"We, ah, met here. At the resort," Julia answered, voice a little unsure as she looked at Luke. "But I haven't seen him around for a bit."

"How could you miss him?" Harry joked.

Luke folded the fabric, tucking it tight to keep it from coming loose. His hand brushed the delicate skin of her wrist and she shivered. He paused. "Ticklish?"

"A bit," she admitted, questions still lurking in her hazel eyes.

His mouth went dry and his mind went blank. He'd thought of a hundred things to say to her the next time he saw her, and now he couldn't think of one.

After an agonizing beat of silence, Julia glanced down. "Oh, my." The corner of her mouth tilted. "Someone is showing a shocking amount of leg."

Grateful for the reprieve, Luke exhaled, following the direction of her gaze, to where his coveralls stopped midcalf. When he'd pulled on the uniform, his jeans had gotten bunched up inside the leg holes and he hadn't bothered trying to fix it, an oversight he now regretted. Embarrassed, he bent down and yanked on the hem of his jeans, pulling them over his exposed shins and ankles. "There." He straightened. "Is that better?"

"Not really." Julia bit her lip, but it didn't stop the smile from taking over her whole mouth. "You look ridiculous."

"Just wait until I put on the goggles."

She laughed.

"If you're laughing at me, I don't blame you," Andie said. She was sprawled out on the floor, rolling up the bottoms of her coveralls.

"We were just discussing how sexy these paintball uniforms are." Julia posed, placing a hand on her waist and popping her hip out to the side.

"Stunning." Andie got to her feet and stuck out a leg. "I had to roll the cuffs on these so many times I look like I'm wearing leg warmers."

"Somebody might be really into that," Luke suggested.

"If they have an eighties fetish, sure," Andie snorted. "Let me go grab my ripped off-the-shoulder sweatshirt and I'll be set."

"What's wrong with liking the nineteen eighties?"

Instead of answering him, Andie gestured at his uniform. "Hey, you're blue too!"

"I am," Luke agreed. The players were divided by uniform color: red and blue. "Looks like we're on the same team."

Andie cracked her knuckles. "As long we kick ass, I'm not complaining."

"Where's your other friend?" he asked Julia.

She eyed him with a hint of suspicion. "Why?"

"Just curious." Luke laughed, and immediately cringed, sure she could hear the note of nervous guilt in his voice. "The three of you seem to be kind of a package deal, that's all." Even though he wasn't lying, exactly—she and her friends did seem to always be together—he still felt like a jerk. But if the reporter missed the paintball match, then his efforts to make sure Zach showed up would be wasted.

"She's in the bathroom, fixing her hair." Julia shrugged. "It looked fine to me."

"Who cares what it looks like?" Andie rolled her eyes. "It's about to be covered in paint in ten minutes anyways." She surveyed the room, taking stock of the other players. "Uh-oh."

"What's wrong?" Julia glanced around.

"I figured out why Kat is primping." Andie gazed across the lobby. "It looks like her pretty boy is on the opposing team." She caught Luke's eye. "I meant Bridget."

"It's fine," he assured her. "You kind of let the 'Kat' out of the bag yesterday." He winked.

"Punny." Andie snorted. "Are you always this clever?"

"I have my moments."

Andie turned to Julia. "Should we officially give up on the character name thing?"

"Probably, since I keep messing up too . . ." Julia fiddled with the elastic strap on her goggles. "What do you think, Luke?"

As GM, Luke would have been steadfastly against the idea. While in play, a character was expected to maintain their assigned role. But this was a different style of LARP; the personas of this game were similar enough to real people it was easy to forget they were pretending.

Which, now that he thought about it, presented a problem all its own, made the situation even more perilous. In most LARPs, the line between fantasy and reality was clearly defined—easy enough when one was pretending to be in a medieval forest or on another planet or even in a Victorian mansion. But the boundaries this rom-com world had were vague, at best. Fantasy and reality blurred.

Maybe it had been a mistake to start calling each other by their real names. If so, it was too late to go back now. And the truth of the matter was, even if they could manage to stick to the fake names, Luke didn't want to. He liked calling Julia by her real name. Even better, he liked it when she called him by his.

Either of these realizations should have set off warning bells. Even more alarming, however, was the fact he wasn't nearly as concerned about the dangerous shift from make-believe to reality as he knew he should be. As the GM for other LARPs, Luke had pulled more than one overzealous player back from the edge. Usually, that meant redirecting the flow of action, breaking up a staged fight before someone actually got hurt.

This time, he'd given up the role of game master. Now *he* was the one in danger of getting in over his head. He needed to be careful. If he let himself get carried away and somehow messed up the sim, he risked more than a bloody nose or sprained wrist. He risked his future.

Luke rubbed the back of his neck, tamping down the worry creeping up inside. "I think it's probably okay," he finally said. "As long as we remember this is all just pretend."

"Right." Julia smiled weakly. "Pretend."

Except there was nothing pretend about the way she made him feel.

"You know what's *not* pretend?" Andie asked, bouncing on the balls of her feet like a boxer warming up for a fight. "The way I'm going to litter that field with red uniforms."

By this point, the room had split into two groups, red and blue congregating on opposite ends of the lobby. Kat finally emerged from the bathroom and joined them, just as Andie cupped her hands around her mouth and yelled, "Red is dead!"

Someone on the other side shouted back, "Oh, yeah?"

Luke recognized that voice. And that phrase.

Apparently, Andie did too, because she immediately moved to the edge of the blue group and hollered, "Eat dirt, Curt!"

Football jersey guy cut through the sea of red. "Make me!"

Zach joined Curt at the front of the red group, eyes fixed on Kat as he replied, "But what if we want to make love, not war?" He reached for her hand, pressing a cartoonishly gallant kiss to her knuckles amid a wave of coos, catcalls, and whistles.

Luke shook his head with a mix of disgust and admiration at the man's confidence and audacity.

"Hey, eighties boy." Andie elbowed Luke in the ribs. "What do they say about love?"

Before he could figure out what she was referring to, she'd already turned back to face her opponent.

"Oh, yeah." The feisty woman mimicked Curt's catchphrase and lifted her chin. "Love is a battlefield."

"Bring it on, baby." Full of bluster, Curt was clearly relishing the combative exchange.

From the gleam in her dark eyes, it was apparent that Andie was enjoying it too. She stepped closer, until she was toe-to-toe with her nemesis. In a low growl she warned, "You're going to regret that."

Forty-five minutes later, out of breath and crouched behind a bunker, Luke was the one feeling regret. Itchy, sweaty regret. Who in their right mind considered this fun? He slumped down, back pressed against his refuge of hay, sucking in giant gulps of air. He should have let the red team have him. He was not a runner. He did not run. They'd been playing for a solid thirty minutes now and he was exhausted.

If this was a video game, he'd be kicking ass. But all of his mental speed and manual dexterity was useless when he ran like a newborn colt who hadn't gotten his legs under him yet. Out in the open, he'd be shot down in a matter of seconds.

Paint-stained casualties lined the sidelines, cheering on their teammates and heckling their opponents. In the distance, he could hear Curt and Andie hurling insults and paint pellets as they chased each other around obstacles. They both seemed to have forgotten that the point of the game was to capture the other team's flag.

Luke gambled and sneaked a peek around the edge of his hay bale. Both flags were still in place, each surrounded by a contingent of guards. He considered the situation. The sooner someone nabbed one of those damn flags, the sooner this would be over. Maybe he should just go for it.

Best-case scenario, he would actually succeed in getting his hands on the flag. Worst case, he would go out in a blaze of glory. Either option was more heroic than hiding behind a pile of hay, and both options would end his misery.

The only drawback to this plan was Zach. The actor had stationed himself at the top of the red flag's tower and was playing sniper. Figures the jackass had great aim. Luke grimaced. Knowing his luck, the moment he stood up, GQ G.I. Joe would nail him with a paintball right to the nuts. He would stay right where he was, thank you very much.

Luke moved to the other side of his hiding place and checked on his team. To his surprise, Julia had taken up a similar position as sniper on the blue flag's tower. Even more surprising? She was good. *Really* good. The girl had skill. Over and over again, red players approached the tower, only to be knocked out with one blue shot. As far as he could tell, she hadn't missed once.

A flurry of movement caught his attention and he shifted his gaze to her flank, where a group of red players was slowly inching up the west side of the blue tower. Kat was in the rear guard position and should have been protecting Julia, but her focus was across the field, on Zach.

Aw, hell. It looked like he was going to have to play hero after all. With a grunt of resignation, Luke jumped up, shouting a warning to Julia. "Behind you!"

She blinked, glancing his way.

"Behind you!" He pointed.

He had no idea if his warning helped or not, because a second later he was thrown to the ground from behind.

"Phew! That was a close one." Harry exhaled, rolling off Luke.

Luke lifted his face, spitting out a clump of grass. Just to his left, two red players cursed as they were pelted with blue paint.

"Nice shot, honey!" Harry bellowed, and Luke realized the man was yelling to his wife, who was hiding behind another hay bale a few feet away. "Come on," the man ordered, grabbing Luke by the arm and all but hauling him to the bunker.

"I got 'em both!" Sally yelled, with gleeful aggression.

"You sure did, babe." Harry reached across Luke to give his wife a hug. "I love you so much."

"I love you, too." Sally leaned over Luke and wrapped her arms around her husband.

And then the two were doing more than hugging; they were kissing. Eyes closed, mouths mashing together, with Luke stuck between them, their paint guns jabbing him in the ribs. "Uh, folks?"

"God, you're so amazing," Harry groaned.

"No, you're amazing," Sally panted.

"You both are amazing," Luke assured them, sliding to the ground. Above him, the make-out session continued unimpeded, and he prayed a red player would come around the corner of the hay pile and take out all three of them. Or at the very least, him.

"Hey." He poked one of them—he hoped it was Harry—in the side. "I think someone is coming." At first it was just wishful thinking, an attempt to call a cease-fire before the couple got too carried away. But a moment later, Luke really did hear footsteps approaching.

He squeezed his eyes shut, bracing himself for the kill shot. Harry and Sally would go down happy, and good for them. But after a few moments of nothing happening—not counting the unsolicited amorous activities going on over his head—Luke risked opening one eye.

Julia stood there, mouth hanging open, as she gaped at the scene in front of her. He imagined what he must look like from her angle, legs sprawled on the ground, with Harry and Sally above him, making out like the world was ending.

"Ah, am I interrupting something?" she asked, lips pursing.

What was that look on her face? Surprise? Horror? Amusement? A little of all three?

"I don't think these two *can* be interrupted," Luke grumbled.

Julia burst out laughing. She came closer, nudging Sally. "Hey."

Nothing.

She poked the butt of her paint gun into Harry's back. "Hey!"

The couple remained oblivious, a moaning, groaning mass of heavy breathing and smacking lips.

"You weren't kidding." She shook her head. "I've heard of a kiss making you forget the world around you, but this is something else."

"God, this is awkward."

The *thhrrrrup* of a zipper opening caught both their attention.

Julia's eyes widened. "I think it's about to get a lot more awkward."

"That's it." Luke thrust his arms up, forcing the two lovebirds to break apart.

"What's the matter?" Harry asked, blinking in dazed confusion.

"Are we under attack?" Sally fumbled for her paint gun.

Watching this tableau unfold, Julia burst into laughter.

"Oh, you think this is funny, do you?" Luke muttered, as Harry and Sally resumed kissing. Thankfully, not on top of him this time.

"What?" Julia gestured at the couple now entwined in the grass nearby. "You don't find this situation humorous?"

"I find it a tad disturbing." He paused, face breaking into a grin. "And yes, I admit, completely hilarious."

"I admit, I was a bit disturbed at the sight that greeted me when I came around that hay bale." She moved closer and squatted down next to him. "The game's over."

"Did we win?"

"Yeah, Kat captured the red team's flag."

"I didn't see that one coming." Luke shook his head. "How'd she manage to pull that off?

"After the sneak attack almost got us—thanks for the warning, by the way—I told Kat that instead of being distracted by Zach she should *be* the distraction."

"So what did she—" He paused as Julia mimed unzipping her coveralls. "Oh."

"It worked." Julia's eyes twinkled, brown and green swirling with mischief.

"I bet it did."

"I came back here to deliver the good news." She pursed her lips. "But then I was the one who got distracted."

"Understandable."

"Hey, where did Harry and Sally go?"

"Horny and Hornier?" Luke glanced around, and sure enough, the couple had disappeared. "If we're lucky, they went back to their room."

She grinned. "They did mention they were hoping this place would rekindle the spark."

"I'd say that's mission accomplished." He shook his head, shrugging. "If love is a battlefield, maybe paintball is couple's therapy."

"Maybe." Julia straightened. "Everybody is headed down to the beach to cool off." She held out her hand. "Wanna come?"

"I would, but there's a problem."

"What?"

Luke winced. "I can't move my legs."

"Are you injured?"

"Not exactly."

"Are they numb from two people making out on top of you?"

"Not exactly."

"Then, what happened?"

"I ran."

"Did you twist something?" Her brow furrowed in concern. "I thought you said you weren't injured."

"I didn't. I'm not. I just . . . I'm out of shape," he admitted. "Really, really out of shape."

Julia plopped down into the grass next to him. "Welcome to the club."

"Please," Luke snorted. "Your legs aren't atrophied skin sacks."

"Gross," she giggled.

His heart did a funny little hiccup at the sound. He liked hearing her laugh. He loved being the one to make her laugh.

"I can't just leave you here," she said.

"Sure you can. Abandon me to the elements. Once I expire, the vultures will come and peck at my pathetic corpse."

"I don't think there are any vultures in Wisconsin."

"Hush. You're ruining my dramatic imagery."

She erupted into giggles again.

Luke wanted to reach out and capture the buoyant sound of her laughter, like grasping at bubbles floating past. "Am I a terrible person if I admit I hate exercise?"

"If so, then we're both terrible. Come on." She offered her hand again. "You can do it."

"Fine." He heaved a sigh and was only a little ashamed that, all joking aside, he really did need her help getting back on his feet. His thigh and calf muscles screeched in protest as he stood. Once he started walking, things got better. He felt a little stiff, but otherwise fine.

By now the other players had cleared the field completely. Luke and Julia ditched their coveralls and goggles in a bin on the sidelines and maneuvered around the obstacle course of hay bales in companionable silence.

"Are you having fun here?" he finally asked, trying to keep his tone light. It meant a surprising amount to him that Julia enjoyed herself, and not just because of her potential influence on her reviewer friend.

"I'm having a good time."

"Good."

"A great time, actually."

"Great," he smiled.

"How about you?" she asked, peering up at him. "Are you having fun?"

"Not as much fun as Harry and Sally were, but yeah."

He was rewarded with another round of giggles.

CHAPTER 17

JULIA

At first, after Luke's postkiss disappearing act, Julia had been wary of seeing him again. He'd skipped out on her at dinner, then missed breakfast. It wasn't the time they'd been apart that bothered her so much as the timing. She'd learned from painful personal experience that these were signals not to read too much into what was happening between them.

Also, she couldn't help but notice one of the first things he did when he saw her today was ask about Kat. Another sign that shouldn't be ignored. Julia had seen the movie *He's Just Not That Into You*. But he was so easy to talk to that when she was with him, she forgot to worry about the stuff that usually fed her anxiety when she was on a date.

Whoa. Julia tapped her mental brakes. Nothing she and Luke had done or said qualified as a date. They'd spent some time together. Had some fun together. *Made out together* . . .

Okay, so maybe a few moments ventured into date-like territory.

By the time they neared the beach, she had a cheek ache from smiling. What she'd told Luke was true; she *was* enjoying herself. She peeked up at him from beneath her lashes. At turns grumpy and goofy, sage and silly, there was an endearing awkwardness about him that she was finding irresistible. She glanced at his hand, wondering how it might feel to hold it while walking along the lakeshore, toes in the sand. Now that would be a date-ish activity for sure.

"There you are!"

Julia turned, surprised to see Sally and Harry waving from the bottom of the trail. She waved back, saying to Luke under her breath, "I wasn't expecting to see those two for a while."

"Me neither," Luke murmured. "Do you think they did it somewhere along the way?"

"If so, bravo to them." Julia suppressed another grin as they joined the couple on the beach.

"We were worried you'd gotten lost," Harry said.

"Sorry. I'm moving a bit slower," Luke admitted, wincing as he smacked his palms against his thighs.

"I didn't hurt you when I knocked you down, did I?" Harry wondered, worry creasing his brow.

"Not even my pride," Luke assured him. "Thanks for saving my tail." He turned to Sally. "And thank you, too. That was some great shooting out there."

"It was pretty great, wasn't it?" Sally beamed. "Not as good as you, though," she said to Julia. "My goodness, you were a regular Annie Oakley."

"It was damn impressive," Luke agreed.

Julia's skin flushed at his praise, heat blooming in her chest and rising up her neck and face.

"Where'd you learn to shoot like that?" Harry wondered.

"I had an excellent teacher," Julia explained. "My father."

"Sharpshooter, eh?"

"How did you know?" Julia wondered.

"Educated guess." Harry chuckled. "Army?"

"Marine Corps." She paused a moment before adding, "Expert." The older man whistled in admiration.

She smiled, though some of the happy glow from earlier dimmed with thoughts of her dad. She loved him, but he didn't exactly inspire the warm-and-fuzzies. A breeze gusted in off the lake, carrying snatches of laughter and conversation. "We should probably go meet up with the others," she suggested.

"You two go on ahead," Sally encouraged, waving a hand toward the crowd gathered farther down the beach.

"Oh? You won't be joining us?" Julia asked, studiously avoiding Luke's eyes.

"We, er, need to head back to the hotel." Harry wrapped an arm around his wife and fumbled for an excuse. "To finish up . . . something."

"We just wanted to make sure you two were okay," Sally explained, blinking rapidly—and not, Julia decided, from the sun and wind.

"Very considerate of you." Luke thanked them, suppressed humor vibrating in his voice as he said, "Enjoy the rest of your afternoon."

"We will!" Sally assured him.

As the couple headed up the trail to the resort, Julia added quietly, "I bet they will."

Luke snorted. "Come on. I'll race you to the beach."

"Really?" Julia glanced up at him, sure the doubt in her tone was stamped all over her face.

"No," he admitted, "but I will walk backward very fast."

"Luke!" she yelped, as he grabbed her hand and stepped backward, tugging her toward the lake. Her skin tingled where he touched her, setting off a string of little sparks zinging up her arm. She let him pull her forward, glancing ahead to make sure he wasn't about to crash into anyone—or anything. "Is that an ice cream cart?" she asked, squinting.

"You're just trying to make me look," Luke accused.

Julia shook her head. "I'm serious. I think they're serving ice cream down there."

Luke turned, gray eyes lighting up with interest. "Okay," he said, dropping her hand. "*Now* I'll race you."

Neither of them would be winning any medals, but a few seconds later they'd reached the spot on the beach where her friends were settled on chairs under the shade of a jolly red-and-white-striped umbrella.

"Nice of you to join us," Andie said. "Want some ice cream?" She elbowed Curt. "He's buying."

"I am?" Curt asked, wiping a pink mustache of strawberry ice cream off his upper lip.

"Losers treat the winners," Andie insisted, sparing Curt a gloating glance before turning her full attention back to her double-scoop cone.

"Fair enough," Curt agreed, another strawberry mustache already forming. He dug into his pocket and forked over some cash with an easy shrug.

"Keep it." Luke shook his head. "I can't claim any credit for that win." He winked at Julia and strode over to where two teens in white paper hats were selling ice cream cones from a pushcart.

"Like that victory was fair, anyway," Zach pouted.

"It's not my fault you got distracted." Kat blinked innocently.

"Sounds like someone is a sore loser," Julia observed, sharing a wicked grin with Kat. Their little plan had been inspired by *10 Things I Hate About You*, which the actor had proclaimed was one of his favorite rom-coms.

"I'll admit, there are worse ways to lose." Zach sighed, lowering his sunglasses to eye Kat's cleavage appreciatively.

"Is that so?" Kat licked her ice cream cone, provocatively sliding her tongue all the way up one side and down the other.

"I might even say it was a win," Zach added in a husky growl.

Kat laughed and lifted her cone to his mouth. The actor proceeded to prove he could be just as suggestive, swirling his tongue around the mound of ice cream in slow erotic circles.

Luke returned, mouth twisting into a scowl as he observed their antics.

Why did he seem so bothered by Zach's interest in Kat? Julia's good mood faltered, but she pushed the gloomy thoughts away and mustered a faint smile. "Is one of those for me?"

"Uh, yeah." Luke blinked and held out a cone. "I hope chocolate is okay. It's all they had left."

"Chocolate is always okay."

He nodded toward the shore. "Wanna take a walk on the beach?"

She glanced at her friends. Kat was busy letting Zach suck ice cream from her finger while Andie and Curt were debating who'd taken out more opponents during the game. They wouldn't miss her.

"Why not." She kicked off her shoes, then handed Luke her cone so she could slip off her socks. Tucking them inside her shoes, she scooted them under one of the chairs.

"Ready?" he asked, handing back her ice cream.

Julia took a taste, savoring the first swipe across her tongue, cold and rich and sweet. Like the sun breaking through the clouds, her mood brightened. It would be nice to spend more time with Luke, especially if they would be alone.

"Ready." She stepped past him and moved toward the water. "Just promise to walk forward this time," she instructed playfully. "And remember to keep your eyes open."

He caught the reference at the same moment he caught up with her, laughing sheepishly. "I only do that when I'm trying to work through a problem."

His adorable self-deprecating smirk made her heart wiggle like one of the resort owner's fluffy-butted corgis. Made her want to lick his face instead of her ice cream. Good Lord, she was ridiculous. Julia shook herself. "You can't walk and think at the same time?"

He bristled. "I *was* walking."

"Not very well, if I recall," she said, provoking his prickly side on purpose.

"I would have been fine if *someone* hadn't been standing in my way," he harrumphed.

"Someone you would have *seen* if your eyes had been open," she insisted, taking another lazy lick of her ice cream and relishing his reaction. It was so deliciously fun to see him get all spiky and out of sorts.

His only response was a smirk that looked both annoyed and amused. But then his gaze dropped to her mouth and his expression froze.

Julia paused midlick, the intensity of those gray eyes stopping her in her tracks. With effort, she forced herself to swallow around the sudden lump in her throat.

Meanwhile, Luke hadn't moved. He stood frozen in place, eyes still on her mouth, while his own cone listed sideways. Then slowly, as slowly as the melting chocolate dripped onto the sand, he bent toward her.

It was just like that first day on the beach, when there'd been this magnetic pull. This feeling drawing her to him. With her shoes off and his still on he seemed even taller, the distance between them stretching and then shrinking as she dug her bare toes into the sand and arched toward him, his lips coming closer . . . closer . . .

A piercing cry from above shattered the moment. Julia fell back on her heels, dropping her ice cream in surprise as a flash of white sped toward her. "Ack!" she screamed, jumping back just as the ivory terror swooped in, snatching up her cone.

Chocolate ice cream rained down, splattering across Luke's face and chest. He blinked. Shook himself. Then glared skyward and shouted, "You evil air weasel!"

"At least it's not poop this time," Julia offered.

He groaned, eyeing the damage. "This is one of my favorite shirts."

"A Pac-Man fan, huh?" She reached out and dabbed at a streak of chocolate on his cheek.

"Yes," he grumbled. "And I refuse to be embarrassed about it."

"Why should you be?" she asked, wiping away another smear. His skin was warm beneath her thumb. "I like Pac-Man."

"You do?" He eyed her suspiciously, shoulders stiffening as if he was bracing for her to make fun of him.

"I do. Who doesn't like Pac-Man?" She smiled gently as the tension eased from his body.

"What's the highest level you've ever gotten to?"

"Um . . . it's been years since I actually played," she admitted. "How many levels are there?"

"Two hundred and fifty-five." He paused. "Technically, there are two hundred and fifty-six, but there's a glitch on the last level that turns it into a kill screen."

"Well, as much as I played, I never made it even close to that far, trust me." She shrugged, tracing one toe in the sand. "I spent a lot of time on military bases when I was a kid. The day care or summer camp or whatever program my parents stuck me in always had some old video games. Usually Pac-Man and Frogger."

"I'm guessing you were probably bored, but I would have loved it," Luke admitted. "Sorry about your ice cream." He held out the drooping remnants of his own melting cone. "Do you want mine?"

"Um, I'm good, thanks." Even as she said it, the cone collapsed, landing in a soggy pile of goo at Luke's feet.

Julia bit her lip, trying hard to suppress the bubble of laughter rising in her throat.

Luke lost it first. A rumble of laughter in his chest expanded outward. When he finally caught his breath, he snarled, "I'm going to kill that winged demon."

"I don't believe you're the kind of person who would commit avicide." Julia shook her head, laughing so hard tears were forming.

He stared at her, nonplussed.

"That's a fancy word for killing birds," she added, suppressing another burst of laughter at his distinct lack of amusement.

"Yeah, I kind of figured that one out." He wiped at his shirt, which only smeared the chocolate more, giving Pac-Man a handlebar mustache.

Julia burst into giggles again.

"You don't think I'll do it, but I will. I'll assassinate that thieving little jerk, and then I'll stuff him and give him to you as a present. You like stuffed animals, right?"

"Not real ones!" Julia wheezed. She was going to get the hiccups.

"Picky, aren't we?" He heaved an exaggerated sigh. "Fine. I won't commit avicide," he agreed, grinning down at her, gray eyes crinkling. "At least not today."

The cheek ache was back in full force, but Julia couldn't help returning the smile. When he looked at her like that, her insides went all light and fluffy. She bit her lip and turned away, inching out into the water until the gentle afternoon tide swirled around her bare ankles. "I appreciate the offer, though," she finally said, struggling to keep the light, playful tone of their conversation. "Do you give all the girls you kiss stuffed animals as gifts?"

He shrugged. "Would you believe me if I said I haven't kissed that many girls?"

"The taxidermy might be part of your problem," she teased.

"I'll keep that in mind." He chuckled. "Though if I was serious about taking that up as a hobby, I might need you to give me shooting lessons. You said your dad taught you?"

"He did."

"I heard you tell Harry he's a marine."

"He *was* Brigadier general. Retired now." Julia kept walking, feet splashing through the water. "Since I never plan to own a gun, learning to shoot might have been a bit wasted on me."

"I think our paintball team would disagree with you."

"I suppose." She tried to suppress the proud smile tugging at her lips. "And I was quite the hustler at carnival games."

Luke shook his head. "Here I am, trying to tempt you with

one measly stuffed animal, and you already have a collection of giant teddy bears."

"My mom got rid of all that stuff ages ago. I only saved one." She grinned. "A jumbo-sized taco."

"A treasure destined to become a family heirloom," he teased. "I'm sure your dad is very proud."

"I don't know about that." Julia laughed, but the happy sound ended on a hollow note. She didn't want to weigh this moment down, didn't want to delve into all the ways she felt like her choices had not been the ones her parents wished she'd made. "He wasn't around a lot when I was growing up, but when he was, he made sure to teach me three things. How to shoot a gun, change a tire, and cook a steak."

"Interesting combination," Luke mused.

"Being independent and self-sufficient was a big deal to him. And I get it. I understand he wanted to make sure I could manage on my own, that I would grow up never having to count on anybody else . . ." Julia hesitated, watching the waves roll in and out, water cresting in frothy white bubbles. "But I also think it might be nice to have someone around to help. To do things for me. Not because I need them to but because they want to. And I'd do things for them. Because I want to."

"If you ever want to cook a steak for someone, I'm here for you," Luke said solemnly.

Julia rolled her eyes and pushed him, forcing him to dodge the waves so his shoes didn't get wet. She knew he was playing around, trying to lighten the mood, but the reality was, the idea appealed to her. She liked the thought of doing something for him. Maybe not cook a steak exactly, but something nice.

"I'll think about it," she finally said, regretting the words almost immediately. It was a foolish idea. She barely knew him. It's not like she could invite him over to her place for a dinner date.

Could she? It was only Tuesday, and yet it already felt like so much had happened between them. At this rate, what would things be like by the time she left on Sunday?

Julia pulled back from that line of thinking. It was just five more days. Things would be the same as they were now. Maybe she'd know him slightly better—assuming of course that anything about the person she was interacting with was the real him, and she had to imagine it was, at least a little bit. She was pretending to be someone else, and yet, aside from hiding the fact that she was the reviewer, pretty much everything she said and did was just her being herself. Especially around Luke. When they were together, she forgot all about her role as a reviewer. She was just a girl . . .

"You mentioned your dad wasn't around a lot when you were growing up." Luke paused, as if testing the temperature of this conversation before wading all the way in. "Were your parents divorced?"

"No, they're still married." Julia shook her head. "Dad's work took him all over the place. As a family, we moved a lot, but not nearly as much as he got bounced around. It was like they would occasionally relocate us to a different hive, and he buzzed in and out." She scrunched her toes, watching the patterns she made in the sand disappear with the tide.

Rather like her parents' marriage. They'd been together for decades but felt nothing for each other beyond a pleasant, tolerant regard. Julia stared ahead, taking in the miles of shoreline stretching before her. No matter how far she walked or for how long, eventually the waves would sweep in and smooth things over. Her footsteps would be erased. Forgotten.

Filled with an aching sadness, she wondered, as she often had before, whether her parents had ever felt something deeper for each other. She wanted to believe they'd started their journey together in love, but that somehow made it worse, knowing feelings that had once been there were gone, washed away over time.

"They're still together, but I'm not sure if they're happy." She exhaled. "They're not unhappy, just not . . . happy."

Luke nodded, gray eyes pensive. It was a few minutes before he spoke, voice so low and quiet it was almost swallowed by the tide. "My parents were definitely unhappy." A sardonic smile curled one corner of his mouth. "Very unhappy."

"Divorced?" Julia asked.

"Yeah." He picked up a handful of pebbles, sending them skittering across the waves.

"I'm sorry." She wasn't sure if an apology was the right thing here. The way he'd answered seemed to indicate he wasn't interested in condolences. But she didn't know what else to offer him.

"Don't be." More pebbles bounced into the water. "You know how you said you thought it might be nice to have someone around to help? To do things for each other because you wanted to?"

"Uh-huh," she said softly, tiptoeing around the sharp edges their conversation had exposed.

He bent and scooped up another fistful of pebbles, this time tossing them into the lake one by one. "My parents weren't really the type to enjoy doing things for each other. Hated it, actually. Always acted like it was some kind of personal insult to have to help each other with anything. I'm amazed their marriage lasted as long as it did."

Her heart twisted at the bitterness in his voice. "How old were you?"

"Eighteen." He wiped his hands on his jeans. "I was fine. But my sister was only twelve. She needed them. Really, really needed them. And they were too selfish to put her needs first."

"I know it may not seem like the right thing to do," Julia began, treading carefully, "but sticking it out isn't always the best option."

Luke jerked his head toward her. "Do you have siblings?"

"Only child," she answered simply. Julia sensed she'd hit a nerve, but she was determined not to let him change the subject.

"I grew up with two parents who stopped loving each other years ago. But they chose to stick it out."

"I admire them for having principles." Luke snorted. "My parents were too selfish for anything like that."

"You're missing my point." A wave crested and Julia kicked at the water in frustration. "What they did was selfish, too. They're not still together because they care for each other but because they didn't care enough to do anything else!"

A muscle rippled in Luke's jaw. His face shuttered, emotions pulling back, as if he'd drawn a curtain behind those stormy eyes.

Part of her wished she hadn't said anything, that she'd kept her mouth shut and her opinion to herself. But it felt worse to leave things half-said, so she soldiered on. "I know it sounds irrational, but I used to *wish* my parents would fight. I wanted to see them angry with each other because then it would feel like they actually cared. Like they were invested in the relationship." She stopped walking, suddenly running out of steam. "Like they were invested in me."

He stared down at her in broody silence.

"Luke?"

"De Morgan's law."

"Huh?" Julia wondered if she'd pushed him off the deep end with her emotional tirade.

"De Morgan's law." He blinked, warmth seeping back into his eyes, thawing the chill. "It's a theorem used in computer programming."

"Oh." Yep, she'd definitely pushed him over the edge. Served her right for indulging in a feelings dump about her parents. He was a guy she'd known for two days, not her therapist.

"For developing logic gates," he added.

There was nothing logical about the current situation. Julia realized her feet were still in the water, the rising surf now tickling her shins. She pointed at the sand, gesturing at the tail of the wave snaking closer to where Luke stood. "Your shoes are going to get wet."

"I don't care," he said. "What you said makes sense."

"Okay . . ." Julia eyed him warily. Luke might think she was making sense, but at the moment, he had her completely confused.

"I'd never considered things from that angle. Your take is the opposite of my view. Yet both conclusions have the potential to be true." He shrugged. "You've given me a lot to think about." He splashed closer to her, shoes squelching in the wet sand. "Thank you."

"Any time," she said faintly, unsure what Luke was thanking her for. She was about to ask, when he bent his head and kissed her. His lips were warm and tasted of chocolate where they brushed against her own, and Julia decided to simply accept this token of his gratitude.

Sometimes it was better not to ask questions.

CHAPTER 18

JULIA

On Wednesday morning, Julia lounged on a chaise in Kat's suite, reviewing plans for the upcoming interview with the resort's owner. "Do you have any questions about the questions I gave you?"

"I'm supposed to write down whatever that lady, Mrs. Whattaburger—"

"Weatherfork," Julia corrected.

"Mrs. Weatherfork," Kat echoed, continuing smoothly, "just write her answers down in here, right?" Kat held up the notepad.

Julia nodded. "Usually, I'd also record the interview on my phone, but since we're not allowed to have our phones . . ."

"I'm sure the owner would make an exception for this," Kat said.

"Besides, don't you need pictures and video of the resort anyway?" Andie asked from her spot on the floor, where she was doing crunches.

"She's right," Kat agreed. "Those 'Take Me!' articles always have fun video clips."

Julia already had plenty of stock photos from the PR packet the resort had emailed her prior to her arrival, but video footage was a component of her review that she'd put on the back burner to figure out later. When was she going to learn that doing that was how she always got burned? It was already the middle of the week; she was running out of "later." "I'll look into it."

"You've been a bit distracted, huh?" Andie teased. She'd flipped over and was now nose to the floor, doing push-ups.

"Yeah, she finally took our advice to have fun." Kat grinned and joined Julia on the chaise.

Julia scooted over. "I've been having a little fun," she admitted, feeling a twinge of guilt. So far, she'd spent way more time thinking about Luke than focusing on writing the review.

"Was that a little bit of kissing I saw happening on the beach yesterday?" Kat asked.

Julia flushed. "I'm surprised you noticed," she shot back.

"I'm an excellent multitasker." Kat grinned, eyes gleaming with wicked innuendo.

"You *both* put on quite a show," Andie snorted. She rolled to her side. "Are either of you planning for a repeat performance this afternoon?" she asked, foot flying up and down in a series of leg lifts.

"What's this afternoon?" Julia wondered. She was having a hard time keeping track of what day it was, let alone what activities were next on the schedule.

Andie rolled to her other side. "Don't you remember what you signed up for?"

"Not really." Julia shook her head. "You were rushing me to finish the itinerary. I picked my own bonus activity, but for everything else I just circled the same stuff you two did."

"Today we're having a beach party!" Kat cheered.

Julia frowned. "We just spent the afternoon on the beach yesterday though."

"This is different," Kat assured her. "There's going to be volleyball and windsurfing and—"

"A sand castle contest," Andie added.

"Sand castles." Julia's lip curled. "Really?"

"It'll be fun."

Julia eyed her friend, currently balanced on her elbows and

toes in a plank position. "I'm beginning to think you and I have a very different definition of that word."

"It's a beautiful day. You don't even have to help build a sand castle," Andie promised. "You can just lay out in your swimsuit on the beach and relax."

"But I didn't pack a swimsuit."

"Who goes to a lakeshore resort in June and doesn't pack a swimsuit?" Kat wondered.

"Someone who doesn't plan to go swimming in the lake." Julia crossed her arms.

"I packed two." Kat beamed. "You can borrow one of mine."

"And I bet we can find a certain someone to keep you company." Andie winked.

"Maybe you should invite Curt to come with us, too," Julia suggested. Turnabout was fair play.

"Why would I do that?" Andie made a sound of disgust, but Julia caught the way her friend's face lit up at the mention of his name.

Kat must have noticed it too. "Come on," she said, sharing a secret smile with Julia. "Let me show you those bathing suits."

A few hours later, settled in with her notepad, a stack of travel magazines from the hotel lobby for research, and a drink from the pop-up beach bar for refreshment, Julia decided that, once again, her friends had been right. It was a perfect afternoon. The sky perfectly clear. The lake perfectly blue.

Her plan had been to review Kat's notes from the interview with the resort owner, content to relax in her beach chair, enjoying the view of the lake and observing the interactions of couples scattered across the beach. Maybe it was the gorgeous weather, but the sandcastle activity proved more popular than she'd expected. She waved to Patrick and David, who were assembling an impressive-looking medieval fortress.

It wasn't long before Andie's competitive streak reared its head, and Julia laughed at her friend's outrageous attempts to sabotage everyone else's castles. Especially Curt's. Julia watched in smug delight. The entire time Andie was taking jabs at Curt's castle, the man stood there with a silly grin on his face, watching her with stark admiration. He was clearly giving Andie the look. And based on the way Andie's smirks were holding less heat and more affection, Julia knew her friend knew it too.

Thinking about the conversation on "the look" that she'd had with Andie and Kat on the forest trail led Julia to thinking about Luke—something she'd been trying to avoid all afternoon. Things had started to get too personal yesterday. Talking with him on the beach, she'd let her guard down. Emotions were getting involved. It was unprofessional. She was here to do a job, one that, if she did well enough, would ensure she still had a job.

Reluctantly, her gaze traveled to where Luke was working on a castle with Kat. Several guys had volunteered to become Kat's worker bees—including Luke. He was kneeling in the sand next to her, long legs folded beneath him, shooting dirty looks at Zach, who was kneeling on Kat's other side and shooting dirty looks right back. As Julia watched, Luke leaned closer to her friend, pointing at something, and Kat's face broke into a grin.

Pinpricks of jealousy pierced Julia's chest. Kat had Zach, as well as an entire battalion of beefcake at her service. Why was she flirting with Luke?

For fuck's sake, stop being an idiot. They were just having fun.

Julia shoved a magazine in front of her face and tried to ignore them. But when a peal of Kat's unmistakable laughter rang out, she couldn't help peeking over the pages again. Luke was helping Kat form a tower from a bucket of sand, his long, competent fingers cupping hers as they patted the sand into place.

The pinpricks grew barbs, making it hard to breathe. Julia

dropped the magazine, tucked her notepad into her beach bag, and headed for the water.

"Where are you going?" Andie called after her.

"For a swim," she bit out, not bothering to look back.

Bare feet pounded in the sand behind her, and a moment later Andie appeared at her side. "Are you sure that's a good idea?"

"You were the one making fun of me for not packing a swimsuit."

"Exactly." Andie laughed. "I know taking a dip in the lake is not really your thing, Jules." She glanced out at the water. "This is Wisconsin in June. It might feel like summer on the sand, but that is a Great Lake and it's still going to be pretty darn cold."

"I walked in it yesterday," Julia pointed out, stomping into the shallows.

"Wading and swimming are two different things," Andie warned her. "It's going to get colder the further you get from the shore."

"Good," Julia muttered. She could use a bit of cooling off. She dove into the waves, gasping as icy water swirled around her. Julia immediately regretted her decision, but with Andie standing there smirking knowingly, her need to be right—or at least not be wrong—reared its head.

"How is it out there?" Andie called.

"It's fine," she lied, clenching her teeth to keep them from chattering, and sucking in a breath while thousands of freezing liquid needles stabbed every inch of exposed skin. "You just have to get used to it," she insisted.

Andie waded in up to her knees and raised an eyebrow.

"Oh, wow." Julia looked past her friend. "Curt's castle is at least three times the size of yours now."

"What?" Andie turned quickly, running back up the beach.

The tide rolled, and Julia drifted a little farther out. She bobbed in the waves, surprised to discover that the water had started to feel a little warmer. What she said must be true; she was getting used to the temperature. That, or a fish had just peed nearby. Wait. Fish were cold-blooded. Would their pee be warm? Did fish pee?

Thanks to a memorable field trip to the Shedd Aquarium when she was in second grade, Julia knew for sure that fish pooped. A fact that reminded her she was currently floating in a giant fish toilet bowl. *Gross.* This was why she didn't swim in lakes.

Distracted by her disgusting realization, it took her a moment to realize something felt different. Even then, she didn't figure out what was wrong until she caught sight of a flash of bright yellow bobbing in the waves a few feet away.

Damn it. She had known she shouldn't borrow Kat's swimsuit. It was too snug in the butt and too loose in the boobs. She'd pulled the strings as tight as she could and tied a double knot at the neck, but apparently that hadn't been good enough.

Julia glanced back toward the beach. Nobody had noticed. Everyone was focused on their castles or on each other and she was the only one who'd been idiotic enough to venture into the lake. Holding an arm over the girls, she reached with her other arm for the top, but it had already floated too far away.

Ugh. Julia dug her toes into the rocks and sand and kicked off, swimming toward the runaway bikini. Her fingers barely brushed one of the ties when a shadow passed overhead. Glancing up, she spotted an increasingly familiar ball of white feathers winging toward her like a missile. On instinct, she ducked her head underwater.

When she resurfaced, the seagull was gone.

And so was her top.

"Thief!" she yelled, smacking the waves with her palms.

Her shout got the attention of a few people on the beach. Wonderful.

She sank lower, waves lapping at her chin.

"What's wrong?" Andie called, her coach voice loud enough to attract the attention of anyone who might not have been looking Julia's way already.

Working her way toward the shore while staying as submerged as possible, Julia pointed toward the sky.

Luke seemed to be the first to realize what was happening. He scrambled forward, scattering sand in every direction, heedless of the structures in his path.

"Hey, that's my castle!" Andie yelled.

"Hey, that's my top!" Kat cried.

"Give that back, you flying menace!" Luke shouted, shaking his fist.

Unimpressed, the seagull circled overhead with its loot, bright yellow strings fluttering in the breeze like an erotic kite. Luke hurried down to the shoreline. "Here." He tossed Julia his shirt. By the time she'd managed to pull it over her head, he was racing across the beach, yelling expletives as he chased after the bikini bandit.

She hurried after Luke, finally catching up to him crouched behind a large rock. "Where did he go?"

"Shh." He put a finger to his lips before waving at her to get low.

Julia hunkered down next to him behind the rock. He was still breathing heavily from the run—and so was she, for that matter. She sucked in air, laughing quietly. "This has got to be the most running I've done in one week in years."

"This has got to be the most time I've spent shirtless in public in years," he muttered.

"Thank you." Julia grinned. "It was very chivalrous of you."

"I'm sure plenty of people would have preferred to see you topless," Luke said, lips quirking. "But they'll have to deal with seeing me instead."

"Life's full of disappointments." Julia laughed ruefully. "And if we don't get that top back, my friend is going to be very disappointed. I was borrowing her swimsuit." She shook her head, baffled. "What would a bird want with a bikini, anyway?"

Luke gestured toward a dip in the sand a few feet away. "I think he's planning to use it in his nest."

"Add a bit of color, huh?" Julia glanced around the edge of the rock. "Is that the same seagull who stole your notebook?"

"Yep," he grumbled. "And your ice cream cone. Little klepto-maniac asshole."

"I think he has an accomplice." She pointed to a second bird. "Ooh, I wonder if it's a lady friend."

"Fantastic. We've discovered the Bonnie and Clyde of the bird kingdom."

The two seagulls fluttered around the nest for a minute before drifting over to a nearby rock.

"Think we can sneak over there and steal the top back?" she wondered.

"It's worth a shot." Luke crept forward in the sand.

Julia followed close behind. They were almost within reach of the nest when both gulls started flapping their wings in a frenzy.

"Abort mission. Abort! Abort!" Luke dove, shoving Julia backward and covering her with his body.

Beneath him, she squeezed her eyes shut as Hitchcock-inspired nightmares involving pecked-out eye sockets dripping blood flashed through her mind. She heard more wing flapping. Eyelids still tightly closed, she pressed her face into his chest and asked, "Are they coming?"

"Um, sort of." His voice sounded odd. Almost strangled.

"Oh, God." Julia cracked one lid open. "Are you okay?" She patted his naked back, frantically feeling for the ripped flesh of talon scratches. "Did they get you?"

"No. But I think . . ." He paused. "I, uh, think Bonnie and Clyde are getting some."

"Some what?" Julia's eyes snapped open, and she shifted, cran-ing her neck and peering over Luke's shoulder. One of the birds was standing on the back of the other. Clyde, by the looks of things. "I'm not sure that's how it works."

"I didn't realize you were so knowledgeable about the mating habits of seagulls."

"I'm not." She punched him in the arm. "Are you?"

They both turned to watch what could best be described as a circus act. As the bird balanced on top began to gyrate his tail feathers around in an acrobatic frenzy, Julia pressed her mouth to Luke's ear and whispered, "I feel like a voyeur."

"That's because you are," he whispered back, attention still on the amorous avian activity. He squinted, narrowing his gaze.

"Do you want me to get you some binoculars?" Julia asked, only mostly teasing. "I didn't realize this was your thing."

"This is not my thing," he hissed, affronted. "I was curious," he admitted. "I wanted to see if Clyde has a . . . um . . ."

"Thing?" Now Julia was curious, too. She joined him in scrutinizing the action. "Hm. I've never thought about bird peen before, but a few minutes ago I was trying to remember if fish could pee, so I suppose it's just that kind of day."

"What about fish pee?" he asked, the question vibrating with barely checked laughter.

Julia met his gaze. He was smiling down at her, humor in his eyes as well as his voice. Suddenly, she was acutely aware of their position in the sand. How she was flat on her back, in nothing but a too-small bikini bottom and his T-shirt, and he was sprawled on top of her. "That was very noble of you, by the way."

"What was?" he asked, mouth drifting closer to hers.

She licked her lips. "How you were ready to sacrifice yourself to try and save me from a bird attack."

"I'm just full of chivalric deeds today," he murmured. He dipped his head, kissing her first in one corner of her mouth and then in the other.

It was a teasing kiss, one that made her ache for the real thing. She pressed her palms into the sand and arched up, bringing her lips to his.

He groaned in response, wrapping his arms around her, grinding his hips against hers. Things seemed to go from zero to sixty when the thick ridge of his shaft pressed between her bare thighs, hard and aroused. Mouth never leaving hers, Luke rolled, shifting their position and pulling her on top of him. His hands skimmed over her scantily clad bottom, fingers gripping the hem of his T-shirt.

Pressed against the warmth of his chest, acutely aware of the fact her breasts were bare beneath the thin layer of cotton, her nipples tightened. He broke off the kiss, inhaling sharply. Julia sat up, and his gray eyes followed the movement, eyes sparkling when they focused on her chest. The way he was looking at her . . . *Whoa.* Heat coiled inside her.

He lifted a hand and brushed the outline of one breast, thumb stroking over the taut peak. The sensation of the soft fabric rubbing against her skin was so intense it was almost painful. His hand shifted to her other breast, and then his mouth was on her as well. She could feel his tongue, hot and wet through the cotton, and then, *Oh, God,* his teeth. Julia moaned, head lolling back, eyes drifting closed.

Just when things were getting *really* good, he abruptly stopped.

"Luke?" Her head snapped up and she blinked. "Is something wrong?"

"Um . . ." His voice was muffled, face still pressed between her breasts. He pulled back slowly and gazed up at her. "Do you feel like we're being watched?"

Julia blanched. When they'd chased after the bikini bandit, they'd gotten so far away from the crowd she'd all but forgotten anyone else was on the beach.

"Though I do suppose turnabout is fair play," he mused.

"Huh?" Julia followed the direction of his gaze. "Oh."

Two sets of beady black eyes stared at them.

"Well, this is awkward."

"Very," he agreed.

"What should we do?"

"You don't think they're expecting us to continue, do you?" Luke asked. "I don't perform well in front of an audience."

"I'll keep that in mind," she joked, feeling a little slaphappy. This whole situation was too bizarre. "Do you want to try and steal back the bikini top?"

Luke kept his gaze trained on the birds, as if afraid that they'd pounce the second he looked away. "I'm not sure that's such a good idea."

"We should have grabbed it earlier, when they were . . . distracted."

"That would have been a good plan." he agreed, smile going lopsided. "But then we, uh, got distracted too."

We did indeed. Julia tried to ignore the pulse of residual heat between her legs, where she still straddled him. "What's the new plan?"

"Depends," Luke said.

"On what?"

"On how mad your friend will be if we don't get her top back."

"I'll buy her a new one."

"In that case, I hope you don't mind my distinct lack of heroism." He met her gaze, lips quirking as he acknowledged his own cowardice. "I recommend we gracefully retreat."

She grinned, equally spineless. "Works for me."

Julia wasn't sure how graceful they were, but somehow they both managed to get untangled and on their feet without much fuss. Slowly backing away from the still staring birds, Julia barely resisted the urge to put a protective hand over her eye sockets. After a moment, when the seagulls didn't react, she and Luke turned around and started the trek back.

They'd been walking for a few minutes when she couldn't help asking, "Do you think that was really what they were doing?" She glanced at him. "Before?"

"I'd rather not think about it." A playful smirk flashed across his face. "But I admit, my internet search history is going to be especially weird tonight."

Julia laughed.

Luke reached for her hand, fingers entwining with hers.

I love your laugh. His words echoed in her mind and her heart squished in her chest like a big, fluffy marshmallow.

A shadow passed overhead.

"Uh-oh," Luke warned, interrupting her happy musings. "The bandit is back."

No sooner had Luke said that, then the seagull swooped down, landing in front of them.

The bird—Clyde, she thought—trotted forward, bikini top in his beak, sunshine yellow strings dragging in the sand.

"What do you think he's doing now?" she wondered.

"Watch out," Luke warned as the gull came closer. "That marauding menace probably intends to claim the other half of his booty."

"Was that a butt joke?" Julia tugged on her bikini bottom, feeling a ridiculous urge to make sure it was secure and safe from panty-snatching pirate seagulls.

But rather than try and steal anything, the bird dropped the top at Julia's feet and squawked once before flying away.

Mystified by this apparent peace offering, Luke and Julia watched silently as Clyde made his way back to his nest.

"Huh," Luke said. "I guess it's a truce." He bent, scooping up the bikini top and handing it back to Julia. "I'm still mad at him, though," he muttered. "Cockblocking sky weasel."

A puff of resigned laughter escaped her. He had a point. The interruption had been frustratingly untimely. Which was for the best anyway, Julia reminded herself, as they started to make their way back. She'd just finished reiterating the fact that she was here to do a job, not get romantically involved.

But when he reached out to hold her hand again, her heart did a rebellious little hop, skip, and jump routine that seemed designed to tell her brain, *Make whatever rules you want, head . . . We're going to break them all.*

CHAPTER 19

LUKE

Luke wanted to do something special for Julia. The thought kept popping up in his mind, making it impossible to concentrate on anything else. Frankly, he was finding it impossible to focus on anything that wasn't Julia. He thought about her constantly.

He woke up on Thursday still thinking about her, and decided to try clearing his head by making some progress on the game engine he was developing for his potential start-up, but all morning he kept catching himself staring off into space. He'd be running through some new code, data streams flowing by, and his mind would shift to Julia—her hair, her smell, how her hazel eyes shifted color when in sunlight or shadow. He'd shake himself and get back to work, only to recall her laugh and how, when she smiled at him, he felt like it was Christmas and his birthday at the same time.

Waving the white flag, Luke gave up trying to get any work done and went in search of his sister. Maybe Pen could knock some sense into him. And if not, at least he could pick her brain about ideas on what to do for Julia.

But when he got to the control room, Luke was surprised to discover the door wouldn't open, which was odd, considering his key card was coded for access to all the resort's offices. He tried again and realized the system was working fine; the problem was that the physical lock had been bolted from the inside. He jiggled the handle. "Pen?"

He knocked. "Penelope, are you in there?" Luke glanced

around the hall. He doubted he'd run into anyone from the sim in this part of the hotel, but he really should be more careful. He'd been so busy enjoying his time with Julia, he'd all but forgotten there was any reason to be a part of the game other than being with her.

Hell, he'd all but forgotten it was a game.

Rustling sounds and incoherent chatter from inside the control room brought his attention back to the door. Luke thought he heard the lower timbre of a familiar male voice. "Jay?" He knocked again. "Open up. I'm locked out."

Scuffling noises. Was that a giggle? Now Luke was getting irritated. His sister and best friend were screwing with him. He knocked harder. "Cut it out, you two."

He pressed his ear to the door. More whispers and rustling sounds. And then the click of the dead bolt being unlatched. The door swung open. Penelope stood there, Jay directly behind her. Luke crossed his arms and glared at his sister and best friend. "I know what's going on here."

"You do?" Jay asked.

A signal passed between his sister and best friend and Luke wondered if their behavior had something to do with that secret project for Mrs. W. they'd been hinting at.

"Luke . . ." Penelope stepped aside as he marched into the room. "We can explain—"

"I get that you two are mad at me for ditching you," he cut her off. "But locking me out?" He closed the door and shook his head. "I thought we were a team."

Penelope's cheeks flushed, and Luke felt bad for going on the offensive. Whatever was happening, she was doing her job, the one he'd asked her to do. He sighed. "I know you wanted me to let you handle this on your own, but I still should have been here for you."

"It's okay—"

"No. It's not okay." He cut her off again. "I've been gallivanting around the past few days, completely ignoring you and abandoning my responsibilities."

Jay snorted and Luke paused. "What's so funny?"

"I've never known you to go 'gallivanting around' before," his friend teased. "And what responsibilities? Pen's got everything under control. She's a great GM." Jay put an arm around Penelope's shoulder. "No offense, but honestly, I think she makes a better game master than you."

"Whenever someone says, 'No offense,' it's almost guaranteed to signify they are about to cause offense," Luke harrumphed. "In this case, however, I am not offended." He turned to his sister, offering her an apologetic smile. "Jay's right. You are a better GM." Penelope's eyes widened in surprise, as if she couldn't believe he'd ever admit to such a thing, and Luke felt like an even bigger jerk. "You're a natural at this."

"You really mean that, don't you?"

Her bewildered smile made his heart ache. Luke was struck by the sudden realization that he rarely complimented his sister. Or anyone, for that matter. Like developing a program or integrating software, he tended to focus on problems that needed to be fixed. If things were working well, they didn't need his attention. "I do. You're more personable. Attentive. The way you spend time with the players and interact with them."

"You're spending plenty of time with one player . . . very attentive." His sister's grin turned sly. "And there has been lots of interaction."

Now Luke was flushing with guilt.

Jay cleared his throat. "I uh, need to go check the hotel email server." Arm still around Penelope, he gave her a quick hug before releasing her. "Go easy on him." With a nod to Luke, he made his escape.

Pen settled into one of the office chairs and spun it around. "How's the plan going?" She steepled her fingers under her chin and studied him. "You know, the plan to play a part in the game so you could keep a close eye on the reviewer?"

"I know what plan you're referring to," Luke grumbled. He collapsed onto the seat next to hers, aware that his sister's shrewd gaze was eating up every bit of his discomfort with a spoon. Comprehension dawned, and he turned to look at her. "You *knew*, didn't you?"

"What?" Penelope didn't play coy for long. "That you were head over heels attracted to the girl from the beach and desperate to find an excuse to spend time with her?" She nodded, smug. "Yeah. I knew."

He scowled at his sister, not a fan of how she'd phrased the situation but not really able to find fault with her summary, either.

"Relax." She grinned. "It's nice to see you focus on somebody else instead of me for a change."

"What's that supposed to mean?"

She ignored his question, adding, "And it's really nice to see you show an interest in someone." Her face softened. "You like Meg, don't you?"

"You mean Julia?" Luke asked, a tickle of pleasure flashing through him at the simple joy of saying her name. "Yeah."

"You've dropped the use of her character name? That's unlike you." Penelope cocked her head. "How did you know?"

"Her real name?" Luke shrugged, avoiding his sister's gaze. "She told me."

"No." Pen waved an annoyed hand, dismissing that topic. "How did you know you *liked* her?"

Luke jerked his head up, bemused. He'd not been expecting that question. "I'm not sure I understand what you're asking."

"I saw you kissing her," Pen admitted. "On the beach."

"When?"

She shot him a look. "There was more than once?"

Luke sidestepped the question. "Was it during the sandcastle competition?" he asked, gut clenching. If she'd caught what they'd been doing yesterday, she would have seen a bit more than kissing . . .

Pen shook her head. "That was Wednesday. I'm talking about Tuesday. After the paintball game. Jay and I walked down to get some ice cream and, well . . ."

"Ah." Julia had smiled up at him as he'd reached for her, his shoes getting soaked by the waves. But he hadn't cared; he was too busy kissing her sweet mouth, savoring the lingering taste of chocolate. Luke shook himself. Was he about to get a lecture from his baby sister? He probably deserved it. When he met her eyes, however, it wasn't censure he saw in her face but curiosity.

"How did you know?" she asked again.

"How did I know *what*?"

"How did you know the time was right? To kiss her."

Now he was flushing for a different reason. His sister was in her midtwenties, a college graduate, for heaven's sake. As much as he didn't want to think about it (and he really, really didn't want to think about it), surely she had been kissed before . . .

As if reading his mind, Penelope blurted, "I've kissed plenty of guys."

Plenty?

"But none of them meant anything to me. It was just for fun."

Luke's throat constricted, but he tried to play it cool. "There's nothing wrong with having a little bit of fun." He almost managed to avoid emphasizing the words *little bit*. Almost.

"I know." Her tone told him she didn't need and wasn't looking for his approval. "But Julia's different. You've only known her a few days, but I can tell she means something to you."

"Yeah, her friend's review could really help boost the success of this resort."

Penelope narrowed her gaze, lips pursed. "My concerns about that statement aside, we've already established the flimsiness of that excuse. You like her, Luke."

"Yes. I like her. I admit it."

"No, you *like her* like her."

"What is this, the third grade?"

"Ha. I don't think you knew what a girl *was* in third grade, let alone liked one."

"I knew you. And I even liked you."

"I don't count. When you were in third grade, I was like three years old. Besides, we've been over this. You're my brother. You *have* to like me."

"I have to *love* you. I don't always have to like you."

"Don't try and derail me from my point with your pedantic nit-picking."

"There's a point to this?" Luke wondered, knowing the question was just going to egg her on.

"Yes, if you'll shut up long enough for me to get to it." Penelope tugged on her hair, a sure sign she was agitated.

Luke decided to keep his mouth shut and let his sister finish.

"Kissing someone you don't really care about is a completely different thing than kissing someone you . . ." she hesitated, pulling on her hair again, "have feelings for."

Luke stared at his sister. Was this a specific question about specific feelings she had for a specific someone? Who?

Those jumbled thoughts faded away as the truth of her words crystallized. Pen was right. Kissing Julia had been different. Not that he'd kissed a lot of girls, but he'd had the occasional girlfriend. Nothing serious. As Pen had said, just for fun. He never really felt like he had time. His focus had always been more on his sister, on making sure she was doing well and had everything she needed. Besides, based on his parents' track record, Luke hadn't been in a hurry for a relationship of his own.

"You're right. But it's not that Julia is different from other girls . . ." He paused, searching for the right words. "It's that my feelings for her are different. Something about her and me together and the way she makes me feel." Luke shifted on his seat. "I'm not sure I can explain it."

"Try."

"Some people might think this conversation between siblings is odd, you know."

"We're not 'some people.'" Penelope scooted her chair closer to his. "Stop stalling."

His sister was right. They'd been through so much together, shared so much. Besides, Luke thought with a pang, it wasn't like Pen was going to ever have a talk like this with their mother or something. That would require too much time and effort on Mom's part.

He pushed the negative thoughts aside. He was still digesting what Julia had said about breaking up being better than staying together, still needed to unpack how that affected his opinion regarding his parents' relationship.

That was another way being with Julia was different. That day on the beach, when Penelope had seen them kissing, he'd told her things he'd never shared with anyone. Luke focused on that. On how he'd felt in that moment, when the urge to kiss Julia had been so strong. He hadn't cared about anything else.

"Kissing Julia is like . . ." He tried to think of a way to put it in words for his sister that wouldn't be too embarrassing for either of them. "Like hearing music."

"What, like a choir of heavenly angels?" Pen wondered.

"Um, no."

"Violins?"

"Nope."

"Then what did you hear?"

"Spandau Ballet."

"Ah, so something classical."

"Not ballet like *Swan Lake*." Luke shook his head. "Spandau Ballet is an eighties band."

"Your geezer tunes. Why am I not surprised." Penelope rolled her eyes, voice teasing. "I'm almost afraid to ask, but . . . what song?"

"'True.' That's the name of the song," he clarified, before she could make another snarky comment. Although, he had to admit, her teasing helped make this conversation seem a little more normal and a little less weird.

"The title has potential, but I don't know it."

"And now *I'm* not surprised."

"Sing it for me."

"Absolutely not."

"Fine. I'll look it up." His sister swiveled on her chair and began typing. "Why that song in particular?"

"I'm not really sure." Luke shrugged. "We started kissing and it sort of came over me." He bit his lip, struggling to define how it felt. "It wasn't the words playing in my head, exactly, so much as it was the music was moving all through me—like the sound was flowing through my veins. And it heightened this feeling that everything was . . . right." He shook his head. "This is stupid."

"No. Luke, no." Pen grabbed his hand. "It's actually the most perfect description of a kiss I've ever heard."

"Really?"

"Yes, really." She paused, the teasing glint returning to her eye. "I'm not sure about the Spandex Ballet—"

"Spandau," he corrected.

"Whatever." She rolled her eyes again. But then she smiled at him, all hint of teasing gone. "It's beautiful, Luke." Her voice was low and raw and sincere. "Thank you for telling me."

"I want to do something special for her," he admitted in a rush. "Something that shows her, in some way, how I feel."

"I think the answer to that is obvious, brother dear."

"What do you mean, obvious? I've been racking my brain for more than a day trying to come up with something." He grinned sheepishly. "It's actually one of the reasons I came looking for you."

"I'm flattered. And I'm also happy to help." Her mouth quirked. "You really can't think of anything?"

He shook his head.

"Even after the conversation we just had?" She looked at him like he was an idiot.

"Penelope," he barked. "Just tell me."

Rather than respond immediately, his sister reached for a file. She flipped it open and began shuffling the papers. "Aha." She smacked a page on the desk in front of him.

Luke glanced at the paper and realized it was Julia's itinerary.

"There's your answer," Pen said, tapping at a spot on the page.

Luke squinted. It was the bonus activity Julia had selected. For her personalized experience, Julia had picked karaoke serenade. His stomach flipped as he recalled the conversation at the break-fast table that morning, how the thought of singing to someone had made him nauseous even then. "No."

"Luke, you have to."

"No way."

"It's too perfect," Penelope insisted, mouth set in a stubborn line. "You already know what song to sing and everything."

He shook his head. But even as he refused, he knew his sister was right.

"Fine," he groaned. "But I think I'm going to need a drink first." He groaned again. "Maybe two."

CHAPTER 20
JULIA

"Red or white?"

"Pardon?" Julia peered around the blank canvas set up in front of her.

A server held out a tray of wineglasses. "Would you prefer red or white?"

"Is 'both' an option?" Andie asked, answering her own question by two-fisting it. She set the glasses down in the tray of her easel.

Julia laughed and selected a glass of white. "Romantic comedies where one of the characters is an artist—go!" Julia ordered, pointing her finger at Kat.

Kat squeezed her eyes shut, thinking. "Oh!" Her eyes snapped open. "Kat!" She giggled. "From *10 Things I Hate About You.*"

"She wants to go to art school. Very good." Julia pivoted. "Andie?"

"Hm." Andie fidgeted with the blank canvas on her easel. "The heroine in *Austenland* keeps a sketchbook. What was her name?"

"Miss Erstwhile," Kat said, then paused, nose wrinkling, "Wait. That was her character name. Her real name was Jane." She grinned. "Kind of like what we're doing here, huh?"

"Yeah, but at least they managed to remember their role-playing names," Julia pointed out. "We gave up on that by like day two."

"The costumes probably helped," Andie snorted. "Though it

also made things more immersive. Harder to remember it was all just a game."

Julie caught the note of caution in her friend's voice and glanced up curiously.

But whatever Andie had been thinking, she let it slide. "Your turn, Jules." She tapped her easel. "Rom-com featuring an artistic character."

"All I can think of is Jane from *Jane Eyre*," Julia admitted. "I don't think that counts."

"Yeah, no." Andie shook her head. "Definitely not a rom-com."

"More like a rom-sad," Kat agreed. "Or rom-traum. Is that a genre?"

"If not, it should be," Andie said, reaching for her wine. She drained one glass and waved the server over, holding up the now empty glass for a refill while starting on the other. By the time the woman had finished pouring a second red, Andie was ready to have the white refilled as well.

"Efficient," Julia noted.

"Always."

"Going for the drunk artist aesthetic, I see," Kat observed.

"No." Andie grinned. "I simply require a bit of liquid inspiration."

"If I was Zach, I'd need some liquid courage," Kat admitted, letting the server top off her glass.

"That's right," Andie purred. "He's going to be our model for the evening."

"He told me the technical term is *subject*, not *model*," Kat informed them with a haughty air of importance. Then she ruined the effect by snickering. "I wonder what it must feel like to stand stark naked and have your private bits scrutinized by a room full of people."

"Cold, is my guess." Andie slipped a bill into the server's apron and winked. "We're going to be seeing a lot of each other this evening." She lowered her voice and added drily, "We're going to be seeing a lot of Zach, as well."

Kat giggled. "I just realized this is like taking dick pics to the next level."

"I'd be fine painting a bowl of fruit or something," Julia muttered.

"Don't worry, I'm pretty sure you'll get to see a banana." Kat grinned.

"And some peaches," Patrick added, matching Kat's grin as he took the easel next to hers.

David waved a greeting and settled behind the last easel in their row. "Is it peach or peaches?"

"Oh, no." Patrick winced with a long-suffering sigh. "Not the peaches debate."

Andie raised a curious eyebrow. "What's this about?"

"Whether one says *peach* or peaches when referring to one's ass," David explained, fiddling with pots of paint on his easel. "Or anyone's ass, frankly."

"I'm going to get some wine," Patrick announced.

"Red for me, please," David called after Patrick, as he moved to chase down the server.

Kat tapped David on the shoulder with her paintbrush. "Tell us more about this great butt debate."

"Well, my grandmother would always say *peaches*, but I think that's because she was talking about cute little baby butt cheeks," David explained. "However, when using an emoji, it's just a peach, right? One peach, singular." He gestured with his hands. "For the whole ass."

"Hm." Julia shared a glance with Andie. "That's a conundrum."

"Quite the pickle, indeed," Andie agreed, picking up her glass again. She glanced up and sputtered, spitting wine. "Speaking of pickles . . ."

Julia turned in the direction of her friend's gaze. "Oh, my." While they'd been getting schooled in the peach debate, Zach had made his grand entrance. He was now standing on a platform in the center of the room, disrobing.

"Looks like I'm just in time," Patrick said, returning with the wine.

David accepted his glass and took a healthy swallow. "Now *that* is a well-groomed peach."

"Mm-hm, very smooth," Kat hummed in agreement.

Andie inspected Zach over the rim of her wineglass. "Do you think he waxes or shaves?" she wondered.

"Both," Patrick guessed.

"Professionally," David added.

Andie nodded sagely. "That explains his nicely peeled banana."

Julia almost spit wine as she burst out laughing. "What does that even mean?"

Kat snickered. "It means you got your fruit bowl after all, Jules."

Once everyone got the produce jokes out of their system, the group settled down and started painting. For the next half hour or so, everyone sipped wine and chatted quietly while jazz music played from speakers set up in one corner of the room. Julia was pleasantly surprised to discover that the whole experience was rather relaxing.

"Maybe it's the wine talking," Andie said, turning to Kat after finishing her second round of twofers, "but painting your boyfriend's penis isn't as awkward as I'd thought it would be."

"He's not my boyfriend," Kat pointed out.

"Your pretend boyfriend, then," Andie said waving her paintbrush in the air as if dismissing the details.

Kat eyed Andie caustically but didn't argue. "Where's *your* pretend boyfriend?"

"Who? Curt?"

"Ha! Then you admit it!" Julia crowed. "I knew you liked him."

"I tolerate him," Andie sniffed. "He's busy with the wedding party tonight. Rehearsal dinner or something."

"He's really here for a wedding?" Julia asked.

"Yep. That was all true. The wedding is Sunday." Andie paused, then added, "He mentioned something to me about being his plus-one."

"Wait, like a real date?" Julia demanded. "Beyond this simulation thing?"

"Plus-ones aren't real dates," Andie argued.

"It's absolutely a real date." Kat tapped her fingers. "There's dinner, drinking, dancing, usually some banging in a hotel room—or a church confessional."

"*What?*" Andie and Julia both demanded.

"Please tell me it wasn't with a priest," Julia begged.

"Please tell me it was," Andie encouraged.

"Not a priest. I don't think." Kat shrugged, brushing it off. "So? Are you planning to go?"

"I'm thinking about it."

"See?" Kat clapped her hands. "I told you true love can happen here!"

"Whoa, slow down. Nobody said anything about true love. I haven't even said yes yet." Andie glanced around the room. "Where's the wine lady?"

Julia grinned. Seeing her usually chill friend get flustered was an unexpected but interesting development.

Even though she'd begun this experience intending to prove her friends wrong and show them it was impossible to experience real feelings while playing pretend, that the kind of love they were hoping to find was a fantasy, Julia had to admit, the longer she was here, the more the possibility was starting to seem, well . . . possible.

"What about Luke?" Kat asked.

"What about Luke?" Julia wondered, heart ballooning at the mention of his name. "I haven't seen him all day," she admitted, deflating a little. "I don't know where he is tonight."

"I do," David said, and pointed.

Julia craned her neck to look past her easel. Sure enough, Luke was standing in the corner of the room by the sound system. "What's he doing?"

"Plugging in a microphone," Patrick said matter-of-factly.

The artsy jazz music cut out, followed by a screech of audio feedback.

Everyone in the room cringed and turned toward the sound.

As if suddenly aware he had an audience, Luke stopped fiddling with the mic and glanced around uncomfortably. "Uh, good evening."

In the center of the room, Zach waved and pointed to his pedestal. Eyes wide with consternation, Luke shook his head adamantly. The awkward standoff continued until, with a huff of disgust, Zach yanked his robe on and marched over to the corner.

"What's going on?" Julia wondered, as Zach pushed Luke forward, sending him stumbling toward the platform. "You don't think he's planning to—"

"Show us his banana?" Andie asked, smirking.

"I think I kno-o-ow," Kat sang, turning her paintbrush into a microphone.

Julia glanced at her friend. "He wouldn't."

"It was the bonus activity you selected, right?" Andie asked.

"Yeah, but I didn't expect . . ." Her voice faltered as she watched Luke step onto the platform.

"Good evening," Luke said again. He cleared his throat. "I would like to dedicate this to someone I wanted to do something special for." He paused, nodding at Zach. A moment later, the first soft strains of a vaguely familiar eighties song filled the room. He shifted in a circle on the platform until he faced Julia. "I think she knows who she is."

Julia watched, frozen, as Luke lifted the mic to his lips. He wasn't singing, exactly, but making a sort of breathy humming sound. She glanced down, discomfited. It was her fault he was subjecting himself to this humiliation.

But as Luke broke into the first line of the song, Julia met his eyes. And once their gazes locked, she couldn't look away. She bit her lip, wondering how it was possible for her heart to be a balloon and her stomach a stone at the same time.

He might not be Heath Ledger in the bleachers, but his deep voice was tender and sincere, if off-key. And that bit of imperfection only made it all the more endearing. Julia's breath caught in her chest as something warm and delicate unfurled inside her.

Andie reached for her hand and squeezed. Eyes still locked on Luke, Julia squeezed back, grateful to have something to hold on to, a link to solid ground, as her world slipped on its axis.

When the song reached its chorus, Luke lowered the microphone. Music still playing, eyes still on Julia, he reached out his hand to her.

"What are you waiting for?" Andie asked

Kat leaned toward Julia and whispered in her ear, "Go to him."

Julia looked at her friends. They both nodded. Andie gave her one more squeeze, releasing her hand with a look that said if Julia didn't join Luke, she was out of her mind.

She *felt* out of her mind. Breathless and scared and excited, she stepped forward to where Luke stood waiting for her on the raised platform, arm still outstretched.

She reached her hand out and he clasped her fingers in his and pulled her onto the platform.

"Hi," she breathed. *The man stands up in a room full of people to sing to you and the best you can do is, "Hi"?* She dropped her gaze, abashed. They were so close that their toes were almost touching.

"Hi." He brushed a thumb across her cheek.

She glanced up, meeting his gray gaze as he rubbed the smudge of paint from her skin. A wave of giddy dizziness washed over her, and she swayed.

Luke reached out to steady her, a smile as tender and sincere as his voice had been curving his mouth. "You okay?"

"I'm fine," Julia lied. Cheek still tingling from his touch, she pulled herself together and realized they both were swaying now, almost dancing to the music. And then his arm was around her waist and they were dancing.

Julia relaxed against Luke, cheek pressed to his chest. After a moment, she tilted her chin to look up at him and smile.

"What is it?" he asked.

"You're so tall my ear is right over your heart."

"Can you hear it beating?" he wondered. "Even over the music?"

"No." She shook her head, still smiling. "But I can feel it."

His gray eyes went dark with some strong emotion. He bent and pressed his lips to her forehead in a kiss that was somehow firm and featherlight at the same time.

Slowly, Julia recalled that even though it seemed like the world had melted away, they were not in fact alone. She stole a sideways glance and noticed that others had decided to join in the romantic moment. Several couples were swaying together, dancing between the easels.

She went up on tiptoe to whisper in Luke's ear, "You want to get out of here?"

He stilled, heat sparking in his gaze as his grin turned playful. "Lead the way."

They scurried out of the art studio, and Julia debated where to go. The lobby was a noisy menagerie of guests. On impulse, she headed for the bank of elevators. Before she could hit the button to head up to her floor, Luke grabbed her hand and tugged her down the hall.

"What's wrong?" she asked, wondering if she'd misread him. Maybe he didn't want to go up to her room with her.

He pulled her into the stairwell and pressed a finger to his lips.

A moment later, Mrs. Weatherfork and her entourage of corgis swept past, skirts swishing and fluffy butts wagging as they continued down the hall.

"That was close," she exhaled. Hand still clasped with his, she turned and pulled him up the steps, laughing as he wheezed and demanded that she slow down. But she didn't slow down, not until they were in her room, their backs against the door, both of them panting from the exertion.

"We're so pathetic," she shook her head, exhaling in mild disgust at herself. "I'm already sweating."

"Never," he declared. He leaned his shoulder against the door and grinned, voice teasing. "You're glowing."

"Is that what this is?" She swiped a hand across her forehead and threatened to wipe it on him. "Glow juice?"

"Hey!" Luke yelped and snatched at her hand, playfully tugging it away from his face.

She giggled.

But as he gazed down at her, the silly mood evaporated.

Julia swallowed. Her heart raced, pulse pounding in her wrist, where his fingers were still locked around her. Luke pressed a kiss to her palm. She shivered, the electricity of his touch igniting a path of nerve-searing need all the way up her arm.

He pulled back and met her eyes again. "*Julia.*" He whispered her name, a desperate, reverent sound. He bent his head and kissed her hand again, lips brushing first her wrist and then her knuckles and then her fingers.

Julia watched, desire careening through her as he nipped at her fingers with his teeth. One by one, he pulled her fingers into his mouth, sucking gently. Each tug pulled at something deep inside her. Her knees wobbled. "I think . . ." she began, swallowing hard as he stroked her with his tongue. "I think I need to lie down."

"Whatever you need." And then they were on her bed—her big, wonderful, king-size hotel bed—and he was stretched out on top of her, one long lean leg pressed between her thighs. "When I look at you," he said, caressing the curve of her jaw with his knuckle, "when I'm with you, I feel . . ." Luke sucked in a breath, his throat working. "It's like nothing I've ever felt before." He lifted her face to his. "I'm going to kiss you now." He dipped his head, then paused, meeting her gaze again. "If that's okay with you?"

"Okay," she echoed, licking her lips in anticipation.

His kisses were sweet, tantalizing nibbles, as if her mouth were dessert, a treat he wanted to savor and make last.

"I have to tell you something," Julia whispered, shivering as his fingers trailed over her hip, his teeth grazing her neck and his hands in her hair. "I might have had a few dreams about you in this bed."

"Really?"

"Yes, really."

"What were we doing?"

"Well . . ." She reached for his hand. "You were helping me decide on a new ranking system."

"I was?" His brow furrowed. "I suppose that makes sense. Ranking systems are one of the first things a developer learns."

Julia giggled. He was so smart, but also so adorably clueless.

He cocked his head and looked at her, mouth curling in a sheepish grin. "You weren't talking about programming, were you."

She shook her head, pulling his hand under her skirt and between her legs.

"Oh," he rasped, comprehension dawning. "*That* ranking."

"You remember, then?" she asked, cheeks burning with a sudden bashfulness even as she grew bolder, splaying his fingers wide and rubbing herself against him.

"Did you reach a verdict?" Luke asked, voice low and strained.

"Not yet," she teased, the boldness winning as she slid their hands into her panties. "I woke up before I could decide."

"Let's see if I can help you make up your mind," he murmured. He caressed and teased, his clever fingers tracing every intimate line, making her ache. Making her want. Making her need.

Julia moaned, hands dropping to her sides, fisting in the sheets as she gave him control, let him take over. She gasped when the rough pad of his thumb brushed over her clit. He stroked her there, back and forth, round and round. Slow, tender circles that made the tension build in deliciously agonizing spirals.

There was nothing clueless about the way he touched her. The way he seemed to learn her body so quickly, as if every twitch of her hips was a lesson, every sound she made a clue. She spread her thighs wider, wanting him closer. Wanting more.

In an instant, he was giving her exactly what she asked for, increasing the pressure of his thumb while his fingers slipped inside, stroking deep within her, fast and hard and sure, until Julia was gasping for breath, whimpering as her release rolled over her in a tsunami of sensation that left her limp, legs trembling with aftershocks.

Julia closed her eyes, the carnal bliss seeping into her bones. Once her heartbeat finally slowed and her breathing returned to almost normal, she glanced up to see him propped on one elbow, staring down at her.

"Well?" He rested his chin on in his hand, the picture of scholarly curiosity. "What do you think?"

"I think that was so much better than my dream." She lolled beneath him, a sated rag doll.

Luke's mouth quirked in a crooked grin. His gray eyes drifted over her, a look of such satisfaction and joy on his face that Julia felt another wave of emotion roll through her.

But this feeling wasn't lust. It was something else. Something more complex. A steel band wrapped around Julia's chest and squeezed. She couldn't breathe, couldn't speak, couldn't do anything but lie there, counting her heartbeats as they hammered against her ribs.

Julia had never believed the kind of moments that happened in movies could happen in real life. The kind where your heart stopped when you caught the gaze of that one person across the room. The kind of moment that made you feel all happy and silly inside. She didn't believe they could be real because she wasn't even sure if love was real.

That wasn't it, exactly. She knew love was real. The kind of love she felt for her friends and family. But deep down, she wasn't sure "true love" was real—the kind that made you say and do ridiculous over-the-top things the way people did in romantic comedies.

"How do you know love exists?" she asked suddenly.

"Hm?" Luke's voice was a distracted muffle against her skin as he dipped his head to nuzzle her neck.

"*True* love," she clarified. Unable to stop, because apparently she'd become that person in a romantic comedy who couldn't help spewing her thoughts and feelings all over the place, Julia pressed on. "The kind that makes your heart swell and breath catch. Makes your skin feel itchy and your eyes tear . . ."

"Sounds like a bad case of seasonal allergies to me," he teased, lips pressed to the hollow behind her ear. The entire time she'd been rambling, he had continued to kiss her, mouth moving over her shoulder, her collarbone, her throat.

"No." She shook her head. "I'm talking about those feelings you see in movies. When the character's face is glowing, lips twitching like they're afraid to smile, afraid because they're both happy and scared at the same time and it's both painful and wonderful—" She broke off, squeezing her eyes shut, struggling against all those exact feelings, even as she asked the question. "Does that actually exist?"

"Love?" he asked, sitting up. "You're asking me if I think true love exists?"

Her body suddenly cold without his against it, Julia swallowed and forced herself to meet his eyes. *Holy shit, yes, true love exists.* There, reflected in his gaze, she saw the look she was giving him. *True love is real.* It was impossible to escape the truth on her own face, and everything fell into place. *It's real, and I know . . . because I think I'm in love with Luke.*

"Yes," she croaked. Accepting this truth seemed to set every-thing free inside her, releasing a torrent of emotion. Julia's heart swelled, the steel band around her chest snapping. Suddenly, she could breathe again. "Yes," she said, inhaling deeply.

When he'd looked at her tonight, time had stopped and she'd felt something shift inside her. No wonder it felt like the earth had moved. She hadn't realized it then, but in that one moment, her world had changed. In that one moment, she'd fallen.

"Yes," she said again, reaching out and pulling Luke back down on top of her. "Because I'm starting to believe true love might be real."

CHAPTER 21

LUKE

Luke let her tug him back down, so close he could see each unique shard of color in her eyes, get lost in the forest of greens and browns. He traced the fine arch of one brow, marveling at the blend of colors. Russet and red and wheat and gold. If her eyes were a forest, her hair was autumn.

When did he start to notice such things—let alone become so fanciful? She inspired this in him. Turned him into some kind of poet who saw the wonder of nature reflected in her every feature. Made him hear music when he touched her. Made him want to sing to show her what was in his soul.

"Wait," he said, shaking his head. He closed his eyes, trying to focus on their conversation and process what she'd been saying. "Did you not believe in love before?"

"True love?" Julia squirmed beneath him in a horizontal shrug. "Not really. I mean . . . how do you find perfect love in an imperfect world?"

"Well, first of all, I don't think there is such a thing as a perfect love," he admitted, turning the idea over in his mind. "Not as you mean it. But I do believe love can be perfect."

She frowned. "But you just said you there's no such thing as perfect love."

"I did."

"Then how can love be perfect?"

"We are all imperfect creatures inhabiting this imperfect

world. Except you." He leaned over, kissing the tip of her nose. "You're perfect."

The tip of that perfect nose crinkled. "I thought you said we are all imperfect creatures."

"I did," he repeated.

She made a grumbly noise deep in her throat and glowered up at him. "Your explanation has a lot of holes."

"It's a sieve," he agreed, unable to hold back a grin. How had he lived so long without the pleasure of riling her up? Of seeing the little pucker of frustration appear between her brows.

"Exactly." She frowned. "It doesn't hold water."

And there was the pucker.

The urge to kiss her there beat hot within his chest, but Luke resisted. "True. But it does retain what's important." He watched her mull that statement over. "It's a metaphor. When you rinse things out in a sieve, the water passes through, but what you're rinsing—"

"I figured that out, thanks."

"Um, right." Luke swallowed. Had she figured out the rest of what he was trying to say, as well? He didn't want to presume to explain further if she saw his point. He knew how much his sister hated it when he did that, and as far as he could tell, Julia wasn't a fan of his "obsession with semantics" either.

"You were saying?" she prodded, a note of hesitation in her voice. Caution, not irritation. Luke could work with that.

"Right," he said again. "Do you know how, in math, a negative multiplied by a negative makes a positive?"

Her lips pursed. "Do not try and tell me love is algebra."

A brow pucker *and* a lip purse. How was he supposed to concentrate? Luke forged ahead, rolling them over so she was on top. "Actually, that's not algebra. It's—" He stopped. Took a breath. "What I'm trying to say is, it's *because* we are imperfect that my theory works."

"Imperfect, huh?" The beginnings of a smile ghosted over her lips. "Didn't you say I was perfect?"

"You are." He reached up, brushing the pads of his fingers along the curve of her jaw, tracing the delicate line from earlobe to chin. "Perfect for me."

"So that's your theory, is it?"

Her voice was teasing now, annoyance giving way to what he thought might be affection. But Luke wanted more than just affection. He wanted all of it—all of her. He suddenly realized this wasn't a game. This wasn't a strategic lineup of situations crafted to result in a particular outcome.

Well, it was—or it had started out that way—but it was not anymore. There was no guidebook for what was happening now, no manual for how he felt, no set of instructions for what he was supposed to do next.

So this is what it means to follow your heart.

Obi-Wan to Skywalker. Gandalf to Frodo. Merlin to Arthur. For the first time, Luke understood the words every wise old sage had muttered to every intrepid hero in the history of forever . . .

When the time comes, you'll know what to do.

And he did. He knew.

His gut tightened, nervous energy pulsing through him like a live wire cut loose. Luke pushed up into a sitting position, leaning back and bracing his weight on his palms. Face-to-face now, with Julia still atop him and straddling his legs, they were almost on eye level.

"It's not just a theory." Luke leaned forward, close enough to share her breath as he said, "It's real." He brushed his lips over hers, once. "What I feel for you is real." He kissed her then, putting everything he was feeling into that kiss.

She moaned and rocked against him.

The movement seemed almost involuntary. A reflex. And that subtle thrust of her hips set off a chain reaction inside Luke, desire flicking on switches everywhere, booting up his entire body. Like a power surge, the contact sent a blast of desire through him. Fireworks went off inside his brain, threatening to knock out coherent thought.

"Whoa," he rasped, pulling back. Also very real? The direction things between them were currently headed. He pressed his forehead to hers, breathing hard. His body was sending out a detailed series of commands, and before the program executed without his permission, Luke needed to get the situation under control.

"This is rather embarrassing," he admitted. "But it's been a while. Since I found myself in this, ah"—he glanced down—"position."

Julia followed the line of his gaze to where their bodies pressed together. "I don't think you have any reason to be embarrassed." She brushed her palm over the hard ridge of flesh straining against his fly. "Nope. No cause for concern." She lifted her chin, an impish smirk tugging at her lips.

The wicked, hungry look she was giving him turned the situation critical. "Ah, yeah. If you keep touching me like that, things are going to get very embarrassing, very fast."

"Oh!" Her eyes widened, and she shifted her hand away. "Sorry."

"Do *not* apologize." He took a slow, measured breath. "It's just, um, I wasn't prepared for things to go this far."

"Ah." Understanding smoothed her brow. "Hm." The pucker quickly returned as she considered their dilemma. "I don't suppose that's on the room service menu."

"No," he said, mouth quirking as a solution came to him. "But there is a convenience store in the lobby."

"How . . . convenient." She matched his grin. "Feel like going shopping?" Her gaze drifted lower again and she bit her lip. "Or maybe I'll just go."

Luke wanted to protest. He didn't feel right putting this on her. But he wasn't exactly in the proper state to roam the halls right now. Not to mention the awkward position he'd be in if word got out among the staff that he was buying condoms at the hotel mini-mart. "Are you sure?" he asked.

"Lately I'm not sure about much of anything," she said cryptically.

Before he could process that statement, she was in motion.

"I'll be right back." Julia hopped up and gave him a quick kiss on the cheek. "Don't move."

"Trust me," he promised. "I'm not going anywhere."

In minutes she returned, cheeks flushed, a little breathless as she hurried through the door. Julia flipped the security latch, kicked off her shoes, and vaulted onto the bed. She opened the paper bag and triumphantly pulled out a box. "Success!"

Then she turned the bag over and dumped it out. Several items scattered across the comforter. Little packages of chips and cookies and a few candy bars. "I also got snacks," she explained. "In case we got hungry . . . after." Her cheeks flushed.

Luke's heart lurched in his chest. She was so damn adorable. "I was worried that by the time you got back, you might have changed your mind," he admitted.

"Definitely not." She handed him the box. "What about you?" she asked, a hint of concern taking her excitement down a notch. "You still, um, good to go?"

In response, he tore the box open. "In the four hundred and fifteen seconds you were gone, all I could think about was how it felt to touch you." Luke stared at his hands. "To be inside you." He flexed his fingers and glanced up at her. "Did you really dream about me doing those things to you?"

"Mm-hmm," she hummed, voice husky. "Right here in this bed." She scooted closer, plucking a bag of chips out of her way.

"Did you dream about anything else?"

"Well . . ." She lowered her lashes and considered him. "In my dreams, you weren't wearing so many clothes." Slowly, Julia began to remove his shirt.

"And you?" he asked hoarsely, body tensing as her hands

brushed against his skin with each button. "How much clothing were you wearing?"

She laughed. "Guess."

His shirt completely undone, Luke tugged his arms out of the sleeves and tossed it aside. At this point, she'd seen him shirtless so many times, he didn't spare a moment for being self-conscious. Besides, he was too preoccupied with seeing Julia to be worried about her seeing him. He reached for the hem of her blouse. "May I?"

She answered him by helping him pull it over her head, continuing to assist him by wiggling her hips as he slid her skirt off. Luke paused, drinking her in. Even though he'd seen Julia on the beach in a bikini, seeing her on a bed, in her bra and panties, was different. Much more intimate. "Were you like this?" he whispered.

She shook her head. "Not quite." Then she reached behind her back to unclasp her bra, sliding the straps off her shoulders and down. He licked his lips, remembering the feel of her nipples growing hard against his tongue through the soft cotton of his shirt.

After their encounter on the beach, he should have thought ahead. Been prepared for the possibility at least. But his thoughts had not taken him this far.

That was a lie. He'd thought about it, he just hadn't believed things would go this far in reality—a truth that he recognized applied to so much more than physical attraction.

"It was more like this," Julia said, lying back on the pillows and removing the last of her clothing.

"I see." And oh, did Luke like what he saw. Rosy nipples, lushly rounded hips, smooth pale skin, russet curls at the apex of her thighs . . . He hurried to pull a condom out of the box. By the time her panties hit the floor, he'd ripped the package open.

"And you were more like this," she added, yanking on his zipper and tugging his jeans and briefs down.

Luke straightened his legs, trying to help her, but his heels smacked into the footboard. "Damn it," he growled.

"What's wrong?" She paused, hovering somewhere around his knees.

He demonstrated by attempting to straighten his legs again, kicking the curved wooden board at the end of the bed.

"Oh." She giggled. "You're too tall for the bed, aren't you?"

"It's not funny." He grumbled. "I hate beds with footboards. Why would a hotel have a bed with a footboard?"

"Hey, I like my big fancy hotel bed," she said, still giggling. "And this mattress is huge. I can't believe you don't fit."

"Welcome to my world." Too annoyed to feel awkward, he handed her the condom and shucked off the rest of his clothes. Then he shifted sideways, shoving cookies and candy bars off the bed was until he was lying across the bed on a diagonal. "That's better."

"It certainly is," she purred, examining every inch of his now naked body. "May I?" She held up the condom, tossing his request back at him.

Mouth suddenly dry, Luke grunted his assent, watching while she rolled it down his hard, thick length.

"Okay?" she asked.

"Okay." He gritted his teeth as she wrapped her fingers around him, sliding the condom snug against his base.

"Okay," she said, straddling him. "Okay," she repeated. Gaze locked on his, Julia slowly lowered herself, taking each inch she'd just been examining. "Okay," she breathed a third time, though it seemed she was saying it as much to herself as to him, sucking in air as she spread her thighs wider and took him deeper.

Luke held himself absolutely still, giving her body time to adjust—hell, giving his own body time to adjust to the tight, sweet grip she had on him. But then she began to move, and he couldn't stop his response, couldn't deny the urge to arch toward her, until finally her body yielded those last exquisite inches.

He was buried inside her now, as deep as he could go. "Okay?" he asked, no more able to stop the teasing grin curving his mouth than the groan that escaped his lips when she picked up the pace.

"Okay," she breathed, head lolling back, exposing her throat. He wanted to press a kiss to the hollow there, longed to fill his hands with her sweet, perfect breasts, bobbing temptingly above him with each thrust. But right now, it was taking everything he had to hold back the explosion building inside him as he let her ride out her pleasure.

"Okay, okay, okay." She was chanting now, that one word, murmured faster and faster, in time to her movements. And then even that was lost to incoherent moans and small breathy sighs.

Something about those sounds unraveled Luke, made him thrust his hips, rocking up into her, hungry for more. He felt her body stiffen, the muscles in her thighs tensing as she pulsed around him, crying out softly.

"*Okay,*" Luke grunted, letting himself go.

And it was better than okay.

It was fucking perfect.

Sometime later, snuggled under the covers and splitting a pack of Oreos while they watched a late-night comedian on the hotel room's flat screen, Luke had the sense that, in its own way, this moment felt pretty perfect too.

"Ugh." Julia glanced down, brushing at crumbs. "We're making a giant mess."

Luke grinned. Yep, imperfectly perfect. "Eating cookies in bed is one of life's small pleasures," he informed her. "Especially when it's not your bed."

He sobered a moment, thinking of how Penelope had told him that once. Ever the optimist, his sister could find something to be happy about even when her entire world was a shit show.

"Luke?"

"Hm," he mumbled, still back in that hospital room with his sister all those years ago.

"What's wrong?"

Noting the concern in her voice, he shook himself. "Sorry." He turned to face her, offering the last cookie.

She took it, eyes still on him as she nibbled one end. "Where did you go?"

"I'm right here." He brushed more crumbs from the blankets, pretending not to understand her.

"In your mind," she clarified, not letting him off the hook so easy. "You were definitely someplace else in your head just now."

He wasn't sure if her perceptiveness was alarming or endearing. But his response was surprising, because he wanted to talk to her, to share more of himself with her. He reached for another package of cookies, using the distraction to gather his thoughts. "I was remembering something my sister once said."

"Oh."

"That didn't come out right." He grimaced. "Being naked in bed with you is not what made me think of my sister." Luke held up an Orco. "It was the cookies." He split the wafers open. "My sister . . . she spent a lot of time in the hospital when we were kids."

"I'm so sorry," Julia said quietly.

She didn't ask for details, didn't press for more information. Which, for some reason, only made him want to tell her even more. "She had cancer. Childhood leukemia. Was diagnosed when she was six. The next three years were hell." He stared down at the two halves of the cookie, remembering how Pen would insist on splitting and sharing with him instead of each of them eating their own. Said they tasted better that way.

Luke swallowed against the pain of all those memories. The agony he'd watched her go through. "No matter how bad it got, though, she always found something to be happy about." He handed Julia half.

"And eating cookies in bed was one of those things that made her happy?" she asked.

He nodded.

"What else?"

He smiled despite himself. "Rom-coms."

"Oh, wow." Julia licked the cream from her cookie. "I bet she would love it here."

"Yeah," Luke agreed. He was threading the needle here. Not lying, exactly, but omitting significant pieces of the puzzle. "She'd design it and then probably want to run the place herself."

Hell. I am going to hell. Should he just tell her everything now?

"I bet you made her happy," Julia said, continuing to lick the cream from her half.

That caught him off guard. "I'm her brother." He shrugged. "I was there for her."

"And your parents?"

He winced. *Now she chooses to be nosy.* "They were there too, of course." He frowned. "But this strange . . . resentfulness seemed to develop. They never directed it at my sister, but it manifested in other ways."

"The other day on the beach . . . you said they were selfish."

"They were." He picked at the filling on his cookie. "My sister went into remission at ten; by the time she was twelve, they were divorced."

"You'd think going through something like that together would make a couple stronger," Julia mused.

"You'd think." He shook his head. "It was too much for them. Her illness. The difficulties of watching her suffer, the exhaustive schedule of hospital stays and treatments, the burden of medical bills." Luke shoved the cookie in his mouth, not wanting to talk about this anymore. Not wanting to spoil this special night by poisoning it with the past. Sharing a little about his sister was one thing, but he didn't want to taint the moment with thoughts of his parents. Those emotional vampires had sucked enough happiness out of his life.

"I can't imagine how horrible that must have been, but I think I can understand . . . a little." Julia said. She stared down at her half-eaten half of a cookie. "The summer before I started college, I got really sick. Nobody could figure out what was wrong with me. For a while, the doctors thought it might be thyroid cancer, but it turns out I had Graves' disease, which actually sounds much scarier than it is."

Sensing she had more to say, Luke waited, silently urging her to continue.

"I mean, it's scary but manageable. It's definitely nothing like cancer. I just need to be on meds for the rest of my life. See a doctor regularly to monitor my symptoms, and get my thyroid checked occasionally to make sure I don't develop cancer later." Julia sighed. "And all that costs money and requires insurance, so . . ." She broke the last bit of her cookie into two tiny halves.

"So . . . ?" Luke pressed gently.

"So you end up being forced to choose what you need over what you want." She considered the fragmented pieces. "And sometimes having to choose can make you resentful."

"Can't it be both?" Luke asked. "What if what you need *is* what you want?"

She laughed, finishing off her cookie. "That sure would make life a lot easier, wouldn't it?"

Her laughter washed over him, cleansing the bitterness from his thoughts. Luke pulled her close, scattering cookie wrappers and crumbs without a care. "All I know right now," he said, brushing her hair away from her face, "is that I need you." He kissed one corner of her mouth, then the other. "And I want you."

Luke woke slowly, disoriented at first as he shifted on a bed that was not his. Details from last night began to download into his mind, and he blinked. *Julia.* Instinctively, he reached an arm out. The space in bed next to him was empty but still warm. He sat up and glanced around.

She must have heard him stirring, because she poked her head out of the bathroom, toothbrush in hand. "Good morning, sleepyhead."

"Morning," he croaked, still groggy. He wondered what time it was. Without the corgi parade at the crack of dawn, he'd slept like a rock. The sex might have had something to do with it, too. His body was relaxed, sated in a bone-deep way that just felt *good*.

Barefoot and wrapped in a fluffy hotel robe, Julia shuffled out of the bathroom. Her hair was pulled up on top of her head in a messy bun that wobbled charmingly as she bounded back into bed. She was fresh-faced and smelled of minty toothpaste and lemony soap.

Mint and lemon. He liked it. He imagined waking up to those scents every day, of her face being the first thing he saw each morning. He liked that, too.

"What are your plans for the day?" she asked.

"Me?" His brain scrambled inside his skull. It wasn't fair that he was expected to think clearly when she was looking at him like that. Early morning sunlight streamed across the bed, lighting up her face, making her eyes glow, the greens and browns of her irises ever shifting, drawing him in. "Uh, I'm not sure."

"Don't tell me you're bored of me already," she teased.

Her voice was light, but he sensed the thread of concern beneath. This bond between them was so new, so fragile.

"Never." He nuzzled her neck. "I've been wanting to do this since last night," he confessed, mouth pressed to the hollow at the base of her throat.

"Mmm." She dropped her head back, giving him better access.

"Yes, just like that." Luke smiled, relishing the way her sounds of pleasure vibrated against his lips.

"What else is on this list?" she asked, as he moved to press a kiss to the tender skin behind her ear.

"Well," he said, tugging at the belt on her robe. He pushed the soft folds of fabric open, revealing her breasts. "Since you asked . . ."

It was a long time before he'd exhausted that list, and when they finally fell back against the pillows, Luke was ready for a nap. He thought he'd been relaxed before, but his bones felt like water now. Julia was lying on her side, snuggled against him, her back to his front. He traced lazy patterns across her bare shoulders. "How about we stay here all day," he suggested.

"Sorry, no can do." Julia laughed, the sound he loved tickling his chest. She rolled over to face him, wide-eyed and bushy-tailed. Clearly, their recent activity had the opposite effect on her. "There's a full day planned."

"Fine," he grumbled in good-natured defeat. "As long as it's not more karaoke, I'm up for anything."

She smiled. "Your singing wasn't that bad."

"See?" He matched her smile. "You admit it was bad."

"I am curious, though." She fiddled with the blankets. "Why *that* song?"

Luke wasn't sure he could tell her what he'd told his sister, didn't know how to explain it to Julia in a way that didn't make him sound like a lovesick fool . . .

Because that's exactly what he was.

"The song is about finding the courage to tell someone you like how you feel," he admitted. "What it's like to be near that person."

"Head over heels," Julia said, not quite singing the words, "when toe-to-toe."

"That's how I felt, the first time we met on the beach. Standing toe-to-toe in the sand with you . . ." Luke paused, struggling to get the words out. "I think I fell then."

"Yeah,, you fell." Her voice had taken on a playful quality. "Literally."

Luke's mouth twitched. He reached for her hand, needing to touch her. "Are you saying you didn't fall for me too?"

"No, I fell *on* you," she corrected, clearly relishing teasing him.

He grinned and decided to deliver some teasing of his own. "You've had your karaoke serenade, but did I ever tell you what *I* picked for my bonus activity?"

"Eating cookies in bed?" she suggested.

He shook his head, mouth quirking as he grabbed the nearest squishy weapon and held it aloft, priming for battle. "Pillow fight."

CHAPTER 22

JULIA

Tempting as Luke's suggestion had been, Julia couldn't spend the day in bed with him. It was bad enough that she ended up missing breakfast and Friday morning's scheduled activities. At lunch, she casually milked her table for details, grateful to Patrick and David for providing a play-by-play of the horseback riding excursion. Julia had thought riding a horse along the beach at sunrise was about as romantic as it could get, but their entertaining commentary painted a picture that was definitely more com than rom.

Afterward, she and her friends headed to the resort kitchen. Julia adjusted the floppy puff of a pastry chef hat, pushing it out of her face. "These make us look like we're in that candy factory episode of *I Love Lucy.*"

"I wish," Andie grumbled. "Then I could eat mountains of chocolate."

"You'll have to settle for a mountain of cookies instead," Julia said, halfheartedly punching a ball of dough. "Remind me why we signed up for this?"

"If I started listing all the romantic comedies with baking scenes in them, we'd be here all day." A seasoned baker, Kat had finished rolling out her dough and was already cutting it into shapes. "As my babcia likes to say, food is an expression of love." She grinned, glancing at the prep table next to theirs, where Harry and Sally were laughing as they worked together. Her grin faltered as their laughter gave way to arguing. "Uh-oh."

The couple seemed to be engaged in some sort of domestic

squabble. Sally was waving a wooden spoon in the air and Harry was defending himself with a whisk. "Think I need to break things up with my referee whistle?" Andie wondered.

"Nah." Julia shook her head. "They're just having fun with each other." She lowered her voice. "You should have seen the two of them go at it after paintball."

A wistful shadow crossed Kat's face. "I wish that was the kind of fighting my parents did."

Julia winced. Kat didn't talk about her folks much, but Julia knew it was a messy situation. She'd told Luke she'd be glad if her parents had been the type to fight more, but that was naive. She might not like the complacent disinterest her own parents had for each other, but it was infinitely better than the volatile household in which Kat had grown up. Was it any wonder that she and her friends liked to escape into the fantasy world of romantic comedies?

She reached out and squeezed her friend's hand.

Kat squeezed back and straightened, as if shaking off the dark cloud of her thoughts. "Baking is rom-com shorthand for bonding time," she said. "We can have some girl talk while connecting over a domestic activity."

"How very patriarchal of us," Andie observed drily.

"Oh, knock that judgmental chip off your shoulder," Julia said. "Baking isn't a gender thing. I've never been good at it," she admitted.

"We know." Kat tittered, watching as Julia tried—and failed—to roll out her ball of dough. "You need to sprinkle some flour over the top so it doesn't stick to your rolling pin." She added a handful of flour to Julia's dough. "And there's nothing wrong with enjoying time in the kitchen. I love baking with my babcia." Kat's blue eyes lit with a warm glow as she tossed a dash of flour in Julia's face. "She promised to teach me how to make kolaczki cookies this year."

"You win." Andie held up her hands in surrender. She wiped

the flour from her cheek and groaned. "Now I'm craving your grandmother's kolaczkies."

"Me too," Julia agreed, her mouth watering at the thought of the buttery fruit-filled cookies Kat's grandmother baked only during the holidays. "Arguments surrounding traditional gender roles aside, Andie does have a point," she added.

"I do?" Andie blinked.

"I think so." Julia waved a hand around, indicating the other prep tables. "Where are all the guys? Why didn't more men sign up for this particular activity?"

"Harry's here," Kat pointed out.

"Only because my wife dragged me," Harry said, grinning sheepishly when the girls turned to look at him. "Sorry, didn't mean to eavesdrop."

"Yes, you did, you busybody." Sally poked him in the ribs with her mixing spoon. "He's annoyed because I wouldn't let him join the group taking a boat out on the lake."

"Ow!" Harry tried to grab the spoon away from his wife. "You can bake anytime you want at home."

"And you can fish anytime we're at home." Sally dodged her husband's attempts to take the spoon and poked him again. "I wanted this to be special. Something we do together."

"We could be fishing on the boat together," Harry countered.

"And end up seasick? Or worse, risk getting attacked by marauding seagulls?" Sally asked. "No, thank you." She turned to Julia. "We saw what happened to you on the beach the other day, poor dear."

"Oh, the great bikini air raid?" Julia asked, flushing. "I survived."

"Now *that* was some romantic-comedy gold." Andie grinned.

"Easy for you to say," Julia grumbled. "You weren't the one whose top was snatched."

"Excuse me, that was *my* top," Kat reminded her, forming the rolled-out dough into shapes.

"And I got it back for you, didn't I?" Julia shook her head, re-calling the escapade, marveling at how the seagull had followed her and Luke, returning the contraband with docile civility. A strange possibility occurred to her. "You don't think a bird can be trained to do that, do you?"

"What creepy weirdo would train birds to steal bikini tops?" Kat wondered, still working the dough.

"Actually, that's genius," Andie snorted. "If someone thought of a way to do that, my hat's off to them . . . or, my top, I should say."

"You're hilarious," Julia observed drolly. "I mean, what if that whole fiasco on the beach was planned?"

"Why would you think so? Because it was so over the top?"

Julia glared at her friend. "Was that another play on the word *top*?"

"Guilty." Andie leaned closer, lowering her voice. "But if it *was* planned, then you better be writing one hell of a kick-ass review of this place, because that is some *top*-notch service right there." Andie grinned, clearly pleased with herself for sneaking one last bit of wordplay in.

Julia pounded her ball of dough, trying to punch down the guilt rising in her chest. Preoccupied with Luke, she'd been completely neglecting her responsibilities and had barely spared a thought for the review.

As if reading her mind, Kat asked, "Where is your serenading, seagull-chasing hero, anyway?"

Julia suppressed another wave of guilt. Hiding her identity as the *TrendList* writer hadn't seemed like a big deal at first, but the charade was starting to feel more deceptive. How would Luke react if he knew she was here to write a story about her experience at the resort—especially now that he'd become an integral part of that experience? "He said he had a few things to catch up on this afternoon."

"Maybe that means he's on that fishing boat?" Andie smirked.

"If he is, his puns are worse than yours," Julia said.

"Impressive, you mean," Andie insisted.

"I have to say, I was impressed by the performance last night," Kat admitted.

"Me too." Andie leaned sideways, holding a spatula to her mouth like a cigar in a Groucho Marx impression. "And we're not talking about Zach's smooth banana."

"Leave his banana out of this," Kat admonished. "I was talking about Luke's singing." She turned to Julia, blue eyes bright with mischief. "But since we're on the subject . . . How was his performance the rest of the evening?"

"Not everything is about the peen," Julia hedged. She hadn't told them she'd slept with Luke.

"Says the girl who got some last night," Kat observed tartly.

Julia dropped the wad of dough she'd been kneading. She should have known she couldn't hide anything from her friends. Not that she was hiding it, exactly. She just wasn't ready to discuss it. Not yet.

Andie broke the awkward silence. "Don't mind Kat. She's suffering from a one-track mind right now." Andie pointed to the counter. "Have you been paying attention to what she's making?"

Grateful for the reprieve, Julia glanced at the shapes lining one of the cookie sheets and blinked. "Are those . . . penis cookies?"

"They are," Kat confirmed, as she shaped another phallic ball of dough. "What can I say? My muse was inspired last night."

"Your muse, huh?" Andie quipped, wiggling her dark eyebrows and waggling the spatula again.

"Yes. My muse." Kat grabbed the improvised prop and smacked Andie on the butt with it. "You know how we joked about making dick pics more romantic by sending flowers with them?" Kat grinned. "I decided to take things up a notch. Instead of sending actual dick pics with bouquets, you can send a box of dick cookies with the flowers."

"A dozen dick cookies with a dozen roses." Andie tapped her

chin thoughtfully. "Now *that* would make for a more interesting Valentine's Day."

"I feel like there should be a better name for them, though." Kat considered her creations. "Dookies?"

"Oh my God, *no*," Julia admonished, horrified.

"You are officially not allowed to name anything," Andie declared. "Ever."

"Fine." Kat crossed her arms. "What would you call them?"

"Cockies?" Andie suggested.

"You're right," Kat agreed. "That is better." She added another finished piece of shaped dough to the baking sheet, a veritable army of cookie cocks awaiting the oven. "Since Julia already got her bonus experience . . ." She paused. "And I'm referring to the serenade," she clarified, shooting a warning glance at Andie. "When do you think we'll get our special activity?"

"What did you choose again?" Julia wondered.

"Stuck in an elevator," Kat said.

"Ah, going for some forced proximity." Andie grinned. "Fun."

"How does this all work, anyway?" Julia wondered. "Couldn't Kat end up stuck in the elevator with someone other than Zach?"

"Unlikely." Andie fiddled with some of the leftover dough. "One of the tasks of the game master is to monitor character interaction. A good GM will decide how and when to put various elements into motion, based on their observations, and even the most oblivious GM could figure out who Kat wants to end up stuck in an elevator with."

"Not to mention, I've been trying to find excuses to ride the elevator with Zach all week," Kat admitted. "But so far, no luck."

Julia tilted her head. "No luck riding the elevator with him or no luck getting stuck?"

"Or no luck getting lucky?" Andie added.

"All of the above." Kat sighed. "I'd just really like some guaranteed alone time with him, you know?"

Andie and Julia exchanged glances.

"What was that?" Kat demanded.

"What was what?" Julia hedged.

"Don't play innocent with me, Jules. I saw you two looking at each other. You're doing that thing."

"What thing?" Andie asked.

"You're judging me."

"We're not judging," Julia said mildly. "We're worried."

"About me?" Kat stiffened. "Why?"

"Zach's an actor," Andie said.

"I know that," Kat snapped.

Andie held up her hands, voice placating. "All I'm saying is, you need to remember what's real and not real."

"Do you honestly think I can't tell the difference between truth and make-believe?" Kat bristled. "I'm perfectly aware that we're participating in a simulation ."

"I've seen it happen before," Andie said carefully.

"I'm here to have fun. Play the game. Live the fantasy. That's it," Kat insisted.

"All I'm saying is, it's easier than you might think for things to get . . . confusing once emotions are involved." Andie placed a gentle hand on Kat's shoulder. "The rules of the game are hard to follow when you mix fantasy and reality."

After a tense beat, Kat relaxed. "I appreciate the warning." Her smile was still a bit stiff as she looked at them, but the anger had left her voice. "And you both should remember to be careful too."

Julia squirmed as her friends' words sank in. Her heart twisted. Just a few days ago she'd wondered at the possibilities. Tried to imagine where things might end up between her and Luke by Sunday. Now it was Friday, and so much had already changed; more than she ever could have imagined. What would happen in a few more days when the game was over?

"Don't worry about me," Andie said, bravado in full force.

"Julia's the one with the lovesick string bean serenading her. It's not like Curt is going to suddenly show up and pull some over-the-top romantic shtick like that."

"I wouldn't be so sure."

Something in Kat's voice caught Julia's attention. She glanced up. "I don't believe it." The timing couldn't have been more perfect. Like a stroke of divine rom-com intervention, Curt was there, skirting the other prep tables as he made his way toward theirs.

"Oh my God." Andie paled. "You don't think he's going to sing, do you?"

Julia noticed the stack of large white poster boards he was carrying. "I don't think that's his plan."

Sure enough, when Curt came to a halt in front of Andie, he didn't sing. In fact, he didn't speak at all. Instead, he held up his stack of poster board. A message was scrawled across the top one in black marker.

Andie read the sign aloud. *"To me you are perfect."* She snorted. "That's not very original of you, Curt."

"At least give the man points for trying," Kat said. "I don't see Zach doing anything like this."

"Yeah, give the lovesick butter bean a chance," Julia encouraged.

"Butter bean?" Andie's brow furrowed for a moment, then she grinned. "I see what you did there. Fine." She blew out a sigh. "If you can listen to your string bean sing, I can read my butter bean's notecards." She waved her hand, indicating Curt should continue.

He eagerly flipped through several more messages, and Andie continued to read them out loud. Soon, his stack had dwindled, the floor around his feet littered with posters.

"*Will you . . . Be my . . .*" Andie paused, squinting at the new message. "*Eno . . . suld?*"

"I think that one's upside down," Julia offered helpfully.

Curt glanced at the board and grimaced. He fumbled around, hurrying to adjust it.

"Oh!" Andie exclaimed, rereading. *"Plus one."*

He nodded, shuffling through the discarded posters on the floor. He picked one up and showed it again.

I'm not a perfect man. Julia smiled softly as she read it to herself. *Maybe not, Curt. But you're perfectly imperfect.*

"All right, Curt," Andie declared. "Yes. I'll be your plus-one."

He beamed and held up the last card. It had doodles of stick people cheering. Julia looked closer and giggled. He'd drawn them in Packers jerseys.

Andie crossed her arms. "What would you have done if I said no?"

He flipped the card over to reveal a crowd of crying stick people, tears spraying from their sad faces.

Laughing, Andie stepped forward, rewarding Curt's efforts with a kiss. Mission successful, he collected his poster boards and retreated from the kitchen.

"Well, that was charming." Kat turned to Andie, a smug grin on her face. "Care to revise your earlier statement?"

"Being someone's plus-one at a wedding is not planning my own wedding to that someone," Andie rambled defensively. "Besides, come on. It's Curt."

Julia exchanged a knowing look with Kat. She wondered if her friends did that to her as well—shared glances when they thought she wasn't looking—acknowledged awareness of the things she was trying to hide from them. Things she was trying to hide from herself.

"Was that your special activity?" Julia asked, skating away from the thin ice of her thoughts.

"The *Love Actually* stunt Curt just pulled?" Andie shook her head. "Nah."

"Then what is it?" Kat wondered.

"I'm keeping it a secret."

"Why?" Kat wrinkled her nose. "It's not a birthday wish. Telling us won't jeopardize your chances of it happening."

"Maybe she's embarrassed about what it is," Julia teased.

"Absolutely not," Andie declared. "I happily own my fantasies . . . I just don't feel like jinxing things by talking about it." Andie's gaze drifted to the cookie sheet. "Besides," she said, dark eyes glinting with humor as she poked at a doughy mound, "I'm spending my afternoon baking edible penises and just had a guy ask me out using flash cards. Do you really think I'm worried about being embarrassed?"

A commotion on the other side of the kitchen drew their attention. The resort owner, followed by her four-legged entourage, was making her way around the room, inspecting the cookies at each table.

"That has to be a violation of some kind," Julia muttered.

"Her outfit?" Kat's eyes widened as she took in the woman's ensemble. "I know. What would you call that color? Orange?"

"I was referring to having dogs in the kitchen, but yes, the dress is also a crime." Julia turned and watched as the woman moved closer. She considered the garishly bright dress, matched with a flowing shawl in the same shade of . . . "Tangerine, maybe?"

"I was thinking apricot," Andie mused. "Or cantaloupe."

"Well, it's some kind of fruit," Kat whispered as the dress in question, and the woman wearing it, arrived at their prep table.

"Good afternoon, ladies," Mrs. Weatherfork greeted them grandly.

"Good afternoon." For some reason, Julia always had the urge to bow or curtsy or something around the eccentric woman.

"I've just come round to peruse the goodies." She lifted a pair of old-fashioned spectacles hanging from her neck by a silver chain and inspected their cookie sheet. "Oh, my." She leaned in for a closer look. "Are those . . . ?"

"Cockies," Kat explained.

Julia swallowed a giggle.

Mrs. Weatherfork shifted her gaze, peering at Kat from behind her glasses. After a moment, she winked. "Well done, you."

Julia bit her lip, determined to keep a straight face. Beside her, she could feel Andie's shoulders shaking with barely contained mirth.

"I shall instruct the staff to be careful when putting your cockies in the oven," Mrs. Weatherfork said sagely, mouth twitching as she added, "I fear these may expand quite a bit in size once they heat up."

And with that, Julia lost it. She held a hand over her mouth, cheek hot against her palm. Her face was probably bright red from trying to hold the laughter in.

"I've been letting all my guests know," the resort owner continued, blithely ignoring Julia and her friends as they snickered like a pack of middle schoolers, "we've added a little surprise to the week's activities. Tomorrow night at the last supper . . ." She paused. "Oh dear. I've just realized how positively maudlin that sounds." She frowned. "Let me rephrase that in a less biblical manner. Tomorrow, at our final evening meal together, I've decided we should have a bit of entertainment."

"Do you think she hired strippers?" Andie whispered.

"That sounds nice," Julia said, beaming at the older woman while elbowing her friend.

"And to make it even more exciting, the guests will be providing the entertainment."

Before Andie could add more speculative commentary, Julia gave her another quick warning jab.

"Which is why I'm encouraging all of you to participate in the talent show!" Mrs. Weatherfork clapped, setting off her dogs, who began yapping up a storm. "Dress rehearsal tonight. Hope to see you all there!" And with that, the woman swept her orange Dreamsicle dress into motion as she and the barking train of corgis moved on to Harry and Sally's table.

"Talent show?" Julia groaned.

"I still think she should've gone with the strippers," Andie said. "I suppose I can show off some of my ball handling skills." She paused, adding, "I'm talking about soccer balls, in case you were wondering."

Kat primly wiped flour off her apron. "Some of our brains don't default to 'pervert.'"

"Says the girl who just rolled out a tray full of dough dildos."

"I've been known to enjoy the benefits of a personal massager," Kat said. "However, I wouldn't recommend using these for that."

"Point to Kat." Julia laughed. "She got you that time, Andie."

"That was good," Andie agreed. "But you're going to have to come up with something better than witty comebacks for the talent show."

"Actually, I have an idea," Kat began, voice a shade nervous as she continued. "If this is supposed to be the place we get to live out our romantic-comedy fantasies . . ."

Andie gasped. "I know what you're going to do!"

"You do?" Julia asked. She turned to Kat, confused. "She does?"

"I do," Andie said, grabbing Kat by the arms. "*Dirty Dancing*. The lift. Am I right?"

Kat's smile was almost shy. "I've always wanted to perform that dance for an audience."

"Do you think you can pull it off in two days?" Julia wondered. "Less than two days, really."

"She knows the whole routine by heart," Andie assured her. "What I want to know is if you think your boy Zach has the arm strength to do it?"

"You managed just fine," Kat reminded Andie.

"Wait, what?" Julia asked.

"We spent a summer obsessed with learning how to do that dance," Kat explained.

"I was Patrick Swayze," Andie clarified. "And I only dropped her once," she added proudly.

"Wow," Julia murmured. "That is quite the mental image."

"It would have blown you away," Andie assured her.

"We've got *our* plans figured out," Kat said, redirecting the conversation. "Which leaves you. What will *you* do for the talent show?"

"Is 'Be a good audience member' an option?" Julia wondered. Her friends' unamused stares were answer enough. "Fine," she yielded. "I'll talk to Luke. Maybe he'll have some hidden talent up his sleeve."

CHAPTER 23

LUKE

Luke rolled up his sleeves, grinding his teeth in frustration. Was it too much to ask that one thing fit right? One piece of clothing that didn't make him look like he'd had a mutant growth spurt overnight? Wanting to look nice for Julia, he'd chosen to wear another shirt from what he'd dubbed the Pen and Jay Makeover Collection, but it was still too short in the arms. He tugged at the cuffs, acknowledging that this wasn't the real reason he was annoyed right now. In his current mood, everything seemed more irritating.

Of all the harebrained last-minute ideas . . . A talent show? Really? Luke stomped through the hotel, searching for his sister. She wasn't in any of her usual spots. As he marched across the lobby, he thought he caught the sound of her voice on the terrace, but it was hard to tell, as it was muffled within a cacophony of barking. Barking that seemed familiar, but much louder.

Much, much louder.

When he stepped outside, he soon realized why. Instead of Mrs. W.'s regular quartet, there were easily a dozen of the yapping puff balls . . . possibly more. *What the hell?* Had Mrs. W. gone on a wild dog shopping spree and added to her corgi collective? Was she planning to turn the resort into a hotel for dogs? Or maybe the furry beasts were like gremlins and had secretly multiplied overnight.

His sister let out a peal of laughter, and Luke paused. He

didn't get to hear that laugh often enough. He hovered in the shadow of the terrace awning, watching Penelope as she and Jay struggled to get the herd of corgis under control. They were both holding several leashes in each hand and had become tangled around each other. The more they tried to unsnarl the mess, the worse it seemed to get.

"Can someone please explain what is happening here?" he demanded.

They jumped in surprise. Jay toppled backward, landing on his backside. Still attached to the tangle of leashes, Penelope was yanked down with him and ended up on his lap. She glanced at Luke, a strange look of panic crossing her face as she struggled to stand.

Perhaps clumsiness ran in their family. Despite himself, Luke chuckled. "Need some help?" He reached for his sister, hauling her to her feet.

"Thanks," she breathed. The corgis cavorted in a circle, leashes wrapping around her legs as if she were a maypole—or their pagan dog goddess.

"Does this have anything to do with the talent show?" he wondered. "Some kind of canine circus act, maybe?"

"You heard about that, then?" Penelope asked.

"The circus act?"

"No." She scowled. "The talent show."

"I'm fine down here, thanks for asking," Jay declared caustically, still on his butt, his feet and hands hopelessly lost in a tangle of leashes.

"Ugh, take these." Penelope shoved the leashes she was holding at Luke and then dropped to her knees to help untangle Jay. "Maybe this was a bad idea."

"I'm still trying to figure out what 'this' is," Luke admitted, juggling more leashes as his sister handed them to him.

"This," she waved at the carousing dogs, "was my idea." She

held out the last leash to Luke before clasping hands with Jay and helping him up. Pen nodded at a sign painted on a sandwich board near the entrance to the terrace.

"*Cuddle with a corgi,*" Luke read. He blinked. According to the sign, the event was scheduled to begin at four—about twenty minutes from now. "You added another event?"

"There was a lull in the schedule, and I thought this might be fun," Penelope said, the barest hint of challenge in her voice.

Not wanting to start a fight with his sister, Luke took a moment to gather his thoughts. He glanced down. She was still holding hands with Jay. They broke apart suddenly, as if sensing where his gaze had landed. He bit his lip, considering.

Normally, he wouldn't have spared the gesture a second thought, but the two of them were acting like teenagers caught smooching under the school bleachers or something . . . which was ridiculous. This was Pen and Jay. Luke shook his head. The idea of anything romantic between his sister and his best friend . . . No. He had to be imagining things. His fanciful romantic thoughts about Julia were making him see things that weren't there.

"Is there a problem?" Pen finally asked, the note of challenge stronger now.

Was she referring to the hand holding or the schedule change?

Jay cleared his throat. "I'm, um . . . I'm going to go check with the front desk on . . . something," he said, hurrying back inside.

"Coward," Penelope muttered. But her accusation lacked heat.

Luke tilted his head and considered his sister. "Just curious. Why so many?" He glanced around at the assembled group of corgis. They'd left off the yapping, thank goodness for small miracles, and were lolling around on the terrace, soaking up the late afternoon sun. "Mrs. W.'s four fur balls not enough for you?"

"Frankly, no." Penelope lifted her chin. There was no mistaking the stubbornness now. "I wanted the guests to be able to spend some time petting and playing with the dogs. If we only had Mrs. W.'s, there wouldn't be enough to go around. Besides," she added, bending down to scratch one of the corgis behind its pointy ears, "you know she'd never let anyone handle her babies."

"Fair enough," he agreed.

Penelope relaxed, the obstinate line of her jaw softening. "Remember when I was sick and the hospital would sometimes bring in dogs for the patients to snuggle?"

"Yeah," he said gently. Something sad and sweet tweaked inside his chest. "I remember."

She shifted, settling onto the terrace patio. One of the corgis she'd been petting hopped up, floofy bottom wiggling against her legs. Penelope laughed. "Those were some of my happiest memories from that time." She continued to pet the dog in slow, soothing strokes. "I wanted to share the joy of that experience with our guests."

"It's a good idea, Pen." He sat down next to her, heat from the sun-warmed bricks of the terrace patio seeping through his jeans.

She glanced up at him. "You think so?"

"I just wish you would have told me about it," he couldn't help adding, as he tied the leashes around the base of one of the heavy wrought iron benches lining the terrace.

She rolled her eyes.

"Where did they all come from?" He gestured to the myriad fluffy bodies surrounding them. Two of the dogs had taken up residence on either side of Luke, a furry fox face resting on each of his knees. "More importantly, where will they all go?"

"They're fosters. I found out about them through Mrs. W." By this point, the corgi in her lap had curled up and fallen asleep, nestling against her like a furry baby.

Luke's mouth twitched. "We're going to end up keeping that one, aren't we?"

She cuddled the dog closer. "That's a safe bet," she agreed, smiling unrepentantly.

He sighed and scratched the two resting on top of him under

their chins. It's not like he hadn't already been considering it. "What about the rest of them, though?"

"I have information for how to sign up to be a foster if the guests are interested. They can't take one home today, but they can get started on the arrangements." She grinned. "And we can always bring more of these cuties back again next time."

"Next time, huh?" He raised an eyebrow. "Let's focus on getting through this time first."

"You're mad about the talent show." His sister cut to the chase.

"You know how I feel about unexpected changes." Luke forced himself to remain calm. His earlier frustration had eased a bit during their conversation, and it was hard to be angry while petting a warm, wiggling ball of fluff. "Arranging for an afternoon cuddling some dogs is one thing, but a talent show? That's an entire production."

"Before you reach for your security blanket and start scribbling in your notebook of doom, hear me out," Penelope said.

Luke realized he hadn't even thought to get out his notebook. In fact, he hadn't thought about his notebook in days. Not since the paintball game. "Don't worry," he said, hearing the disbelief in his own voice. "I don't even have it with me."

Penelope gave him a side-eye full of *Who even are you?*, but she let it slide. "I admit, at first, when Mrs. W. told me what she wanted to do, I wasn't sure of the idea myself." His sister grinned. "I can never decide if her eccentricity is brilliantly bananas or just bananas."

"I've wondered the same thing," he admitted. "That woman really needs to stop introducing new ideas into the mix on a whim."

"That woman signs our paychecks," Penelope pointed out. "And it's our job to create the experience she envisions."

"But you can't spontaneously introduce new data and expect the program to run without a glitch," he grumbled.

"I recall you once telling me there will always be glitches." His sister smiled encouragingly. "What is it you like to say? 'Nothing is ever perfect. But things can be—'"

"Imperfectly perfect," Luke finished, flushing. Those were his own words. He wasn't lying when he told Julia he believed that. It's not like his sister knew about his private conversation. Still, it didn't stop him from feeling exposed. "Was this the secret plan you've been sneaking off to discuss with Mrs. W. all the time?"

"The talent show?" Penelope shrugged. "She told me about it a few days ago. Everything will be fine. It's not as big of a change as you seem to think. We'd already planned for a fancy reception with dinner and dancing. This is just adding something a little more than dancing."

Luke harrumphed. He scratched the dogs bookending his knees harder behind the ears, until their paws were thumping in time to his movements. "Well, there's no way I'm going to perform in front of an audience."

"You already did, last night," Penelope reminded him. "How'd that go, by the way?" She nudged his leg with her foot. "Did she like the song?"

A smile Luke couldn't control tugged at his mouth, taking over his whole face.

"That good?" Penelope whistled, which led to the entire fleet of corgis turning her direction in unison, pointy ears quivering. "I see why you might be uncomfortable with the idea of an audience," his sister acquiesced, as the canines continued to scrutinize her. "But you did it once, you can do it again."

"I'm not singing again. That was a onetime, never-to-be-repeated-in-this-lifetime deal."

"Well, if that's not an option, let's think," Penelope mused. "It's a talent show. What are you good at?" She paused, grinning impishly. "Besides annoying me."

"Ha ha." Luke considered the question. What was he good at? Computers . . .

"And before you suggest it, I don't think anyone is interested in seeing you write code in real time."

Luke's mouth pinched. He was not about to admit that was exactly what he'd been considering. He grimaced. Thinking of a talent, something he was good at—especially something others would be interested in—was hard. As with programming, it was easier to focus on the flaws. They stood out more.

"What about a *Zelda* speed run?" He perked up at the possibility. "My latest record for *Breath of the Wild* is—"

"Absolutely not. No video games." Penelope shook her head. "The point is for people to be entertained, not put to sleep."

"Hey." Luke covered the ears of the dog he was petting. "Careful with the euthanasia euphemisms."

Penelope blinked at him, unamused. "You could always do something with a partner. Why don't you ask Julia?" she suggested.

"How do you think I learned about the talent show in the first place?" Luke griped, irritation returning. "I really enjoyed getting blindsided by this change. She asked me if I had any tricks up my sleeve." Julia's question had taken him by surprise, and he'd panicked, making up some nonsense excuse so he could escape and find his sister.

"That gives me an idea!" Penelope grinned. The dog in her lap rolled over and she cooed at it, rubbing its furry belly. "I mentioned how much the dog visits meant to me when I was in the hospital, but do you remember something else that made me happy back then?"

"Oreos?"

"Well, yes, that was about the only food that didn't make me want to barf. That and lime sherbet. But that's not what I'm referring to." Penelope leaned her head on his shoulder. "Do you recall the name of that old magician who would come by the children's ward one Sunday a month?"

"Herb?"

"Yes!" Penelope beamed. "The Amazing Herbdini. You were fascinated with him."

"I was not."

"Were too," Penelope insisted.

And, in that moment, bickering the way they had when they were kids, it was like going back in time. Luke swore he could feel the scratchy nubs of the chair he would nap on in Pen's hospital room, hear the beep and hum of machines, the tense murmur of voices beyond the door, and as always, smell the astringent burn of disinfectant, which seemed permanently singed in his nasal passages, no matter how many walks he took around the gardens in the pediatric wing. At least he got to go outside for some fresh air. Most days, Pen couldn't. Most days, she couldn't do much of anything.

His sister turned her head and bit his shoulder.

"Ow!" His thoughts jerked back to the present. "Geez. You win. I was fascinated with old man Herbdini."

"Don't do that." Penelope stared up at him, solemn eyes the identical shade of gray as his own.

"Do what?" he asked.

"Go back there," Penelope said quietly. "It's fine to talk about the good stuff. Sometimes. But don't get sucked in by the bad stuff."

"You're right." Luke put an arm around his sister and watched as three of the dogs played a game of tug-of-war with their leashes. He checked the knot he'd tied around the bench, making sure it was still secure. His day was busy enough without having to chase a dozen escaped corgis across the resort lawn. "And yes, I did look forward to Herb's visits. He knew some cool tricks. It's been years since I've tried any of them, but a magic act is a great idea for the talent show."

"I do have them sometimes, you know."

"Yeah, I know." Luke glanced down at his sister. She was smiling, but he didn't miss the catch in her voice. He tightened his hold, pulling her closer. "You've done a great job taking over this week, Pen. I don't say it enough, but I appreciate all you do."

"Stop it." Pen sat up abruptly.

"Stop what?" he asked, truly bewildered. "What did I do wrong this time?"

"You're not Dad. I'm not Mom." His sister shook her head. "I know you appreciate me. I don't need to hear you say it."

"But I should say it." Luke shifted, turning to face her. "You deserve to hear it."

"Whatever." Penelope blushed. She scooted the dog off her lap and stood up. "Guests are going to start arriving any minute now." She waved at him to go. "They want to cuddle corgis, not you."

Luke scrambled to his feet. "Are you sure I can't get one cuddle?" He held his arms out to her.

Even as she rolled her eyes, Penelope leaned toward him. "Not bad," she said, squeezing him tight. "But corgis are better. Fluffier butts."

"I'll try and work on that," he promised.

"And you'll ask Julia to do the magic act with you?" Penelope pressed.

If she's still talking to me. Luke cringed inwardly. He might need a bit of magic to convince Julia to be his partner. After what they'd shared last night . . . And this morning, taking off on her like he had, wasn't his best moment. He needed to find her and apologize.

He gave his sister a reassuring smile. "Abracadabra."

CHAPTER 24

JULIA

The "stage" for the talent show was a sizable dais in the center of the gazebo, with a circle of folding chairs fanning out from the raised space. Julia sat with the other performers waiting their turn, attention drifting from the act currently onstage. The interior of the gazebo was spacious and elegant, with twinkly fairy lights dripping from the rafters. Near enough to the lakeshore that one could hear the crashing waves, the spot had a moody, romantic vibe.

Too bad all that romantic ambience was going to waste. She glanced at her friends, seated on folding chairs on either side of her. They'd arrived for the rehearsal only to discover that their partners were all MIA. Maybe Luke was going to bail on her again. He hadn't seemed overly excited about the prospect of performing in the talent show when she'd asked him about it. In fact, the man had taken off like a bat out of hell. She shrugged. She'd signed them up to perform together. If he didn't show, maybe she'd be off the hook.

Julia turned to Kat. "How does Zach feel about the *Dirty Dancing* idea?"

"He seemed really into it." Kat sighed. "Honestly, a little too into it."

"Why do you say that?" Andie wondered.

"He told me he needed go work on his 'Patrick Swayze look.' Whatever that means."

"It means he's staring at himself in the mirror while making sexy faces. Or feathering his bangs with hair spray." Andie snorted. "Probably both."

Kat laughed. "You're probably right." She nudged Andie. "What about Curt? Is he busy doing more wedding party stuff?"

Andie lifted one shoulder in a noncommittal shrug. "Possibly. He was rather vague on the details." She wrinkled her nose. "I swear I heard him say something about dance practice."

"Ooh, maybe they're going to do one of those flash mob dances at the wedding." Kat grinned. "I've always thought that would be fun to do."

"As your future maid of honor, I hereby declare that to be a *hell no*," Andie said.

"Hey!" Julia poked Andie. "Who decided you get to be the maid of honor?"

"You will *both* be my maids of honor," Kat announced.

"What?" Andie shook her head. "You can't have two maids of honor!"

"It's my wedding." Kat crossed her arms. "I can have whatever I want."

"How about you figure out who you're going to be marrying at this hypothetical wedding before we get too wrapped up in the details," Julia suggested.

"Too late for that," Andie snarked affectionately.

Julia laughed. It was true. Maybe it was because she was a florist, but when it came to wedding planning, Kat didn't have a list of ideas, she had an entire book. Her friend wanted the happy ending so bad.

If she was being honest with herself, they all did. Their own version of it, anyway. Julia wasn't sure what her version of happily ever after looked like, exactly, but she knew it wouldn't be like what her parents had. She wanted to be with someone who made her *feel*. Immediately, her thoughts turned to Luke. There was no question she had many feelings where he was concerned. But could she trust those feelings? Could she trust *him*?

She replayed the events of the past few days and wondered if the "romanticness" of their moments together was causing her doubt. The kiss in the rain, the make-out session on the beach as the waves crashed, the goofy, sweet things he said . . . It all seemed too good to be real. Imperfectly perfect, to use Luke's expression.

What if he was an actor after all? The suspicion had crossed her mind more than once this week. She'd even gone so far as to wonder if it was possible to train a seagull. But why would he do that? What would be the point?

Julia tried to shove the negative thoughts away. She had a habit of assuming the worst, and it had destroyed more than one relationship. Take, for example, any guy she'd dated in college. The better things seemed to be, the more she would second-guess and overanalyze. It was like she was *looking* for a problem. Waiting for something bad to happen to give her a reason—an excuse—for having doubts. Proving herself right.

This time, she had to hold out hope she was wrong.

"Earth to Jules," Andie called. "Come in, Jules."

"Huh?" Julia blinked.

"Oh good, you're not having a stroke," Kat said drily.

"I told you she was just tuning out the train wreck onstage." Andie winced as the couple singing a country music duet together hit a particularly sharp note.

"Sorry." Julia shook her head. "I guess I got lost in my thoughts."

"Well, I hope you found what you're looking for," Kat said, pointing. "Because someone is looking for you."

Julia caught sight of Luke on the other side of the gazebo. Her heart flip-flopped. "Stop that," she hissed, pressing a hand to her chest.

"What?" Andie cocked an eye at her.

"Nothing." Julia stood. "I'll be back." She made her way around the outside of the circle, past the clumps of people practicing their acts. She took her time, moving casually, when what she really wanted to do was run into his arms and wrap her legs around him while sucking his face off. She also had the urge to demand what the hell did he think he'd been doing by taking off on her earlier.

Face sucking first, though.

But she didn't do any of that. "Hey," she said, opting for an attempt at playing it cool. She crossed her arms and waited for him to make the next move.

"Hey," he said back. "Sorry about earlier. You, uh, caught me off guard. But I had some time to think and I was wondering . . . Would you like to do a magic show together?"

"Magic, huh?" She paused, considering. "To be honest, I didn't appreciate your disappearing act."

"I know. I really am sorry." He cleared his throat nervously, only adding to the awkwardness that she found irresistibly adorable. "You asked me if I had any ideas up my sleeve, right?" He grinned, throwing his arms out dramatically and pulling a bouquet from one of the cuffs. "For you," he said, presenting her the flowers with a flourish.

Julia took the bouquet. Completely charmed despite herself, she sniffed the blooms, hiding a smile. He'd won her over, but she wanted him to work for it a little more. "Hmm," she hesitated, voice teasing now. "You're not going to try sawing me in half or anything like that, are you?

"Definitely not," he assured her.

"Would you wear a cape?"

"Um . . ."

She raised an eyebrow in challenge.

"Yep," he capitulated. "I'd love to wear a cape."

"Deal." She beamed at him, not ashamed to revel in how quickly he'd surrendered to her wishes. "Should we shake on it?"

"I've got a better idea," he said, leaning in to press a soft kiss to her mouth. Electricity crackled between them. "Now *that's* magic," he whispered.

Julia giggled.

"Oh, God," he groaned. "That was corny, wasn't it?"

"Very," she agreed. It was the most ridiculous, corniest thing in the world he could have said, and Julia loved it. Her heart squished. "You want to hear something else that's corny? You make my heart feel like a marshmallow."

"What?" He chuckled in surprise, a low rumbly sound in his chest.

"It's true." She dropped her gaze, studying the petals on the flowers. "When you look at me, my heart puffs up. It gets all squishy and I feel warm and sweet inside."

"Oh," he breathed.

Embarrassed by her revelation, Julia risked a glance at him.

He was smiling down at her, gray eyes shining like a sunny sky after rain. "Have I ever told you I love marshmallows?"

Squish.

Julia was about to go up on her tiptoes and kiss him again when Penelope, the game master, approached. She was holding a clipboard and looked like she meant business.

"You two," she pointed. "You're going to be on deck soon. Are you ready?"

"Um, we haven't really had a chance to practice," Julia admitted.

"No problem," Penelope said easily. "I know this was all kind of last minute. We'll just have you do a quick entrance and exit on the stage for now. As long as you're sure you'll be ready tomorrow night."

"We'll be ready," Luke assured her.

Was it Julia's imagination or did he just exchange a strange glance with the woman? She shook her head. She was doing that thing again. Looking for trouble when there wasn't any. But when

Penelope grinned up at Luke, her gray eyes bright with mischief, something clicked into place.

"Holy shit."

"Pardon?" Penelope blinked at her.

And there it was again, that same twinge of recognition Julia had felt when meeting Penelope on the first night. That was why the woman had seemed so familiar. Julia had recognized those eyes. Eyes that looked so much like Luke's.

"You're his sister, aren't you?"

If Julia wasn't sure before, the uneasy glances passing between Penelope and Luke, as well as the guilt written all over both their faces, was proof enough. The marshmallow in her chest turned into a brick. "I can't believe I was such an idiot."

"Julia—" Luke began.

"No." She stopped him, not wanting to hear his excuses. "I can't believe I didn't see it before. I mean I did, but I kept ignoring it." She looked at him then, the warmth she'd felt moments ago draining away. "This is all fake." She laughed bitterly. "I know it's all *supposed* to be fake, but I thought you . . . I thought we . . ." She stopped, choking back the rest. "I mean, come on. Who says stuff like 'Whoops-a-daisies'? That's straight out of *Notting Hill*."

"Whether you want to believe me or not, I've been saying that stupid phrase for years," Luke explained, jaw tight. "But you're right; I did get it from *Notting Hill*. I told you my sister loves rom-coms. That wasn't a lie. After watching that movie together, I said 'Whoops-a-daisies' when I did something clumsy, as a joke. But it made her laugh, so I did it again, and what started as a joke stuck."

"What about us? Are we a joke?" Julia took a breath. "What the hell, Luke? Your sister is the game master, the GM or whatever. Why didn't you just say so?"

"That's my fault," Penelope cut in.

Julia turned to look at her. She'd been so focused on Luke, so entrenched in his betrayal, she'd almost forgotten the other woman was standing there.

"I don't know if you've noticed, but my brother can be, ah, a little awkward."

"Thanks, Pen," Luke grumbled.

"Joining the game has been a way to socialize more. Get out there and meet people."

Luke's sister seemed so sincere. And Julia had to admit, the explanation was plausible. She turned to Luke. "Are you playing the game as one of the actors?"

"No." He shook his head emphatically. "I was never one of the actors."

Like his sister, he seemed sincere, his words ringing true.

"Julia," he said quietly, reaching for her hand. "I was never playing a game with you."

And damn it, there went her heart again. Squishy, gullible, asshole heart.

"I'm, um . . . I'm going to let you two sort this out." Penelope met Julia's eyes. "I'm sorry if it seemed like we lied to you. And my brother can be mad at me for saying this, but I've never seen him look at anyone the way he looks at you." She paused, a sardonic grin identical to the one Luke made teasing her lips. "And he never, ever, sang to anyone else."

Julia watched Luke sister's stride away, returning to the center of the action onstage.

"I should probably tell you, I know about the review."

Ice flooded Julia's veins. She froze. "What review?"

He took a step closer and lowered his voice. "The one your friend is doing for *TrendList*."

"Oh. Right." She forced herself to breathe slowly. "My friend." Of course, being the brother of the game master, he would know about that. Or would think he knew.

"I hope that doesn't make things weird for you. Because, what my sister said? It's the truth. I've never done anything like that for anyone before," he admitted, almost shy as he met her eyes again. "I've never felt like this about anyone before."

Squish. She wanted to be wrong, but Julia couldn't help the nervous feeling in the pit of her stomach warning her that something about this whole thing with Luke was still off. Maybe that had more to do with her than with him. Even if it turned out he was as real as it gets and was not lying to her, she was lying to him. Or, if not lying, then withholding relevant information. And wasn't that also a form of lying? If she was being honest, yes, it was—which meant she'd been lying to him as well.

Julia could come clean right now, tell him about *TrendList*, explain how *she* was the one here to do a story on the resort—and oh, by the way, she'd been letting her friend pretend to play that role—but something held her back. Maybe it was because she sensed Luke was still holding something back, too.

Or maybe it was because she feared that none of it mattered anyway. She'd known, going in, that this whole thing was supposed to be a fantasy. No matter what she might be feeling right now, in less than two days she'd be back in Chicago, and who knows what would happen then? She should just embrace the moment and have fun.

Deciding to do just that, Julia did what she'd meant to do a few minutes ago, before everything went off the rails. She got on her tiptoes and kissed Luke.

"Are we okay?" Luke asked.

"Okay." She nodded, warmth stealing through her again as she recalled the last time he'd asked her that question. She was okay for now, and she convinced herself that was enough. Decision made, Julia led Luke back through the crowd of people, over to where she'd been sitting with her friends. Kat was absent but Andie was still there, bobbing a soccer ball on her knee. "What'd I miss?"

"What'd *I* miss?" Andie shot back. "I'd say I wasn't spying on you, but I totally was. What was going on with you two and the GM?"

Julia hesitated, not sure what to say. It wasn't exactly her secret to tell.

"Oh, you mean my sister?" Luke asked.

Well, that took care of that.

"The game master is your sister?" Andie asked. She dropped the soccer ball and it went rolling.

Stretching one long leg out, Luke stopped the ball's progress. He handed it back to Andie, glancing around. "I'd prefer you keep this information to yourself, if that's all right."

"Sure." Andie bounced the ball on her knee again. "It's none of my business." She stopped, dark eyes sharp and unyielding, as she added, "Just don't hurt my friend."

In the awkward silence that followed, Kat returned, accompanied by Zach. "Look who I found!" she declared.

"A bit late to the party," Luke observed, his tone sharper than Julia had ever heard it.

She turned to look at him, but his attention was focused on Zach, gray eyes hard and cold as steel. Julia knew Luke wasn't fond of the actor, that had been obvious from day one. At first she'd assumed he was jealous, figured he'd wanted to be the one spending time with Kat. But that wasn't it. There was something else here, an undercurrent of tension. Whatever it was, Julia didn't like it.

"Perfection like this takes time," Zach said, adjusting his collar. "You wouldn't want me to give anything less than my best, right?"

Dressed in black slacks and a black button-down silk shirt, it was clear the man had been doing exactly what Andie had predicted. "He's right, Luke." She tugged on his arm, surprised at the tension in his body. She stifled a nervous giggle. "I bet he was feathering his bangs with hair spray for at least an hour."

"Close." Zach winked. "I know how important it is to make sure I leave a good impression." He wrapped an arm around Kat's waist. "Especially when I have such a *special* partner."

"Zach and I are going to go practice the lift," Kat announced abruptly. She switched back to her fake British Bridget voice and added, "But first we're going to *take* the lift."

Andie chuckled. "I see what you did there, cheeky girl." She sobered and poked Zach in his silk-sleeved arm. "Remember to stay out of her dance space, Johnny."

Kat stiffened, blue eyes shooting warning daggers.

"Aw, come on," Andie protested. "I at least get points for the movie reference." She waved her hand. "Go on, get out of here, Baby."

Kat shook her head, mouth twitching with loving disgust, before she made her exit, dragging Zach along with her.

After they left, the tension diffused, and Julia almost choked on the gurgle of relieved laughter that bubbled up.

"You two want to blow this Popsicle stand?" Andie asked.

"I thought it was 'blow this *pop* stand,'" Julia said.

Luke shook his head, brow wrinkled in thought. "I believe the expression is '*popcorn* stand.'"

"Any bets the answer is 'D, all of the above'?" Andie grinned. "And popcorn is an excellent suggestion. I heard they were setting up a popcorn machine in the lobby. They're doing a movie night."

"What's playing?" Julia wondered.

"Shouldn't it be obvious? We're at Notting Hill Resort," Andie pointed out. "What movie do you think is playing?"

Julia glanced at Luke, that marshmallow feeling spreading all through her as he gave her a knowing smile.

By the time the film ended, Julia was stuffed with popcorn, cozy from snuggling with Luke, content in the tender afterglow of a good rom-com, and ready for bed. She sighed, enjoying the feel of Luke's arm warm around her shoulders as they joined a small crowd of other guests waiting for the elevator.

"This damn thing must be broken again," someone grumbled, poking the buttons in irritation.

"Again?" Julia met Andie's eyes and knew they were both thinking the same thing. "Ah, maybe we should take the stairs." She glanced at Luke, wondering if she should ask if he wanted to come up to her room.

"Can we escort you ladies?" Curt asked.

Nicely done, Curt. Julia smiled, nodding approvingly. He'd shown up during the movie, around the time Hugh Grant's character spills juice on Julia Roberts. Ironically enough, Curt had proceeded to spill his soda all over Andie, and the two of them had left to get her cleaned up.

Julia had honestly been surprised when they'd returned not too long after. Apparently, Andie was better at following the no hanky-panky rule than she was. And better than Kat was, as well. When they reached their floor, Julia pushed open the stairwell door to reveal Kat and Zach locked in an embrace on the elevator's threshold, their entwined bodies jamming the door.

There was no telling how long the two of them had been at it . . . Long enough for a few wardrobe malfunctions to happen. Kat's sweater was a pink puddle on the elevator floor and Zach's linen dress pants looked like they were about to drop. He stepped backward into the hall—and there they went.

Apparently, Zach's version of Johnny Castle went commando.

"Oh my," Andie whispered.

"It's not like we haven't seen it all before," Julia whispered back, as the elevator door slid shut behind the oblivious couple, leaving them to carry on in the hallway.

"Oh, yeah?" Curt asked.

"He was the model when we did paint night," Andie explained.

"Technically, he was the subject," Julia couldn't resist adding. "It was all very tasteful."

"I'd like to *change* the subject," Luke muttered.

"Should we go back downstairs?" Julia asked under her breath, not sure why she was trying to be quiet when it was clear that Zach and Kat were too busy getting busy to hear anything.

"What if someone else comes?" Andie hissed.

Curt snickered.

Andie punched him. "I mean, I know we're dealing with two exhibitionists here, but I don't think voyeurism was part of Kat's bonus activ—"

The elevator dinged, and a second later the door slid open, releasing a deluge of corgis.

"Uh-oh."

"Oh shit."

"This is bad."

Julia wasn't sure who said what, but she had to agree. This was indeed very, very bad. She stood shoulder to shoulder with the others, still huddled in the doorway of the stairwell, watching in suspended horror as Mrs. Weatherfork observed the tableau before her.

"*Mister Zachary Brennan!*" the woman bellowed, voice booming as she stepped into the hall.

Julia was surprised the wineglasses on a nearby room service cart didn't shatter. The sound was enough to set off a torrent of yapping, canine alarm bells. That got her friend's attention. Kat shifted away from Zach and took in the scene around her. Julia and Andie waved awkwardly.

"I believe this is yours?" Mrs. Weatherfork asked, holding out a bundle of pink fabric.

Kat nodded meekly, face flushing the same color as her sweater.

Zach turned toward the stairs to make his escape, and they got a front-row seat to the frontal view.

"Don't worry," Andie reassured Curt. "We already saw that, too."

"Stop right there, young man," Mrs. Weatherfork commanded.

Zach listened to his boss and froze, pants at his ankles, while the corgis ran circles around him, still barking.

The cacophony had begun to draw guests from their rooms. Doors opened and curious heads peeked out into the hall.

The owner of the resort ignored all of this as she stared her wayward employee down, bosom heaving. "You are aware we have strict rules regarding player intercourse—"

Another snicker from Curt.

"I've warned you about this," Mrs. Weatherfork continued. "Put your heart and soul into your performance, not your"—she paused and glanced down—"cockie." She sighed and hushed her dogs. "Oh dear, I find we are in quite the pickle."

This time it was Andie who snickered.

"Pull your damn pants up!" someone yelled from down the hall.

Zach bent awkwardly, tugging on his trousers.

"Party pooper!" another voice called.

"I don't want to fire you, but I have to consider my bottom line." Mrs. Weatherfork glanced up and down the hall, clucking her tongue. "Perhaps, if you'd avoided such a public display, I might have been able to overlook it." She released a long-suffering sigh and pressed the button for the elevator. When it arrived, she swept inside, corgis on her heels. She gestured for Zach to join her.

The actor flashed Kat an apologetic smile but did as he was told. As the doors slid closed, he blew her a kiss and winked.

Curt whistled. "You gotta admit, the guy has balls."

"I assume you mean that in the figurative sense?" Andie quirked a brow. "Though I suppose the literal interpretation applies here as well."

Julia ignored them and hurried toward Kat, standing alone in front of the elevator, looking a little shell-shocked. "Hey." She reached for her friend, pulling her in for a hug.

"You don't think she'll actually fire him, do you?" Kat wondered.

"I think it's possible," Julia admitted.

"But it's all my fault!" Kat wailed.

"I doubt that," Luke protested. He left the stairwell and joined them in the hallway, Andie and Curt close behind.

"But it's true." Kat's lip quivered. "I forced Zach to come up here with me."

"Forced?" Luke made a dismissive noise in the back of his throat. "Does he seem like the type of guy who would do anything he didn't want to?"

"No," Kat sniffed.

"From what I observed, he appeared to be a willing participant," Andie added drily.

"Oh yeah," Curt agreed. "Very willing."

Kat flushed and glanced around. "How much did you see?"

"Enough to know he was enjoying it," Andie said. She patted Kat's shoulder. "As one of the actors, he knew the rules. Don't blame yourself for the consequences of his actions."

"She's right," Luke said. "If anything, he owes you an apology."

Julia glanced up at Luke, grateful for his soothing words to her friend. She reached for his hand. "Change in plans?"

He smiled in understanding, bending to press a soft kiss to her cheek.

Curt bade Andie a similar farewell.

Their good-byes said, Julia and Andie looped their arms around Kat and headed down the hall.

"Do you ladies need anything?" Curt called after them.

"Ice cream!" Andie shouted. "And lots of it." She glanced over her shoulder. "Send it to the Princess Suite."

CHAPTER 25

LUKE

Luke finished checking his props and peeked through the curtain that had been rigged at one end of the gazebo to create a backstage area for those queuing up to perform. He was surprised to see almost every seat filled. Aside from the guests not participating in the talent show, he recognized many of the resort staff as well as a large group of people he wasn't sure about.

"Showtime in ten," Penelope announced, coming up behind him and tapping him on the shoulder. "All set?"

"Almost." He peeked through the curtain again. "Who are those people?" He pointed to the cluster of guests he hadn't seen before.

Jay moved to join them. "Oh. That's the rest of the party for tomorrow's wedding. They've been arriving all day."

"Why are they here?"

"For. The. Wedding." Jay looked at Luke like one of his mental files had been corrupted.

"That's not what I meant. Why are they *here*? In. The. Audience."

"You'll see." Penelope grinned.

"You two know I hate surprises."

"It's nothing to worry about." Penelope shook her head in exasperation. "The bride had a special request for her bonus activity, and we're making that happen."

"Listen to your sister," Jay said, munching from a bag of popcorn.

"Where did you get that?" Luke wondered.

"I had the popcorn machine brought down from the lobby." Jay tossed a kernel up in the air and caught it in his mouth. "Thought it would be a nice treat for the audience."

"A nice treat for you, you mean," Penelope scoffed.

Luke was pleased to note that his sister sounded just as exasperated with his friend as she had been with him. "Yeah, Jay."

Vijay threw a piece of popcorn at his head. Luke opened his mouth and caught it.

"No throwing food backstage," Penelope ordered. She nudged Jay through the curtain. "Stop acting like a child and go manage the guests for the wedding; make sure everyone is settled." She turned to Luke. "Showtime in five." She pushed him toward the roped-off section of the audience that had been reserved for performers. "Go."

Luke grumbled, but he went. He owed his sister for yesterday. When Julia had put together that he and Pen were siblings, he'd thought that was the end of any chance he had with her. Pen had stepped in and saved the day. His sister might have stretched the truth, but nothing she'd said had technically been dishonest. And when Julia had asked him point-blank if he was one of the actors and he'd said no, technically that also had been the truth.

But "technically" wasn't making his conscience feel much better. It had been eating at him all day. He'd spent most of the afternoon practicing the magic act with Julia. On the surface, they'd had a great time together, laughing and talking and generally enjoying each other's company. But an elephant-size shadow of doubt had lurked in the room.

He'd hoped to smooth things over with her last night, to spend time convincing her of the very real nature of his feelings . . . but that plan had been a bust once her friend the reviewer had been caught in flagrante delicto with Zach.

Perhaps it was for the best. Considering what Luke had been doing with Julia—what he still wanted to do—he was far from a place to judge. But it wasn't like he was getting paid to be with her. Another technicality his conscience wasn't buying.

Luke slid into the chair Julia had saved for him. She smiled and his heart lurched sideways. He didn't deserve her. Didn't deserve her forgiveness for hiding things. Wasn't worthy of the affection shining in her beautiful hazel eyes. But he was discovering that when it came to Julia, he was greedy and unprincipled and would take whatever he could get. Whatever she was willing to give.

"Nice cape," Julia whispered.

"Like it?" Luke adjusted the bright red satin monstrosity over his shoulders. "I borrowed it from Mrs. W."

"Are you a magician or a vampire?" Andie asked.

Julia and her friends snorted with laughter.

"Maybe he's a vampire magician," Kat suggested, leading to more giggles.

"Maybe," Luke agreed. He leaned closer to Kat. "Sorry you don't get to perform tonight," he told her. "Julia mentioned you'd been looking forward to doing that dance."

"Thanks." Kat sighed.

"I'm still willing to be your Swayze," Andie offered. "I'll even try not to drop you this time."

"I appreciate it, but I'll pass." She sighed again. "It's just not the same."

Kat was clearly disappointed. Luke didn't know how much last night's debacle with Zach might affect her review, but at this point he couldn't make himself care. However it might impact the success of this opening week and consequently affect Mrs. W.'s decision regarding the bonus, it didn't seem to matter as much anymore. Had mattered less and less since this game started . . . since he met Julia.

Luke frowned. He was far from joining the Zach Brennan fan club, but it was too bad Mrs. W. had to fire the guy. Kat really seemed to like him. An observation that also made him wonder whether Zach leaving might be for the best. It was clear she was forming an attachment to the actor. But was that necessarily a bad thing? How was it any different than what was happening between him and Julia?

The lights over the audience dimmed, and conversations died away as Mrs. W. took center stage. Dressed in a rhinestone-studded gown, she needed no spotlight. Hundreds of small bits of reflected light turned her into a human disco ball.

"Good evening, my fellow romantics," the resort owner welcomed her audience. "Love is in the air tonight. I can feel it. As I stand here, I can't help but think of tomorrow, and the two souls who will be joined together in this very spot. Before the vows are taken, before bread is broken, before the deed is done, the bride and groom have one last night. And per the bride's request, they've decided to share it with you. Kicking off our talent show this evening, I am pleased to introduce soon-to-be newlyweds Jack and Diane and their entire bridal party!"

As the audience broke into applause, a line of people dressed in long, puffy white gowns and veils appeared from behind the curtain and made their way down the aisle to the dais.

"I knew it!" Kat whispered in triumph.

Luke glanced at Julia, confused.

"Kat was betting they were planning a group dance number," she explained.

The music started, and everyone turned their attention to the stage. Eighties fan that he was, Luke immediately recognized the opening keyboard notes of Madonna's "Like a Virgin." The dancers weren't professional by any means, but they were committed, and it was obvious they'd been practicing. The moves were well timed and in sync.

It wasn't until the song got to the chorus and all the "brides" lifted their veils that Luke realized when Mrs. W. had said the entire bridal party, she meant *everyone* . . . bride, bridesmaids, groom, and groomsmen too. Based on the reaction from the audience, he wasn't the only one taken by surprise. Hoots, hollers, and whistles zinged around the gazebo as the dance continued, everyone onstage giving it their all as they writhed and thrusted in wedding gowns. Frankly, he was impressed by how committed they were to the source material.

As the song wrapped and the audience clapped, Andie fanned herself. "Is it just me, or did it suddenly get hotter in here?" she wondered.

A moment later, Curt appeared, veil askew. He made his way toward them, struggling with the frothy layers of his dress. He landed on a chair next to Andie in an explosive puff of white tulle. "Did you see me up there?"

"You were amazing!" Andie laughed, adjusting Curt's veil and giving him a kiss. She turned to Kat and declared, "For the record, this future maid of honor's answer remains the same. Hell no."

"Spoil sport." Kat pouted.

Mrs. W. had returned to center stage and had just begun to introduce the next act when a shout from the front entrance of the gazebo caught everyone's attention. Along with the rest of the audience, Luke shielded his eyes from the stage lights and watched as Zach Brennan strolled down the aisle.

What the hell was he doing here?

"I thought he was fired," Julia said quietly to Kat.

"He was . . ." Kat replied, her voice fading away as Zach moved to stand in front of her.

Dressed head to toe in Johnny Castle black, the actor held out his hand.

"Oh my God, you have to say the line," Andie demanded. "Kat, make him say the line."

Zach cocked a smile. "Nobody puts Baby in a corner."

Andie laughed in triumph as Kat beamed and took Zach's hand, letting him lead her to the stage.

"He certainly knows how to make an entrance," Luke

grumbled. But he had to admit, the guy could really dance. After hoisting Kat high in the air for the iconic lift, the actor swung her into an elegant bow before sweeping her off the stage in a flurry of thunderous applause. "And apparently, an exit," Luke added, when the pair didn't return to their seats.

"I think I know what they're doing," Julia said in a teasing singsong voice.

"Well, let's hope they make it to a room first this time."

Julia laughed.

"We're up soon," Luke said, standing. "We should probably get ready."

During the next transition between acts, Luke and Julia quickly made their way to the backstage area. Behind the curtain, the last of the performers milled about nervously.

On stage, Mrs. W. was addressing the crowd again. "I hope everyone has enjoyed their stay at Notting Hill this week. I appreciate you being here. After this next act, there'll be a brief intermission. But stick around for our last performance, because I promise it's going to be magical!"

"Ugh," Luke groaned. "I didn't know we were the grand finale."

Penelope shushed him. As the polite clapping signaling the end of the current act began to fade, she fiddled with a panel of switches. The lights on the stage dimmed. "You've got five minutes to set up," she ordered. "Go!" she barked, sliding the curtain aside and waving them out.

Luke glanced at Julia and she followed him, helping lift the little table of props and carry it down the aisle and onto the stage. He almost tripped on the cape a few times, and it was a damn good thing he was so tall, otherwise he would have fallen on his ass or face for sure.

They'd barely managed to get the tablecloth settled into place when Mrs. W. hustled over, pet parade in tow. "I'm excited to see you in action."

"Don't expect too much," he warned, suddenly apprehensive under his boss's avid scrutiny. Luke maneuvered his cape around the corgi obstacle course and handed Julia a deck of cards, then focused on laying out the rest of the props.

"Always so modest." His boss chuckled and turned to Julia. "I have this man to thank for bringing the magic of rom-coms to my resort."

Julia glanced between Luke and Mrs. W., confusion knitting her brow. "Because of his sister?"

"Penelope has been a godsend, no question." Mrs. W. patted Luke on the shoulder. "But he's the brains that made everything work."

Beside him, Julia stilled. Luke's heart leaped into his throat.

"I see." She was staring at him now, hazel eyes frosty as the woods on a winter morning.

"Listen to me, chattering away," Mrs. W. tittered. "Intermission is almost over, I better let you two finish setting up." Oblivious to the bomb she'd just dropped, his boss herded her squad of corgis to a row of cushions lined up in the front of the audience.

"Julia, I can explain," Luke began, his hushed voice vibrating with urgency.

Spine straight, her entire body stiff and cold as a mannequin, she refused to look at him. "Better make it fast," she bit out, mouth barely moving, wooden smile frozen in place like some creepy ventriloquist's dummy.

He glanced at the crowd as they began to return to their seats. What could he say? "None of this was planned . . . not at first."

Mrs. W. finished settling her brood and held up a finger.

They had one minute. How the hell was he supposed to explain the clusterfuck of events that had led them to this moment in less than sixty seconds? "When I met you on the beach, I mean. I didn't know." Luke licked his lips. "And then I found out about the reviewer—"

She jerked her head toward him. "You know I'm the reviewer?"

"*You're* the reviewer?"

Her façade cracked. He could see a dozen thoughts flash across her face in a nanosecond.

Luke's heart beat faster as the pieces fell into place. It made sense. The way she'd always been more interested than her friend in how the game worked, the questions she asked the other guests. *That fucking notepad she always carries around.*

He was an idiot.

To Julia's credit, though, she didn't treat him like one. She didn't try to weasel out of her accidental admission or backtrack from the truth. She simply nodded. She glanced down at her hands, and a sad, wry smile crept across her face. "Cards on the table." She set the deck down and met his gaze. "I guess we *both* were pretending after all."

He reached for her, but she backed up, shaking her head.

"I don't want to play this game anymore." She took another step away from him, and then another. She turned, stepping off the dais and running down the aisle, disappearing into the shadows.

Luke cleared his throat and sketched a quick, embarrassed bow before rushing off the stage. His instinct was to chase after her. He knew she was furious. He needed to find her. To talk to her. To try to make her understand. But understand what? He wasn't sure *he* understood everything that had happened.

Distraught, Luke shifted direction. Maybe he should talk to Pen first. She could help him make sense of things before he tracked Julia down and ended up making the situation worse. As he slipped behind the curtain, he plowed into Vijay and Penelope. Luke was so befuddled that it took his brain a moment to register what he was seeing.

His best friend and his sister backstage. Alone in the dark. Kissing.

And not just any kiss. Not an *Oh, you're so cute and I love you like a friend* kiss.

It was a *kiss* kiss. An *I hear music when you touch me* kiss.

"What the hell is going on?" he demanded.

Jay jumped back, shielding Penelope with one arm.

Did Jay think she needed protection? From *him*? Hurt and anger clawed at Luke's chest as he stared at them, stunned into silence.

"Luke." Jay held up a hand. "Let me explain."

"Explain why you're sneaking around behind my back and taking advantage of my sister?" Luke snarled.

"He is not taking advantage of me!" Penelope protested. "For once, mind your own business and stay out of mine."

"How long has this been going on?" Luke asked, chest heaving with the effort to breathe, as everything seemed to be crumbling around him, burying him under the rubble. *"How long?"*

His sister notched her chin up, stubborn jaw he knew so well clenching in defiance. "None of your business."

He flinched as if she'd slapped him. When he turned to Jay, his friend—his best friend, who was more like a brother to him— refused to look him in the eye. Luke stood motionless, staring at two of the most important people in his world, wondering how they'd suddenly become strangers. He turned back to his sister. "Where's Julia?"

"What?" Penelope blinked at him in confusion. "She's gone?"

"You didn't see her leave, did you," he bit out. An accusation, not a question. "Too busy letting my best friend shove his tongue down your throat."

"That's enough." Jay seemed to have finally found his voice.

Luke glared at them, simmering with a rage he recognized was out of proportion to the current situation. His nerves were already frayed, and unexpectedly discovering the two of them together like that, he'd snapped.

Beyond the muffled quiet behind the curtain, he could hear Mrs. W. apologizing for the sudden cancellation of the final act of the evening. In a moment, the show would be over. The audience would be cheering, the gazebo filling with the happy buzz of people preparing to celebrate. Luke couldn't handle that now. He couldn't handle any of this. On impulse, and more to be spiteful than anything else, he grabbed Jay's bag of popcorn and fled.

His mind a muddled mess, Luke let his feet take over, muscle memory and habit leading him down the path to the beach. This time of year, sunset was late, but since the resort was along the west coast of Lake Michigan, the sun rose in the east, over the lake, and set beyond the hotel, in the west. Which meant that although it was barely twilight, the beach was already shrouded in deep purples and dark blues of the coming night, the sky over the lake bruised.

Luke felt bruised. He kept walking, waiting for the waves to weave their spell, for the rhythmic pull of the tide to loosen the knots in his thoughts. Eventually, his pathetic legs demanded a rest and he hunkered down.

The evening air had turned chilly. Luckily, he was still wearing the ridiculous cape. He tucked it tighter around himself, laughing at the picture he must have made. Tall, awkward, skinny guy, glittery bloodred cape flapping in the wind as he roamed the empty beach. Maybe Kat was right. He was a vampire magician. Though that character sounded more like something from an angsty teen drama than a rom-com.

Tension inside him relaxing the tiniest bit, Luke opened the popcorn bag he'd stolen from Jay. He'd just reached into the bag when a familiar screeching sound brought him up short.

"You have got to be kidding me." He turned, and sure enough, to his left stood his thieving feathered foe. "Isn't it past your bedtime, Clyde?"

The gull cocked its head at Luke and hopped forward a few steps, leaving a trail of hash marks in the sand behind him.

"Coming to steal my snack?" Luke asked. "Guess what. I stole it first." It had been juvenile of him, but better than punching

Jay, which Luke had felt a sudden urge to do as well. "Here." He tossed a few pieces of popcorn in the seagull's direction. "Let me save you the trouble."

Clyde scooped the popcorn up in his beak and hopped closer. Luke tossed out a few more kernels for the bird before scooping a handful for himself. For a few minutes, they watched the waves, munching in companionable silence.

"This is nice, Clyde," Luke said, nodding to the bird. "I'm glad I ran into you this evening."

Good lord, he'd gone off the deep end. Thinking about sharing companionable silence with a seagull? He was becoming more eccentric than his boss. *Ugh, his boss.* That was another situation Luke needed to figure out. He'd royally screwed up tonight. Julia had waved goodbye to him, and he might as well wave goodbye to that bonus.

How the hell was he supposed to demonstrate he'd successfully proven the fantasy of a romantic comedy can feel real when he couldn't even convince himself?

The thing was, it *had* felt real. In the middle of this charade, where everyone was pretending, Luke had believed he'd found someone, had even started to think he had a chance at a happily ever after. And that might be the most painfully ironic thing about this entire messed up situation.

Luke shook his head and set the popcorn bag aside. He leaned back, palms pressing into the cool sand as he watched the horizon blur, the sky over the lake turning ever darker. He thought about Julia, about the walk they'd taken on this beach.

At the time, they'd both been hiding things, but what they shared that day had been honest. They'd opened up to each other, revealed parts of themselves. And there was no denying there was something special between them. He knew that much was true.

But he also knew she'd lied to him. Right to his face. Luke understood why Julia didn't tell him who she was at first. Hell, he'd been doing much the same. And they'd both had their reasons. What he couldn't understand was why she'd kept up the deception.

A flurry of movement startled him, and his hands slipped. His back smacked into the ground. *"Clyde."* Luke gritted his teeth. While he'd been distracted, the asshole had swooped in and snatched the popcorn bag.

"I was sharing that with you," Luke called after the bird, who was scampering up a grassy hill, contraband clamped in his beak. "I thought we had a truce!"

Clyde's abrupt abandonment hurt more than Luke cared to admit. He stood up, brushing sand from his palms, and hurried after the kleptomaniac seagull. "You have a problem, Clyde. You know that? I swear, you'll steal anything that isn't nailed down."

Luke topped the hill and realized it was the same spot he and Julia had ended up the other afternoon, when the little thief had taken off with her bathing suit top. Clyde was dragging his loot to the rocky outcrop where his nest was hidden. The gull released the bag and flew to the nest where the other gull—Bonnie, Luke assumed—sat perched.

It was like watching a tag team in action. As soon as Clyde had settled himself in the nest, Bonnie made the short flight to the popcorn bag. Luke chuckled. "You sly devil. She really is your partner in crime."

Careful not to startle the bird, Luke reached out and turned the bag over, dumping out the remaining popcorn. Then he crept closer to the nest, a hunch forming. At Luke's approach, Clyde stood, wings spreading in warning. "Easy buddy. Easy," he said soothingly.

Glancing down at the nest, his suspicions were confirmed. Secured within the cozy hodgepodge of beach debris were three speckled seagull eggs. "Congratulations," he said, lifting his hand in a mock toast and backing away slowly. After a moment, the bird relaxed, resettling himself over his brood.

Luke realized that Clyde had brought the popcorn back to the nest for Bonnie and had taken over egg-sitting duties while his partner enjoyed her snack. "I owe you an apology." Staying a safe distance from the nest, Luke eased down. "You are quite the gentleman," he commended Clyde. "At least somebody around here gets to have a happy ending."

The bird let out a low squawk.

"That sounded awfully judgy, Clyde." Luke stared at the gull, whose beady black eyes stared right back. "But you make a good point. I should have been more of a gentleman myself. Not just with Julia, but with my sister, too."

Another squawk.

"You're right. I do owe them both an apology." He sighed. "I need to fix things with Penelope first; maybe she can help me figure out what to do about Julia." If anyone asked Luke why he was talking to a bird, he'd probably deny it. But it felt good to work through things with someone . . . even if that someone happened to be a seagull.

Bonnie finished off the last of the popcorn and ambled casually past Luke on her way back to the nest. As his partner settled in beside him, Clyde flapped his wings and squawked dismissively.

"Rude!" Luke declared. "I got the hint. I'm going." He stood, the ostentatious fabric unfurling around him. A noise that sounded disturbingly like a bird laughing drifted from the nest. He whirled around, cape flying. "This isn't even mine, I'll have you know."

Feeling completely absurd and strangely comforted at the same time, Luke bade Clyde and Bonnie and their growing little family good night. He smiled to himself. The sweet picture they made, cuddled up in the nest together, fortified his resolve to make things right in his own life.

CHAPTER 26

JULIA

⌒

Julia marched up the path from the gazebo, back to the hotel. She could have stayed and talked to Luke. Demanded answers. But what good would that do? He'd had the chance to be honest with her and had chosen to snake around the truth.

How did that saying go? "Fool me once . . ."

No. It wasn't worth risking her heart to hear more excuses. When she'd first made the connection between Luke and Penelope, she'd been so quick to accept their explanations. She'd capitulated so easily. Because she wanted to. She still wanted to. Even when she knew this had all been a game to him.

Was she the reviewer? Yes, you bet your sweet ass she was. And she was ready to purge her emotions in a scathing review.

But by the time Julia reached her room, she'd reconsidered that plan. Even in the midst of her anger, she knew she was better than that. She may not have the intestinal fortitude to stick around and face Luke, but she wasn't going to rip apart this resort just because her feelings had been hurt.

Having talked herself down from engaging in petty revenge journalism, Julia decided she couldn't sit in her hotel room and brood. This was her last night here. She should grab a drink at the bar downstairs or take a walk along the beach. Maybe do both. She ditched the heels she'd been wearing to play magician's assistant and slipped on some sandals.

Two perfectly chilled glasses of buttery chardonnay later, Julia was feeling more chill. Her legs were a little buttery, too. She slipped off the bar stool and wandered onto the hotel terrace for some fresh air.

Outside, the summer night was alive with conversation and laughter. Couples were seated at quaint candlelit tables, enjoying soft music and a sweet breeze blowing in from the lake. Julia's smile was bittersweet as she soaked in the romantic atmosphere. It would have been lovely to spend time here with Luke this evening.

A pang of acute loneliness hit her. But it went deeper than simply wishing she was with Luke tonight. Her reaction to his subterfuge stemmed from more than her disappointment at being lied to—and she recognized he hadn't outright lied, just withheld relevant information. Julia wasn't such a hypocrite that she could ignore the fact that she'd done the same. She'd let him believe Kat was the reviewer.

That's what hurt most—that, given the opportunity to be fully honest with each other, they'd both chosen to hide. To play pretend. How could any meaningful relationship develop with such a false foundation? It was a house of cards. And that's what she was really mourning. Not just losing the chance to spend her last night here with Luke but also losing the chance at having something more with him, something that went beyond this week of fantasy.

She hadn't known where things were going to go with Luke after this week ended, but the possibility had been there. Now that possibility was gone, hope for something more snuffed out like one of the candles dotting the tables, lighting the blissful faces of the couples all around her.

With an indulgent sigh of self-pity, Julia walked to the edge of the terrace and propped her elbows on the ledge. The twilight sky was magnificent, a blurred mesh of indigo and violet over the lake. In addition to the lovebirds on the terrace, more couples strolled along the beach below.

Julia had no way of knowing how many of the pairings were

made here as part of the fun and how many had arrived together like David and Patrick or Harry and Sally, but everyone seemed so *content*. How could she write a review tearing this place down when it delivered exactly what it promised? As upset as she was, she couldn't deny that all week long she'd felt like she was living in a romantic comedy, even as she actively tried to dismiss those feelings.

Lost in her thoughts, she continued to scan the beach, enjoying a bit of people watching. Someone had built a bonfire on the shore, and as she looked closer, she realized the couple snuggling in front of the cozy-looking blaze was Andie and Curt—and they seemed cozy, indeed. Their faces were glowing, and from more than the flames.

Julia noted that while he'd ditched the veil, Curt was still in his bridal dress from the dance number. She grinned, laughing softly. A quiet joy lit inside her for her friend. Curt wasn't like any of the guys Andie typically went for . . . he was much closer to their age. In fact, he might even be younger than they were, silly and carefree. He was unpolished, a bit rough around the edges, and from what little Julia knew of his life, it seemed far from set.

Andie usually got involved with men who had retirement funds and corporate haircuts. Julia wasn't sure why her friend was drawn to that type. Was it a yearning for stability? Andie's parents had a great relationship. Julia and Kat had often discussed how they envied their friend and the kind of household she grew up in—with parents who loved and respected each other. She knew that appearances weren't everything, but as far as she could tell, Andie's parents' marriage was as happy and real as it seemed.

True, Andie's dad was several years older than her mother, and she did have two much older stepbrothers . . . Julia blinked. For the first time, it finally clicked. Consciously or unconsciously, Andie was following in her mother's footsteps and choosing to date men like her father. How had Julia never made that connection before? It wasn't a bad thing, necessarily, but it did cut Andie off from playing the field a bit more, from seeing what else was out there.

Here, in the safety of the rom-com fantasy bubble, Andie had allowed herself to be open to new possibilities—and in doing so had opened her heart. If Julia needed proof that Notting Hill could provide the experience people who love romantic comedies wished for, her friend's budding opposites-attract relationship was a prime example.

Mentally sidestepping dissecting her own budding relationship—one that had been nipped in the bud before it could fully blossom—Julia's thoughts turned to Kat. She wondered how things were going with Zach. His unexpected appearance tonight had been wildly romantic, if a tad cheesy. Besides, Julia had already discovered she had a penchant for romances with extra cheese.

As if her thoughts had conjured her friend, Kat came running up the stone steps of the terrace. Julia took one look at Kat's tear-streaked face and knew whatever had happened, those were not happy tears. She shifted away from her spot at the ledge and met Kat at the top of the stairs, holding out her arms for a hug.

⁓

Upstairs in the Princess Suite, after commandeering a bottle of that chardonnay from the bar, Julia poured them each a glass while Kat shared what happened with Zach after their dramatic exit from the stage.

"I knew he was an actor. That part didn't bother me. I was perfectly happy to let him shower me in attention for a week." Kat took a gulp of her wine. "Oh, wow, that's good." She sniffed and downed the rest.

"Easy there," Julia warned. "I had two glasses earlier, and it's good, but it's also strong." She refilled Kat's glass, asking gently, "So what went wrong?"

"You and Andie believed Zach was assigned to me because the hotel assumed I was the reviewer. But I convinced myself he was spending time with me because he wanted to." Kat shrugged, sipping her second glass more slowly. "I didn't tell you this before, but last night, when we finally got stuck in the elevator together, I asked him about it."

"You asked Zach if he knew you were the reviewer?"

"He admitted he'd heard something. And you were right. That girl, Penelope—the game master or whatever—did assign him to me. But Zach said none of that mattered because he enjoyed being with me. And then one thing led to another, and you know what happened after that." Kat blushed.

"I'm confused," Julia admitted. "How did we go from making out in an elevator last night to you crying as you ran up the steps tonight?" She paused, a suspicion forming. "That whole Johnny Castle routine . . . You don't think the hotel planned it, do you? Oh, God. What if they fake fired him?"

"I wish that was what happened," Kat said ruefully. "Then maybe I might feel less pathetic." She sank lower into the plush cushions. "I thought he came back because he cared for me. He wasn't working for the resort anymore, so his motivation had to be pure, right?"

"I'm sensing this is a rhetorical question," Julia said carefully.

"Give the lady a prize." Kat's tone was bitter. "He came back because of that stupid review. After we left the stage, I thought we were going to have a romantic night, maybe finish what we started in the elevator . . . but all he wanted to do was talk about *TrendList*." Kat knocked back the rest of her wine. "Kept going on about what a fabulous performance our dance had been and wasn't I blown away by his surprise entrance at the talent show. You would not believe how many times he asked me if I wanted to write his name down so I would spell it right in the review. Spoiler alert—it was a lot."

"Oh, Kat." Julia's heart ached at the defeated note in her

friend's voice, the way she seemed to shrink into herself. "I'm so sorry."

"At first, I thought it was me, you know? My typical need to self-sabotage."

Julia began to protest, but Kat stopped her.

"You know I do it; don't try and pretend otherwise." Kat shook her head. "It's a game I play with myself. Some misguided attempt to avoid disappointment. I date jerks because I know, in the end, things will never work out. And that's how it started with Zach. Why not have some fun with a hot guy in a relationship that I know is fake from the start?"

"And then you started to fall for him?" Julia guessed.

"Don't I always?" Kat asked. "In case it wasn't clear, that was another rhetorical question," she added drily. "It doesn't matter how obviously wrong a guy is for me, I always end up falling for him. In fact, I think the worse he is for me, the harder I fall." A burst of mocking laughter escaped her. "How do I expect to find Mr. Right if I'm always chasing after Mr. Wrong?"

Julia wasn't sure what to say to that. She knew Kat didn't want or need platitudes. She needed a friend. An honest one. "It's true, your track record isn't the greatest . . ."

"That's putting it nicely," Kat said, grimacing. "My radar is broken. I'm broken."

"You are *not* broken." Julia set her wineglass down and scooted closer.

Kat stared into her empty glass, twirling the stem between her fingers. "Growing up, the way my parents treated each other . . . the way they treated me . . ." She swallowed. "I don't think I know how to love someone right." She looked at Julia, blue eyes filled with a tired sadness, a world-weary acceptance more suited to someone way beyond her years. "I don't think I know what love looks like or what it should feel like."

"Bullshit," Julia declared.

Kat blinked.

"You do have a tendency to fall for guys who are wrong for you. I'm not going to argue with you there." Julia took Kat's glass and set it aside, then reached for her friend's hand. "But I think maybe your choices have less to do with your 'radar' and more to do with the fact that you don't believe you deserve love."

Julia expected Kat to get defensive. Instead, she cocked her head, face guarded but curious.

"You think you don't deserve better than the jerks you pick to date, and that's simply not true. You have such a big heart. I've seen it over and over again in our friendship. You think you don't know how to love? I say that's bullshit, because I know otherwise. I've seen it in the love you give to me and Andie. The love you have for your grandmother . . ."

"I do love you both, and I love my babcia—I'd be lost without her, without you—but that's different than romantic love." Kat pulled her hand out of Julia's grasp, studying her fingers. "I got into the floral business because I enjoyed helping make the special moments in peoples' lives feel even more special. Flowers are supposed to be the language of love. I thought I'd see proof of love all the time." She shrugged. "And sometimes, I do. But more often, I see assholes sending *Sorry for banging the secretary; it will never happen again* bouquets to their wives while simultaneously ordering *Thanks for the awesome BJ; let's do it again soon* bouquets for said secretaries."

"You're right. There are a lot of assholes out there," Julia agreed. "I have to admit my own faith in romantic love is at an all-time low right now."

"Why?" Kat straightened, brows furrowed with concern. "Did something happen with Luke?"

Julia laughed and refilled both their glasses.

"That bad, huh?" Kat asked. She picked up her wine, swirling the golden liquid. "Well, I've got no other plans tonight, so why don't you tell me all about it."

Whether it was the booze, the fact that misery loved company, or the simple peace of unpacking her sorrows with a dear friend, as Julia shared the details of how her own evening had taken a wrong turn, her heartache eased a bit, the weight of her thoughts lightened, and the long night ahead became a little brighter.

CHAPTER 27

LUKE

It was fully dark by the time Luke made his way back along the beach toward the resort, the night sky lit by a fat full moon hanging low on the horizon. The sand glowed with a pale luminescence and the waves crashed softly. The effect was all achingly beautiful, a night tailor-made for romantic moments. Too bad his most intimate moment this evening was spent with a seagull.

A bonfire was blazing along the shore. Luke recognized Julia's friend Andie and waved, but she didn't notice—too wrapped up in her own intimate moment with Curt. He shook his head, smiling to himself as he recalled the antagonism between those two at the start of the week. Who could have seen that coming? His sister, probably. Which was another surprise entirely, and one he should have seen a long time ago.

A lot had happened this week that he couldn't have predicted. Luke sighed and started up the steps to the hotel. A few couples still lingered on the terrace, talking in low murmurs, flickering candlelight casting their faces in light and shadow. He didn't see Pen and Jay among them. He headed upstairs, bracing himself as he knocked on the door to his sister's suite.

It took a moment for her to answer, and every second he stood there in the hall he debated hightailing it out of there and escaping to his own room. But before he could convince his feet to move, the dead bolt clicked and Penelope opened the door.

"Luke." Her face was guarded, eyes wary.

He hated that his sister felt like she had to hide things from him, hated that he'd been the one to make her feel that way. "I owe you an apology."

"You do." She opened the door further, inviting him in. "And you owe Jay one, too."

Luke drew up short, struggling with his initial shock at seeing Jay in his sister's room. "You're right." He swallowed. "I owe you both an apology for my reaction earlier."

Penelope gestured for him to take a seat and moved to join Jay on the sofa in the suite's sitting area. Luke settled into the chair across from them, acutely aware of how the position made him feel like he was facing off against them. They were supposed to be a team. Three peas together in a pod.

Maybe his rage earlier had been more than the reaction of a protective older brother, more than a bubbling-over of his frustrations with Julia. Maybe he was scared of losing them, that if Pen and Jay were together, things would change. Peas were meant to come two in a pod, after all.

Luke realized he wasn't worried just about Pen getting hurt. He also was afraid of how this change in her relationship with Jay would change her relationship with him. He wouldn't be as important to her anymore, wouldn't be the one she went to for help. But even if all that were true, he couldn't let his fear get in the way of his sister's happiness. He wouldn't. "I was taken by surprise," he admitted. "And I reacted poorly."

"Jay and I owe you an apology, too. We shouldn't have hidden . . ." Penelope paused, reaching out to clasp hands with Jay. "*Us* from you." She took a breath. "But based on your reaction, can you understand why we were hesitant to let you know?"

"Pen, I—"

She cut him off. "It might be hard for you to accept, Luke. But I'm more than your little sister. More than that sick little girl in the hospital."

"I'm well aware of that." He scowled.

"Are you?" She stared at him, gray eyes steely with challenge.

"Sometimes I'm not so sure. I haven't been that sick little girl in more than a dozen years. I've graduated college, helped you build this project, and now I'm even running it, and I think I'm doing a pretty good job—"

"You're doing a great job," he rushed to assure her.

"Let me *finish*."

Luke flushed, but he shut his mouth and waited for his sister to continue.

"What I'm trying to say is, I'm doing okay by myself. More than okay. That big secret I've been working on with Mrs. W. . ." She bit her lip. "It wasn't the talent show."

"Oh?" Luke felt like he was standing in an open field, waiting for the next chunk of sky to fall on him.

"We've been discussing the possibility of expanding the experience. Developing new events, like a holiday-themed one for the winter season."

He held himself in check. "Any particular reason I was excluded from this discussion?"

"Well . . ." His sister straightened her shoulders, as if gathering courage for what she was going to say next. "Mrs. W. wants to hire me full-time. Beyond this contract. She asked if I would be willing to spearhead the program and run themed experiences at the resort year-round." Penelope glanced at Jay. "Jay plans to stay here, too. Mrs. W. asked him to be her head of marketing."

Luke turned his attention to his best friend. "Is that so?"

Vijay cleared his throat. Maybe it was Luke's snarky response, but something nudged his friend into action. Jay leaned forward, speaking for the first time since Luke had entered the room. "Not just for the immersive experiences, but for the entire resort."

"How nice for you." Luke couldn't keep the acid from his tone this time. How had all this been happening right under his nose? Disappointment and betrayal simmered in his gut, but he quelled the urge to snap, keeping the angry words trapped behind his clenched teeth. "Is there a reason you felt you needed to go behind my back?"

"It's not like that," Penelope objected. "Working on this game has been a dream come true for me, but I know it was supposed to be a onetime thing for you—your dream is to launch your own start-up." She shrugged. "I didn't want the possibility of developing new projects here to make you feel like you had to stay and help, out of a sense of responsibility or obligation." Her voice dropped. "That's kept you from going after what you want long enough."

"I don't regret it, Pen, and I don't resent you for any of it."

"I know," she said gently. "I told you, you're not Dad. I'm not Mom."

"You will always be my little sister," Luke said, heart aching.

"But I'm more than that, too."

"Damn straight she is," Jay stood. "She's an amazing woman, and I hope she will be my wife." He stared at Luke, chin jutting out with stubborn purpose. "I want to marry your sister."

"You do?" Luke asked, bewildered.

"You do?" Pen echoed, equally bewildered.

"I do." Jay spun around to face Penelope. "We've known each other a long time. You were my best friend's sister, and for years I thought of you as a little sister, too. But then something changed. I've always loved you, but that love shifted, grew, became something else. I started noticing all these little things I'd never really paid attention to before, each one making me love you a little more. The way you make that soft little sigh at your favorite part in a movie or song. The way you dissect your sandwiches and eat them in layers. The way you love watermelon but hate anything watermelon-flavored."

Luke swallowed an affectionate chuckle, torn between wanting to witness this tender moment between two of the people he loved most in the world and wanting to fade into the wall so they could share this moment alone. He settled for being as quiet and still as possible.

"There's a line in one of those rom-coms that you love so much: 'When you realize you want to spend the rest of your life with somebody, you want the rest of your life to start as soon as possible.'" Jay dropped to one knee, reaching for Penelope's hand. "Pen, I've known for a long time. For me, it's always been you. But I waited. I waited because I didn't want to be selfish. I wanted to give you space to live your life, a chance to meet other people— time to figure out what you wanted."

"I know exactly what I want." Penelope slipped off the couch to kneel across from Jay. "So stop waiting and trying to give me what you think I need and just marry me already."

"Yeah?" Jay asked.

"Yeah," Pen said.

And then his sister and best friend were kissing and Luke wished he could perform a disappearing act for real. He glanced down, realizing he was still wearing the ridiculous cape. Maybe he could toss it over his head and they'd forget he was in the room. Wait—that might not be the best idea. Luke cleared his throat awkwardly.

Penelope laughed and let Jay help her to her feet. Together, they turned to face Luke.

"Congratulations," he said, truly meaning it. "I'm sorry I acted like such a jackass. To be honest, if you asked me, I couldn't imagine anyone ever being good enough for Penelope."

His sister made a noise of protest and Luke hurried to add, "Jay, you'll never do better than Penelope." He turned to his sister and grinned. "But Pen, you could do a lot worse than Jay."

"Thanks, man," Jay said drily. "I'm going to head to the bar and grab us some champagne to celebrate." He gave Pen a quick kiss before shooting a warning glance at both of them. "Don't kill each other while I'm gone."

Luke chuckled, the moment of familiarity easing some of the remaining tension in him.

Penelope laughed too, then paused. "I just realized something," she said. "I've become a romantic-comedy trope." She beamed, love shining in her gray eyes as she watched Jay leave the room. "I'm the girl who falls for her brother's best friend."

"Guess I should have seen that coming, huh?" Luke teased, a shade tartly. The sting from all they'd hidden from him had dulled considerably, but the wound was still there. He'd get over it though. His sister was happy, and that's all that mattered.

"Now then," Penelope said, grin turning sly. "It's your turn."

"My turn for what?" he asked, knowing that when his sister got that look on her face, he was in trouble.

"I got my happily ever after, so it's only fair I do what I can to make sure my big brother gets his happy ending too." She settled back on the couch. "We need to discuss your plan."

"My plan?" Luke raised his eyebrows.

"For how to fix things with Julia, of course." Penelope rubbed her hands together.

"I was hoping you could help me with that," Luke admitted, scrubbing a hand over his face. "I really screwed things up."

"Every romance has to go through a dark moment," Penelope assured him. "The important thing is you have to be willing to put in the work to reach the light on the other side."

Luke grimaced. "You make it sound like I'm dying."

"You kind of are," Penelope mused. "The old you, the person you were before you met Julia."

"Jay's proposal must have affected your brain," Luke teased.

His sister ignored that comment. "What are you going to do?"

"I don't know. I mean, what should I do?" He leaned forward. "I was thinking now's the time to go big. I think I need a grand gesture."

"I'm not so sure." Penelope cocked her head, thoughtful. "I think what's needed here is a sincere grovel."

"Come on, Pen," Luke said. "I've only got one shot at making things right with Julia before she leaves. I've watched enough rom-coms with you to know the best way to win her back is to apologize with a grand gesture."

Penelope looked like she was going to argue, but then she shrugged. "It's your call." She sighed and crossed her arms. "Tell me your plan."

CHAPTER 28

JULIA

Julia woke Sunday morning with a pounding head. She sat up, immediately regretting it as the room spun and the wine-soaked contents of her stomach sloshed threateningly. She closed her eyes and breathed slow and deep through her nose. The pounding continued and she realized the sound wasn't just inside her throbbing head.

She braved opening one eye. When the walls stayed where they belonged, she opened the other. She was still in Kat's suite, the bottle of chardonnay lying on its side, empty. Their wineglasses, also empty. Kat was asleep on the couch next to her, face smashed into the pillows.

Her friend was so quiet, Julia was tempted to check for a pulse. She settled for a pinch. She nipped Kat in the arm and her friend groaned, twitched, and went still. Well, at least she'd gotten a response. Kat wasn't dead. The pounding continued and Julia growled. Kat might still be alive, but whoever was beating down the door was about to meet their maker.

Julia gingerly rolled off the couch, testing her balance before venturing across the room. Her hangover wasn't too bad, just enough to be irritating, making her want to stab whoever it was that was *still knocking*. She started to reach for the door of the suite but had the presence of mind to stop and check the peephole before ripping it off its hinges.

"Andie!" Julia exclaimed, catching a glimpse of her friend's short, dark locks.

"Jules?" Andie called through the door. "What are you doing here?"

Julia unlocked the door and opened it. "Impromptu sleepover." She turned and headed back to the couch.

"I thought you might be having one of those . . . but in someone else's room," Andie noted pointedly. She paused when she caught sight of the tipped-over wine bottle and Kat, still sprawled on the couch. "Rough night?"

"Ended up that way, yeah." Julia collapsed back onto the couch.

"I'm sorry I wasn't here for it." Andie opened the suite's mini fridge and pulled out two water bottles. She handed one to Julia and placed the other against the back of Kat's neck.

"Aah!" Kat cried, gasping for breath and clutching at the bottle. She moaned and slowly shifted to a vertical position, like a ship's sail being raised. "Actually, that felt good," she conceded, resting the bottle against her neck again.

"I've gotta say, I was not expecting this." Andie clicked her tongue and fussed over them like a mother hen, cleaning up the wine bottle and glasses and wiping Kat's mascara-stained cheeks with a tissue. "When you left with Zach last night, you looked so happy." She took a seat in the chair closest to the couch and handed Kat the tissue. "What happened?"

Kat dabbed at her eyes a little more. "Zach is a fame-hungry asshole is what happened."

Andie turned to Julia for clarification.

"He got wind of the rumor that Kat is the *TrendList* reporter," Julia explained.

"I'm still confused," Andie confessed.

"He's convinced my glowing review of his *Dirty Dancing* routine is going to, I don't know, launch his Hollywood career or something."

"Oh, so he's delusional," Andie snorted.

"One of his many faults, yes," Kat agreed. She opened the water bottle and took a swig.

"I think the man has more faith in the power of that website to get him a job than I do," Julia added.

"Well, clearly his employers think so too," Andie said, gesturing at the sumptuous décor surrounding them. "All week long they've been catering to Kat." She glanced at Julia. "I see now why you didn't want them to know you were the reviewer."

"Yeah, well, that cat is out of the bag." Julia groaned. "And no, I'm not trying to be punny."

"What *are* you trying to be?" Andie wondered.

"Honest." Julia shrugged. "I told Luke the truth. Explained I was the one writing the review for *TrendList*."

"Did you explain *why* you kept that fact hidden?"

"I didn't actually get to that part," Julia admitted. "But things ended in disaster anyway, so I don't think it really matters." Her throat felt tight, voice clipped.

"Oh, that man is going down." Andie punched her fist into her palm. "I warned him not to hurt you," she seethed.

"Relax, Justice League." Julia reached out and patted her friend's knee. "It's my own fault for getting carried away."

"But isn't that the point of this whole experience?" Andie stood. "To get carried away?"

"As long as we still remember it's a game," Kat said quietly.

"Some of us allowed our feelings to seep into the fantasies." Julia shared a smile of commiseration with Kat before turning her attention back to Andie, her tone brisk. "I'm not saying that's necessarily a bad thing; there are exceptions to every rule." She nodded encouragingly at her friend. "How was your night with Curt?"

Andie collapsed back into her chair with a gusty sigh.

"Someone else have an impromptu sleepover?" Julia prodded.

"He made a bonfire for us." Andie wrapped her arms around herself. "On the beach." Her face glowed with the memory.

"I know," Julia confessed, a playful grin lifting the corner of her mouth. "I saw you two in action."

"You did?" Andie blushed.

"Oh my God, I didn't see *that*," Julia quickly amended.

"Was that your bonus activity?" Kat purred. "Sex on the beach?"

"No!" Andie's blush deepened, cheeks turning a bright sun-burned pink. "But I did want a romantic night under the stars."

"Aw, that's so sweet," Kat cooed.

"It was." Andie's dark eyes shone with affection. "He's sweet."

"Are we still talking about Curt?" Julia teased.

"I know he comes across as a doofus, but there's more to my butter bean than meets the eye."

"You really like him, don't you?" Kat asked.

Andie nodded. "I hope you don't mind that I'm staying for the wedding today."

"After all the work he did to get you to be his plus-one?" Julia laughed. "I think we'd mind more if you didn't stay."

Kat shared a grin with Julia, then paused, frowning, "Do you need us to stick around to give you a ride home?"

"No, I wouldn't do that to you." Andie shook her head. "I have no idea how late the reception will go. Besides . . ." She bit her lip, uncharacteristically shy. "Curt offered to drive me home."

"Back to Chicago?" Kat asked.

"He said that he'd be happy to do it." Andie beamed.

"Doesn't he live in Milwaukee?" Julia wondered. "With his mom?"

"I found out more about that. It really is a temporary situation. He's building a house and moved back home until it's finished."

"Uh-huh," Kat said.

"I know. At first my BS detector was triggered too, but I believe him. He showed me a bunch of pictures and plans and talked way too much about it in way too much detail for it to be a line.

And if it turns out he made it up, I'm impressed enough by his commitment to consider rolling with it at this point."

Kat shot Andie a look.

"I'm kidding," Andie assured them. "Seriously, though, I'm still living in an apartment my parents own . . . How much different is that than living in your mom's basement?"

"I'd argue very," Julia said. "Your parents aren't under the same roof as you, for one."

"Yeah, and except for rent, you cover all your own expenses," Kat pointed out.

"Except that," Andie agreed, snorting. "And we all know my coaching salary is not enough for me to swing a place on my own. I've spent the last five years living pseudo independently."

"Where is this coming from?" Julia wondered.

"It's just been something I've been thinking about lately." Andie paused, fingers twisting in her lap. "Maybe that's part of why I usually date older guys . . . It's easier for me to let someone else be the adult in the relationship." She shrugged. "I'm realizing if I want something to work out long term, we *both* need to be adults."

"Wow." Kat shook her head. "One week at this place is better than a year of therapy. Who knew pretending to be in a romcom would lead to all these breakthroughs about our relationship issues?"

"Huh?" Andie glanced at Julia.

"You missed a lot last night," was all Julia said, too physically and emotionally exhausted to rehash the discussion right now. Her head throbbed and she winced, pinching the bridge of her nose.

"Are you feeling all right?" Andie asked.

"As well as I can the morning after a few too many glasses of chardonnay," Julia said, waving a hand dismissively. "I'm fine."

Andie frowned. "Did you take your thyroid pill this morning?"

Julia groaned. "No, Mom."

"Come on." Andie stood and pulled Julia to her feet. "Let's get you to your room. After your meds and a shower, you'll feel much better."

"What I need is some coffee. And lots of it," Julia grumbled, letting Andie lead her toward the door.

"Brunch will be starting soon. You can have all the coffee you want then," Andie promised. She turned to Kat, in full coach mode as she pointed at her and ordered, "You. Go pamper yourself with a nice hot bath in that big luxurious tub and meet us downstairs in an hour."

An hour later, Julia entered the dining room of the Notting Hill Resort one last time. She took a breath. Her head definitely felt better. Andie hadn't been wrong about the shower, and it was true, if Julia missed the window when she usually took her medication, she felt off the entire day. She spotted her friends seated at what she'd started to think of as their usual table. David and Patrick were there, too. A bittersweet pang wafted through her as she crossed the room.

"Why the glum face?" Patrick asked, brows creasing in concern as she took a seat across from him.

"I'm just a little sad thinking about how everything is coming to an end," Julia admitted. "Look, I know David and Patrick aren't your real names, and I understand this whole week was a game, but I just want to say I'm happy to have met you both."

"Oh," David said, clutching his chest. "You are just the sweetest." He hopped out of his chair and hurried around the table to give Julia a quick hug.

"Meeting new people is one of the best parts of these experiences," Patrick said. "And the hardest."

"Goodbyes are always hard," David agreed, returning to his seat.

"Especially when you meet someone truly special," Patrick added.

Julia jerked her head up. But Patrick wasn't looking at her; he only had eyes for David.

"Wait a minute," Andie said, leaning forward and eyeing the two men curiously. "Did you two meet at something like this?"

"Guilty as charged." David chuckled. He reached for his partner's hand and they entwined fingers.

"It was my first role-playing adventure," Patrick explained.

"Yes, my little LARP virgin," David said affectionately.

Patrick sighed good-naturedly and continued, "We got paired up for a few activities, and things sort of happened from there."

"But how did you know?" Julia asked, unable to stop herself. "I mean, how did you know that what you were feeling was real? That it was going to last beyond the end of the game?"

The two men exchanged a look full of memories.

"We didn't," Patrick said. "Not at first."

"But we were both willing to take the risk and find out," David added. "As much as we enjoy the fun and excitement of playing pretend, at the end of the day—or the week—when we return to our real lives and our real selves, that's when we know what we have is real."

"It's true," Patrick agreed. "All the heightened emotions and passionate moments of the fantasy are icing on the cake for what we have back in the real world. It's all the normal, boring stuff, the quiet moments at home, that create the foundation for a lasting relationship."

"I'd argue life with me is never boring," David countered playfully, "but he's right. The trips and games are thrilling, and they make romance seem easy. It's the other stuff, like figuring out whose turn it is to take out the trash and who was supposed to buy toilet paper, that takes work. And honestly, I don't think anything is more romantic than caring enough for another person to be there for the everyday stuff."

"Yeah, but it's more than shopping and chores," Patrick cautioned. "It's also apologizing when you're in the wrong. Putting the other person's needs first. Making their joy a priority."

David sniffed, visibly tearing up as he pulled Patrick in for a kiss.

Andie leaned in to plant a kiss on Curt. Julia knew her friend was not a crier, but in this moment, she looked like she was on the verge of turning on the waterworks.

Julia felt herself tearing up too. David and Patrick had described it perfectly. *That* was what she was looking for. That was the kind of happily ever after she wanted for herself.

She was so lost in her thoughts it took her a moment to realize that Penelope, game master and Luke's sister, was approaching their table, accompanied by the guy Julia had seen backstage last night. Penelope took a moment to greet everyone at the table, her gray eyes lingering apologetically on Julia.

Pasting a smile on her face, Julia steeled herself, not sure what to expect from this surprise visit. She tried to ignore the flash of disappointment when she realized that Luke wasn't with them. For a moment, she regretted storming off last night. So many things had been left unsaid.

"I want to thank you all for being a part of this event," Penelope began. "The very first of its kind at Notting Hill, but not the last. I'm pleased to announce we have several other rom-com-inspired experiences in the works."

"Really?" David asked, interest clearly piqued. "Such as?"

"We can't disclose the details yet," the man with Penelope said, "but I have a feeling you'll find them quite to your liking." He winked and held out a hand. "Vijay Chandran, marketing and PR for Notting Hill Resort."

"Well, aren't you a tease, Mr. Chandran," David said, shaking the man's hand.

"Vijay is fine. Or Jay." He smiled pleasantly. "We do have a newsletter you can sign up for to stay informed on all upcoming events."

"Clever segue," Patrick noted, shaking Jay's hand as well.

"Oh!" Penelope perked up. "That reminds me: Don't forget to stop by concierge and pick up your cell phones." She grinned. "And please feel free to take as many pictures of the resort as you'd like."

"And post them to all your social media accounts and tag us, of course." Jay grinned. "There's also an evaluation form we'd appreciate you filling out," he added. He glanced around the table. "Your feedback will help ensure our next event is even better."

"It's not like this one could get much worse," Kat muttered from Julia's left.

Julia sputtered into her coffee. Kat, apparently, was still dealing with some residual anger. Not that Julia blamed her friend. Another wave of disappointment hit her. She'd held out hope that Luke would make an appearance, give them both a chance to clear the air, but clearly that wasn't going to happen. Which was probably for the best. She kept her smile pinned in place while Penelope and Jay wrapped up their conversation and moved on to the next table.

Once they were gone, she turned to Kat. "I know the stuff with Zach sucked, and I'm sorry it ruined your experience here."

"Why are *you* sorry?" Kat asked. "You weren't the one pretending to be into me."

"Yeah, but it's because you were pretending to be me that the whole mess with Zach happened in the first place." Julia hesitated. "Maybe if he didn't think you were the *TrendList* reviewer, he would have—"

"He would have *what*? Liked me for me?" Kat's laugh was sharp and self-deprecating. "He would have been cozying up to you, instead."

Julia didn't argue. Instead, she asked earnestly, "Did you really have a miserable time?"

Kat fiddled with the pleats of her cloth napkin. "No," she finally admitted. "If we pretend those last few hours of last night didn't happen, I had a great time." She grinned, mood brightening. "Like when my grandmother watches *Titanic*."

"I'm not following."

"She still owns a VCR and watches that movie on VHS. It comes on two cassettes, so Babcia only watches the first tape, because it's not until the second one that everything goes to hell."

Julia giggled.

"What about you?" Kat asked.

"What about me?" Julia hedged.

"What kind of review are you planning to write?"

"An honest one." Julia took a sip of coffee, gathering her thoughts. "Last night, I was ready to rip this place to shreds. But then I reminded myself I'm better than that. I'm a better person and a better journalist." She wrapped her hands around the mug. "My job was to assess whether this resort can pull off making people feel like they've been living in a fantasy world for a week."

"Like Disney," Kat suggested.

"Exactly," Julia agreed, laughing. "Nobody expects to leave Disney World believing it all was real. They just enjoy the fantasy while they're visiting. Did the resort deliver the magical experience of being part of a romantic comedy? Yes, it did."

Kat shifted her gaze to where Andie and Curt were leaning toward each other, foreheads pressed together as they talked softly. "Some of us are going home with better souvenirs than others."

"True, but we're all bringing home some great memories." She grabbed Kat's hand and stood. "Let's go get our phones and take some pictures."

Out in the lobby, Julia and Kat joined the crowd of people hovering near outlets, charging up their phones. Looking around, she felt an odd sense of loss. All week long, this area had been filled with conversation and laughter, but now it was almost silent as everyone fixated on their electronic devices, encased in invisible bubbles, oblivious to the world around them as they checked messages and caught up on emails.

Last night, couples had stared intently into each other's eyes. Today they stared intently at their screens. She sighed wistfully. It really was time to let go of the fantasy and head back to reality.

After going over her notes for the "Take Me!" review, Julia convinced Kat to help her take some pics. She snapped a few of Andie and Curt, and of Harry and Sally, too. She even got Patrick and David to agree to a few pictures. They were tickled to discover her secret and were happy to provide their contact info so she could reach out later with any follow-up questions for her review. With all their experience traveling the world and participating in role-playing adventures, they were going to make a great resource.

She was wrapping things up with a video in the resort's grand foyer when Kat, who was filming for her, suddenly froze, staring, eyes wide.

"What?" Julia asked. "Do I have something on my face?"

Kat shook her head. She pointed at a spot above and behind Julia.

Slowly, Julia turned and glanced up.

There, at the top of the landing overlooking the foyer, was Luke. He stared down at her and lifted something over his head. It took Julia a moment to realize it was a Bluetooth speaker.

"It's not a boom box, but you gotta give him points for creativity," Kat said.

"Are you still filming this?" Julia hissed.

Kat nodded, blue eyes gleaming. "Oh, you better believe I am."

Music suddenly blasted through the foyer, filling the quiet lobby with sound.

Heads snapped up as guests tore themselves away from their screens.

Kat cocked her head. "Is that the same song from—"

"Wine and paint night? Yep." Either Luke was a one-hit wonder or he was trying to make a statement. She shook her head. As the song played, he continued to stand on the balcony, staring down at her, holding the speaker over his head, *Say Anything* style.

"Stay here, please," she told Kat. "I need to have a word with John Cusack."

As she marched up the steps to the balcony, Julia reminded herself this was not real and she was not living in a romantic comedy and she would not—under any circumstances—be falling for another scripted scenario. She reached the top of the stairs and Luke lowered the speaker, the sweet, awkward half smile curving his lips almost her undoing.

Julia couldn't deny that she was completely charmed by the ridiculousness of the moment, even as she recognized it was too much. It was over the top and she was done with the fantasy. She couldn't trust his adorable smile and hopeful gray eyes—she wasn't sure she could trust herself.

He turned off the music and set the speaker down. "Can we talk?"

"I'm listening."

He moved toward her, and she backed up a step. It was instinctive. Self-preservation. A need to protect herself, protect her heart.

Luke halted midstep, stricken, gaze darkening with a wounded look that gutted her. He licked his lips, throat working.

"Don't," she said, shaking her head. "Don't say anything."

"But—"

"I changed my mind." She held up her hand, while inside her chest a fist tightened around her heart. "I don't want you to say anything."

"Julia—"

"Please, don't." She closed her eyes. "I don't want to hear what you have to say, because I just realized it wouldn't matter what you said right now." She opened her eyes and met his gaze. "I'm not going to believe you. I can't."

She could see the struggle on his face, the need to defy her request and spill whatever promises, excuses, explanations he'd planned to accompany this elaborate gesture. She sucked in a breath. That's what this was. A grand gesture. The last move in the game.

A game she was done playing.

He'd lied to her, but she'd lied, too.

"You didn't have to do that," she said, gesturing toward the speaker. "What we had—the funny first meeting on the beach, that amazing kiss in the rain . . ." She paused, reaching out to touch Luke's cheek. "Our night together." Julia could hear the pain in her own voice. That pain was real, and it scared her. "It was perfect." She smiled softly. "Imperfectly perfect."

He reached up to press his hand over hers, but she pulled away.

"Goodbye, Luke."

Julia turned and hurried down the stairs. And no matter how much she wanted to, she didn't look back. More than anything, she wanted to believe that what they had shared had been more than a game, was more than being swept up in the fantasy. But at the same time, she was scared to believe. Because that would mean that, by choosing to walk away from him, she was walking away from their chance at having something real.

CHAPTER 29

JULIA

Julia spent the drive home alternating between patting herself on the back for walking away from Luke and kicking herself in the ass for not listening to what he had to say. Kat had earned bonus friend points for putting up with Julia's ranting the entire ride to Chicago. To make up for it, Julia insisted that Kat let her buy dinner, promising not to utter the words *Luke* or *rom-com* the rest of the night.

By the time Kat dropped Julia off at her apartment, it was after eight, and Julia was exhausted. She fumbled to get her key in the lock, grateful to be home. Dumping her suitcase in the corner, she collapsed face-first onto her miniature bed. She hated traveling. This trip had been only an hour or so by car, and she'd been miserable. How was she supposed to do this for a living?

But she *was* doing this. If she wanted to save her job and to continue be able to afford healthcare, if she wanted to avoid telling her parents they'd been right all along, then she *had* to do this. Which meant, she needed to start writing that review.

She flopped onto her back, gaze tracing the ductwork snaking through the rafters of her loft ceiling. The familiar view was comforting, but it did nothing to ease the ache inside her chest. Julia closed her eyes and visualized the acres of mattress she'd had at Notting Hill. She didn't miss the bed. She missed the man she'd shared that bed with.

Her phone chimed and Julia scrambled to check it, heart swelling with hope.

But it was a text from Andie. A quick note to let Julia and Kat know she'd made it home fine. Curt hadn't decapitated her and buried her in his mother's basement.

Her phone chimed again with another message and an image came through. A picture from the wedding. Curt appeared surprisingly dapper in the more traditional groomsman wear of a three-piece suit, and Andie looked adorable tucked against his side, a flower crown on her head and laughter in her eyes.

Julia grinned at the picture, happy for her friend. At least somebody got the rom-com ending they were hoping for. With a sigh, she dug out her notepad and got started.

On Monday morning, Julia showed up for work at her usual time. She'd hit Send on the "Take Me!" assignment late last night—or rather, early this morning. Sometime during the beastly hour of three a.m.

She'd been tempted to call in sick. Not just because she needed the sleep. She legitimately felt ill, terrified to hear what Cleo thought of her article. The problem was—regardless of whether her boss loved it or hated it—Julia feared either outcome.

At half past nine, Cleo summoned Julia into her office. Julia's stomach churned. On one hand, she was relieved she wouldn't have to wait all day to find out the fate of her future. But at the same time, she felt like a defendant in a trial, where the jury's ruling had come back so quickly that everyone wondered whether the fast decision meant really good news or really bad news.

"Julia!" Cleo waved her inside and gestured at a chair. Julia hoped the giant smile on Cleo's face meant good news. If not, her boss was a closet sadist.

Julia took the seat indicated before Cleo changed her mind and had her doing more stretching exercises. Come to think of it, maybe her boss was a sadist after all.

"Julia," Cleo said, giving her name enough weight to make it feel like it should be a whole sentence.

"Yes?" Julia asked, breath sticking in her chest.

Her boss rested her clasped hands on the desk and stared at her, giant smile still in place.

Julia continued to hold her breath. If Cleo didn't say something soon, she was going to pass out. *We'll see if you're still smiling then*, Julia thought crossly.

Cleo leaned forward the tiniest bit. "I love it," she declared, slapping the top of her desk with both palms.

"You do?" Julia exhaled, refilling her lungs with big gulps of air.

"I do." Cleo nodded. "It was such a damn delight. Warm and witty. Informative but playful. The spotlight interviews you did with some of the guests might have been my favorite part."

Julia grinned, glad she'd thought to include that angle. "Most of the names I used are the fake ones the guests were given to role-play, but I still made sure to get signatures of consent from everyone I included in the story."

"Excellent." Cleo leaned back in her chair. "Reading about Harry and Sally, the empty nester couple, reminded me how much I love rom-coms. As soon as I finished your article, do you know what I did?"

"Um, called me into your office?"

"No. First, I contacted that Mrs. Widowpork—"

"Weatherfork," Julia corrected automatically. Figures she'd finally get it down only after she'd left.

"That's the one. I called her up and booked a stay." Cleo drifted over to her shelf of photos. "My thirtieth wedding anniversary is coming up, and this is exactly what I need to rekindle the spark with Mr. Chen." She pulled a frame down and showed it to Julia. "This is our wedding photo."

"Your dress is lovely," Julia said, admiring the image of a younger version of her boss exchanging vows.

"I still have it, you know. I'm hoping one of my grandbabies will wear it one day." Her boss set the picture back on the shelf and returned to her desk. "Your story on the resort did exactly what *TrendList* hopes every "Take Me!" review will do. Inspire the reader to visit!" Cleo clapped her hands. "Julia, I'm delighted to officially offer you a position on the 'Take Me!' staff. Congratulations."

"Ah, thanks." Julia swallowed.

"Are you ready to get started?"

She dug her notepad out of her purse. "I'm ready."

"I hope so." Cleo chuckled. "Now that you've dipped your toes in the pool, we're going to toss you into the deep end." Her boss booted up her laptop. "But not too deep. For this first round of assignments I think it's best we schedule you for a few quickies."

"Pardon?"

Cleo glanced up. "Quickies are day trips." She slipped on a pair of reading glasses and peered closely at the screen. "It looks like we've got leads on locations in Dayton, Ohio; Duluth, Minnesota; and Davenport, Indiana."

"All in one week?" Julia flinched, staring at the list of cities she'd scribbled down. "That's a lot of travel."

"Comes with the territory." Cleo shifted her gaze from the laptop to Julia. "The segment is called 'Take Me!' As in *Take me there!* or *Take me on vacation!*"

"I get it," Julia said. "But what about stuff closer to home? Shouldn't we have a segment dedicated to cool places to go in the city?"

Cleo frowned. "Doesn't Chicago already do something like this? I've seen a feature similar to what you're describing on the news."

"It is similar," Julia agreed. "But this would be different. Better."

"How so?" Cleo's voice was full of challenge, but Julia caught the spark of interest in her boss's eye.

"The bit you mentioned on the news is . . . well, like the news.

It's dry. The concept I'm proposing would be more engaging. Have the energy and freshness *TrendList* is known for."

"What about the 'Take Me!' position?" Cleo wondered.

"I was so desperate to avoid getting fired I thought I was willing to do anything. Take any job you offered. I was thrilled when you suggested I pitch a story idea, and I'm so grateful to you for the opportunity."

"But . . ." Cleo prodded.

Julia inhaled. "But, I'm starting to realize I'm not the best person for this job . . . Or maybe this job isn't a good fit for me." She bit her lip. She was taking a huge risk, but in her gut she knew this was the right move for her. "It's a great job. So many cool opportunities. I feel like an idiot for not wanting it. Especially after you were generous enough to give me a chance."

"Then why the change of heart?"

"One reason is my terrible motion sickness," Julia admitted.

"Yikes." Cleo laughed. "Sorry." She sobered. "That's not funny."

"You can laugh," Julia assured her boss. "It is kind of funny. Another example of my warped luck. I needed a job and the only position available requires doing something that makes me violently ill."

A wry smile ghosted her lips. "Another reason is I hate traveling. And not just because I get sick. As a kid, I never felt like I had a place I could claim as my own. A place I belonged to. But ever since I moved here, that's changed. Chicago is my adopted hometown. I want to explore every nook and cranny. Discover all the things that make the place I call home special."

"I have to admit, that does sound enticing," Cleo mused. "One problem. I'm not sure 'Take Me Home!' has quite the same ring." Her boss tapped her fingers thoughtfully. "Let's say you were in charge of this feature. What would you call it?"

"Good question." Again, Julia found herself struggling to breathe, afraid to hope. She flipped through her notepad, frantically searching for ideas she'd jotted down in the past, skimming scraps of brainstorming sessions and daydreams. "My mission would be to cover more than what's trendy. Go beyond what's popular with tourists. The news can do that stuff. I want to reveal the hidden treasures of the city to the people who live here and might not realize all there is to enjoy right under their noses."

"Get the word out about all the local places people love," Cleo summarized.

"*That's it*," Julia exhaled, inspiration striking like lightning. She grinned, face splitting into a smile that felt as big and bright as the sun after a storm. "I'd call it 'Local Love.'"

On Friday afternoon, Julia texted her friends to make plans. It had been a hell of a week and she needed their holy trinity of comedy, carbs, and cocktails to be her salvation tonight. She also wanted to celebrate. The past few days had been long and stressful, but rewarding, too. "Local Love" would make its official debut on the *TrendList* website this weekend.

Only one meal was up to the challenge. Sushi.

She ordered two of all their favorites from the tiny but awesome sushi bar around the corner from Andie's apartment. While Julia spread everything out on the table in front of the couch, Andie opened a large bottle of Sapporo and Kat started the movie. It had been her turn to pick this time.

"After everything that happened, I can't believe you went with *Dirty Dancing*," Julia declared, working her way through her second rainbow roll. "It's not even a romantic comedy."

"Excuse me, but that classification is up for debate," Kat argued. "And it's *because* of what happened that I picked it. I need to reclaim one of my favorite movies as my own."

By the time Johnny delivered the "Baby in a corner" line—looking infinitely sexier than Zach, they all agreed—Julia felt like a stuffed turkey. "I don't think I've ever been this full in my life," she groaned, rubbing her swollen belly.

"You say that every time we have sushi," Kat reminded her, finishing off the last piece of her shrimp tempura roll.

"This time I mean it."

"Uh-huh," Kat and Andie said together, their tone indicating that neither of them was buying it.

"I'm serious. I don't think I can move. You'll have to roll me out the door like Violet Beauregarde."

Andie poked her with a chopstick.

"Stop," Julia warned, shoving the chopstick away. "You're going to pop me like a big blueberry balloon."

"Have you started taking walks like we discussed?" Andie asked.

"*You* discussed," Julia grumbled.

"Hey, you're the one who told me you wanted to improve your fitness," Andie reminded her.

"It was a lapse in judgment. I've recovered my senses," Julia said, though at this point she was teasing Andie. She'd asked her friend for help and had meant it. When she'd said her week at Notting Hill had been the most exercise she'd had in a long time, it wasn't an exaggeration.

Memories of commiserating with Luke about being out of shape flooded Julia's mind. A silly grin tickled her lips as she thought of how endearingly self-deprecating he could be. How much he'd made her laugh. She imagined what it might be like to work on improving their fitness together. Julia could think of plenty of fun activities that would get their heart rates up.

"Hey." Now Kat was poking her with a chopstick. "Knock it off."

"Why are you both attacking me?" Julia jerked away from the wooden utensil of torture. "I'm literally just existing."

"You were thinking about *him*."

"I was not."

"Yes, you were." Andie shook her head. "I know the look. You were totally mooning over him just now."

Julia blew out her lips dismissively. "What are you talking about?"

"Daydreaming. Woolgathering." Kat set her plate and chopsticks aside and stared at Julia. "Mooning."

Julia snorted. "In my day, that word meant waving your bare ass around in public."

"Your day was the same as my day," Kat scoffed. "And I've mooned more than my fair share of people from the window of an L train."

"I remember." Julia giggled. "We had some good times in college."

"We did," Kat agreed, grinning.

"Do you ever want to go back?" Julia wondered.

"To college?" Kat's smile turned into a grimace. "Hell no."

"Why?" Andie cocked her head, studying Julia. "Do you?"

"Not really, no." Julia sighed. "I do miss it sometimes, though. Everything seemed easier then. To still have your future in front of you."

"My babcia is eighty-seven and she'd tell you *she* still has a future. You're twenty-six. Trust me, your future is still in front of you." Kat nudged her shoulder against Julia's. "Where is this coming from, anyway? I thought things were going well."

"They are," Julia agreed.

"Aren't we celebrating your new job tonight?"

"We are. We did." Julia groaned and rubbed her sushi-stuffed belly. "I'm excited about this job. Frankly, I can't believe it's happening. But I also keep having doubts. Maybe it's the echo of years of my parents asking me these questions, but I can't help wondering if my life is headed in the right direction. Did I choose the right career path. Am I going to meet the right person . . . Your standard, garden-variety esoteric shit."

"Hm." Andie reached for the bottle of Sapporo and poured

some into her glass. "You know what happens when you take enough right turns?"

"What?"

"You end up back where you started." Andie handed the beer to Julia.

Julia stared down at the bottle, considering her friend's words as she traced a finger over the star on the label. "Interesting point." She refilled her glass and passed what was left in the bottle to Kat. "Do you think that's my problem?"

"What?" Andie studied Julia. "That you're going in circles?"

"That I'm back where I started."

"Why do you say that?" Kat wondered.

"It's hard to explain." Julia puckered her brow in thought as she searched for the right words. "It's like there's this hole inside me, an empty space that I can't seem to fill." She rubbed a hand over her chest. "I can ignore it for a little while, get lost in my work, but I can't forget about it." She dropped her hand and sighed. "I can't stop wondering if I made a mistake. Took the wrong turn."

"You need to pivot," Andie surmised.

Julia looked at Andie over the rim of her glass. "Meaning?"

"When I have my players do pivot drills, I make them keep one foot stationary and use the other to shift direction. This way, they can see every option available to them before committing." She stood, demonstrating by turning in a circle, stockinged foot of her stationary leg spinning slowly on the hardwood floor. "The goal is to stay grounded and maintain your current position while finding the best way forward." Andie pivoted again. "Sometimes all it takes is a small change in direction to change your perspective."

"Listen, Andie, if you ever get tired of coaching soccer you might want to consider becoming a life coach. I'm completely serious." Kat blinked. "Do you happen to have any sage advice for me?"

"I'm sorry." Julia squeezed Kat's hand. "You've had a pretty crappy time of it too, and I'm making everything about me."

"Don't be sorry," Kat ordered, squeezing back. "Tonight, everything *should* be about you. You need us. We're here. There've been times when we've done the same for Andie, and plenty of times you've both done the same for me."

"Exactly," Andie declared. "We're going to help you figure out how to pivot." She sat down next to Julia. "If you could change anything in your life right now, what would it be?"

"If I could change one thing?" That was an excellent question. Julia contemplated possible answers, thoughts drawn to the hole in her heart, probing the weight and shape and depth of it. "The truth? I'd keep everything exactly the same as it is right now, except Luke would be here."

"In my apartment?" Andie's nose crinkled.

"How can you be so smart and still have a brain full of dandelion fluff?" Kat *tsk*ed, shaking her head. "She means here with her. In this city. Chicago." Kat turned back to Julia. "Are you sure? Sometimes what you think you want turns out to be all wrong."

Kat's voice held a faint dash of bitterness, and Julia ached for her friend. "I hear what you're saying, but I just want to talk to him." The hole in her heart burned with the sting of regret. "I wish I'd stayed and listened to what he had to say when I had the chance."

CHAPTER 30

LUKE

The July sun was bright overhead, shining down on the Notting Hill terrace. As the warmth seeped into his shoulders and back, Luke stirred, realizing it was already past noon. He logged off his laptop and twisted in his chair, stretching his spine. Over the past month or so, he'd established a new routine. Work on the plans for his start-up in the mornings, followed by a walk down to the lake. Then he'd have lunch with Pen and Jay and spend the afternoon helping solve any problems they might be having, either with the resort website or with the simulation software. In the evenings, he'd usually take another walk along the beach, mentally reviewing his notes from the day.

By all appearances, it was a pleasant, organized, simple life. But Luke recognized it for what it was—a holding pattern. Come fall, Penelope and Jay would be rolling out their new experiences at the resort and they wouldn't need his help anymore. Truth be told, they really didn't need him now. Pen and Jay made a great team.

At first, the realization had only amplified his sense of being kicked out of the pea pod, a useless third wheel. It took a bit of time and self-reflection for Luke to move past his initial distress regarding the shift in the dynamic between his sister and his best friend. He eventually got over himself, but that didn't make being around their lovey-doveyness all day any easier.

While planning romantic-comedy experiences for others, his sister and best friend had gotten their own happy ending. He wasn't jealous, exactly, but it was hard not to feel the sting, like a bit of salt rubbed in an open wound. The hole in his heart. Seeing them together amplified his own sense of loneliness, and it made Luke acutely aware of what he was missing.

After rejecting his grand romantic gesture, Julia's glowing review of Notting Hill had surprised Luke. Ironically, the resort likely would have succeeded regardless of what her review said. Even before the *TrendList* feature went live, bookings had begun pouring in—many from LARPing aficionados who'd heard about the resort via word of mouth, thanks to Patrick and David.

To date, Pen and Jay had run two more sessions of the rom-com sim, each time expanding the player capacity a little more. Business at the resort was booming, and Mrs. W. was over the moon. But it wasn't the impressive registration numbers that had his boss swanning about the hotel for weeks in a colorful, silken cloud of gloating satisfaction. And it definitely wasn't the revenue. As she'd told Luke, the woman really didn't give a fig about money.

He shook his head, recalling the morning she'd called him into her office to celebrate. It was a week after the first session had wrapped, and Julia's "Take Me!" review of the resort had just posted on the *TrendList* website.

His boss had handed him a mimosa, plopped a corgi in his lap, and told him congratulations, he'd earned his bonus. When she rattled off the amount she was transferring to his account, Luke was stunned, unable to do little more than suck down cocktails as fast as she poured them. By the time the shock had worn off his brain, Luke realized that while his boss had kept refilling his glass, she'd stopped bothering to mix the drink, and his "mimosa" was now nine-tenths champagne with a splash of orange juice for color.

"Do you know what convinced me this experience was successful?" Mrs. W. asked.

Luke set his glass down and tried to collect his thoughts. "You found someone who believed the fantasy was real?"

"Exactly." Cheeks flushed pink with drink, she beamed. "And that someone was you."

"Me?" Luke asked, wondering if he'd misunderstood. His mind was slow, his brain soggy and saturated with champagne. "What makes you think so?"

"Oh, this and that." Her gaze turned mischievous. "I wondered, when you told me you'd decided to participate in the simulation, what was really going on."

"I was just trying to do my job," he assured her.

"I'm certain that's what you told yourself. And maybe you even believed it for a bit." Mrs. W leaned back, supremely confident in her assessment. "But soon enough, you realized you were falling in love."

Luke sputtered.

"Against all odds," she continued, ignoring his attempts to deny what she was saying. "Over the course of the week, you met someone and fell for her, despite everything." She gazed at him over the rim of her glass, expression sly. "And trust me, I tried to add a few obstacles myself."

What is that supposed to mean? Ideas sloshed together and his eyes widened. "That night at the talent show. You mentioned my job at the resort on purpose."

"Did I?" Mrs. W. asked, her tone indicating a confession, not a question.

Luke studied his boss. Sitting in her overstuffed office chair, one hand idly stroking the corgi curled in her lap, champagne in the other hand, Mrs. W. looked like she was auditioning to be a Bond villain. "Why would you do that?"

"I thought it best to get everything out in the open." She clicked her tongue. "Can't build a relationship on a false foundation."

"Who said anyone was trying to build a relationship?" he demanded.

The look Mrs. W. gave him told Luke she saw right through his bullshit. But just in case he didn't interpret the message correctly, she opened the laptop on her desk and turned the screen toward him.

Luke glanced down, swallowing hard when he saw the video of himself holding the speaker over his head. There was no denying the lovesick look on his face. That was a man who wanted a relationship. His heart contracted. "This might not be the best example to prove your point."

"What makes you say that?"

"Romantic comedies are supposed to have a happy ending, right?" He nodded at the screen, throat tight. "Well, this one didn't."

"My dear boy . . ." Mrs. W. smiled tenderly. "What makes you think this story is over?"

And just like that, his boss transformed from Bond villain to fairy godmother. Sometime later, Luke had left her office covered in corgi fur, a little tipsy, and very bemused.

He'd fulfilled his contract and earned the bonus. Finally, he had the time and money he needed to devote to his start-up. His sister was safe, secure, and supposedly happy. And yet here he was, a month later, still hesitating.

Reflecting on that afternoon when Mrs. W. had handed him his future on a silver platter, Luke wondered if he wasn't the problem, the obstacle that had been in his path all along. Not the lack of money, not the concern he had for his sister, but himself.

He tapped his pen against his notebook. If he was serious about launching his company, eventually he was going to have to stop planning and start doing. He needed to take the next steps, do things like register domain names, secure an office space, and hire a team. It was daunting, to have what had only been a dream for so long finally on the verge of becoming a reality.

That was the irony of dreams: they appeared more attainable when they were out of reach.

The high-pitched yapping of an excited canine barreled through his thoughts and he glanced up. Penelope was making her way across the terrace toward him, her fluffy, faithful new companion in tow. Luke shook his head. By some miracle, his sister had managed to control herself and had adopted only one fur ball from the legion of corgis she'd brought to the resort.

And even though Cuddle with Corgis had continued to be a part of the rom-com experience, Pen had resisted the temptation to add any more companions to her personal entourage. Luke's teasing that she was going to turn into Mrs. W. probably helped. While Penelope had limited herself to one dog, their boss had adopted at least another three—possibly four. At this point, Luke had lost count. He just got out of the way when he heard them coming.

"Have you taken your walk on the beach yet?" Pen asked.

"Am I that predictable?" Luke asked, squinting up at her.

"Do you really want me to answer that?" she shot back.

"No." They both knew he already knew the answer. "And not yet," he added. "I was just about to, though."

"Do you mind if Crumpet and I join you?"

"I don't know," Luke said slowly, a teasing grin tugging at the corner of his mouth. "I'm not sure if I can handle such a shocking deviation from my routine."

His sister laughed. "Challenge yourself."

"If you insist." With a beleaguered sigh he slipped his laptop into his bag and followed his sister down to the beach.

A few minutes later, Pen had talked "Uncle Lukey" into holding Crumpet's leash. Luke would never admit it, but he loved it when his sister referred to him as her dog's uncle; the fox face and fluffy heart-shaped rump had grown on him. "So, what did you want to talk to me about?"

His sister glanced at him from beneath her lashes. "Am I that predictable?"

"Do you really want me to answer that?"

"Fine," she snorted. "You got me."

Crumpet scampered eagerly toward a large chunk of driftwood that had washed ashore overnight, and Luke paused to let the dog investigate. "What's up?"

"Jay and I finalized plans for the holiday sim." Pen brushed some sand from the top of the wood and sat down. "We're going to turn the pond into an ice rink and use the paintball field for snowball fights. And there will be hot cocoa and candy cane cocktails and gingerbread house–making contests . . ." She grinned. "It's going to be great. I'm talking epic, greeting card–level perfection here."

You were perfect. Julia's words echoed in Luke's mind.

"Wow." He sank down next to his sister. *Perfectly imperfect.* "Hard to picture all this winter stuff in the middle of summer."

"Christmas in July, right?" Penelope laughed. "But Jay wanted everything ready for the website so we can start booking the holiday season now. And then there's the New Year's Eve party to plan."

Luke wrapped the dog leash around a broken limb sticking out of the log. He thought about the months ahead, picturing the days turning colder, the nights longer. All of it happening without Julia.

"What do you think?"

"Huh?" Luke blinked.

"For New Year's Eve. We're thinking of making that its own separate mini-experience. A weekend event."

"Oh. Sounds fun." He frowned. He didn't want to face those long, cold nights alone . . . didn't want to ring in a new year without her.

His sister studied him carefully but didn't say anything.

That first week after Julia left, Penelope had tried to get him to tell her what happened, but Luke had shut his sister out. It had been too painful to think about, let alone talk about. By the time he'd finally felt ready to open up, she'd stopped asking him about it.

Crumpet sniffed between their feet and sneezed.

"What happened, boy?" Luke glanced down. "Did you snort some sand?" As glum as he felt, he couldn't help smiling at the goofy dog's antics, his heavy heart lifting a fraction.

Penelope laughed and pulled a baggie of dog treats from her pocket. She held one out to Crumpet, scratching him behind the ears while he made short work of his snack. "I'm assuming by that point you'll have launched your start-up." Penelope said casually, attention still on her pet.

"That's the plan." Luke swallowed. A plan that wasn't moving forward, because he was stuck in neutral.

"Have you given any thought to where you want to open your office?" she asked, the casual tone a bit more forced this time.

Luke shrugged. "Probably somewhere in town."

"Here?" Penelope looked at him, face aghast. "In this dinky vacation town? Why would you do that?" She shook her head. "You need to go to Milwaukee . . ." Her gaze turned sly. "Or Chicago."

He snorted. "I can't go to Chicago."

"You sound like Crumpet," Pen teased. "Did you get sand in your snout too?" She reached up and mussed his hair. "Of course you can go to Chicago. I know Mrs. W.'s bonus was big enough to let you open your company on the moon if you wanted to. Or California. Isn't that where all the cool tech kids go to launch their start-ups?"

"I'm *not* moving to California." The idea of being that far away, on the other side of the country . . . He might as well be on the moon. Thinking about it made Luke's stomach heave.

Penelope's eyes narrowed shrewdly. "I had hoped we were finally past the overprotective big brother routine."

"We are," Luke spluttered. "I am."

"Chicago, then." She raised her brows in challenge. "Unless you have another reason for not wanting to live there."

"More like someone who doesn't want me living there," Luke mumbled.

"What's that?" Pen tilted her head, cocking her ear toward him.

"She doesn't want me there," Luke growled.

"Who? Julia?"

Hearing her name out loud like that, for the first time in weeks, stole Luke's breath. He nodded curtly, belatedly realizing his sister had craftily maneuvered him into having the conversation he'd been avoiding.

"That's ridiculous," Penelope scoffed. "Have you tried calling her?"

He shook his head.

"Not even once?"

Another shake.

"Then how do you know?" she demanded, exasperated. "What happened between you two?"

"You were right." Luke forced the words past the lump of regret lodged in his throat.

"I was?" Penelope blinked in confusion. "Well, of course I was." Her face pinched. "What was I right about this time?"

"The way I handled things before she left."

"Ah," Penelope said, understanding and sympathy filling that one sound to overflowing.

"I don't know what I was thinking. Trying to impress her with some big, showy, grand gesture."

"It was easier," Penelope said simply.

"Excuse me." Luke glared at his sister. "But getting up in front of a crowd of people and declaring my love was hardly easy."

"Oh, so you declared your love?"

"No." Luke scowled. "She wouldn't let me get that far." He kicked at a pile of sand, startling Crumpet. "She told me she didn't want to hear what I had to say."

"Why would she?" Penelope scoffed. "You weren't being real with her. I told you to be sincere." She ran her hand down her dog's back in slow, soothing strokes. "But you had to play the game. Hide in the fantasy." Pen shook her head. "It's easier to take risks that way. You think, by letting the fake version of yourself make mistakes, you won't have to suffer the consequences of your choices." His sister glanced up, gray eyes reflecting more than the same color back at him. She understood. She knew.

"Pen?" Luke asked gently.

She turned away, gaze shifting to stare out at the lake. "When I was sick, it felt like my entire life was narrowed down to that one thing. Everyone I knew, everyone I cared about, was preoccupied with managing my health. It didn't matter what I did or said, it wasn't me people saw—it was my illness." Her shoulders stiffened. "The cancer may not have taken my life, but it had *taken over* my life, and I hated it."

Luke wrapped an arm around his sister, squeezing those shoulders that had carried so much, so young.

"Maybe that's why I became obsessed with romantic comedies," Pen continued, seeming to talk more to herself than to him. "The problems always seemed . . . silly. Life was silly. And simple. You could count on what happened next. Two people would stumble across each other's path, a bunch of ridiculous stuff would happen, the situation getting more and more ridiculous until finally they realize they love each other. Bam. Kiss. Happily ever after. Roll credits."

Luke chuckled. "Yeah, but what happens after the credits roll?"

"Who cares?" She fed Crumpet another treat, giggling as he licked her palm. "I sure didn't. Not when I was a kid and there was always another rom-com to watch, always another happy ending I could escape into."

She turned to look at him, face sobering. "But as I got older, I realized it was after the credits rolled that was the most important part. That's when things get real. When I got better and we were past the cancer, Mom and Dad—" Her mouth worked. "I think they pretended for so long, while I was sick, that when things were finally *normal* and they could be real with each other . . . they didn't know how."

"Maybe because they were too busy being selfish assholes," Luke said gruffly. His sister would not waste one moment of her hard-earned happiness on their parents. He wouldn't allow it.

"You're right." Pen sagged against him in deflated acceptance. "I mean, it sucks, but you're right."

Luke sucked in a breath, thinking through his sister's words. He clenched his jaw, considering. "Yeah, but you're right, too."

She tilted her chin and looked at him curiously.

He shook his head. "Julia said something that got me thinking."

"You talked to Julia about Mom and Dad?" Penelope's eyes widened.

He squirmed uncomfortably. "It just sort of happened."

She grinned. "I get the feeling a lot of things 'just sort of happened' between you two."

And he thought he'd been uncomfortable before. Luke grimaced.

"Oh, wipe that broody scowl off your face and tell me what she said," Penelope urged.

He dug the toe of one shoe into the sand. "She mentioned her parents were still together but she didn't think they loved each other."

"Ouch." Pen's mouth pinched in sympathy.

"All this time, I was mad at Mom and Dad for not trying hard enough to make it work. And while I still think it's true that they were selfish assholes who loved themselves more than anyone else and that's why they didn't want to try . . . at least they were honest enough to admit it."

"Damn, Luke." Penelope's voice was hoarse as she reached for him.

He hugged his sister tightly, struggling against the sudden sting of tears. "I will always love you enough to fight for you," he said fiercely. "Always." He eased his hold on her and wiped his eyes. "And Vijay will, too," he added. "If I didn't think so, I wouldn't have been so chill about his marriage proposal."

"That was you being chill?" Penelope laughed. "You need to let me fight my own battles," she reminded him, rubbing at her tearstained cheeks. "Besides, it's not me you have to worry about fighting for."

Luke's throat tightened; there was that lump again.

"Stop being a daft prick and tell her how you feel."

He jerked back in surprise. "What the hell, Pen?"

"Enough with the pearl-clutching." She rolled her eyes. "I was quoting *Notting Hill*, you idiot."

"Oh."

"Seriously, though." She leaned into him, nudging him with her elbow. "Go to Chicago and find Julia and be honest with her. No more games."

Luke wanted to. He'd been wanting to do exactly that since the moment Julia walked away from him. But he hadn't. He wasn't sure how. Problems in gaming programs were so much easier to deal with than people. With people, it's not like he could identify the broken piece of code, fix it, and hit Refresh.

If he dug deeper, Luke knew that much of his hesitation stemmed from fear. What happened if he admitted his true feelings and she walked away again? Or worse, what if she said she felt the same and they decided to make a go at a relationship together? Once she had a chance to really get to know him, would she still love him? All of him? Or would she start to find him intolerable?

"Pen," Luke blurted out. "Am I intolerable?"

"Only sometimes." She flashed him a smile. "But I'm your sister. I have to love you anyway."

"That's what I'm worried about," Luke admitted. "There's nothing forcing Julia to put up with me, no reason she has to love me."

"That's what makes love so amazing." Penelope squeezed his

hand. "When someone *sees* you—the real you. And loves you just for you."

Luke nodded.

"You won't know unless you try," she added quietly.

He nodded again.

"I need to head back. Jay's going to be wondering where I wandered off to." Penelope reached for Crumpet's leash and tugged it loose. "Are you going to join us for lunch?"

"I'll be along in a minute." Luke stood. "Do you mind if I have a few of those dog treats?"

She cocked her head, mouth curling in amused disgust.

"They're not for me," he assured her.

She shrugged and handed him the bag, then waved and jogged back up the beach toward the resort, Crumpet trotting along at her side, heart-shaped rump bobbing merrily.

Tucking the treats in his pocket, Luke turned and headed in the opposite direction. Before long, he reached his destination—a now-familiar spot. He climbed up the grassy dune, careful not to move too fast. Rather than approach the nest, he paused at the top of the little hill and pulled out the treats, crouching down and setting them on the sand next to him.

It didn't take long for his friends to realize they had a guest.

His friends. Luke chuckled at himself. And he thought Mrs. W. was eccentric.

Luke watched as the adult birds left the nest together, moving in a syncopated rhythm, keeping their young sheltered between them. The baby chicks were covered in a fuzzy silver down. As soft and tempting as they looked, he knew better than to touch an animal's young.

Ever since the night of the talent show, he'd been coming to visit the nest every few days, checking on Bonnie and Clyde and their little clutch of eggs. He'd grown protective of the mischievous pair, and when the eggs had hatched, Luke was honored that they trusted him enough to let him near their precious babies.

He'd joked with Julia about looking up on the internet how seagulls procreate, but Luke had done some research on things like egg incubation period and what foods were safe for the birds to eat. Considering the way they stole anything and everything in sight, he wasn't sure what he was worried about. He'd also learned that gulls mated for life, and he found something about that very comforting.

A series of little squeaks and chirps let him know they'd finished off their snack.

"Sorry, that's all I've got for you today."

The squeaks grew louder.

"I'll bring more next time, I promise." He stood, brushing sand off his hands. "Though next time might be a little while," he admitted. "Remember that pretty lady you stole the bikini top from?"

Clyde tilted his head, and Luke swore the bird understood exactly what he was saying.

"Well, she stole my heart. And I need to go make sure she's been taking good care of it."

For all he knew, she'd abandoned his heart, and any thoughts of him at all, when she left here. But he couldn't believe that. He wouldn't. She'd asked him if he believed true love was real . . . and he did. Because of her. And it was worth fighting for. *She* was worth fighting for.

That didn't mean he wasn't still scared as hell. Fighting for his sister was one thing; fighting for Julia, for himself—for what they might be together—was another. Luke stared out at the lake, a sense of wonder and fate washing over him at the thought of these same waves crashing on the shores of the city Julia called home. Penelope was right. He needed to take a chance. Make a move toward his future.

Which meant he was headed to Chicago.

CHAPTER 31

JULIA

Every July, Chicago celebrated its well-documented passion for good food with an epic celebration known as the Taste. For five days, locals and tourists alike flocked to Grant Park, a gigantic, gorgeous spot along the city's lakeshore, for the chance to sample all that the city had to offer. Everything could be found, from iconic items such as Chicago-style hot dogs and Eli's cheesecake to more bizarre offerings like shark burgers and fried alligator nuggets.

Julia was having a *Pinch me* moment—one of those surreal moments where she couldn't be sure that what was happening to her was actually real. Since moving to Chicago, she'd looked forward to attending the Taste each summer, excited to grab her favorites and explore what was new. So when *ChiChat*, a leading local talk show, invited her to represent "Local Love" and appear on a panel during the Taste, she'd said yes without a second thought.

She did experience a brief moment of doubt when she arrived at the pavilion where the panel was being held. She hadn't realized how *packed* the event would be. Julia had navigated the crowds at the Taste enough to know how wildly popular it was, but she'd never stopped to consider that the speaking events would be busy, because she'd never attended one herself. She'd always just come for the food.

Aside from the sheer size of the crowd, she wasn't sure why she was so nervous. She just couldn't shake this strange sense that something big was going to happen—which was stupid. Of course something big was going to happen. Something big *was* happening. She was speaking on a panel at one of the biggest events in the city, and the whole thing was being filmed live for one of the most watched local TV shows.

In the end, Julia had nothing to worry about. The other panelists were entertaining and informative and the hour flew by in a pleasant blur. Outside, away from the shade of the pavilion, it took a few minutes for Julia's eyes to adjust to the bright afternoon sun.

A cacophony of smells and sounds overwhelmed her senses. One scent in particular caught her attention, and Julia groaned. Stomach grumbling, she followed her nose to her favorite vendor at the Taste. She'd been so nervous about the panel, she'd done the impossible and had momentarily forgotten about her annual tradition.

Ever since her first visit to the famous food festival, Julia had made it a point to visit the booth run by a little family-owned restaurant based in Greektown. But it wasn't the gyro on a stick or the baklava ice cream that lured her, it was the divine perfection of feta fries. Crispy, golden-brown potatoes served piping hot and sprinkled with crumbles of creamy, salty feta cheese . . . heaven.

They were too hot to eat yet, so she decided to head toward the fountain and find a spot to enjoy her treat. She wove through the maze of people, the aroma wafting from her little grease-stained paper carton of ambrosia making her stomach cramp with anticipation. The jewel of Grant Park, Buckingham Fountain, was a lovely island of calm amid the chaos. The rushing water drowned out the crowds and the air around the fountain was drenched in a cooling mist, providing a welcome respite from the heat and noise.

She'd barely lifted the first fry to her lips when a shadow passed overhead. Julia glanced up, a shiver of déjà vu running through her when she caught sight of the seagull. She dropped the fry and the bird dove, landing at her feet with a squawk of excitement and snatching it up. She grinned and tossed the bird a second fry. She knew she shouldn't encourage the little thief, but she couldn't help it. Her heart contracted with bittersweet memories.

Again, Julia was struck by the overwhelming sensation that something was about to happen. Her entire body hummed with expectation. And in that moment, she knew.

Luke.

She glanced up, not surprised at all when she immediately caught sight of his tall form. His height made him impossible to miss in the sea of bodies. As she watched him pace around the fountain, another ripple of déjà vu tingled down her spine. A vision bloomed in her mind. She would call out to him and he would stop, turning toward her voice. Then his gray eyes would meet hers and the crowd, the city, the *entire world* would fade away.

Of course, that's not how it works. Not in real life, and especially not in *her* life. Julia called out to Luke several times, but the fountain, which so effectively drowned out the noisy crowds, also made it almost impossible to hear someone yelling your name.

The oblivious man continued to walk the circumference of the fountain. Sacrificing her fries, Julia set them down next to the seagull. "It's your lucky day, buddy." She dashed off, chasing after Luke. His long legs easily outpaced hers, and eventually Julia gave up. But she was *not* going to give up on him.

The moment might not be playing out in perfect rom-com-movie fashion, but she'd learned to appreciate the imperfections. Luke had taught her that. She decided to wait him out. On his next pass, she'd be ready.

As he circled the fountain again, Julia realized his eyes were closed. She laughed in exasperation, watching as people scurried to dodge the clueless man. Shaking her head, she shifted her position. Unlike their first meeting, which had been a complete accident, this time Julia purposely ran into him. Well, technically,

Luke ran into her. She just happened to make sure she was in his way.

"*Oof!*" he cried, colliding into her. Luke stumbled, but because she'd been braced for impact, Julia held steady and they didn't go down. He opened his eyes, the apology he'd begun to mumble coming to an abrupt halt. "Oh," he breathed. His notebook clattered to the concrete, pages flapping in the Lake Michigan breeze. "It's you."

"It's me." Julia swallowed a bubble of nervous laughter as she took in his bewildered expression. "Were you expecting someone else to bump into you?"

Luke shook his head. "No, I—" He paused, staring down at her. "Did you do that on purpose?"

"Guilty as charged," she admitted unrepentantly. "When are you going to learn to stop walking around with your eyes closed?"

"I told you, it helps me think," he grumbled, bending to retrieve his notebook.

"What were you thinking about?" she asked, leaning against the iron railing surrounding the fountain.

He tucked his notebook into his back pocket. "A lot of things." "Like what?"

He rubbed a hand across his chest—over his heart. Julia smiled to herself, wondering if he was feeling the same hopeful ache she was. And then she recognized the video game character on his T-shirt and her smile widened.

Apparently, she wasn't the only one who noticed. "Dude," a man passing by said appreciatively. "Love the *Zelda* shirt."

Luke muttered a distracted thanks at the guy, then cleared his throat and turned his attention back to Julia. "Like moving to Chicago."

"You're thinking of moving here?" Julia asked, breath hitching. She hadn't been expecting that.

"To launch my start-up," he explained. "Yeah."

"How long would you be staying?" she asked carefully.

Luke dipped his chin and met her eyes. "Indefinitely."

"Oh." She swallowed. Suddenly hot, Julia tilted her face toward the cooling mist wafting off the spouts of water. "Strange . . . you happening to be here today."

"I came here to see you," he confessed.

"You did?" She shifted, turning to face him, one hand still gripping the railing, as if that would support her through whatever happened next.

"A Chicago talk show mentioned some panel you would be appearing on. I had the time and place and everything." He ran a hand through his hair. "This will probably sound creepy—at best cheesy—but I took it as a sign."

"I keep telling myself I don't believe in signs," she said, "but I might have to change my stance on that. And I've discovered I like cheesy." She cocked her head, watching him curiously. "If you knew I was at the panel, why didn't you come find me there?"

"I considered it," he admitted. "Thought about bursting through the crowd with an epic apology."

"Like Hugh Grant?"

"Exactly." A shy smile tugged at the corner of his mouth. "But I didn't want to jeopardize my chance to speak to you with another attempt at a grand gesture." He exhaled, breath shaky. "I'm afraid I'm going to screw this up," he admitted. "Or screw it up *again*. I already screwed things up by not being honest with you from the start."

"I wasn't honest with you, either," Julia reminded him. "I kept coming up with excuses not to tell you. Made lists of reasons for why it was okay to keep who I really was hidden. But it wasn't okay." She leaned closer. "It was wrong, and I'm sorry."

"I'm sorry, too. Sorry for everything. I shouldn't have tried to win you over with something showy." His shoulders lifted and dropped. "The thing is," he continued, "I will likely screw up again. No . . ." His smile turned tight and self-deprecating. "I will *definitely* screw up again. I will mess up and be imperfect." He reached for her hand. "But I'm hoping it is an imperfect you can accept." He pressed a kiss to her knuckles. "An imperfect that is perfect for you."

"Luke," Julia said hoarsely. His honesty had completely disarmed her, stripped her of her planned defenses.

"The last time we saw each other, you told me you didn't want to hear what I had to say," he blurted, meeting her gaze.

"I remember."

"This time I want you to know I'm serious."

"Serious about what?" Julia's heart hammered, every muscle tense as she braced herself. At the hotel, she'd refused to hear what he had to say because she wanted to keep her heart closed to him. Now she was afraid to let him back in. But as she looked at him, Julia realized that Luke was already in her heart and had been since that first collision on the beach.

Still holding her hand, he dropped to one knee. He placed his other hand on top of their joined fingers and looked up at her. "Do you think you could tolerate being with someone like me?"

"Tolerate?" Julia echoed, giggling. Her laughter subsided as she stared down at him, trying to decide if he meant what it looked like he did. It was Luke, though, so better to ask him directly. "Are you asking me to marry you?"

"Um, no . . ." He faltered. "Should I be?" Frowning, Luke got to his feet. "See? I told you I would screw up. I was just . . ." He gestured at the ground. "The kneeling thing, it's something you always see at the end of romantic comedies, you know?" He held up a hand. "And I'm not trying to pretend we're in one. This isn't a game to me." He ran a frustrated hand through his hair. "I simply got this urge to do it, to go on one knee—not to propose—I mean, I *do* love you . . ."

"You love me?" Julia blinked. If this were a movie, she would press Pause so she could absorb the moment.

"By now, you must know I do." He snorted. "I'm not that good at pretending."

"Maybe neither of us are." Julia smiled. "Because I love you, too. I tried to tell myself I didn't, that I'd just gotten wrapped up in the fantasy." She shook her head. "But *that* was the lie. Not my feelings for you."

Luke's eyes lit with joy. "I love you," he said again. "And by some miracle, it appears you love me. I want to be with you forever, but . . . marriage doesn't make any sense right now."

"Oh, good." She breathed a sigh of relief.

"Though maybe," Luke continued, voice growing contemplative, "this could be a proposal."

"What?" Her heart stopped. Julia wasn't sure she could take much more of this roller coaster. "Why?"

"I just said I love you, that I want to be with you forever. And you love me. What's preventing us from making that happen? After all, Jay asked Penelope to marry him."

"Your sister is getting married?" Julia tried follow Luke's leap-frogging thoughts. "Good for her."

"It *is* good. She's very happy." A tender smile warmed his face. "And Bonnie and Clyde had babies, three of them."

"The seagulls?" she asked, wanting to be sure she wasn't misunderstanding him.

He nodded, beaming like a proud godfather for a moment, then sobering. "So what's my problem? Is it the scared part of me making excuses again?"

"I don't think you're scared. I mean, of course you're scared. I'm scared." Julia's heart kick-started back into high gear, beating so fast she felt like she'd just run the Chicago Marathon. "The idea of marriage is a scary thing, especially for two people who haven't known each other long. Your sister and friend have known each other their entire lives, right?"

"Basically."

"And we've only known each other for about a week."

"Well, actually we've known each other longer than a week. It's been over a month since we first met."

She was considering bopping him in the head for *Well,* *actually*–ing her, when he continued.

"But your point is valid." He grinned, eyes crinkling in the corners the way she loved.

Julia thought of those crinkles deepening with age, laugh lines from years of happiness together . . . She shook her head, laughing. "Now you've got me thinking about it."

"When I came here today, I only knew two things."

"Only two?" she teased.

"Two very important things." His gaze was intense now, the gray of his eyes piercingly bright, like the sky over Lake Michigan on a December morning. "I knew that, one, I love you. And, two, I want to be with you."

"Luke." Julia sucked in a breath.

"I had to find you and tell you. I want to be with you. Like I said, forever. Though I admit, until this conversation, proposing marriage never occurred to me." He ran a hand through his hair, gathering steam. "Why would it? It's preposterous. Of course, I've just concluded the idea is not without merit. But I don't have a ring. Perhaps the hypothetical is enough for now?"

As he rambled, Julia bit her lip, affection bubbling up. "Luke?"

"Yeah?"

"I don't need a ring to know our love is real, okay?"

"Okay," he echoed. As the word left his lips, he paused, a knowing gleam sparkling in his gaze, and she knew the memory of their night together was washing over him, too. "Okay," he repeated, voice raspy and raw.

"And we don't have to get married." She tilted her chin, equal parts playful and hopeful as she considered him, "Not yet, anyway. Is that okay?"

"More than okay." Luke gently brushed the hair away from her face before he bent down and pressed his mouth to hers. Like that first time when he'd kissed her, in the woods after a rainstorm, it was soft, and slow, and sweet. And even though there was no tender power ballad rising to an emotional crescendo as they drew closer together, no fireworks exploding in the night sky the moment their lips touched, not even a magical sunset, it still felt perfect.

"I'm having a *Pinch me* moment," she whispered.

"Huh?"

"What's happening right now . . ." She stared up at him. "Us. This is for real, right?"

"For real," he confirmed, voice barely more than breath, featherlight but heavy with purpose. He lowered his head to kiss her again, promising, "For real and forever."

ACKNOWLEDGMENTS

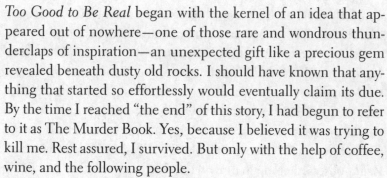

Too Good to Be Real began with the kernel of an idea that appeared out of nowhere—one of those rare and wondrous thunderclaps of inspiration—an unexpected gift like a precious gem revealed beneath dusty old rocks. I should have known that anything that started so effortlessly would eventually claim its due. By the time I reached "the end" of this story, I had begun to refer to it as The Murder Book. Yes, because I believed it was trying to kill me. Rest assured, I survived. But only with the help of coffee, wine, and the following people.

My amazing, patient, understanding editor, Jennie Conway. Thanks for merrily coming along for the ride when I called you out of the blue and suggested we drop everything we'd been working on to chase this wild idea instead. You are a consummate professional who navigates the process of taking a book from concept to product with ease and empathy, and I am so lucky to have you in my corner.

Shout-out to the team at St. Martin's Press, especially Marissa, Naureen, and Kelly. Thanks for being my book cheerleaders!

Much appreciation for my agent, Pamela Harty, for always being just a phone call away. Your experience and wisdom helps me keep my mind on the big picture and my eye on what's in front of me.

To my fantastic plotting retreat buddies: Sonali Dev, Lynne Hartzer, Clara Kensie, Heather Marshall, and CJ Warrant for their help brainstorming romantic comedies. Heather, your reminder of "Whoops-a-daisies" was epic. I am in your debt.

Many thanks to my beta readers Erica O'Rourke and Lynne Hartzer for giving up their valuable time to provide insightful critiques.

Heaps of gratitude to Christine Palmer, for surprising me with a lovely survival basket of wine and treats to sustain me during my week of living as a hermit in a cottage on the lake.

Hugs to my Golden Heart sisters, always a source of great comfort, more so than ever during these trying times. Rebelle island is my safe harbor, an island of calm in a sea of uncertainty.

Much love to my family, including my mom, Linda (I promise, the next book will be dedicated to you!), my brave and beautiful daughters Aishtyn and Gwyn (thanks for putting up with cranky deadline mom who for weeks on end you only knew as that bedraggled lump on the couch), and my husband, Hugues, a six-foot-four-inch, video game–playing, Pac-Man T-shirt-wearing, *Zelda*-obsessed computer guy who, due to quarantine and being around each other 24/7, may have shown up in my hero more than I planned. Thanks for providing such great source material.

Speaking of quarantine, trying to write a funny, happy, feel-good book in the midst of a pandemic has been a series of challenges—all of them difficult—but none of them insurmountable. I managed to get this story down on paper, but it happened slowly, one paragraph at a time. Anne Lamott's "Bird by bird" comes to mind . . . though in my case, the bird was a bikini-snatching scene-stealing seagull named Clyde.

Finally, dear Reader, whoever you are, wherever you are, whatever state the world is in when you read this, I hope you find an escape within these pages, I hope this story makes you smile. Thanks for spending time with my book.

—*Melonie Johnson*

ABOUT THE AUTHOR

Heather Stumpf

USA Today bestselling author MELONIE JOHNSON—aka #thewritinglush—enjoys sipping cocktails that start with the letter *m*. Declared a "writer to watch" by *Kirkus Reviews* and a "fizzy, engrossing new voice" by *Entertainment Weekly*, her smart, funny, contemporary romances include *Too Good to Be Real* and her award-winning Sometimes in Love series: *Getting Hot with the Scot*, *Smitten by the Brit*, and *Once Upon a Bad Boy*. A former high school English and theater teacher, she spends her days in her *Star Wars* office, dreaming up meet cutes. She lives in Chicagoland with her husband, their two redheaded daughters, and one very large dog.